W9-BEU-112

OCTAVIA GONE

ALSO BY JACK MCDEVITT

OCTAVIA GONE

AN ALEX BENEDICT NOVEL

JACK McDEVITT

Margaret E. Heggan Public Library
606 Delsea Drive
Sewell, NJ 08080

SAGA PRESS

LONDON SYDNEY **NEW YORK** TORONTO NEW DELHI

SAGA PRESS
AN IMPRINT OF SIMON & SCHUSTER, INC.

1230 AVENUE OF THE AMERICAS, NEW YORK, NEW YORK 10020

This book is a work of fiction. Any references to historical events, real people, or real places are used fictitiously. Other names, characters, places, and events are products of the author's imagination, and any resemblance to actual events or places or persons, living or dead, is entirely coincidental.

Text copyright © 2019 by Cryptic, Inc.

Jacket illustration copyright © 2019 by Stephen Youll

All rights reserved, including the right to reproduce this book or portions thereof in any form whatsoever. For information address Saga Press Subsidiary Rights Department, 1230 Avenue of the Americas, New York, NY 10020.

SAGA PRESS and colophon are trademarks of Simon & Schuster, Inc.

For information about special discounts for bulk purchases, please contact Simon & Schuster Special Sales at 1-866-506-1949 or business@simonandschuster.com.

The Simon & Schuster Speakers Bureau can bring authors to your live event. For more information or to book an event, contact the Simon & Schuster Speakers Bureau at 1-866-248-3049 or visit our website at www.simonspeakers.com.

The text for this book was set in ITC Veljovic Std.

Manufactured in the United States of America

First Edition

2 4 6 8 10 9 7 5 3 1

Library of Congress Cataloging-in-Publication Data

Names: McDevitt, Jack, author.

Title: Octavia gone / Jack McDevitt.

Description: London ; New York : Saga Press, [2019] | Series: An Alex Benedict novel ; 8

Identifiers: LCCN 2018058597 | ISBN 9781481497978 (hardback) | ISBN 9781481497992 (ebook)

Subjects: | BISAC: FICTION / Science Fiction / High Tech. | FICTION / Science Fiction / Space Opera. | FICTION / Science Fiction / General. | GSAFD: Science fiction.

Classification: LCC PS3563.C3556 O28 2019 | DDC 813/.54—dc23

LC record available at https://lccn.loc.gov/2018058597

For Robbi Jo McDevitt

o o o o o o o o o o o o o

Acknowledgments

I'm indebted to Walter Cuirle, Michael Bishop, and David DeGraff for technical assistance.

o o o o o o o o o o o o o

PROLOG

1424: RIMWAY CALENDAR.

The *Larry Corbin* was barely fifteen minutes out of Ventnor Station, still charging its hyperdrive unit. Both moons were visible, one in the rear, the other off to port. Adarryl Perry had just gotten out of his seat, intending to go back to the cabin to talk with his passengers, when Thwanna, the AI, lit up. *"Captain,"* she said, *"message from the station."* She put it on display:

> Adarryl, we just got word that Rimway has lost
> contact with Octavia station. It's the research
> unit orbiting the black hole KBX44. They'd been
> receiving daily transmissions, but the transmissions
> have stopped. Their orbit takes them behind the
> black hole periodically, which cuts everything off
> for thirty-one hours. That just happened two days
> ago. But they've been clear for almost twenty hours,
> and there's nothing from them. You're closest.
> Please divert. Be informed they also have a shuttle.
> Report back as soon as you see what's happening.

I'll let you know if we hear anything more.
Brentway.

"Thwanna," he said, "how long will we need to get there?"
"Just a couple of hours. Riding around in the system trying to find the station, though, will probably take some serious time."

"Give me a minute." He switched back to cruise, got up, and went into the passenger cabin. All four of his passengers were there. A romantic comedy, *Love on a Wing,* had just started. It's a clever show in which the goddess Athena shows up in a Greek theater to enjoy a play that features her as a principal character. Perry had seen and enjoyed the film several times. The lead actor, of course, falls in love with the goddess. He watched for a few moments and then stopped it. "Betsy," he said, "gentlemen, we've run into a problem. There's a possible emergency. Communications from a research station orbiting a black hole have broken off and they want us to go take a look. Sorry, but we don't have any options. I can take you back to Ventnor Station if you want, and they'll set up another ship for you. But it could take a while. Or if you prefer, stay here and go with me. Your call. Better if you stay on board, just in case there's a problem out there and they need help. Either way, you'll be compensated."

Mark Friedman was Betsy's husband. "Sounds good," he said. "Did you say they were orbiting a black hole? That doesn't sound very smart."

"They're doing research. Been there more than a year."

"Interesting," said Mark. He was not the sort of person Perry would have taken for a retired hangball coach, except that he was extremely tall. He didn't have the polished moves of a onetime athlete. But he looked like a leader. Perry had needed only a quick glance to realize he was a guy to whom people would pay serious attention. He had black hair and a face that might have belonged to the leading man in *Love on a Wing.* "Those are kind of dangerous, aren't they? Black holes?"

"Of course they are, love," said his wife. Betsy was slender and attractive, also with black hair and a mischievous gleam that never left her eyes.

They were headed for a new home on the recently established Kolmar colony. Perry couldn't imagine why anybody would want to move out to a place so removed from the rest of the Confederacy. "They just want us to take a look and make sure everything's okay," he said.

The other two passengers, Aaron Prentiss and Virgil Henderson, exchanged glances. They both shrugged. "Let's do it," said Aaron. "We have plenty of time before we're due at the Omicron. And we'll get a chance to add a black hole to the act. That sounds golden." They were a comedy team who'd been making appearances for the opening of their new movie. Perry didn't recall the title. Aaron was a small, thin guy who played the dunce.

Virgil was probably twice his size, the excitable part of the team who usually wound up paying the price for Aaron's stupidity. A growing look of concern was shadowing his features, much as it often did during a movie. "Captain, the black hole isn't anywhere near Kolmar, is it?" That was where they were headed.

"No. No need to worry. But you guys should stay belted down. We'll be making our jump in a few minutes."

Aaron wasted no time checking his seat belt.

"You say they've been out here a year?" asked Betsy.

Perry nodded and started toward the bridge. "I'll be back. We have to get moving."

As he left the passenger cabin, Virgil was saying that, whatever kind of research it was, he couldn't imagine how it could be any use to anyone. "It's just asking for trouble." He was managing to sound scared.

Perry took his seat on the bridge. "Thwanna," he said,

"inform Ventnor we're on our way." He locked in his own seat belt and glanced at the green lights that told him his passengers were secure. Then he warned them they would begin to accelerate in a moment. He heard the movie come back on. "Okay, Thwanna, let's get moving again."

They adjusted course, turning in the direction of the black hole, and began to accelerate. "Thwanna, Adam said they were blocked off from communicating for thirty-one hours. Is that really because of the black hole?"

"Yes, Captain. It disrupts any transmissions, radio or hyper-comm, that pass close to it. There is one period of approximately thirty hours during each orbit in which the station is cut off from all contacts."

"That's when they lost touch with it."

"That seems like an odd coincidence." Ten minutes later she told him they were ready to go under.

"Do it," he said.

The smaller moon, Dura, was visible outside his starboard window. He watched it disappear as they slipped into hyperspace.

Life was routine over the next two hours. They watched the rest of the Athena movie, and then Perry made a light lunch available. Mark and Betsy showed signs of being disappointed that Aaron and Virgil were different from the characters they played in the comedies. Perry had met them on an earlier flight. Away from a performance, they were ordinary people. They'd all been interested in visiting the bridge during the early minutes after the launch. Now of course if they looked out the windows there was nothing to be seen except occasional mist and unbroken darkness.

Mark fell asleep in his seat. The others simply sat and talked until Thwanna informed them they should secure their harnesses while the *Corbin* prepared to return to normal space. It did, and as far as Perry could tell, they were all disappointed when they looked out the windows and were still greeted by little other than black space and a sprinkling of stars.

He gave Thwanna a few minutes to check their position. Then: "How'd we do?"

"Still working on it, Captain. It'll be another minute."

"Take your time." He sat back and closed his eyes.

Thwanna came back: *"We're close. Maybe twenty billion kilometers. Ready to accelerate and recharge the Korba."* The Korba was, of course, the star drive. *"We'll need to go down one more time to get within range."*

He directed his passengers to belt down again. Then Thwanna made a moderate course change, after which they started to add velocity. And the Korba began recharging.

Perry had been out here before, bringing supplies to the station, but he felt his own energy level rising. He'd never been involved in a rescue mission before. Betsy and Mark had seemed happy enough. They'd get a reduction in their travel costs as compensation and be able to talk about the black hole at every party they attended for the rest of their lives. And Aaron and Virgil might get some publicity.

So much for the good side of this. But he wondered what could have happened to the guys on Octavia? Hell, they were probably okay. What could possibly go wrong screwing around with a black hole?

They submerged again and after a minute or two came back up. *"We'll need a couple of days to get the rest of the way in,"* said Thwanna.

"Good enough." Perry notified the passengers they could leave their seats and wander around as they liked. Then: "Thwanna, do we know who's currently on board Octavia?"

"Yes, Captain. The tech guy is Rick Harding. And there are three scientists from DPSAR, Delmar Housman, Archie Womack, and Charlotte Hill."

"What's Dipsar?" asked Betsy. Perry was surprised. She'd

opened the door from the passenger cabin and was standing directly behind him.

"Hi, Betsy," he said. "It's the Department of Planetary Survey and Astronomical Research. It's headquartered on Rimway."

Harding was a pilot and an engineer. Perry had met him a couple of times, had even shared a mission with him when they'd both taken visitors to Toxicon. He'd never heard of Womack. Housman was apparently pretty well known. And he'd seen Charlotte Hill, who'd stopped at Ventnor Station on her way to Octavia a year or so ago. She was a knockout. Hard to forget.

"Why are you smiling, Captain?" asked Thwanna.

Caught in the act. "Octavia," he said. "They put some of the smartest people in the Confederacy out here and they get lost."

Betsy returned to the passenger cabin and Perry followed. Aaron asked if the captain had ever seen a black hole.

"Technically," he said, "nobody ever sees a black hole. But yes, I've been out here before."

Mark looked up. "If you can't see the black hole, Captain, how can you find it? I mean, how do you know where to take us?"

"We knew the general direction from where we started. And we know what the angles to several stars are from the position of the black hole. So all we have to do is get to the intersection of those angles and we will have arrived."

"Which stars?" asked Betsy.

"There are six of them. Castor, Procyon, Pollux. I don't recall the others. But there's no problem. We've got it locked into our course. If you look out the port-side window you can see Pollux. It's the brightest star in the sky."

"That *is* beautiful," said Betsy. "Bright red."

"Yeah."

"That's good," Mark said. "We wouldn't want to run into the black hole."

"Don't worry. No way that's going to happen."

The conversation attracted Virgil's interest. "What kind of research were they doing with the black hole, Captain? You have any idea?"

"I'd be guessing. Why don't we ask Thwanna?"

"Who's Thwanna?"

"Oh, she's the artificial intelligence who helps out." Years before, on his first flight as a captain he'd joked about how the AI was present to keep him from wrecking the ship. He still remembered the expressions he'd seen on the faces of his passengers. He'd never said anything like that again. "Thwanna," he said, "why don't you introduce yourself?"

"Hello," she said. *"Betsy and Mark, I'm glad to meet you. And, Aaron and Virgil, we've met before. You might recall I'm a long-time fan."*

They all looked around, trying to decide where the voice was coming from. The speaker was directly over the door that led onto the bridge. Mark and Betsy said they were glad to meet *her.* Aaron said how he could never forget a beautiful woman and Virgil told him she was an AI so she couldn't really be beautiful. That led to an argument between the comics that could have come right out of one of their movies. When they'd finished the routine, Mark repeated his question about the black hole.

Thwanna took a few seconds. Then: *"They're doing general research, Mark, but it looks as if the specific purpose of the project is that they hope to demonstrate there really are wormholes. Which they've done."*

Mark looked at Perry. "What's a wormhole?"

Betsy stepped in: "I'm not sure. But I think they're more or less tunnels, right? Through space. To another place. Sort of like traveling through what they call hyperspace."

Perry let her see that she had it right.

"That," said Thwanna, *"is probably as good a hypothesis as any. Though some physicists think a wormhole can take you across the universe in a half hour. Or even to other universes. If there really are other universes."*

"But what does that have to do with black holes?" asked Virgil.

"Theoretically," Thwanna continued, *"wormholes are created by a black hole. Don't ask me about the science. Nobody really understands it. Anyhow, they've been looking for one for a long time. But apparently the research is seriously expensive. They have to build a giant cannon that fires pods or something. The black hole creates space-time distortions in the area. The distortions form the tunnel, or the wormhole. The analysts can tell everything is working properly if they can find the pods after they've been fired. The cannon is huge, hundreds of kilometers long. That makes it expensive. It's too big to be moved so it has to be built on the spot. Theorists always claimed the theory should be valid, and it turns out it apparently is."*

"So they *did* find one?" Mark asked. "A wormhole?"

"Yes."

He grinned. "What do you do with it? With a wormhole?"

"That's always been the issue," said Thwanna. *"It has no practical use. Maybe you can cross over to another universe."*

Mark shrugged. "But what's the value in that? This one has more real estate than we're ever going to be able to use." He started to get up, apparently headed for the washroom. "Back in a minute." But he was too tall for the cabin. Almost bumped his head.

Betsy laughed. "Talk about crossing to another universe. Some of us have trouble getting to the bathroom."

Perry took advantage of the time to get more details on Octavia. Everybody was interested, so he stayed with them in the passenger cabin while Thwanna showed pictures of the station and explained its analytical capabilities. Physics was

not his strength and most of it went over his head. His mind was adrift somewhere about a beautiful young woman he was trying to get involved with back at Ventnor Station when Thwanna started talking about the cannon.

She put up a picture of what appeared to be a thin protracted gun barrel. *"It's more than six hundred kilometers long, mounted on a frame that has thrusters. Octavia uses them to control its position. Its purpose is to accelerate pea-sized probes up to about half light speed and eject them into the area where they think the wormhole is forming. I don't know how they make that determination. It has something to do with quantum activity. The tunnel forms inside the space-time continuum. There is nothing complicated about the probes. Activate them and they beep an ID code until they exhaust their power."*

"I still don't get it," said Betsy. "Why does it prove anything simply because we activate them?"

"Oh. We don't activate them. They do analysis of their surroundings. If they meet the parameters of a wormhole, they start signaling. They activate themselves."

Mark jumped in: "Sounds good."

"Brilliant." Betsy looked genuinely impressed. "Did they ever find any of the pods?"

"They did," said Thwanna. *"They claim they've established the existence of a wormhole."*

"Where's the cannon?" asked Aaron. "Is it close to the station?"

"It's only fifty or sixty kilometers away from it."

Perry had thought about applying for the tech job on Octavia. The money was good, but it would have meant settling in for a twenty-month assignment in unknown country. He was concerned at first that Marinda Barnicle, his boss, had been unhappy when he showed no interest. It left him wondering if she was trying to get rid of him. The truth was that he was enjoying his life on Chippewa too much to take on that kind of assignment. He'd have liked the extra

money, but his mom had always told him that money wasn't everything. Wasn't even very much in a society when the essentials were guaranteed. He didn't want wealth; what he wanted was time, hanging out with friends, partying, living the good life. And maybe, now and then, taking on a goofy assignment that didn't create problems.

Pollux was brighter out here than it was from Chippewa. He also picked out Castor and Procyon. But it was Pollux that dominated the sky. It was nine times the size of Earth's sun. (Perry was originally from Earth.) "Where is it?" asked Mark. "The black hole?"

Perry had done some catching up on what they could expect. "We're still pretty far out," he said. "We can't really see anything yet. In fact, we won't be able to see it at all, but we'll get some of the effects it causes. It'll take a couple more days to get there."

They watched more movies, did some electronic jigsaw puzzles, played bridge while Perry watched. And eventually a dark portion of the sky emerged, surrounded by moving lights. The sky itself grew twisted and distorted. They'd all seen images of black holes before in documentaries and movies. It was even possible to create virtual images to occupy a living room and scare the kids. Still, knowing this one was for real did have a disquieting effect. Even though he'd been here before, Perry was affected by it. "Thwanna, let's see if we're close enough to talk to them. Go to broadcast."

A blue lamp came on. Betsy and Mark both came out of the passenger cabin and stood behind him in the doorway. "Octavia," he said, "this is the *Corbin*. Do you read?"

He got nothing but static.

"Octavia or shuttle, is anybody there?"

They waited, wrapped in silence. Finally Betsy laid a

hand on Perry's shoulder: "I guess not," she said.

"They might be on the other side of the black hole," said Perry.

Mark was staring out at the troubled sky. A substantial portion of it had no stars. It was just dark. And that of course was the black hole. There was a constellation at its edge that looked like someone with a gun. The same constellation was visible on the opposite edge of the disk. He pointed it out to his passengers. "It's the same group of stars," he said.

"In two different places?" asked Mark.

"Strange things happen when you get a gravity overload."

"Captain," said Betsy, "can we see the station anywhere?"

"Not yet."

Perry flipped a switch. "Thwanna, open a channel to Ventnor."

The AI's green activity lamp lit up. *"When you're ready, Captain."*

"Corbin to Ventnor. Message for Adam Brentway: We've arrived in the KBX44 area. Have begun search. Nothing visible yet. Will get back to you when we have something. Perry."

Betsy was obviously intrigued by the object. "Where is the event horizon?" she asked.

"Out at the edge of the darkness," said Perry. "Keep in mind we won't be able to see any part of the black hole directly."

"Even if we get closer? Not that I'd want to."

"Love," said Mark, "if you got close enough to see it we might be in trouble."

"Actually," said Thwanna, *"an event horizon isn't a physical condition you can look at. It's the place where the gravity is so high that nothing can escape from it. Not even light."*

"Sounds spooky," Betsy said.

"How big is it?" asked Mark. "The black hole?"

Perry passed the question to Thwanna. *"It's about twenty kilometers across."*

"Is that all?" Mark's brow turned wrinkly. "I thought these things were seriously *big*."

"They're seriously *massive*," said Perry. *"Heavy."*

"What *is* the mass? Is it heavier than Kolmar?"

Again, Perry let Thwanna take it: *"Compared to one of these things,"* she said, *"Kolmar would have the mass of a small pickle."*

Mark frowned. "She's not serious?"

"I suspect she is."

"Incredible. I can't imagine why anybody would want to get anywhere close to something like that. I understand about the wormhole. But who really cares? Why do we need another universe? What's the point?"

Thwanna enjoyed talking with passengers. *"It's not so much what you do with a wormhole as what you can learn from it. It provides an insight into the structure of the space-time continuum. It's what they call blue sky science. It might not have a practical value but it reveals something about the cosmos."*

Mark laughed. "Well, I don't think I'd want to go through life without finding out about that."

Perry responded with a polite smile. "Says the guy in the starship. If we didn't do blue sky science, we'd never have gotten off Chippewa. In fact, I guess we'd still be sitting on a beach near the Atlantic Ocean."

"There's certainly truth to that," said Thwanna. Her tone suggested that the captain was showing an edge in his voice and maybe should stay calm.

They saw nothing. And finally it was time to sleep. He didn't get much rest that night. Too excited. They all had breakfast together in the morning, and of course the black hole continued to dominate the conversation. It was still too far to see anything other than blurry stars. "Sorry about the long ride,"

Perry told them "We didn't want to take a chance surfacing too close to this thing."

"I'm in favor of that," said Aaron in his squeaky character voice.

Betsy returned to the passenger cabin and put the HV screen on again with their telescope's view of the sky. Virgil sat down in the copilot's chair. He said how happy he was that they'd had this opportunity, that Perry had a great job. "If I had my life to live over," he said, "I think I'd train for running one of these things."

Perry was surprised. He sounded sincere.

"Captain," Virgil said, "why'd you become an interstellar pilot?"

Before Perry could answer, Thwanna was back: *"Captain,"* she said, *"I think I have something."*

"You found the station?"

"No. The cannon." She put it on the display. It was not striking, just a thin rod floating in the night.

"Excellent. The station should be nearby."

"I understand that. But if it's there, I can't see it. Not anywhere close. Certainly not sixty kilometers."

"Let me try." Perry bent over the controls and pressed a button. "Rick, you there anywhere? Calling Octavia. Rick Harding." They waited, listening to the silence. "Rick, this is Adarryl Perry. Hellooo."

"Rick's the onboard pilot, right?" asked Virgil.

"Yeah. He's the guy you'd want if you ever got in trouble out here. We'll have to give it a while, I guess."

Where the hell are they? He tried again with the same result. And called Ventnor again. "We're on-site. We've got the cannon, but no sign yet of the station. I'll get back to you as soon as we locate it." He signed off. "Thwanna, let me know when they respond." He got up, stared out at the sky for a few moments, and started for the passenger cabin.

Virgil smiled and rose easily out of his chair. "Love this

low-gravity stuff." He followed Perry into the passenger cabin, where the captain told everyone about the cannon.

"But we haven't found the station yet?" Betsy said.

"That's correct."

"Well, I guess we just have to be patient."

"I'll let you know when we get something more." Perry knew that conditions near the black hole were seriously abnormal, but somebody should have been able to get back to him. It was possible that they still didn't have a good angle to the station. Black holes had a long history of screwing up radio transmissions and sightings. For example, sometimes you got echoes of your own radio transmissions. And the last time he was out here, Perry had seen his own ship on the far side of the black hole.

Sitting in the pilot training program years before on Dellaconda calculating distances in light-years was considerably different from experiencing them, from actually crossing the sky. The reality was, of course, that he *wasn't* really experiencing them. The subspace thrust technology the *Corbin* used was, as far as he could understand, pure magic. The universe, he'd come to realize, evaded human understanding. And probably always would. Humans might know the rules, have a grip on physical law, and even make the math work, but the senses that had evolved on Earth would never grasp the realities.

Thwanna continued transmitting the same message every two minutes: *"Octavia, do you read? This is the* Larry Corbin. *Please respond."* She was also scanning the area and increasing her reach as they drew closer to the black hole. *"Captain, I see no sign of them."*

They *had* to be there.

The station would have appeared as a cluster of lights. But there was nothing other than occasional groups of stars. As Perry watched, an asteroid passed. It wasn't much more than a blur in the window but it was unnerving. "Close," he told Thwanna.

"It's okay. I was tracking it. No reason to be concerned."

"If we have any more like that, give me some advance warning." The sky was full of rocks orbiting the black hole. Some simply slid down in a gradual path toward the fireworks scattered across the darkness. One riding almost with the *Corbin* was bucking the tide. It had probably just rolled into the neighborhood and was trying to use its velocity to get clear. But it was losing the battle. "Thwanna," he said, "we still have nothing?"

"Negative, Captain. Just the cannon."

"How about the shuttle?"

"Negative. No indication of that either."

They were sitting buckled in their seats eating turkey sandwiches with cranberry sauce and coleslaw. "Are we going to go into orbit at some point?" asked Mark.

"No," said Perry, "it's too unstable out there. Stay belted in unless you have to go somewhere. There shouldn't be any surprises, but let's just play it safe for a while."

"You don't think," said Betsy, "that this thing might have periodic eruptions, do you? Maybe that's what happened to the station."

"I don't think so. I've never heard of a black hole erupting or becoming unstable. Thwanna, you know of anything like that ever happening?"

"No, Captain. We should be okay as long as we keep an eye on the traffic."

Mark looked uncomfortable.

"There's no need to worry," Perry said. "Thwanna tracks everything."

They all took a moment to concentrate on their lunch. Then Virgil asked whether Perry thought humans would ever be able to do a manned flight through a wormhole.

"That's a good question. I'll have a better idea after we find out what kind of shape the probes were in after they got recovered, provided that actually happened."

They finished their meals. Mark suggested they watch a movie. Maybe the Edgar Martin comedy they'd been saving.

Perry returned to the bridge. "Still nothing?" he asked Thwanna.

"That is correct," she said.

At that time, Edgar Martin was just launching a career that would leave its mark across the Confederacy. He played himself, as a writer for a stiff-necked comedian. He and a small group of friends spent most of their time trying to gain the attention of people who could boost their careers or who looked like potential sexual partners. But they consistently compromised themselves with false claims. Luke Hogart, for example, a guy who was always making a mess of one of his assorted public relations jobs, loved to portray himself as a onetime firefighter. When he did, he inevitably, toward the end of the show, found himself facing a desperate situation, someone trapped on a ledge, perhaps, or, as on one classic occasion, a woman who had fallen into a cage at the zoo and was pleading for help as a gorilla closed in. Hogart, of course, stands and watches, later claiming that he tried to get into the cage but it was locked. Fortunately, the woman is not injured. But she does get annoyed.

Perry always enjoyed Martin, so he joined his passengers. It had been running about three minutes, just time enough for Edgar to begin telling a lovely young woman at a party that he'd had an unusual career as an artist when the lights blinked and the AI's voice came through the speaker: *"Captain, we have something you might want to see."*

Perry nodded. "Be right there." He got up and went back onto the bridge.

Somebody shut Edgar Martin down.

• • •

They were approaching the cannon. It was on the display screen again, but clearer this time. *"I thought you might want to get a good look at it,"* Thwanna said.

Perry sat down and activated the radio. *Last chance,* he thought, *if they're not here they're not anywhere.* "Rick, this is Adarryl Perry aboard the *Corbin.* Please answer up. Are you there anywhere?" He switched over and got static. Then: "Octavia, can you hear me?"

Behind him the door opened and closed. He cut down the volume of the static and looked back at Mark. "We have a problem?" Mark asked.

"No. I think Thwanna just wanted to give us a look at the cannon."

"Oh," Mark said. "Holy cats. Yeah. That thing's *enormous.*"

"It is pretty big."

"There's still no sign of them?"

"No. But we're in a loud area. Maybe they're just not getting the signal. Or we're not getting theirs."

"You don't give up easy, do you?"

He pointed at the copilot's seat. "Mark, relax. We're going to move in closer, and we'll be braking."

"Okay."

Perry passed the message to the passenger cabin. Moments later the *Corbin* turned slightly to starboard and began to decelerate. The cannon grew larger. There was no sign of damage anywhere. He took over the controls and started to brake.

"It's tumbling," said Mark. "Look at it."

It was, but slowly. *"There's too much activity here,"* said Thwanna. *"They would have had to make constant adjustments to keep it aimed at the target. Whatever that was."*

It descended below the frame and then rose again as Perry drew closer. He continued until it filled the windows, only a couple of kilometers away, an endless tube encased in a cube-shaped frame. He lined up alongside it, matched its velocity, and went into cruise. He couldn't quite stay with it, though, because it would have required matching its tumble, which would have made everyone ill. *"I estimate,"* said Thwanna, *"that no adjustments have been made in its course in at least a week. Probably longer."*

"Are you saying," asked Mark, "that they've been sucked into the black hole?"

"I'm just saying they should be somewhere in this area."

"What do you think, Captain?"

Perry sighed. "I think they're gone."

I.

1435: 11 YEARS LATER.

However magnificent the seas and forests of other worlds,
However dazzling their sunlit skies,
However wide their beaches,
There is no view from any place in God's vast cosmos
That matches the moonlight falling on one's own front porch.
—WALFORD CANDLES, "HOME AT LAST," 1199

I can't remember a happier time than the day Gabe came back. Alex and I had assumed he was dead, along with the other twenty-six hundred passengers and crew on the *Capella*. It simply disappeared more than a decade ago and nobody had any idea what had happened. Funerals and farewells were conducted, and eventually families and friends went on with their lives. But a few months ago it surfaced. It had gotten tangled with a time warp. On board only about three weeks had passed, so the passengers and crew were shocked to discover that the outside world was eleven years older. Gabe and the others had returned though, and that was all that mattered.

We picked him up during the rescue operation and

returned to Rimway, where we docked at Skydeck. Alex asked Gabe whether he would like to stop and have a drink to celebrate, but he shook his head. "Just take me home," he said. "I'll celebrate when we walk in the front door."

Gabe was seated beside me in the skimmer a couple of hours later as we descended through the clouds. "I can't believe this happened," he said. "Thank God it's over." He looked back at Alex. "Are you still living on Rambuckle?"

"No. After the *Capella* disappeared, I decided it was time to go home."

Gabe let us see he was amused. "So one good thing, at least, has come out of this. You're living here now, right? In the country house?"

"Yes, we've set up a business here."

"It'll be good to have you home, Alex."

"I've been here a long time. Thanks for turning the property over to me. Anyhow, we'll clear everything out. Soon as I can decide where I'm headed. It should only take a few days."

"No, no, no. You're not listening to me. You can't do that. You've been living here too, right? Not just running a business?"

"I have been, yes."

Gabe looked my way. "And you, Chase?"

"I have a cottage near the river," I said.

"I don't see any rings. You guys aren't a couple, are you?"

I'm not sure my cheeks didn't redden a bit. There'd been a time when Alex and I had made a connection. But it had been brief, and it was long ago.

"No," I said. "I just work for Alex. For Rainbow." I'd been Gabe's pilot before the *Capella* took him away. It was a flight he'd invited me onto, a combination of business and vacation, but fortunately I'd declined. Although it occurred to me that if I'd gone along I'd have been more than a decade younger.

"Well, anyhow," said Gabe, "there should be plenty of room at the country house. There's no reason you should leave, Alex. Stay there, please."

Alex hesitated. "Sure, Uncle Gabe. If it's really okay with you."

"Of course it is." He was suddenly looking out the window at the river. "I've never seen the Melony look so good."

"That's because *you're* home," I said.

"Is Jacob still there?"

The AI. "Yes," said Alex. "Of course."

"So what kind of business does Rainbow do?"

"Nothing's changed. I still deal in antiquities." Alex showed a touch of discomfort. "I hope that's not a problem."

"It's okay. Do what you have to. Don't worry about it." Gabe had never approved of selling artifacts to private collectors. They should be available to everyone. Not stored away in the homes of the wealthy. But fortunately, on this occasion, he showed a flexibility that allowed him to confront his new situation with a let's-not-get-excited attitude.

Minutes later we arrived over the country house. "It doesn't look any different," Gabe said. We touched down and climbed out. Then he stood admiring the building, the walkway, and the surrounding trees. "It's hard to believe what's happened."

We did a round of hugs and kisses, then climbed onto the porch, and the door opened. *"Hello, Gabe. I can't believe you're back."* It was Jacob, the house AI, who was so excited he could barely contain himself. *"It's so good to see you again. Are you okay? You look great."*

"Hello, Jacob. How've you been?"

"We missed you. Maybe you should think about retiring. Just hang around."

We went inside. "What've you been up to?" Gabe asked Jacob as the door closed behind us.

"Watching Bellarian plays." Jacob loved the theater and spent a lot of his time in virtual box seats.

Margaret E. Heggan Public Library
606 Delsea Drive
Sewell, NJ 08080

"Bellarian?" I said. "Where are they from?"

"Fourth millennium. Bellarius was the first world to produce its own shows."

"Maybe we could attend some together," said Gabe.

"I can arrange that. I'm planning on watching Graveyard Shift *tonight, if you're interested. It's a comedy."*

"I'll need a couple of nights to settle in, Jacob. But sure, let's set something up."

We carried everything to his quarters in the rear. Gabe was looking around the apartment, shaking his head, commenting that it was hard to believe he'd been gone over a decade. "By the way," he added, "did we ever find out what happened to Octavia?"

"That happened," I said, "just before you left. Am I right?"

"That's correct. Just a few weeks earlier."

"No," said Alex. "They never got any answers. It had to have gone into the black hole, but the people who were running the program claimed that just wasn't possible. There was a major commotion at the time when you guys disappeared too. The media were full of rumors about a connection."

"So they never came up with anything at all?"

"Not anything definitive. Mostly all they had was speculation."

"You think it could have also gotten tangled up in a time warp?"

"I've no idea, Gabe. According to the experts, you need a star drive unit to make that happen. The station had thrusters but that was all. The search parties found nothing. They put together a commission that decided the only reasonable solution was that one of the four crew sabotaged the place. That caused a lot of anger. Members of the commission took considerable heat. Eventually the media suggested they were trying to conceal a defect in the station. But they went over other stations of the same model and found nothing."

"Now that I've had some experience being stranded myself," said Gabe, "I can tell you it's seriously unsettling. We knew for about a week that something had gone wrong and it was scary. We thought we were going to be there forever. I'd hate to think something like that happened to the people on Octavia." He settled into the sofa. "I knew one of them."

"Really? Which one?"

"Del Housman. We grew up together. Both members of the Explorers back in grade-school days. We never really lost touch. Until Octavia happened. You met him. We had him over to the house a couple of times when you were there."

"I have no recollection of him. But you had a lot of visitors."

"What was he like?" I asked.

"He was a good guy. A lot of the other kids treated him like a nerd. But he shrugged it off. They got especially annoyed with him because he refused to believe that AIs were actually alive. I think he's the reason I figured out that the house didn't really care what happened to me. That the voices were all automatic." He paused for a smile. "He was always popular with the girls though."

"He looks pretty ordinary," I said.

"I guess. But that didn't matter. He was a charmer. They loved him."

Gabe had provided a home for Alex, who'd lost his parents in a hurricane when he was two years old. He was tall, with black hair parted on the left in a style we didn't see much anymore. He had intelligent blue eyes that reflected the patience derived from so many years digging into dozens of archeological sites around and beyond the Confederacy. There was an intensity in his manner that tended to draw attention whenever he entered a room. Alex was just coming in off the porch when Gabe came through the door carrying a captain's cap. "It's Deirdre Schultz's," he said. She had been the *Capella*'s commanding officer.

"Beautiful," said Alex. I understood. It was already valuable and would become, in time, priceless. "How did you persuade her to give it to you?"

"I just offered to replace it. She laughed and turned it over. Wouldn't accept any money."

"That was generous of her."

Gabe couldn't avoid shrugging, as if she'd have done it for anyone. "She told me I was her public relations guy." She'd signed an authentication. "I think she suspected that if she let me have it, it would eventually wind up in a museum."

"She read you pretty well," said Alex.

The laughter continued, and neither said anything about what must have been on both their minds: that Alex, left to his own inclinations, would have eventually sold it to the highest bidder.

"You know," Alex said, "leaving Rimway was probably the dumbest thing I've ever done." They shook hands, both looking as if they had finally put the old quarrel behind them. "And thanks for this." He looked up at the house. "I'm going to call Joyce Bartlett and have her take care of whatever legal formalities are necessary to return everything."

"Who's Joyce Bartlett?"

"My lawyer."

Gabe looked puzzled. "Oh. I get it. You're talking about my will."

"Yes."

"Holy cats, Alex. I hadn't thought about that. I mean, from my perspective, I've only been gone a couple of weeks. And by the way, call me Gabe, okay? We're both adults now."

"Gabe." Alex was testing it. "Sounds strange."

"This whole business has been pretty strange."

"I know. You were officially declared dead three years ago."

"So this place is now yours?"

Alex nodded. "Yes. It is. But you'll have it back pretty quickly."

Gabe stared out at the trees, the carefully trimmed bushes and the sculpted lawn. "You took good care of it," he said.

"Of course, Gabe."

"I won't have you leave it. It's your home. Has been for years."

A worldwide celebration was staged two nights later. Passengers, families, and crew arrived at thirty-six sites around the planet, and one at the space station, to share drinks and memories and to say thanks to those who'd been part of the rescue effort, as well as to President Davis.

Telemotion technology enabled them to embrace and shake hands. The Andiquar group met at the Miranda Hotel. The event broke every Rimway record for total number of viewers and participants. And for at least those few hours, we became a global family.

An army of Gabe's old friends and relatives descended on the country house during the next few days. They took him out to luncheons and dinners, and spent time with him just sitting around talking about what, for them, were the good old days. Since for Gabe the good old days had been only three weeks earlier, there was a fair amount of disorientation on both sides. "We held a funeral service for you," Alex told him.

"Did anybody come?" Gabe asked.

Alex got an uncertain look in his eyes. "I can show you some pictures."

"Let's let it go."

Veronica Walker was standing beside Alex. She was an elementary-school teacher with chestnut hair, brown eyes, and a killer smile. I watched her squeeze his hand as he spoke to his uncle. They'd met at an auction when she'd outbid Alex for a lamp that had belonged to Wally Candles, the poet who'd become famous during the Ashiyyurean War. "Gabe," she said, "I'm glad to meet you. I've heard so much about you. I wonder if I could have you come by the school and talk to my kids?"

"Sure. Would that be about archeology?"

"Whatever you like. But especially about why history matters."

Alex and I had no problem adjusting to Gabe's return. We'd both missed him, and getting him back became a gift of immeasurable substance. I was happy to note that whatever resistance Gabe had mounted against his nephew's habitual salvaging of historical artifacts and putting them up for sale to private collectors did not show itself during the weeks that passed after he came back. If he was still embarrassed by Alex's profession, he refused to show any indication of it.

But there were some difficult moments.

Alex updated him on a few family deaths, including two great-grandparents on his mother's side. And there was his cousin Tom Benedict, an MD who'd died on the primitive world Lyseria, where a plague had broken out and killed almost the entire colony. Tom had gone to help in spite of dire warnings by friends and relatives. After a long struggle, he became one of the casualties. Eventually the plague was neutralized, but not in time to save him.

Gabe and Tom had been close, had spent a lot of time together, and had taken the young Alex on camping trips and boat rides back in the early days. They'd also taken him along on a couple of interstellar tours, which Alex told me had changed him forever. "They gave me a passion for history. For artifacts, especially. I loved touching them, touching *history*. I especially liked an artifact when I had a name to go with it."

• • •

I got a surprise the next day when Gabe informed me that April Rafferty would be arriving at about noon. A shadow had crept into his eyes. "Except," he said, "that her name isn't *Rafferty* anymore. She's April *Dutton* now."

April Rafferty had been his fiancé eleven years earlier, when he climbed aboard the *Capella* and disappeared into the night. They hadn't set a wedding date when it happened, but it had been obvious they weren't going to delay it much longer. April had been heartbroken when the ship was lost. She'd waited, praying that someone would figure out what had happened and provide a reason to keep up hope. But after a few weeks without contact, everything turned negative. Whatever had occurred, the experts said, *we may never know, but it's obvious we'll not see them again.*

The Confederacy went into shock. It was easily the worst interstellar disaster ever. The *Capella* had disappeared and taken everyone with her. April had come to me because I was a pilot and she thought I might be able to offer a ray of hope. Interstellars had been occasionally disappearing over the centuries. A few came back after having suffered minor engine damage of some sort, combined with a communication blackout. But that sort of thing was extremely rare. So when she showed up at my cottage one evening a few days after the incident and asked whether I thought there was any chance that Gabe was alive somewhere and whether there was any possibility he'd be found, I said nothing to give her hope. I thought a claim in which I had no confidence would do nothing except extend the pain.

April arrived exactly at noon. I told her how good it was to see her again. She responded by saying much the same thing. She hadn't changed, except that maybe some of the vibrancy that I remembered was gone. But that was natural after so many years. I let Gabe know and led her into my office. His office door opened in back, he came forward, and I tried to figure out how to get out of the way. I recall saying something about how I hoped she was happy with whomever it was she'd married.

Then Gabe arrived. They exchanged warm smiles. "April," he said, "you won't believe this but it's only been about three weeks since I saw you."

"That's what I've been hearing," she said. "Gabe, I missed you."

They moved into a cautious embrace while I excused myself and left the room. The last thing I heard was Gabe asking whether she was okay.

II

Celebrate whenever and whatever you can. Wed, bring
forth a child, repair a broken door, cut the grass, and do not
waste the opportunity to beat the drum with friends and
throw a party. It is the essence of life and joy.

—CHEN LO COBB, "CAREFUL WHERE YOU WALK,"
FROM *COLLECTIBLES*, 614

A few nights later, we threw another party. We cleared several
rooms, brought in a band, served drinks and side dishes, and
danced well into the night. I'd hoped that Gabe might have
invited April and her husband. But he said nothing either to
Alex or to me. I'd thought about making the suggestion but
realized it would be a terrible idea. So I kept my distance.

Guests included a couple of archeologists from Andiquar
University; people from several museums, including Argus
Konn, who'd traveled halfway around the globe to attend;
and historians, one of whom was writing an archeological
book that featured Gabe in a prime role. There were also a
few family members and old friends. And there was someone else from his earlier days: his pilot, Tori Kolpath. My
mom. I watched them fall into each other's arms. For me it
was the highlight of the evening. She'd come from the other
side of the continent to be here. And when she began talking
about her reaction to his reported death, tears rolled down

her cheeks. Gabe told me later it was the only time he'd ever seen that kind of emotional outburst from her.

Fenn Redfield, a police commissioner who'd been only an inspector when the *Capella* vanished, was also present. He'd helped Alex on several occasions and also, to Gabe's surprise, became his longtime tennis partner. Gabe had never known Redfield to play tennis.

We all sat down to prep for the banquet. Alex kicked things off by introducing Gabe to a round of enthusiastic applause. "He was the man," he said, "who made it possible to uncover the truth about Christopher Sim." Sim, of course, was remembered as the George Washington of the Confederacy, the legendary hero who'd held the Mutes at bay during the war years. Gabe spoke for a few minutes about how happy he was to be back with old friends on solid ground.

Amanda Ornstein, one of the University Museum directors, commented how quiet everything had been while he was gone. "All the excitement of the old days," she said, "kind of subsided. I don't know if Gabe ever thought of himself as a driving force, but I think we came to realize how much we needed him."

Gabe looked up from his drink and smiled. "You want some old-time excitement, Amanda?"

"Of course," she said. Amanda was tall, serene, a onetime actor who still attracted the attention of males despite her advanced age.

"Good enough." Gabe grinned. "I was going to let this go for a while, but this is probably as good a time as any. Give me a second. I'll be right back." He finished his drink, got up from the table, and left.

Amanda looked toward Alex. "I didn't mean to start anything."

"It's okay. He's still making some adjustments."

Quinda Arin, another of Gabe's longtime friends, just

stared at the door he'd passed through. "It's really nice having him back. I don't think I ever appreciated him until we'd lost him. Alex, do you have any idea what he's talking about?"

"None whatever. But apparently he's got something hidden in his room."

Amanda asked her audience if anyone knew whether Gabe planned to resume his archeological career. Several hands went up, and the answer was a resounding *yes*. Several of our visitors had posed the question to him, and in each case Gabe had responded with enthusiasm. Of course he was. There was some inconsistency about the nature of his next project, but details didn't matter.

Eventually Quinda approached me. "You think he's okay?"

"Sure." I thought about saying I'd go check, but that was silly. He was gone longer than we expected. We all assumed he'd gone to get something, but when finally he came back, his hands were empty and he looked frustrated. His eyes settled on Alex and me. "I had an artifact back there. A silver trophy. I think it was on the shelf in the closet. You guys by any chance know what happened to it?"

We'd kept his quarters pristine for a year or so. But gradually we'd begun using it for storage of artifacts owned by our clients. They were usually for sale, and they sent them to us to ascertain their value and arrange delivery when they were moved.

"A silver trophy?" asked Alex.

"Yes. The owner was, I think, Angela Harding. She wanted me to figure out whether it was an artifact. Possibly from a high-tech civilization. There was an imprint using characters I'd never seen before and wasn't able to track."

Alex thought about it. "I don't recall seeing anything like that in there."

Gabe turned toward me. "It was shaped like a flower vase, widening toward the top. It had a cone image in front and three lines of characters that didn't match any known language. How about you, Chase? You ever see it?"

Yeah, I'd seen it. Four or five years ago. "I remember it."

Gabe's eyes grew intense. "What happened to it?"

"I returned it."

"To whom?"

"Its owner. I think she had a receipt."

"You *think*?"

"Gabe, it's been a long time. But yes, I wouldn't have given it to anyone who couldn't prove she was the owner."

"Did you run it by Alex?"

"I think at the time he was out on a project."

Alex broke in: "Gabe, who did it belong to?"

"Angela Harding."

"Give me a minute," I said. "I'll check it."

"Please do. We need a contact."

I left the room and walked down the hallway to my office. The door opened for me and I went inside. "Jacob, check out Angela Harding for me, please."

I sat down and started some soft music.

"I have her, Chase."

"Did she pick up a silver trophy several years ago?"

"That is correct."

"Was she the owner?"

"Yes."

"What was the source of the trophy?"

"That is unknown, Chase."

"Do we have a receipt?"

"Yes, we do."

"Print a copy, please."

Amanda was still overseeing a conversation between Gabe and the audience when I got back. "We have it," I said, and handed him the receipt.

"Good." He looked over at Alex, who nodded, suggesting

he'd told his uncle I wouldn't give anything away without getting the appropriate paperwork. "Alex, you know who Angela Harding is, don't you?"

"I have no idea, Gabe."

"She is Rick Harding's sister."

Alex's brow creased. "The name rings a bell."

"He was one of the people lost on Octavia."

"Oh. Right."

Amanda had finished her remarks and was part of a small crowd that had gathered around us. "I knew Archie," she said.

"Archie Womack?" The question came from several people.

"Yes."

Everyone turned and looked at her. They said they were sorry to hear it and asked whether they'd been close. Alex was visibly surprised. "I don't recall your mentioning it at the time."

"He was a good man," she added. "He had a special interest in orphans. I don't know how many of them got through Andiquar University thanks to his support."

"You came to know him through the museum?" somebody asked.

"Actually, no. We belonged to the same bridge club. Over the years we got closer. He was at the house a few times. We had lunch together occasionally. I'm pretty sure you met him once." That was directed at Alex.

"Really?" He was trying to reach back, but he produced nothing. "I remember getting introduced to a lot of your friends over the years." He shrugged. "I just don't remember."

Her eyes closed and she shook her head. "I'm sorry he's gone. I wish they could pin down what happened."

"So do I," said Gabe.

"The best they could come up with," said Amanda, "is that they got attacked by pirates. Or kidnapped by aliens."

"You don't buy into either, I assume?"

"We don't have any pirates. And in either case, if someone

they didn't know showed up, they'd certainly have sent a message. No, wait, I take that back. There was a period of about thirty hours every few months that they were blocked off. That the black hole got between them and anybody they could have contacted. And that was when it happened."

"Interesting," said Alex. "Any reason someone would have wanted to attack them?"

"None I've ever heard of."

"That would be worth looking into, Alex," said Fenn Redfield. "I take it you've never gotten involved."

"No, not really. No way I could."

Fenn asked Gabe what he knew about it.

"Not much. If my memory serves me right, the Octavia tech, Rick Harding, was the owner of the trophy. Angela said she found it in a closet after the station disappeared. She brought it in here and asked me if I'd ever seen anything like it before."

"Had you?"

"Not at first glance. Unfortunately I never had time to work on it. I can tell you there's no record anywhere, in any known age, of a set of characters that looked like the ones on the artifact."

"So it might have been legitimate? A product of an alien civilization?"

"Possibly."

Alex looked puzzled. "If it was, why did he have it in a closet?"

"I think you just asked the right question." Gabe looked seriously unhappy. "Unfortunately I don't even have a picture of it."

We drifted back into the party. But Gabe and Alex spent much of the rest of the evening in what was obviously a serious conversation. The truth was there was no way those two were going to walk away from a lost artifact. But Gabe had committed to join an archeological team that was preparing to leave for the Korkona, a star system that had housed a failed colony during the sixth millennium. And Alex was facing a trip around the world in two days to attend an antiquities conference. So I got the assignment of taking the first step. "Chase," said Gabe, "do we have a contact for her?"

"For Angela Harding?"

"Yes."

"She lives in Newbury. Or at least she did when she retrieved the artifact." I passed the question to Jacob.

"Negative," he said. *"There is no listing for anyone by that name currently living in Newbury. Nor is there a forwarding address for the Angela Harding who formerly lived there. She seems to have dropped off the listings in 1431."* Four years earlier. Newbury was about sixty kilometers west, a quiet little leisurely town.

"Okay." Gabe shook his head. Nothing's ever easy. "Chase, see if you can track her down. That okay with you, Alex? I don't want to be taking over your assistant."

Alex grinned. "I don't exactly think of Chase as an assistant. But sure. Do whatever you need."

"Right. Okay. If you can locate her, we'd like to recover the trophy, if possible. And if you can, let's get more information on Harding. It would be especially helpful if we could find out where he got the thing."

"Gabe," said Alex, "you probably remember this better than we all do, but when nobody could explain how a space station could disappear, even one circling a black hole, rumors started showing up. Harding was the tech. The station had thrusters. Could he or someone else have used them to send the station into the black hole?"

"I've no idea," said Gabe. He passed the question to me.

"I doubt he could have used the system to steer the thing into the hole. It was a station, not a ship. He'd have had to destabilize it, get it out of orbit. It would have taken a while, and it's hard to believe the others would have just stood around and watched."

"There were also rumors," said Amanda, "that DPSAR figured out what happened but kept it quiet."

"Somebody wrote a book," I said. "The title was *Lost on Octavia*. It claimed that a bomb had been planted on the station."

"How could that have happened?" asked Gabe. "They were out there for what, a year and a half? And they weren't changing the personnel."

"There were periodic visits by supply vehicles. Mostly bringing food and water. The problem is they couldn't find a motive for anyone, so the author invented one. Blamed it on religious extremists who thought we were breaking into divine territory. But she could never point the finger at anyone specific."

Gabe sent me a tolerant smile. "When did Angela come back for it?"

I checked the receipt. "Midsummer, 1429." Six years ago.

"I guess she got tired of waiting for me." A bird—I think it was a turik—landed on a windowsill, flapped and squawked in the moonlight, and fell off. We all glanced at it and watched it fly away. Then Gabe continued: "Chase, if you can catch up with her, see if you can find out whether she ever learned whether it was actually an alien artifact. Was it *real*?"

"Okay."

"And by the way, apologize for my not getting back to her."

"I already did that. At the time, she didn't realize you'd been on the *Capella*."

"I hope she didn't get rid of it," said Gabe.

Alex was not happy. "You said you didn't get any pictures of the thing."

"That's correct, Alex. I was on the run at the time."

"That's the first thing we do, Gabe, when something like that comes in."

Gabe's expression hardened, and I thought the old animosity between the two might break out again, but he didn't say anything. In case he was thinking about it, I jumped in: "If she does have it, and she's found out it's a legitimate alien artifact, do you guys want to make an offer?"

They looked at each other. "If she tells you it's legitimate," said Gabe, "and she still has possession of it, tell her we'll be in touch. If she's sold it, see if you can find out to whom."

It was getting late. Alex got everyone together in the conference room. "Something else we need to take care of," he said. He looked over at Gabe, who was talking with Amanda and Fenn. "Uncle Gabe, would you come forward, please?"

Gabe looked around him as if Alex was actually speaking to someone else. That was Amanda's cue to take his arm and escort him to his nephew's side.

"Gabe," he said, "I'd like to remind you that you're surrounded by friends and family who've come together not only to show you how pleased they are to have you back but also because we have something for you."

He stepped aside and was replaced by Hiram Olson, head of the archeology department at Andiquar University and a longtime friend of Gabe's. Hiram was a tall, wide-shouldered man with the electric features of a comedian. He could in fact play almost any role needed. On that evening, he was dead serious. He reached down and took a package from beneath the table. He removed the wrapping, revealing a gold-framed plaque. "Gabriel," he said, "eleven years ago, you inspired a search that made it possible for Alex to unearth a previously unsuspected piece of history. One of the keys that led to that happy result was the classic poem 'Leisha' by Walford Candles, written during the Mute War."

He held the frame where everyone could see it. The poem was inscribed on the plaque, beneath Gabe's name and above a visual of Christopher Sim's *Corsarius*.

• • •

Amanda took him aside a few minutes later. "Gabe," she said, "I'm not supposed to tell you this, but you're on the inside track for the Fleminger Award this year." For anyone who doesn't know, the Fleminger is granted for special achievement in support of historical research. The recipients have been frequently associated with archeology.

A few minutes later Gabe approached his nephew and said thanks. "It wouldn't be happening without you."

III.

The terror of the graveyard
Is not that it waits at the end of life's journey,
But that it becomes, as time goes by,
The resting place of family and friends,
Of so many who matter.
—WALFORD CANDLES, "LIGHTS OUT," 1212

If the trophy had actually been an alien object, and Angela Harding had disposed of it, it would almost certainly have shown up on the datanet. So when I got home, I showered, got into my pajamas, sat down, and asked Carmen to run a search. She found nothing.

So we looked for the background of the Angela Harding who *had* lived in Newbury. She arrived there in 1427, lived a quiet existence for four years, and dropped out of sight. That's not especially unusual. A lot of people, with an interest in maintaining a level of privacy, keep as much of their data off the net as they can.

"Do you see anything of value?" asked Carmen.

"Not yet. I wonder if she has an avatar?" Most people do. But of course the reader already knows that. We can go to one and experience the illusion of talking with the actual person. We can get that individual's opinion on just about anything. All kinds of information about accomplishments is accessible. Of course, there's no guarantee about accuracy, but then, as most of us realize, it would take all the fun out of the exercise.

But again Angela was a negative. There *was* an Angela Harding in Piedmont, a large island eighty kilometers off the coast. But she was only nine years old. "Maybe she's related?" I said.

"I'll check." I watched while Carmen contacted the parents and asked if there was another branch of the family located in the area. They said not that they knew of. The child had a grandmother in Andiquar, but there was no familial connection with anyone else of that name.

"All right. Let's try a general search."

Carmen needed only a moment: *"There are approximately six hundred persons named Angela Harding spread around the planet. That doesn't take into account the possibility that she got married and changed her name."*

There *had* been an avatar, but it was taken down in 1429, about the same time Angela returned to the country house and recovered the trophy.

The most curious aspect of all that was that she'd removed contact information. I wondered why. Unfortunately it meant that instead of just calling, I would have to visit Newbury and start looking for her. In the morning, I notified Alex. "I won't be going in today," I told him. "I'm headed for Newbury."

"All right," he said. *"Did you find her?"*

"No. No sign of her yet."

"Okay. Good luck. When are you leaving?"

"In about fifteen minutes."

He started talking to Gabe. Then he was back: *"Good. Can you hold for a second? Gabe wants to ask you something."*

Gabe picked up. *"Chase? My schedule has changed. You mind if I go along?"*

• • •

He and Alex were both waiting when I touched down at the country house. At first I thought I was going to have *two* passengers. But Alex signaled no. "Hate to miss it," he said. "But I have to get out of here this afternoon. Let me know if you find anything."

Gabe climbed in, we waved good-bye, and lifted off. "What's the plan?" he asked.

"The only thing I can think of is to head for the last address we had and see if we can track her from there."

"Sounds good."

A light rain began to fall as we swung west and flew out over the Melony. The wind picked up, and sailboats were taking advantage of it to get to shore.

We didn't talk much. Gabe seemed to have something on his mind. Maybe April. I made several efforts to find subjects that would interest him. Finally I decided to ask him directly: "You going to see her again, Gabe?"

"See who?" He knew damn well who I was talking about.

"April."

"She invited me to stop by for a visit. Said I'd like Craig. Her husband."

"Oh."

"He's a judge. She couldn't resist telling me."

"Are you going to take her up on it?"

He was looking off into the distance. "I don't think it's a good idea. Anyhow, I'm pretty busy right now." He fell silent again. Moved around in his seat. Adjusted his belt. Went back to staring out at passing clouds. And then sighed. "Best thing I can do, Chase, is to stay out of her life."

We both knew that. But it hurt.

The hunt for intelligent life has been a mainstay of space science since the first moon flights nine thousand years ago. We haven't found much. The Ashiyyur, who lived among a relatively close cluster of stars, have been pretty much the entire game. There've been a few worlds with ruins, but on the whole life seems to happen on only a small fraction of even the most ideal worlds, filled with water and sunlight. And on the rare occasions that a technically advanced culture showed up, once they developed explosives they showed a tendency to use them. The Ashiyyur were the only ones we'd found who seemed to have survived through eons of advanced technology.

"Gabe," I said, "why do we care so much about finding aliens?"

"I guess because the universe seems so empty. For thousands of years, we rode around the Orion Arm and saw *nothing*. If you read the histories of the period, people seemed to be convinced that they were probably alone. I mean, those years were seriously depressing. They *did* find an occasional world with trees and squirrels, but they were rare." He turned and stared at me. "Why am I telling *you* all this stuff? You know this as well as I do."

"The thing that amazes me," I said, "is that when we finally *did* find somebody, we got into a war with them."

"Yeah. That was dumb." We were approaching a small town surrounded by forest. "Is that it?"

"Next one over." We kept going and a few minutes later came out of the rain, saw Newbury, and started down. The town consisted of about two hundred homes, a town hall, a theater, a church, a school, and a couple of bars. We descended into a field behind 716 Thornberry Avenue, Angela Harding's home as recently as 1431, four years earlier. Some kids were playing cards in a tree fort. As we touched ground, they stopped and waved.

The house was an attractive gold-and-white two-story villa with lots of windows, a cluster of palm trees, a swing, and a fountain. We climbed out and Gabe led the way to a timber fence. We passed through a gate into the front yard, checked the number, and climbed four steps onto the porch, where

we introduced ourselves and explained that we were looking for Ms. Harding. A minute later the door opened and a
congenial young man appeared. He was probably just at the
end of his high school years. He smiled but shook his head.
"Sorry. I don't think I can help you. I don't know anybody by
that name."

"She lived here, in this house, a few years ago," said Gabe.

"Oh. Well, come on in. Maybe Mom knows her." He backed
away to make room for us. We went into an interior filled
with fabric furniture and a table that might have served for
doing puzzles or playing games. We heard a woman's voice
from another room: "Who is it, Mack?"

"I'm not sure," he said. "They're looking for—" She
emerged, wiping her hands on a towel. Her hair was brown
and a bit disheveled. She pushed it back away from her fore-
head and inspected us with matching brown eyes. "They're
looking for a Ms. Harding, Mom. Is she the lady we bought
the house from?"

Mom shrugged. "I've no idea. We never met the owner."
Her tone suggested she had no interest in hunting through
paperwork. "Sorry."

Gabe glanced at me. *Take it.* "Ma'am," I said, "maybe your
AI could help?"

"Allie came here with us."

"Oh. May I ask how long you've been here?"

"About five years." She looked around the room, indicating
she had better things to do. "Listen, I don't want to rush you
people, but I'm busy at the moment, and I don't think I can
be of any help."

"You never heard her name at all? Angela Harding?"

"Not that I can recall." She opened the front door and stood
aside. "I hope you find her."

We took the hint. "She was probably the wrong person to
ask anyhow," I said after we got outside.

"Why's that?"

"I never met the people I bought my place from, either. I suspect that's generally true. Let's try the neighbors." The homes on Thornberry Avenue were not far apart. You could walk to whatever was next door in a couple of minutes. So they probably knew each other fairly well.

The house on the opposite side of the road was one of the more stylish properties in the area. It rose three stories, with an arched doorway and side panels, sliding glass walls, neatly cut terraces, and a swimming pool off to one side. We crossed over, followed a pebbled walkway through the garden, climbed a stairway onto a veranda, and were greeted by an AI. *"Good afternoon,"* she said. *"Can I be of assistance?"*

Gabe identified himself. "We are trying to locate Angela Harding. She lived across the street a few years ago."

"Just a moment, please. Let me consult." A German shepherd appeared on the street. It stopped and looked toward us before moving on. The AI was still consulting when a skimmer rose from one of the properties at the east end of the avenue, turned in our direction, passed overhead, and faded into the distance. Then the door opened and a stout bearded man looked out at us. "You're looking for Angela?"

"Yes," said Gabe.

"Come in." He backed away and we followed him into a lushly furnished living room, dominated by a three-piece sectional dark leather sofa. A beautiful young woman sat in one of two matching chairs. He took a seat in the other and left the sofa for us. "Are you relatives?"

"She was a client," said Gabe. "I need to talk to her about a project we were working on."

"I see. May I ask the nature of the project?"

Gabe made up something about an effort to improve funding for area schools. Our host responded with a tolerant smile. "She lived across the street, but she moved four or five years ago." He looked over at the woman. "You have any idea where she is, Ari?"

"No," Ari said. "She's still in the area somewhere, or at least she was. But I've no idea where she actually lives." Ari's black hair was cut short. She had classic features.

We did a round of introductions. Then Gabe picked up the thread: "Do you guys by any chance know whether she got married? Maybe changed her name?"

They passed the question on to their AI.

"No, Mr. Benedict," she said. *"Sorry, but it was never mentioned in my presence. I'm not aware whether she ever married."*

Gabe got up. "Okay. Thank you. Maybe one of the other neighbors will have something." We started for the door.

"Wait," said Ari. "I have a better idea. Angela had a pretty close friend you might try talking to."

We stopped in our tracks. "Who's that?"

"Esther Horn. She owns a bake shop across the street from the Burrows School."

"That's the one on the edge of town?" I asked. We'd passed over a school coming in.

"Yes. The bake shop is right across from the main entrance. They've tried to close it a couple times. People worry that the kids are getting too much sugar. But it's still there."

It was a weekend, so the school was closed. But the bake shop was open. We landed in an adjacent field and a couple of minutes later were taking a long look at Esther Horn's cherry-flavored croissants. She was a tall blonde who managed to look genuinely happy to see us. Her cinnamon-colored eyes had a depth that suggested a serious level of intelligence and, if called for, tenacity. It was easy to imagine her confronting school authorities who were trying to close her down. "Sure," she said, "I remember Angela. She used to come in here all the time."

The shop was stocked with oversized brownies; olive oil cake; lemon, banana, and peach muffins; zucchini bread; strawberry shortcake; apple and cherry pie; chocolate cake;

and a variety of cookies. No wonder the school authorities were worried.

"Can you help us locate her?" asked Gabe.

"She's a long walk from here. What's going on? You guys salesmen?"

"No." Gabe thought about what he wanted to tell her. "We may have some good news for her."

"Really? Well, glad to hear it." We indicated we'd like some buns. She put them in a bag and handed them to me. Gabe made the payment.

"Do you know where she lives?" he asked.

"Oh, yes. But it's going to take you a while to get there."

"We were given the impression she was in this area."

"Oh, no. No. She lives on the west coast."

"Really?"

"That's correct."

"Can you give us an address?"

"I don't like to give out personal information. You want to tell me specifically why you want to contact her?"

"She was a client. I lost touch with her years ago. I owe her something."

Her eyes darkened. "How about I pass your name and code along to her, and she can get in contact with *you*?"

"Okay." Gabe gave her the information. "Tell her it's important. She'll know what it's about." He reached into the bag, removed one of the buns, and took a bite. "It's good," he said.

"You can't go wrong with cinnamon buns, Mr. Benedict."

"Esther, how long has it been since you've seen her?"

"A couple of years. I don't think she's been back here since her wedding." She was looking past us, her mind somewhere else. "I miss her."

"Did you know her brother?"

"Rick? Yes, I knew him." She hesitated. "We were pretty close at one time. I was horrified about what happened to him at that space station. Terrible. He was a decent guy." She

took a long deep breath. "I assume you know about that."
Gabe nodded but said nothing. "He used to come in here all
the time." She smiled at the bag. "He loved cinnamon buns. I
haven't heard anything for a long while. Did they ever figure
out what happened?"

"Not that I know of," said Gabe.

"Well, if they haven't figured it out yet, I don't guess it's
going to happen." She tried another smile, hoping to reassure
us that everything was all right. "He was away a lot. Spent his
time traveling around out there." She glanced up at the ceiling. "Periodically he came home. More or less. His intention,
as he explained it to me, was to live a life of leisure. He never
stayed long, though. I don't think he ever stayed more than
a few months before he took off again."

"To do what?" asked Gabe.

"He was a pilot. Interstellars." A customer came in and
bought a chocolate cake. We got out of the way until he'd
left. Then Esther picked up her narrative: "I should mention, by the way, that he enjoyed mountain climbing. He
was out there one day when they had a landslide. Some girl
troopers got caught in the path of the thing. Rick ran into the
middle of it and helped get them out. He saved, I think, four
of them. Got them huddled down somewhere until the danger was past. They were lucky he was there. That was how
he was. Always put other people first."

"Thanks, Esther," Gabe said. Another customer was coming in the door.

"The town put up a memorial to him."

"He sounds like quite a guy," I said.

"He was."

"Where's the memorial?" asked Gabe.

"Just go out the front door and turn left. It's on the south
side. In Branson Park. It's in the center of the park. You can't
miss it." She bit her lip and her eyes closed briefly.

"You okay, Esther?" I asked.

"Yeah," she said. "I'm fine."

"One more thing: Do you know her married name?"

"It's Montgomery."

We climbed into the skimmer and lifted off. "Gabe," I said, "you really want to go look at the memorial?"

"Yes."

"Why?"

"Not sure I can give you a reason that makes any sense."

"Give me one that doesn't."

"We're trying to decide whether this guy brought a major deep-space artifact back with him and forgot to tell anybody about it. The more we know about him, the easier it will be to figure it out." I said okay and turned south. There were several parks. I called in to the town and asked for directions to get to Branson. *Immediately to your left. It's directly in front of the wainscot-and-plastene building with the pillars. Do you see it?*"

"I do. Thank you."

The building with the pillars was a courthouse. We descended into a parking area and came down near a statue of a woman. The engraved name was Madeleine Branson.

"I should have realized," I said.

"You know her?" asked Gabe.

She was a poet. From the previous century. "Yes," I said. "I didn't realize she was from around here."

Madeleine stood with a tablet in one hand, looking toward the sky, her other hand shielding her eyes. "Yeah," said Gabe. "I think I remember reading her work when I was in college."

"She wrote about living for the moment. Don't take anything for granted. That's something I think we all learned when you went missing."

A sign bearing Rick Harding's name pointed toward the center of the park, where a cluster of trees circled a fountain. We followed a pebbled walkway past a few benches. Off to one side, a half-dozen kids were throwing a ball back and forth. Most of the benches were occupied. People were reading and talking. Two older guys had fallen asleep. A woman sat holding an infant. And a couple of chess games were underway.

We passed the trees. The fountain lifted a steady stream into the air. It fell back with a soft gurgle into a circular pool. Several wooden seats were available.

The sound of the water and the kids with the ball and the occasional gusts of wind disturbing leaves somehow emphasized the overall silence of the place. Gabe seemed completely absorbed by it. The moment bore a striking resemblance to an afternoon on Orpheus when he'd unearthed a thousand-year-old statue of the beloved Barlus Ocotto. In the same year, we'd entered a temple on Lycaeus that dated back to the fourth millennium. In both instances, Gabe had grown quiet as we approached. It was as if he could reach back into those long-gone years and visualize what life had been like in those ancient places. I recalled once he'd tried to explain himself, that it was a matter of living inside the experience, rather than simply trying to solve an issue.

And finally we arrived at the Harding statue. He wore a captain's uniform and looked up past the trees. The sculptor had managed to infuse a sense of penetrating vision locked on the infinite. An inscription was carved into the base of the fountain:

Richard K. Harding

1386–1424

The world will never be the same

Later we learned that the memorial had been financed primarily by donations from the parents of the girl troopers whose lives Harding had saved.

IV.

Life is a romantic business. It is painting a picture, not doing a sum—but you have to make the romance. And it will come to the question how much fire you have in your belly.

—OLIVER WENDELL HOLMES II, LETTER TO OSWALD RYAN,
JUNE 5, 1911 CE

As soon as we got back in the skimmer, we ran a search for Angela Montgomery, sister of Rick Harding. But we got nothing. We lifted off and flew back home through bright sunlight and warm temperatures, hoping to hear from Angela. But the speaker remained silent. "You know," said Gabe, "we haven't checked to see whether Rick Harding has an avatar."

"Sounds like a good idea."

It turned out there were more than a hundred with that name. We were able to get rid of the surplus by adding "Octavia" to the search. Gabe asked if I was interested in participating in the interview. "Of course," I said. He was having no hesitation about involving me in the investigation, which was a distinct change in his manner. In the days when I was his assistant, I functioned as not much more than a secretarial aide. I answered incoming calls, was responsible for the paperwork, and took him wherever he wanted to go, whether it was the University Museum or what was left of the colony world Lyseria. But I didn't do much that was serious. He would not have thought of asking me to help with tactical or strategic issues, as he was doing now. And I understood that not much time had passed for him since then. So this wasn't an evolutionary change. He'd stepped away from the person he used to be. Or maybe it was that I'd come a considerable distance from those years and he'd noticed.

We made the connection and moments later the Harding avatar appeared on the control panel view screen. He delivered a charming smile in my direction and more or less nodded at Gabe. *"Hello,"* he said. *"My name's Rick Harding, but I suspect you know that. Can I help you?"*

Most people groom their avatars. They tend to be taller than the originals, with smoother features, brighter smiles, and a suggestion of higher intelligence in their overall appearance. This one though looked very much like the guy in the online photos. For that matter, like the statue in the park. Except that he wore a button-front V-neck aquamarine cardigan and khaki jeans, not showing off the uniform with which most interstellar pilots adorned their avatars.

He was seated in a luxurious two-piece indigo sectional with his feet propped up on a round ottoman.

We went back and forth on the introduction and then I turned it over to Gabe while the avatar let his eyes show where his interest lay. Gabe caught the message and couldn't quite hide his amusement. "Rick," he said, "after the loss of the Octavia, an unusual object was found in your home, something that looks like a silver trophy. It's inscribed in a language no one recognizes. It was eventually found by your sister Angela. Do you know what I'm referring to?"

"Yes, I recall something of that nature."

"Where did it originate?"

"Interesting."

"What is?"

"You're the second person to ask me today about that."

"Really? Who was the other one?"

"Alex Benedict."

"Okay. I should have guessed. So where did the trophy originate?"

"I'm not certain. My information is that it is from the Ocean-side Hotel on Elysium. It was what they call a 'one of a kind,' a unique gift from the hotel to a guest. It's intended to be an object that always recalls good times."

"Tell us about Elysium."

"It's a prime tourist site, in the Kollio system. Long ride, but it's a pleasant place. The Oceanside Hotel is located in a beautiful area. It looks out not only at an ocean but at a ringed giant and a huge moon. It's a few days' travel from Chippewa, where we were based."

"Based with whom?"

"Orion Express."

"So you were a pilot for a touring company?"

"That is correct, yes."

"Where are you from originally, Rick?"

"Dellaconda. My family moved to Rimway when I was a kid."

"And you've been living here ever since?"

"Except the six years I spent on Chippewa."

"The language on the trophy: Do you know where it's from?"

"It's purely fictitious."

"It's made up?"

"Yes. As far as I know."

"Why on earth would they do that?"

"It was part of a game they played. They selected an Occupant of the Month, and if you won, you got an award in this language. The awards were in different formats, usually plaques and trophies, but there were also framed photos of the winners, usually standing out on the beach looking at the sea. Or a demitasse. Engraved data was always in the created language, which they called urbanic. *The winner also received a certificate stipulating that he'd won. The certificate was in standard, of course. With a supposed translation of whatever was engraved on the award itself."*

Gabe cleared his throat. "Can you tell us what the inscription means? The one on the silver trophy?"

"Yes. It provides my name and the date of the award, says I'm recognized by Oceanside as a highly talented human being, and that the language is fictitious."

"It says the language is fictitious?"

"Yes."

"Rick, where is the certificate now?"

"I don't know. I had it in, I think, a desk drawer when I left for the Octavia mission."

"Do you know whether the language was consistent? For example, would 'highly talented' look the same on all the awards?"

"I have no way of knowing."

Gabe exhaled and closed his eyes. "Incredible," he said. "Chase, you want to take it?"

"Sure. Rick, what other tourist spots did you go to? Other than Oceanside?"

"A lot of places. I've been to Arabella, Quiseda, Zhonpour, some others."

"What was the name of the vehicle you used?"

"There were several. The Moonlight, *the* Loriston, *the* Venture. *They had different capacities. The* Venture *was the smallest. A Corpsman model. It was a yacht. Maximum six passengers."*

"Did these ships all belong to Orion Express?"

"No. The Venture *was mine."*

"What happened to it?"

"I sold it."

"To whom?"

"I don't have that information."

Gabe and I exchanged glances. "Do you have any close friends in this area, Rick?" I asked. "Near or in Andiquar?"

"Of course. I have plenty of friends here."

"We'd like to get more information about you, if we can.

We're interested in doing a book detailing the life of a star pilot. You'd be a good central figure."

"Why is that? I've never done anything exceptional. In fact my interest was more in interstellar tech than in piloting."

Gabe was impressed by the modesty: "Being an interstellar technician as well as a pilot is fairly exceptional, Rick. That's exactly why. Not to mention the girl troopers. If we tell your story, we'd be relating pretty much what interstellar pilots live with. What it's like to be away from friends and family for extended periods. What it's like to cruise past a giant star. You know what I mean."

"Well, that sounds good to me."

"Can you give us some names? People we can talk to who've been a significant part of your life?"

He gave us nine names, including Esther's. When he was done, we assured him that if we were able to finish the project, we'd see that they all got copies of the book. Then I looked over at Gabe. He was done.

"Thank you, Rick," I said.

"Glad to help, Chase." He actually managed to look as if he was interested in our getting together for an evening. *"Hope to see you guys again sometime."*

When he was gone, Gabe looked pleased.

"What?" I asked.

He sat back in his chair and gazed at me with that smug look I was once so familiar with. "I don't believe a word of it."

"Why not?"

"Hotels want to be noticed."

"You're saying—?"

"The Oceanside wasn't going to go to all that trouble with an artificial language that accomplished nothing except preventing potential customers from reading it."

"Maybe they thought the winners would show their prizes around a lot."

"That's what they would like. Except you would want to

find a way to get the hotel's name out front. Putting everything in an artificial language is more likely to scare potential visitors off."

"Makes sense," I said. "I have a suggestion. When we get a chance, let's call Skydeck and find out if the *Venture* is in dock, and check to see who owns it."

"And then," said Gabe, "we ride up and talk to the ship's AI."

We'd have an advantage that we didn't have with the avatar: AIs can't be rigged to lie.

The speaker released its musical alert as we descended toward the country house. It wasn't Angela Montgomery, though. "Good morning," I said. "Rainbow Enterprises."

The caller was Clem Wayfield, one of our clients. *"The antique lamp I left with you last month,"* he said, *"has it sold yet?"*

"Clem," I said, "I'm not in the building. But I'll be there shortly. Give me a few minutes and I'll get back to you."

"The lamp belonged to Johan Bester. You really don't know whether it's been sold or not?" Bester was a minor politician who'd run for a governorship in the last century.

"I don't, Clem. I'll check and get right back to you. That kind of information is not accessible when we're out of the building."

We touched down as Wayfield gave me an exasperated okay. Jacob opened the front door and said he was glad to see us. *"Were you able to locate the silver trophy?"*

"No," said Gabe. The place was empty. Alex had gone off to his antiquities conference on the other side of the world.

I checked on Bester's lamp. It had not moved yet. I called Wayfield and he expressed his dismay at what he perceived as our lack of interest. *"Maybe,"* he said, *"it could use some publicity."*

"I'll take a look, Clem. I'll get back to you later."

I called Skydeck Ops. "Is there a *Venture* currently in operation?"

"*Negative,*" they said. "*I don't see anything like that anywhere in the system. Not currently.*"

"But you *did* have one?"

"*Years ago.*"

"What happened to it?"

"*It was sold. It's now the* Mary Kaye.*"

"Can you give me the name of the current owner?"

"*I'm sorry. That's a privacy issue.*"

"Can you tell me if it's docked now?"

"*It's not.*"

"When do you expect it back?"

"*I'm sorry, Ms. Kolpath. That information isn't available.*"

"Can you let me know when it returns?"

"*It's a private vehicle, ma'am. I can inform the owner of your interest and ask him to get in touch, if he wishes.*"

Gabe came into my office a few minutes later. "How'd we make out?" he asked.

"They weren't much help."

"Did you ask them to let us know when the thing's in port?"

"Privacy concern."

"Where've I heard that before?"

"Gabe, why do we care about this so much? About the trophy?"

"Are you serious?" He sat down in one of the armchairs. "If that thing is *real*, it means that Harding, or somebody, may have discovered a civilization that we don't know about. Maybe it's gone, maybe it's still out there, but we just don't know. If it exists, if they're still alive, it would be the biggest news of the millennium. A third interstellar society." He leaned forward. "And I don't want to go crazy on this, but there could be a connection with Octavia."

"Blame it on the aliens," I said.

"I'm serious. We just don't know."

• • •

Gabe took me to dinner that evening at Molly's Top of the World, located on the peak of Mount Oskar. I asked him about his upcoming mission.

"We're going to Bowman's World." It was one of the planets orbiting Solanik, Rimway's closest neighbor. "Earth is supposed to have dispatched a few ships during the fifth millennium to go out and set up a colony. There's no record that it actually happened, but there are references to the effort in some of the literature from the period."

"Has anybody gone out to look?"

"Of course. There've been several missions."

"And—?"

"They haven't found anything. At the time the colonials left Earth, if they really did, it was in the middle of the millennium. A turbulent period. The whole story may just be a myth, or they might have lied about their destination and gone somewhere else. Or maybe the people doing the missions weren't thorough enough."

"So you and your colleagues are going to try again?"

"Yes."

"How many of you are going?"

"Just two of us. Ed Baxter will be with me."

"That seems small for that kind of mission. How much digging can two guys do?"

He laughed. "Not much. We won't be doing any digging. We're just going to do a quick survey and try to decide the most likely place they'd have tried to settle. Then, if we turn anything up, we'll send in a team."

"Who's providing the transportation?" I was wondering whether he hadn't asked me to go because he didn't want to offend Alex. Or put me on the spot.

"The WWAA," he said. That was the Wide World Archeological Association. "They'd like to settle the matter."

"Sounds as if it could be an interesting trip."

"I hope so." Our dinners arrived. Fried chicken for him, meat loaf for me. "I should be back in a week or two."

When we'd finished and returned to the country house, he asked me to let him know if Angela called. "I'll be leaving tomorrow, but you have my code."

"Absolutely," I said.

"I hope we get something on the trophy." He went to his quarters, supposedly to retire, but he was gone only a few minutes when I heard the piano. I checked on Wayfield's lamp. It still hadn't moved. I informed him and suggested we might want to lower the asking price. He wasn't happy.

I called it a night and returned to the cottage. In the morning, when I arrived at the country house, Gabe was gone.

V

The saddest of words spoken by men,
Most feared, most painful,
Haunting all our years,
Is not fail, or die, or lose,
But good-bye.

—WALFORD CANDLES, "THE LONG TWILIGHT," 1215

I'd been working in the country house almost thirteen years, most of it under Alex's direction. He spent a lot of time on the road, and I suspect I was alone in the building as often as not. Nobody lives close to us. No other human habitation is visible through any of the windows. Nevertheless, I never felt a sense of solitude. Maybe that was because of Jacob; maybe it was because Alex was forever calling in with assignments, asking me to run over to the Bannerman Artifact Center to get an esti-mate on the value of a ninth-century car, or to visit someone who was interested in details about a three-thousand-year-old tablet that had once belonged to a dictator on Toxicon. But that morning, with Gabe and Alex both away on their projects, I could feel the emptiness of the place.

We'd been having disruptive weather off and on for sev-eral days. It was growing increasingly turbulent, so much so that I'd decided if it didn't ease off, I'd pass on going home that night. Thunder and lightning were so severe I was almost ready to hide under a table. Rain pounded the building. There wasn't much work to be done. I finished it before noon and was playing chess with Jacob when he told me we had a call. *"It's for Gabe,"* he said. *"From an April Dutton."*

From April? Uh-oh. "Put her through, Jacob."

He made the connection. "Hello, April? This is Chase. I'm sorry, but Gabe isn't here."

She appeared in the center of the room, wearing a light blue jacket and gray slacks. She was standing on a lawn under threatening skies. *"Chase,"* she said. *"I hope I'm not interrupting anything."* Thunder shook the building and the image faded for a few moments. Then she was back.

"No, not at all. What can I do for you?"

"Is Gabe okay?"

"Yes, he's fine. Why do you ask?"

"There was something he said that's had me worried." She hesitated. *"Will he be back today?"*

"No, April. He's off on an interstellar mission. We don't expect to see him for a week or two."

"Okay." She sounded simultaneously disappointed and relieved. *"Maybe it's just as well. He said how, because of that space-time thing, it had only been about three weeks for him since we'd been together. Chase, I can't imagine what he must have gone through."*

I got out of my chair, came around in front of the desk so we were within arm's reach of each other. "He's good," I said. "I can transfer you to him if you want. He's probably at the terminal waiting for a flight to the space station." She looked uncomfortable. "Are *you* okay, April?"

"Yes. I'm all right. But don't connect me. Just tell him I called. That I was worried about him."

"I'll tell him."

"Thank you." And she was gone.

I looked out at the storm. Thunder rumbled overhead.

April hadn't gotten over *him* either.

• • •

I've never really loved anyone. *Romantic* love, that is. I've gone through occasional flings, but I've never been in a relationship that would have been capable, had things gone wrong, of tearing me apart.

To be honest, I've never been convinced serious love affairs actually happen. The ones I've observed from a distance inevitably seem to wear out over time. They suggest a kind of quantum entanglement in which the participants talk themselves into a condition that exists only on a temporary basis. Maybe I'm wrong. I don't know.

Maybe I've just never met the right guy. There've been a couple in my life that got my chemistry going. Alex was one of them. But I just haven't seen anyone yet who could have the kind of effect that shows up in romantic movies. I was surprised back in the old days when Gabe told me about his engagement with April. Odd. I'd always thought he was too smart to fall in love.

The storm eased off that afternoon. Alex called shortly before dinnertime to make sure everything was okay. The media were describing it as one of the severest storms the area had seen in living memory.

The skies cleared in the early evening and gave us a bright full moon. I was in the conference room watching *The Julie Edwards Show* and getting ready to go home when Angela called.

She stepped out of a glimmering light, smiled, and said, "Hi, Chase."

Nice effect. "Hello, Angela." It had been about five years and I'd forgotten what she looked like.

"It's good to see you again," she said. *"I was surprised to hear you were looking for me. What's going on?"* Lush red hair enveloped her shoulders, and she had a body that might have belonged to an athlete. It made me wonder if, like her brother, she'd been, or still was, a mountain-climbing enthusiast.

"I guess, first, I should tell you that Dr. Benedict isn't here just now. He's off on an expedition of some sort. He'd want me to assure you he'll get back to you, but it'll be a while."

"Well, I guess that can't be helped."

"When he got home, your trophy was one of the first things he asked about."

"That's nice to hear. I hope you're not going to tell me it really was a relic of some sort."

That past tense did not sound good. "I hope nothing happened to it."

"I tossed it. I think I invited you to keep it if you wanted it. But you didn't look interested. Nobody was."

"Angela, it wouldn't have been ethical for me to keep it."

An embarrassed look swept across her features. *"I'm sorry. I wasn't trying to blame anyone."*

"I know." I took a deep breath. "Dr. Benedict will be interested in what you have to say about it. Do you mind if I record the conversation?"

"Not at all." She reached out, brought a chair into the picture, and sat down. *"Are you telling me it actually* was *an alien artifact?"*

"We don't know. It might have been. That's the reason Dr. Benedict wanted to get another look at it. What did you do with it?"

"People I'd shown it to laughed at the idea it might be alien. And once I found out it wasn't really silver and seemed to have no value of its own, I just put it in the trash."

I closed my eyes for a moment. "When was that?"

"Three or four years ago."

"Were you sure it wasn't silver?"

"I showed it to a metallurgist. That's what she told me. It wasn't silver, but she didn't know exactly what it was. There just didn't seem to be any point keeping it. The only thing it did was remind me of Rick."

"She didn't know what it was?"

"No."

That sounded like a good reason to have hung on to it. But I let it go. "We were in Newbury the other day, hoping to find you, and we discovered the memorial they've erected for your brother."

"Oh yes. It's beautiful, isn't it? I thought somebody would put up a memorial for all four of the people who were on Octavia, but I guess that's not going to happen."

"Well, it's early yet, Angela. Things like that take time."

"Tell me again why you were looking for me? You think the trophy might actually have been an alien artifact?"

"It's possible." I glanced out at the moon. "If Rick had found another civilization somewhere, did he seem to you like a person who'd have kept that quiet?"

"Not at all. It's been a while since I've thought about it. But no, he'd have loved to come up with that kind of discovery."

"What can you tell me about him? What kind of guy was he?"

"He was serious. Didn't talk much, except when he was running tours for Galactic. I was on board one of them once, and I almost didn't know him. He talked and laughed with the passengers. He was the perfect pilot to have for a long-term flight. After he retired from doing all the tours, he went back to being kind of somber. Even more than he'd been. He became even more intense after he started working for the Quantum Research Group. But that was who he was."

"How did he get assigned to Octavia?"

"I don't know. I never understood it. He liked being around people. Women, especially. When he told me about getting assigned to the space station, I was shocked. But he said it was just what he wanted."

"Angela, why did you leave Newbury?"

"My husband. I got married."

"What does he do for a living?"

"He's an endocrinologist."

"May I ask where you live now?"

"Castleton. It's on the west coast."

"It must have been hard, leaving Newbury."

"Actually I wanted to get away from what had happened. Get to a place where they didn't have a statue of my dead brother in the center of town. I don't know. Maybe that's not it at all. Maybe I just needed a change. Harkin was willing, so we took off."

"Harkin's your husband?"

"Yes."

"You met him in Newbury?"

"No. He was from Andiquar. We were dating while he was going through medical school. When he graduated he got an invitation to help set up a practice in Castleton. I was all for it." She closed her eyes. *"One person at the University Museum told me it was probably a joke of some sort."* She was talking about the silver trophy again. *"She said there was no record of any such language. I just got tired keeping it around the house. Was that a mistake? Do you think it might actually have been worth something?"*

"No," I said. "Probably not."

"Well, whatever. It's gone."

"One more question, Angela. Rick owned an interstellar yacht."

"That's correct."

"He eventually sold it, right?"

"Yes. When he came back from the Orion Express job."

"Do you know who the buyer was?"

"I have no idea, Chase."

"Okay. Something else: Rick's avatar said he had a certificate from the Oceanside Hotel on Elysium. It explained what the trophy was about. That the hotel had issued it. Did you ever see it?"

She needed a minute. *"No,"* she said finally. *"I don't recall anything like that. If I had, I wouldn't have started running around thinking I had something from aliens. There was a lot of junk in Rick's place. I just pretty much tossed everything."*

VI.

There is no adequate definition for love,
No description that warns of its effect,
No analysis that encompasses the look in a woman's eyes,
Or the passion that overwhelms a man's senses.
Love is all that matters,
All else is decoration.
— WALFORD CANDLES, "EMILY," 1193

I went back to the cottage, where I lay most of the night staring at the ceiling. Eventually I gave up trying to sleep, got up, and watched the sun rise through my kitchen windows while I ate a breakfast of grapes and raisin bread. Then I put on the news and collapsed into a recliner. The president was unhappy about charges of corruption he was receiving. That was apparently the only thing that was happening, but it was enough finally to put me under.

I spent the next two days organizing accounts at Rainbow. When I arrived on the third day, Jacob informed me that Alex had gotten home during the night and was asleep in his quarters. I wandered into my office and went to work. Alex walked in a half hour later with a cup of coffee.

I was recording auction results. We'd finally gotten a decent offer on Wayfield's lamp. "Anything of significance?" he asked.

"Not much. Belklavik claims he found a two-thousand-year-old bracelet in a collapsed house on Traygor that they'd like us to move. They also have a monitor dug out of what they think was a courthouse that's about a thousand years older. They're asking a lot, but I'll leave that to you."

"Okay. The bracelet might work. Does he have confirmation?"

"From the archeological team? Yes."

"Good.

"How'd the conference go?"

"Okay." He sat down.

"That exciting, huh?"

"I can't get Octavia out of my mind."

"You have any ideas?"

"Not really. I tried reading the paper that Housman produced. 'Quantum Passage.'" He took another sip of the coffee.

"That was submitted from the space station, wasn't it?"

"Yes."

"Did you understand it?"

"Not much of it. It won the Exeter Award."

"Posthumously."

"Yeah, I know. At least he lived long enough to see it published."

"You think they sent him a copy?"

"Oh, sure. There's no way they wouldn't have done that. He probably even knew he was a candidate for the award."

"I guess."

"They published his paper a couple months before the station disappeared."

"So what did you get from it, Alex?"

"Just that wormholes are crazy."

"Why'd you bother? I've never known you to show an interest in physics."

He shrugged and finished his coffee. Then he got up and looked at the cup. "You want any?"

"No. It keeps me awake all day."

He grinned, left the room, and came back with two cups. "Can't afford to have you sleeping on the job." He put it down in front of me. "Chase, have you ever heard of Sola Kylin?" I'd heard the name but couldn't pin it down. "She wrote *Down the Wormhole* a few years ago."

"Oh yes. I remember. She claimed that black holes are *alive.* That you can't trust them to just stay in place and let you alone."

"That's correct."

"I think it was a best seller."

"She says that black holes are exceedingly complicated structures. And when you add the quantum effect, you get a very strange creature."

"That's crazy," I said.

"That's what all the physicists said too. But she was at the top of the charts for six months."

"Alex, that would suggest that stars are alive too. You don't buy any of this, do you?"

"Of course not. She mentions that we've gone through eras when people believed the planets they lived on were alive. Remember *Kelia?*" His eyes narrowed. "It sounds ridiculous but I couldn't resist asking Benjamin about it."

"Benjamin Holverson?" He's a physicist who's been a client and a friend for a good many years. "What did he say?"

"About black holes being alive? That it's lunacy. Life is too complex to be able to operate in that kind of crushed condition."

I picked up the coffee. "Even if it *were* alive, I don't see how it could reach out and create a problem for something in orbit."

"Kylin says it can manipulate gravity. That at those levels it wouldn't take much to draw in an orbiting station. Just for the record, though, I'm not serious about this."

"Good."

"By the way, did you know that Harding's trophy wasn't the only link we had to Octavia?"

"No, I wasn't aware there was anything else."

"You know who Charlotte Hill is, right?"

"Sure. The only woman on board."

"She was apparently an extraordinarily good chess player. And she owned an unusual set. Her family brought it with them when they moved to Rimway a few years ago. The chess set was aluminum, and the design hasn't been around for a thousand years." He raised his voice slightly. "Jacob, can you show us a picture of it?"

The set appeared on the coffee table by the window. It was similar to the classic Staunton chess pieces that had been available in all cultures since the beginning of the space age. Probably before that. But there were differences. The pieces were more compact, the queen's crown had lost its sharp edges, and the king's no longer had a cross. The knight looked annoyed, and the bishop's edges were more curved than the Staunton model. The black-and-white coloring was somewhat faded. "As far as I know," Alex said, "there isn't another one on the planet."

We handle substantial numbers of artifacts in our listings, and I probably don't pay as much attention to them as I should once they've gone on the block. Unless there's a problem. There'd been several chess sets over the years, but with one or two exceptions they'd always been the standard model, of interest only because of the owner's identity. And my involvement usually had to do with verifying certification. "I don't recall our ever having access to it. Did we sell it or something?" I asked. "The chess set?"

"No. It disappeared after her death. Charlotte's mother, Olivia Hill, contacted me a year or so ago to find out if we might have any idea what had happened to it, whether we might have seen it on the auction listings. She was hoping to get it back."

"So you've been looking into it."

"Yes." He was smiling. "I got a response while I was on the road. From Paul Holton." Holton was a long-time client. He put the message on-screen: *Alex, Kimberley Morris has it. She tells me she got it from one of Charlotte's friends. She lives in Traymont. Link attached. She does not seem anxious about selling. Let me know if I can do anything more to help."*

Traymont was a time zone away.

Outside, a mollok was hanging from a tree limb gazing in at us. He was smiling at something, and when Alex waved at him, he waved back. I couldn't resist going into the kitchen for a banana. Alex was frowning when I returned with it. "You do that," he said, "and it'll be out there every morning."

"Special credit at salvation." I opened the window and tossed the banana. The mollok caught it on the fly, chittered happily, and began peeling and eating it.

Alex rolled his eyes. "Jacob," he said, "connect us with Kimberley."

I gave him my chair and backed off so I'd be out of the conversation. After a minute we heard a woman's voice. *"Mr. Benedict?"*

"Yes."

She blinked on in front of my desk. *"I'm Kimberley Morris. What can I do for you?"* There was a shyness about her that clashed with a pair of expressive amber eyes. Her hair was dark and cut short, and she wore a golden knit crop top and soft blue jeans.

"Ms. Morris, I understand you own a chess set that once belonged to Charlotte Hill?"

"That's correct, sir."

"Would you be interested in selling?"

"Well, I've thought about it."

"How much are you asking?"

"I really hadn't planned on selling it, Mr. Benedict. I have an

interest in chess sets used in celebrated matches. I have the set from the Confederate Championship game last year. And the one used by Ronnie Jamison when he took down the Arkon AI."

"That was the last millennium, wasn't it?"

"Common Era 9416." Jamison was the last human to win a world chess title anywhere in the Confederacy.

"And you have others?"

"Oh yes, Mr. Benedict. Charlotte's set is the first one that has a purely historical context."

"Call me Alex, please. Our interest in the chess set is that Charlotte Hill was the daughter of a client."

"Oh, I'm sorry to hear that. I assume nobody ever got to her with an explanation of what happened?"

"No. They've never been able to figure it out."

"I see. And her mother would like to get the chess set?"

"Yes. It would mean a great deal to her. I have to tell you though that she doesn't have a lot of resources."

"That's unfortunate, Alex," Kim said. *"I can certainly under-stand her pain, and I'd like to be of help. But the set was expensive for me, and I've acquired a fondness for it. I'm really not anxious to let it go. Not without adequate compensation. What kind of offer is she prepared to make?"*

"May I ask how you obtained it?"

"I bought it from Mary Stroud. She was a friend of Charlotte's."

"How did she come to have it, do you know?"

"Charlotte gave it to her when she left to go to Octavia. She knew that nobody on the station would be a decent opponent, and if she played the AI, that would be purely electronic. Mary was supposed to take care of it until she got back."

"Before we begin discussing compensation, be aware that Charlotte Hill designated her parents as heirs. She left every-thing to them. So unless Mary Stroud can show a formal transaction providing ownership, it would belong legally to Charlotte's mom."

"That can't be right."

"It's correct. Have you a document anywhere transferring ownership?"

"Look, Mr. Benedict, let's try to keep this reasonable."

"I'm in favor of that. May I ask how much you paid for it?"

Kimberley hesitated. *"Two thousand markers."*

Alex nodded. And I knew the look in his eyes. He'd researched it and she was well over the line. "Okay. I'd have preferred to arrange things so you didn't lose any money, but that's obviously not going to work. Our lawyer will be in touch."

"Wait. How much are you offering?"

"I'm sorry to inform you, but the chess set won't command anything like what you paid for it."

"What's your offer?"

"We'll go to four hundred. That's our top figure."

"Make it six."

"I tell you what: we'll go with five. That's it."

Alex sent the payment. Several days later we got a call from Gabe. As he liked to phrase it, he was back in town. Though in fact he was standing in the Starlight Hotel, on Skydeck.

"How'd the project go?" said Alex. "Did you find anything?"

"We figured they'd have settled near water."

"And—?"

"Bowman's World has a ton of oceans, lakes, and islands. Anyway, to keep it short, not really. Listen, I've got to run. Just got time to make my shuttle. See you in an hour."

Charlotte's chess set arrived that afternoon. We opened the package, took out the board, removed a plastene box, opened it, and examined the pieces. Aside from the slight difference in the design, the set was ordinary. Until Alex showed me the date engraved on the underside of the board. With Charlotte's first name. "It was her tenth birthday," he said.

"I'm surprised she didn't get a set with more glitter. Pieces designed like people in pressure suits or something. If you want to get a kid excited about a game, you have to do better than conventional pieces."

"I think her mom was expecting her to do exactly what she did: grow into a serious chess player."

"What's that got to do with the set?"

"You don't play chess, do you, Chase?"

"Actually, I do."

"Ever compete in a tournament?"

"No. Not that I can recall."

"People who play the game seriously won't stand for anyone changing the way the pieces look. Do that, substitute guys in space suits or whatever, and everything changes. Don't ask me why. But you don't see the board the right way if you're playing with cones or mythical beasts or whatever. I suspect Charlotte's mom understood that."

"Alex, where are we headed with this?"

"Nowhere, I guess. Charlotte was an extraordinary woman. She graduated from Andiquar and earned her master's in physics two years later. Del Housman became her mentor. One of the top physicists in the Confederacy."

"He must have been impressed by her."

"One way or another, yes. It cost her." Housman had been responsible for getting her the Octavia assignment. Alex cleared his throat. "Chase, would you call Olivia and let her know the package has arrived? Find out if she wants it shipped."

Ordinarily I'd have passed the call to Jacob, but in that case I couldn't resist being the person to deliver the news. I moved the set into the conference room, placed it in the middle of the table, and opened the curtains, exposing it to sunlight. I took the pieces out of the box, set them up, and made the call.

An AI answered: *"It is good to hear from you, Ms. Kolpath. Olivia will be here in a minute."*

It was more like ten seconds. She blinked on and was about to say something when her eyes locked on the set. A huge smile took her over. And finally she looked up at me. *"Thank you,"* she said.

"You're welcome. Alex was glad he was able to help."

"It's just the way I remember it. Please tell him I'm grateful. How much do I owe you?"

"It's five hundred markers plus fifty. Our commission."

Olivia had sparkling green eyes and auburn hair, and it was easy to see where Charlotte had gotten her looks. "That's a surprise. I thought they'd want a lot more. When can I get it?"

"Your call. We can ship it this afternoon. Or you can pick it up yourself."

"I'll be there in an hour."

She and Gabe arrived almost simultaneously. Alex picked him up at the spaceport and was helping him with his luggage as Olivia's skimmer descended into the parking area.

I was standing at the front door when it opened for them. They were trading introductions, and Olivia seemed especially pleased to discover Gabe knew more about her daughter than simply that she'd been a victim in the Octavia incident. "Yes," she said, "that was her. She was smart. She'd have had a brilliant career as a physicist if—" It was as far as she got before waving it away.

Charlotte might have been the most celebrated member of the Octavia team. And it was not only because she looked so good. She'd done a few interviews, and I guess everybody had been struck by her animation. She'd obviously been enthusiastic about the assignment and thought of Octavia as the opportunity of a lifetime. With a little luck, she said, they were going to open a door into another universe. She'd piloted the shuttle that had gone out in the shadow of the black hole to look for the pods fired into the disrupted time-space continuum by the cannon. It became fairly obvious why Olivia Hill had contacted us about her daughter's lost chess set. "Her passion for the game," she told me that afternoon, "stayed with me. In a way it's kept her alive."

Though Housman gave her no particular attention in his prizewinning account, Charlotte had been largely responsible for their success, because after months of getting no results, she'd gone deeper than theory suggested and came back with the pods.

We helped Gabe inside with his bags. Then Alex led Olivia into the conference room while I accompanied Gabe to his apartment. He asked what Charlotte Hill's mother was doing here. I explained and he was obviously pleased. "Good for Alex," he said.

After Gabe got settled, I returned to the conference room. Alex and Olivia were seated at the table, admiring the set. Olivia was fondling one of the white knights. She put it down, removed the other pieces, and put them back in the box. Then she lifted the board so she could inspect the date on its underside. "Excellent," she said. "Beautiful. Now, you said five hundred fifty?"

Gabe walked in the door and closed it quietly behind him.

"It's yours," said Alex. The display of generosity was unusual. He could be benevolent on occasion, but not normally where business transactions were concerned. Rainbow Enterprises for him was strictly an accounting operation.

"No, no," she said. "You can't do that."

"It's not a problem." Alex directed her attention toward Gabe. "Gabe, by the way, is my uncle, and he taught me early that I should not accept money from beautiful women." Gabe managed to keep his surprise hidden.

Olivia delivered an alluring smile that let us know she had doubts about the story. "I can't believe I actually got it back. I haven't seen it for about fifteen years. Charlotte took it with her when she moved out of the house."

"I'm glad we were able to help," Alex said.

"I can't let you do this, Alex. I insist on paying. Please?"

"It's no problem," Gabe said. "There was no expense involved." He glanced at Alex, waiting for him to break in and divert the conversation in another direction.

"How did you manage that? When I spoke with him, Paul told me the price would be high." Paul was the guy who'd put us on track to find the chess set.

"We got lucky." Now that it had become clear that Alex was just going to let everything play out, Gabe was obviously enjoying himself and I could see he was proud of his nephew.

Olivia was about to protest again, but Alex broke in: "You've already paid enough, Olivia. Your daughter gave her life for scientific research, which is a sacrifice for all of us. It's enough."

VII.

Look at the night sky and know the meaning of infinity. We talk
of many universes as if some could be walled off from others or
simply placed on the far side of a nonexistent zone. Ridiculous.
There is only one universe. And it has no borders.

—Randall (Endgame) Telifson, comments during
graduation address at Horwitz University, 4311 CE

I never really discovered whether it was connected with
Olivia, but in the morning Gabe was all about wormholes.
"Housman *did* establish that they exist, right?" he asked.

"Actually," I said, "they'd had evidence of their existence
for thousands of years. But actually pinning one down took
a while. I don't know why that was. But yes, he was the guy
who found it."

"And what kind of result did we get from the discovery?"

"How do you mean?"

"What did we learn?"

"Well, there *was* one major breakthrough."

"And what was that?"

"It happened two years after Octavia disappeared."

"So what was it?"

"We have the media coverage, Gabe. If you like I can run
it for you."

We went into my office.

• • •

Two years after the loss of Octavia, DPSAR put a mission on board the *Claymont* and sent them out to examine the wormhole. As a result of Housman's work, they knew where one opening into the wormhole was, so it had become simply a matter of inserting probes that would do analytic work. The probes were more complex than the ones Housman and Charlotte had used. Stacy Harper showed one of them to her audience on the day of the breakthrough.

Harper was an Earth reporter from the Interstellar Network, on board the *Claymont* with the scientists. She held one of the probes in her hand. It was about the size of a comm-link, or maybe a flattened tennis ball. It had a drive unit and an autocontrol. They were planning to release eighty-six of them that day. The probes would enter the tunnel and begin immediately to analyze interior conditions. And to search for exits. *"They'll be able spot an opening,"* she said, *"which will become visible when struck by light penetrating the mist and the distorted space that form the wormhole. When that happens, the probe will exit into the other universe, spend about thirty minutes photographing everything in sight. Then it will return into the wormhole, if it can, and come back to us. When it arrives, we'll be able to see what it found."* She was sitting with one of the physicists, identified as Cornelius Giusando, of MIT. *"Cornelius,"* she said, *"is it true we don't have radio contact when they're in the wormhole?"*

"Sometimes we do, apparently," he said. *"At least, Housman's experience bears that out. But you can't depend on it. And most of the time the answer is no, you have nothing. We're still trying to figure out what the laws are inside that thing. We've got a long way to go."* He looked pleased, a guy in the right place at the right time.

She returned his smile. *"Cornelius, do you really think there are other universes?"*

"It's still all guesswork, Stacy. That's an issue that has evaded

us for a long time. Nobody knows. But I'll tell you the truth. I'll be surprised if we're the only one."

Stacy was attractive, as all the female pundits are, and obviously quick on her feet. She was usually involved in covering politics, but she had no trouble adjusting to physics. She was also blessed with a sense of humor, and understood when the conversation was getting overly technical. "If there really is another universe, Cornelius, what would we expect to find? Will it be like ours?"

"Maybe," he said. "The big question is whether the laws of physics would be the same." Cornelius was small, with something of a weight problem and features that wouldn't have stood out in a crowd. But his manner generated a sense that he understood what he was talking about.

"What might be different?" she asked.

"Everything. But all you'd need to prevent a universe from developing could be one variant. Gravity, for example. It wouldn't take a major alteration to prevent stars from forming. Or maybe light would move at a different velocity."

"Like what?"

"How about a hundred kilometers an hour?"

"Is that really possible?"

"I don't see why it wouldn't be."

"So if you rode your skimmer you'd probably exceed light speed?"

"No, that wouldn't happen."

"Why not?"

"Nothing can travel faster than light. So your top speed would be a hundred kilometers."

"But that's only a physical law, right? Maybe it's different in another universe. Maybe somewhere nothing can travel slower than light."

Cornelius's eyes widened. "You know, you might have a point. Let me think about it."

Stacy smiled and let it go. She looked down at the probe,

which she'd set on a table. *"Cornelius, if we were able to ride in this thing, and we reached an opening, what would it look like?"*

"Hopefully, the wormhole would simply have a hole looking out into sunlight. Or starlight."

"Okay. And if we cross over into a different universe, how will we know that's what it is? That it's not part of this one?"

Cornelius checked the time. *"We'll be starting in a few minutes. But as to your question, if it functions like this one, if the rules are the same, we won't know. At least not until we've had a chance to do some analysis. But the general view is that if it's a different universe, we'll be able to pick it up pretty quickly. Gravitational waves will be different. Radiation. You name it."*

"Do you expect any surprises?"

He grinned. *"How about a black-and-white universe? No colors?"*

"Is that really possible?"

"Maybe."

I stopped it for a moment. "He's got a surprise coming," I said.

"What?"

"Stay tuned."

"I have one more question, Cornelius."

"Fire away."

"What if there is no other universe? Everybody's so excited about multiple universes that we don't talk much about the possibility that ours is the only one."

"Stacy, a lot of cosmological theories would go down the drain if it were to turn out that ours is all there is. But I don't think, whatever happens, we're going to be able to establish that we're alone. Not today, anyway. What we may find out is that the wormhole goes nowhere. But I guess that's not the same thing."

A light rain was falling against the windows. And I could hear birds chirping. Despite all the missions I'd been part of, I'm not sure I ever appreciated more the sounds of that morning.

Stacy thanked Cornelius for his help, then turned and faced us. *"We're about to launch. Stay on board."*

They ran ads for a detergent, for the recently released White Hawk skimmer, and for Colonial Cough Medicine. Then we were informed about upcoming programs. Finally Stacy was back. Cornelius was gone, and we could see two guys through a large window. They were at opposite ends of a long room, both talking into microphones.

"Where's the surprise?" asked Gabe.

"It's coming." It had been a long time since I'd watched this. "By the way, it gets a little scary."

Stacy smiled at us. *"Okay, here we go, everybody."* She vanished and we watched swirling dark clouds take over the center of the office and begin to expand. *"We're seeing the wormhole entry as it would look if we were sitting inside one of the probes. If it's nighttime where you are and you'd like to get a realistic image, turn off the lights."*

The clouds twisted and writhed. "It looks as if it's trying to swallow us," said Gabe. It opened and closed and churned and roiled. A large mouth. I pushed back in my chair. "What *is* that?" he asked.

"I'd guess it's what space looks like when it gets distorted."

We were getting sucked inside. I hung on to my chair arms as we slipped between the lips into darkness and gas. The probe's navigation lights came on. The gas lit up, and suddenly Stacy was back, smiling broadly. *"We've had a successful launch, ladies and gentlemen,"* she said. *"We are now inside the wormhole. Radio contact is breaking down so we're losing our picture."* The churning darkness faded and Cornelius appeared beside her. She turned toward him. *"Everything okay?"* she asked.

"So far."

It was all gone and the ship's lights came back to normal. *"How long will this take, Cornelius?"*

"We don't know. Our probe might already be headed for an exit. On the other hand it may go all the way to the end of the tunnel. Assuming it has an end. That might take a while."

"You're kidding. I mean about whether it has an end."

"The problem here, Stacy, is that we just don't know what's going on. We know the tunnel goes considerably farther than we'd originally thought because it was ejecting pods from the Housman team a lot farther out than we'd anticipated. And that's just length in our local area. We're in strange territory here."

The conversation continued. I knew that the first results were still a few minutes away, so I fast-forwarded until Cornelius raised two fingers to an ear. "One of them's back," he said. "They're looking at the pictures now."

"Do we have access to them?"

"Let me check." He produced his link and spoke into it. Then, after a moment: "Okay. We have it."

A bright star-filled sky appeared across the ceiling. "I don't recognize any of the constellations," said Stacy.

"I'm not surprised. We're far away from Earth. But it's all local. The probe didn't go anywhere new. But that's pretty much what we— Wait." He pressed his ear again. "We've got another one."

Gabe looked at me questioningly. Was this the surprise?

"Not yet," I told him. "We need to fast-forward some more." I ran past more negative results until I recognized a moment when Cornelius's face changed. And Stacy tugged on his sleeve. "They're telling me we got something," the physicist said. "Picture coming up."

Gabe leaned forward in his chair, his attention riveted on Cornelius and Stacy. The picture revealed more churning space. Then it darkened and went black.

Cornelius said, "They're saying that we may have another universe."

The picture stayed black.

Stacy leaned over and spoke into her partner's link. "We got nothing."

"That's what they're reading," said Cornelius. *"That place has no stars."*

"Holy cats," said Gabe. "Hard to believe. What about the other probes?"

"Most of them got to the end of the tunnel and emerged and came out near the black hole. Five others found exits along the way. Three of them led back into our universe. The other two took them out under that starless sky."

"The same place?"

"Maybe. They have no way to tell. If they were different universes, it suggests that stars are an unusual feature."

"Okay, Chase. That's a good show. But it's been a few years. We must have made some advances since then."

"None that I know of. We've gone back a number of times, but the results don't change. Some exits come out under starless skies. Two of the places that have stars have been identified as ours. There are seven or eight more with stars that we simply can't identify. But you'd expect that. Our universe is pretty big. We haven't seen that much of it yet."

"I assume people were shocked when they saw the places with no stars?"

"There was a fairly strong reaction. I remember somebody on one of the networks asking what's the point of having a universe if it doesn't have any stars? The media went crazy.

"Every show brought in cosmologists, quantum physicists, theologians, you name it, to talk about it. The major issue surfaced immediately: Could we be sure it wasn't our universe that the probes had blundered into, and just locked onto a part of the sky that was empty? Is there an area somewhere in which no stars exist? According to most astronomers, considering the wide angle lens the pod has, the answer is no. It had gone into a universe with no light."

VIII.

Think not in terms of ultimate success,
Of plaques hanging on the wall
And trophies glittering on a shelf.
Concentrate rather on the first step,
The first obstacle,
And find a way to cast it aside.

—TULISOFALA, "MOUNTAIN PASSES,"
TRANSLATED FROM ASHIYYUREAN BY LEISHA TANNER, 1202

Several days after our visit from Olivia Hill, Gabe came into my office carrying two packages. "What have you got?" I asked.

"Some artifacts. Do you have time to take these over to the University Museum?"

"I'm a little bit on the run, Gabe. Do they have to go today?"

"No. It's all right. Let it go. I'll take them."

I was involved in an afternoon of boring, purely administrative routine details, and I didn't want to go home with them still hanging over my head. That was the only reason I dodged his request. "It's okay, Gabe," I said. "I've got it."

"No, Chase. Finish your work."

I looked at the packages. "What are they?"

"A picture and an electronic log. I picked them up on a research outing a couple days before I got on the *Capella*. In fact, come to think of it, you were with me at the time."

It had something to do with the ninth-century biologist Daniel Grantner. That's *Rimway's* ninth century, of course. What I remembered mostly was that we'd gotten something, but two days later Gabe was gone.

Grantner had been originally from Chippewa. He'd come to Rimway as a teenager, and eventually written numerous tracts on human behavior, primarily concentrating on why a creature capable of such compassionate behavior could also commit acts of extreme cruelty. In his view, it came down to a clash among forces released by the empathy gene, the basic drive for survival, and a human capability to overlook reality. "In other words," he once added in an address to a graduating class, "being stupid."

His most celebrated work is *Life As It Is*. Gabe had gone through a library in the town where Grantner had lived. I couldn't remember the name of the town, but he'd come across the electronic log, which had belonged to him. It contained a first draft of *Life As It Is*, notes on several of his seminal works, an avatar, and photos of Grantner and his family. When we showed it to the librarian, she told us it was of no use that she could see, and we could have it.

The library also owned a framed portrait of him, which had found its way into a storage room. Gabe was invited to take that as well. "Poor woman," Gabe had said. "She has no idea." He was still talking as if that had happened only a few weeks ago.

"Is that what you have in the packages?" I asked. "The log and the portrait?" The portrait depicted Grantner as a young man, probably in his mid-twenties, kneeling by a tree with a Dalmatian at his side.

"Yes. I spoke to Amanda at the museum a few minutes ago. She's pretty excited." He grinned. Amanda would be walking on the ceiling.

"What's going on?" It was Alex's voice. I hadn't noticed him standing in the doorway.

"I'm headed for the museum," said Gabe, "with a first draft of *Life As It Is—*"

It was as far as he got. "Daniel Grantner's book?"

"Yes. It's in a log."

"And what else?"

"An avatar. Letters. You name it." Gabe couldn't resist smiling. Alex's attention focused on the packages. "Gabe, those would be worth a fortune. You're *donating* them?"

"Sure."

He came the rest of the way into the office and slowly lowered himself into a chair. "Is this what you were really doing when you said you were out wandering around on Bowman's World?"

I thought about jumping in and changing the subject at that point but decided to stay out of it.

"No. I got them eleven years ago."

"They've been here all this time?"

"Yes."

"Okay, Gabe. They're yours, so you can do what you want with them. You'll get no objections from me."

"Funny. I thought I was just getting one."

"I'm sorry. Let it go."

Gabe kept his voice level: "Maybe it's not such a good idea that I'm here."

"No. I just hate seeing us throw away this kind of money."

"I'm not throwing it away. I never had it." He picked up the two packages and walked out the door.

Alex turned in my direction. His displeasure was palpable. He left the room without saying another word. I walked over to the window and watched Gabe climb into his skimmer. Moments later it lifted into the sky. He never looked back. I hated seeing these two guys at odds with each other. And I'd have loved to be with Gabe when he turned the Grantner log over to Amanda.

• • •

He came back with an expression that tried to project casualness while concealing a smug sense of accomplishment. The world was his oyster. "Hi, Chase," he said, pausing at my office door.

I said hello. He smiled and turned away, but I knew he was expecting me to stop him. "How'd it go?"

"I thought Amanda was going to have a heart attack. You know Grantner never had an avatar anywhere on the net. Other than when he was about twelve years old."

"I think I *did* know that. You might have mentioned it to me when we were coming home that last time."

"Okay. Anyhow, yes, everybody down there was pretty excited." He was glowing.

"Well, congratulations."

"Thanks, kid. Congratulations to us both."

"Have they offered to give you your job back?" Gabe had been a professor in the archeology department at the university to which the museum was connected.

"Oh, they did that two weeks ago. I'll be starting in the fall."

"Beautiful." It reminded me of something I'd forgotten. "When you were missing, the news media reported that your PhD was in history, not archeology."

"That's correct."

"How come you're in the archeology department?"

He grinned. "I think it's because I'm lazy."

"You want to explain that?"

"Chase, we have thirteen thousand years of history. A lot of it's missing. Places and times where we don't really know what happened. But most of it is on the record. It's just overwhelming. It's hard to make it interesting for students when there's so much out there. So when I got the opportunity to jump ship, I took it." He sat down. "More important issue: Is Alex okay?"

"He's good," I said.

The glow was gone and discomfort was settling in. "It was my fault. I should be used to it by now." He pushed the tab on his commlink. "Alex, you busy?"

A pause. Then: *"Hang on. I'll be right down, Gabe."*

Gabriel started for the door. "Why don't you wait here?" I said, making it a point to look up at the clock. "I've gotta go. Past my quitting time."

When I ran into them the following morning, they were eating an amicable breakfast, and it was obvious whatever ill will had surfaced was gone. I was happy they weren't discussing the Grantner documents. The conversation was mostly about local politics where they were generally in agreement.

Eventually, somebody brought up Octavia. "I was interested," Gabe said, "that so many people thought the station had been grabbed by aliens. There was still a lot of excitement about it when I got on the *Capella*. I was surprised, when I got back here, that nobody had figured out what happened. You think there could possibly be anything to the alien theory?"

"Well," said Alex, "I'd guess that anything that doesn't violate physical law is possible. But I'd be more inclined to accept the idea that they all fell asleep, the system broke down, and they got sucked into the black hole."

"Well," said Gabe, "if that was really what happened, I would understand why DPSAR would want to keep it quiet. Incidentally, I heard that you're a member of the Maracaibo Caucus. Is that true?" The Maracaibo Caucus is, as anyone living close to Andiquar knows, a group of Ashiyyureans and locals who joined together in an effort to maintain a shaky peace back in the days when we were not comfortable with each other. Those times have changed, although the presence of an Ashiyyurean, or a Mute as they're more commonly referred to, still makes people nervous.

They resemble oversized mantises, extremely tall, with

leathery flesh. Their faces are vaguely humanoid, with arched diamond eyes. When they smile, even with the best of intentions, people tend to leave the room. In a hurry.

They unnerve everyone. But their appearance, despite the fangs, the eyes, and the tall pointed ears, is not the main cause. The real problem is that human minds are open to them. No secret is safe when a Mute's at the table.

They communicate telepathically with each other, and while they can read us, they require translator boxes to talk to us.

"Yes," said Alex. "I joined the Caucus three years ago."

"How long have they been around?"

"Only a few hundred years."

"I didn't mean how long we'd known about them. I seem to recall reading somewhere that they had offworld technology forty thousand years ago."

"Yes," said Alex. "That's about right."

"Have they encountered aliens anywhere?"

"Just us. They've come across a few dead civilizations. As we have. But nothing that's still functioning."

Gabe's eyes narrowed. "I've some questions I'd like to ask. Do you think you could get me in to see them?"

IX.

*We all treasure the golden meeting, the first encounter with a friend,
with a brilliant mentor, with the lover of a lifetime. And, incredibly,
we usually recognize the experience from the first moment.*
—REV. AGATHE LAWLESS, *SUNSET MUSINGS*, 1402

Alex made the call to the Maracaibo Caucus. They said sure,
come on down. The language was considerably less formal
than had been the case in my previous encounter at the Caucus. Even though I've spent considerable time with Mutes, and
established friendships with some, they're still disconcerting.
Especially the part where they automatically read my mind.

When that happens, you spend most of your time trying
not to think of aspects of your life that are less than elegant.
Which means, of course, that your worst moments are all
you *can* think of. It's why you seldom run into Mutes at parties.

Alex and I went with him. We arrived in the late afternoon
at Kostyev House, which was once a Dellacondan embassy.
A flat, gray structure that resembles an abandoned school
building, it's located near the capitol. We descended into a
landing area two blocks away, walked across a broad green
park, and entered through the front door between a pair of
white pillars. A tube took us up to the third floor, where a
wall panel admitted us into a carpeted corridor. We passed

carved doors, and murals portraying Mutes in sedate pos-
tures contemplating approaching storms, strolling past fruit-
laden tables, or simply standing in contemplative poses.
Particularly noticeable was a portrait in which one of them
gazed down at a chessboard.

"You think," I asked, "that Mutes play chess?"

"I doubt it," said Gabe. "How do you play any kind of
game, except maybe bingo, if the players can read each other's minds?"

"That was going to be my question."

"Let's try to stay on target here," said Alex.

We passed several offices. One was Trotter and Smythe, a
prominent legal firm; another was a transit corporation that
arranged vacations. The others showed names, but nothing I recognized. And then, near the end of the corridor, we
reached a set of double doors marked MARACAIBO CAUCUS.

Alex activated his commlink and one of the doors opened.
We walked into an office. It was nothing out of the ordinary.
An empty desk, circled by a large sofa and a couple of fabric armchairs. A wooden table stood before two square windows that looked out over the city. Somehow the sky seemed
grayer than it had when we were on the street.

We heard voices from an adjoining room. Moments later
it opened and a young man, probably not more than twenty
years old, entered and closed the door behind him. His eyes
settled on me but he spoke to Alex. "It's good to see you again,
Mr. Benedict. Why don't you and your guests be seated? Roka
Kailan will be with you in a moment."

He waited while Gabe and I took chairs and Alex relaxed
on the sofa, which almost engulfed him. "My name's Jerry,
by the way. If you need anything while you're here just tell
the AI." He smiled and then reacted as if he'd heard something. The door behind us opened and a Mute came in.

He had a huge prothorax and large bulbous dark eyes that
inevitably put humans into a kind of spotlight. "Welcome,

Alex," he said, speaking through a gold-colored locket that hung on a chain around his throat. "I'm happy to meet your uncle Gabriel and to see Chase again."

"Hello, Roka," said Alex with a smile. Introductions were always a bit awkward with someone who can read your mind.

Roka wore a long rust-colored robe with a red sash over his left shoulder. He was tall and moved with easy grace. But Mutes find it difficult to smile, and he was no exception. I'd almost learned to relax in the presence of the Ashiyyur, but I couldn't recall having met Roka before and I could feel my mind opening and every private thought drifting out into the daylight. Including my failure to recognize him. "It's okay, Chase," he said with a smile that was almost innocent. "I've blocked myself off. Nothing's coming through."

Our understanding of Mutes is that, because of their communication method, the basic context created by a culture in which telepathy rules, nobody lies. They *can't*. There's no point in it. As much connection as I've had with them over the years, I still have a hard time understanding how their interactions work with each other.

"I wish we could manage more time together, Roka," said Alex as the Mute sat down beside him.

"My feeling exactly, Alex. What can I do for you?"

"You know of Octavia?"

"The lost station? Yes, of course. Is there news? Has anything changed?"

"No. Unfortunately not. They've made no progress."

Roka's eyes darkened. They generated a chilling look. "We did not have anything to do with it."

"We have to consider every possibility. But that's not one we've given much credence. I can see no advantage, no reason, for your people to make off with a space station."

"Had it happened," said Roka, "it would probably have been influenced by a desire to discover how we might travel through wormholes."

"Except that I'm pretty sure your people know that if we'd gained that kind of technology it would have been yours for the asking."

"Alex, I don't know whether that's true or not."

"We would not have kept it from you. But you know nothing about it?"

"We do not."

From a society that, as far as we knew, couldn't keep secrets, that seemed to settle the issue. Unless Roka was willing to lie to humans. That thought crept into my head despite every effort to push it away. I looked across the room at him, and believe it or not, he was smiling at me. He wasn't reading my mind, but he knew exactly what I was thinking.

"The real reason we came was to get a sense of whether DPSAR had run a complete investigation."

"If you're asking, Alex, whether they came here to question us, the answer is yes. They did. I wasn't here at the time, nor was anyone else who's currently here. But I know one of the coordinators who *was* present when the investigation was conducted. So you'll understand I was, in effect, also present. And yes, they wanted to know whether we had any vehicles in the area at the time, whether it was possible we could have had someone out there and not known about it? Did we understand that we should not take their questions in an offensive manner, but did we have any *pirates*? I think that was the term they used. It would of course be impossible for us to have pirates running around and not know of it."

Gabe got into it at that point: "Roka, please understand that our ability to communicate is fairly clumsy compared to yours. DPSAR didn't have many options on the table. Either some nonhuman power had taken the station, or there'd been an equipment breakdown of some kind. The station was supposed to be impermeable. There could be no equipment failure without adequate warning."

"That's what they claimed," said Roka. "But even the

highest-tech equipment is not perfect. And why couldn't there have been *human* pirates?"

"We haven't completely eliminated that possibility. Let's get that off the table, though. I have a question for you."

"I am at your service."

"If an attack had been committed by an Ashiyyurean, would it have been possible for him, or her, to hide it from everyone else?"

Those large dark eyes fastened on Gabe. "Yes," he said. "Provided the individual never returned to live with the rest of us."

"How about if he was unstable? Would it be possible then?"

"For him to hide what he'd done? No. For one thing, we have very few persons who become deranged. One of the reasons for that is that everyone around them learns very early what is happening, and we are consequently able to intervene."

"I suspect that's one of the things the investigators wanted to know."

"I'm sure that's correct. More significantly we cannot hide who we are. We literally live inside each other's minds."

"Roka," said Alex, "the most likely possibility seems to be aliens. We've both had interstellar flight for thousands of years. The only high-tech aliens we've encountered have been each other. Am I correct?"

"That is correct, Alex."

"Nevertheless, there are millions of worlds out there that neither of us has visited."

Roka nodded. "That's certainly true."

"You have any theories," asked Gabe, "why intelligent life is so rare?"

He took a moment to consider the issue. "It seems obvious enough. Give a creature intelligence and it begins to acquire knowledge. The knowledge leads to advanced technology and probably a tendency to use their developments in a way that exhausts their planetary home. It almost happened with us, and we know you also came close. We've seen a substantial number of dead civilizations over the years. As a rule, they have little staying power. The basic key to their eventual collapse has been the development of the printing press. Knowledge spreads too quickly among a species not yet equipped to handle it. Once that happens, we have seen no one who survived more than a few centuries. Other than yourselves."

"That doesn't seem to have happened with you either," said Gabe. "The Ashiyyur had aircraft and electricity before we were even thinking about building pyramids. You were slow getting to the stars, but there's no record of your people threatening their own world."

"I think we were fortunate."

"How do you mean?" I asked.

"We communicate through direct mental contact. It probably results in a higher level of empathy than most other intelligent life-forms. Lust for power, for example, is rare. Possibly nonexistent. Because one cannot hide it. And we all recognize that it is linked to stupidity. It would serve only to draw the contempt of our associates. Consequently, we are not going to attack each other.

"For the same reason, negligence that leads to planetary destruction through runaway population growth or corrosion of natural resources cannot hide itself. We were much slower to develop advanced technology than other species because we weren't fighting wars and consequently had less use for it. By the time we learned to manipulate atomic power, we were well beyond the point where anyone would have thought of converting it into a weapon. And please don't be offended."

"It makes me wonder," said Gabe, "how *we* managed to survive."

"It was close," Alex said. "Vasili Arkhipov saved us from a nuclear war."

"Oh yes." Gabe smiled. "The *Arkhipov* was one of the first interstellars."

"What did it do?" asked Roka.

"Not the starship," said Gabe. "The man."

Roka nodded, inviting him to explain.

"Several years after we'd invented atomic weapons, there was a standoff between two major powers. They were quarreling over an island. One was shipping weapons to the island while the other sent a fleet of warships to establish an embargo. The incoming freighters were accompanied by three submarines with nuclear missiles. If I remember this correctly, the three submarines each had a captain and there was a senior officer in overall command. In order to use the nukes, all four had to agree. Arkhipov was the guy who said no."

"It's fortunate," said Roka, "one of them was intelligent. I hadn't heard that story before. You were lucky."

"It makes me wonder," I said, "how we managed to get into a shooting war with your people?"

The Mute paused. "I think the problem was that both sides were sitting in interstellars with no knowledge of each other. Probably, had we been close enough for the telepathy to work, we would have realized you were only acting out of fear, that neither side constituted a willful threat to the other. It won't happen again."

"There's not much question you're right," said Alex. "The whole thing was probably just a massive communication breakdown."

We'd learned a few weeks earlier that Kormin Broder, who'd been one of our clients for almost ten years, had passed away. Kormin was a collector of antiques that had a connection with famous writers. He also owned three hardcover classics that had been signed by the writers: Gasper Mendez's history of the Ashiyyurean War, *Conflict Resurrected*; Timothy Zhin-Po's

Night Thoughts; and Wally Candles's poetry collection *Rising Water.*

Kormin's family had asked us to convert the antiques into cash. Alex put everything up for auction. The best offers for the books all came from the same source, the Collectors' Library, which was located in Salazar, forty minutes away on the Melony River. I was present but out of sight when Alex closed the deal with the library's owner, Chad Barker. After they disconnected he asked me to take care of the shipment. "Best," he said, "is to take them out to him personally. We don't want to risk any of those books getting lost." It had happened once before.

That was good by me. I'd never met Barker but I'd seen him twice during negotiations. It was odd; somehow he'd become one of my favorite guys. He seemed intelligent, friendly, blond, good-looking. If there are any other qualities that matter, he possessed them too.

A half hour later I was on my way. I picked up the Melony and followed it directly to Salazar, where I descended into a parking area that served the library and several other small businesses on the north side of the city.

A force-field screen floated above the rooftop, identifying the building and providing pictures of books currently available, including novels by Ellen Tier and Beaumont Savage and a collection of Hikari Hanyu's plays. *The Great Expansion* had been given the center position. Rees Cleever's classic novel *Road to Nowhere* was prominently displayed. As was *Return to Paradise*, described as a discussion of the evolution of human morality. I wasn't familiar with the author, though the book had originally appeared two thousand years ago. Another title dated all the way back to the third millennium, Tad Daley's celebrated *Apocalypse Never*, which has been credited as one of the major players in the denuclearization of Earth. Gabe maintains that, had we not managed eventually to get rid of nuclear weapons, none of us would be here today.

I got the shipment out of the skimmer and took it inside. The store's entire stock was available for inspection. A visitor could put whatever she wanted on-screen, effectively turn pages, and look at covers. But the books themselves were in a separate storage place. They could be brought out and shown physically to a customer, but they couldn't be handled or even touched until ownership was transferred.

Barker was behind a counter, talking with a middle-aged man. Another customer, a woman, was waiting, apparently having a discussion with an AI. I wandered through the store, looking at what they had available. Barker glanced my way. When our eyes touched, he smiled and indicated he'd be with me in a minute. The middle-aged man was short and heavyset. He was clearly an academic type, a professor of literature or history, probably, at Salazar University, on the southern edge of the city. They were agreeing about something, the professor nodding and Barker providing information. Then Barker exited through a door and came back a minute later with a book. The professor studied it and obviously approved. He handed over payment and the deal was done. The two shook hands, the professor continued examining his prize, and finally he left, still turning pages.

The woman waved for me to go ahead. So I went up to the counter.

"May I help you, ma'am?" Barker asked.

"I'm Chase Kolpath," I said. "From Rainbow Enterprises." I handed him the books.

"Oh," he said as his face lit up. I remember wishing that it was my presence that had generated that effect. He put the package on the counter, opened it, and lifted each volume, nodded, and then placed them all back down. "Thank you." He produced a receipt and handed it to me. "What was your name again, please?"

"Chase Kolpath."

The door opened and another customer walked in.

"Thank you, Ms. Kolpath. You know what these are, right?"

"Yes."

"I appreciate the prompt service." He hesitated. "If you don't mind my asking, are you an associate of Mr. Benedict?"

"Yes, I am."

"And you came all the way out here from Andiquar? Instead of simply shipping them?"

It's not that far, but I could see what was happening. "We wanted to make sure they got here okay."

"Ms. Kolpath, I know it's a bit late for this, but I hate to see you just turn around and go back. May I take you to dinner? If you haven't eaten already? There's an excellent café right across the street."

Let the heavens open, the rains pour down,
Let the oceans roll in and scatter their empty shells,
Let the mountains erupt, and the fire boil forth,
We don't care.
We know why these things happen
And we fear them no more.
—WALFORD CANDLES, "NIGHT DREAMS," 1201

The café was the Prime. It was an elegant club with a beautiful view of the Melony. The menu had no prices because its customers weren't supposed to be concerned with trivia. A young woman served as hostess, which is expected in the better restaurants. There were real waiters, which is also rare. When we walked in, a piano player was in the middle of "An Evening with You."

Jasmine candles illuminated the interior. The place was crowded; the hostess informed us a seat would be available in a few minutes. "Is it always like this?" I asked.

It was just after six. "I guess we didn't time this very well." Chad's eyes brightened. "They need a VIP section."

The walls were covered with prints from the previous century. Some were art deco; others were landscapes and portraits of people in formal dress. I wondered if Chad knew any of them, and managed to look surprised when he said he didn't.

Eventually we found our way to a table, ordered, and sat back. The pianist was doing "Love in the Elms." A young couple that was just leaving danced the last few steps. Others applauded.

"I noticed," he said, "that you're a star pilot."

"How did you know?"

"I looked you up." He hooked his hands together and braced his chin on them. His smile lit up the room. "I didn't want to go out with a strange woman."

"Especially to a place like this."

"How'd you get started, Chase? Why'd you become a pilot?"

"My mom was one."

"Really? Is she still doing this stuff?"

"No," I said. "When I got my license, she talked her boss into giving her job to me. Then she retired."

"Her boss was Alex?"

"It was Gabriel Benedict. Alex's uncle."

"Oh, okay."

"Actually, she didn't retire exactly. She wanted to spend time with my father."

"And she never went back?"

"No. She tells me that life on the farm is the ideal existence."

"So your dad's a farmer?"

"Not exactly. I was overstating things a bit. They just have a place in the country. A few goats and a dog."

"Goats?"

"My mom's always had a thing about goats. Don't ask me why."

"So what does your father do?"

"Physical workouts, mostly."

"That's it?"

"He concentrates on enjoying life. He says how you only get one shot and you shouldn't waste it working."

Chad's grin kept getting larger. He couldn't decide whether I was serious. "How about you?" he asked. "You thinking about heading into the countryside yourself at some point?"

"I don't think so."

"You going to stay with being a pilot?"

"Probably. I've never really thought seriously about going in another direction. I enjoy what I do, and I have a good boss."

Our drinks arrived. Chad raised a glass in my direction. "Here's to you, Chase, and to Gabriel and Alex. If you didn't work for them, I'd probably never have met you."

A few nights later, Alex took Olivia Hill to dinner. The following morning he told us how much he'd enjoyed it. "She's a treasure," he said. "She belongs to the National Historical Society, writes poetry for their magazine, and is one of the funniest people I've ever met. She has a picture of Karen Bianchi on a bookshelf in her living room."

"Who's Karen Bianchi?" I asked.

"A close friend of Charlotte's. And another avid chess player. I guess that's no surprise." Alex fell silent for a moment. "She blames DPSAR for what happened and suspects they're hiding something."

"You think there's anything to that?"

He sat quietly for a moment, stirring his breakfast. "Probably not. But I wish we could do something."

"You did the right thing last week," Gabe said.

"What was that?"

"Not charging her. You not only swallowed your commission; you paid for the chess set."

"Come on, Gabe. How could I have taken her money? I'm just glad we were able to get it."

Gabe had ordered an upgrade for his printer. It arrived, and I took it back to him. He was in his office, looking through reports on current archeological efforts being made across the Confederacy. When you have fourteen worlds politically joined—probably seventy colonies and way stations where efforts to establish permanent outposts have a broad history ranging from dazzling success to crash landings, with all that happening across a sweep of ten thousand years—you're going to have a lot of archeological sites. "You setting up another mission, Gabe?" I asked.

"I don't know. I've been thinking about it. Something I can get in before I go back to the university." Gabe loved teaching. Seminars were his style. His classroom presentations morphed into conversations with students. It was his tactic for igniting enthusiasm.

"Anything particular in mind?"

"To be honest, I don't feel like doing any more interstellars for a while. I'm tempted to go to Ironda and just do some digging." Ironda was a small continent on the other side of the world, named after the politically anarchist group that had initially settled there. The problem with an anarchic perspective, of course, is that anything it establishes is likely to have a short life span. The Irondans were at odds with one another for half a century before the movement collapsed. The turmoil, however, increased the value of artifacts. Especially personal items associated with the leaders, all of whom tended to be authoritarian. Gabe had always been fascinated by them.

"You want me to go along?"

"I'm probably not going to bother, Chase. At the moment I'm more interested in the Octavia business. Did you know there's a science museum in Calvekia that used to have a virtual display of the place? Patrons could sit inside the space station and watch what was going on. They shut it down after Octavia got lost. I asked them if they could set it up for me."

"Are they going to do it?"

He delivered that in-charge smile. How could they not?

It reminded me of a time when my mom was his pilot and I was just going along for the ride, that we'd gone to the museum in Calvekia to donate artifacts. It's a long ride, down the coast, fifteen hundred kilometers south of Andiquar. I think there were several artifacts but the only one I can remember clearly was a radio from the twenty-third-century CE that he'd found at the site of the original Mars colony. And there was something connected with Marcellus Rienke. A notebook computer. For those who don't follow classical theater, Rienke was the fourth-millennium playwright who's best known for *The Night That Victor Arrived.*

"Why'd they shut the Octavia display down?" I asked. "I'd think there'd have been a lot more interest in the thing after it disappeared."

"I'd have thought so too. But I guess the interest just fell off."

"Is Alex going?"

"Yes."

"You guys are still hung out about the space station, aren't you?"

"I think we both feel that the families of the people who were lost deserve an answer. So do a lot of other people with connections to it."

"I doubt you'll get one by going down to the museum. What's its name?"

"The Corvey Institute. And you're probably right. But it's worth trying. If we watch them at work, see how they operated, we might come up with an idea. You want to come along? We need a driver." He smiled. The skimmer doesn't need much help.

"Sure," I said. "When are we leaving?"

"Tomorrow."

Calvekia was an hour and a half from Andiquar. We left in the late morning, rising into a bright sunlit day, turned south, and headed down the coast. Gabe settled in with something from the skimmer's library. Alex had brought some reading along on his commlink. "What is it?" I asked.

He grinned. "*Wormhole Research for Nitwits.*"

"How's it going?"

"It's okay. Brackett, the author, says that some black holes have wormholes. Or at least one does."

"I think we already know that. We're not planning on going through it at any point, are we?"

That caught Gabe's attention. Alex laughed and traded glances with him. "No," Gabe said. "Not really. If I recall, there was a lot of excitement about the research when they first put Octavia in orbit." He shook his head. "That just seems like a month ago. You weren't much older than a kid."

Nobody spoke for several minutes. Then Gabe started breathing loudly, the way he does when he thinks a conversation has gone off the rails. "You know," he said, "we've had interstellars for thousands of years, and most of the galaxy is still unknown country. I'm not sure I understand why there's so much enthusiasm about finding a way to cross over to Andromeda. Let alone find a new universe." He looked in my direction. "I'm talking here preferably about one with stars."

Nobody likes to talk about this, but we live in a dark age for science. And it's never going to change. We still talk about research, but it's really, as someone once said, not much more than stamp collecting. Scientists get excited by life-forms nobody's ever seen before, and add them to the catalog. And we visit new worlds and record the differences among them and whatever else we encounter. Blufield has a wider oxygen-nitrogen split than any other Earth-type planet. Parmentier has the widest ranges of temperatures. Barnicle has the highest mountain. And that's what constitutes serious science today. The remaining questions that have evaded us for thousands of years are still there, and probably always will be: How big is the universe? Does it have an edge? And if so, what would that look like? And what came before the big bang? I guess the bottom line will always be whether life has meaning.

I don't think there's been a serious scientific break-through for centuries. And I suspect that was the reason for the enthusiasm about wormholes. Most of the people who used to become scientists are now probably training as architects.

The Corvey Institute is located in the center of Crystopolis. Cities on Rimway, of course, and for that matter throughout the Confederacy, are generally unlike cities on the home world. They are not crowded, they are not tight clusters of skyscrapers jammed together, and they are not places where kids grow up thinking that concrete is the natural condition of the ground, where trees and bushes are occasional orna-ments and fields are connected to sports.

Crystopolis is a typical example of the interstellar city. Groves, meadows, and parks are everywhere. There are only a handful of modest-sized towers, all rising with a kind of simplistic utility, all surrounded by greenery. Columns are rare, in fact almost nonexistent, as are domes, arcades, cornices, and porticos. We do seem to have a taste, though, for spires. Trolleys run almost silently. Some cities use them on bridges to connect rooftops, though Crystopolis is not one of them.

We came down in the institute's parking area, went inside, and made our way to the director's office. The secretary's desk invited us to be seated and informed us the director would be with us shortly.

"You know him, Gabe?" Alex asked.

"More or less. I've been over here a couple times as a guest speaker. When I called yesterday, though, I couldn't get past the AI."

"How long's it been shut down?" I asked.

"They tell me we're the first people who will see it in about two years, other than science or historical groups."

"Good thing we have you with us," said Alex.

The curtains were drawn in Malcolm Denver's office, which was decorated with framed certificates expressing appreciation for his work in archeological and scientific fields and framed photos depicting him conversing with persons of obvious significance. There was also a family portrait of him standing on a beach with his wife and two kids. And a gilded engraved cup denoting him as the winner of the 1431 Harbor Trophy. We'd been there about ten minutes when he came in, immediately recognized Gabe, and extended his hand. "It's good to see you again," he said. He was a thin, placid man, well into his later years but still with a long way to go. His hair was steel gray, his eyes stern, and his manner distant. He was casually dressed, with a blue shirt pulled loose over pale gray pants.

"Good to see you too, Malcolm. It's been a while. This is my nephew, Alex. And our associate Chase Kolpath."

He smiled politely in my direction without softening his expression, and adjusted the curtains to let more light into the room. Then he sat down in an armchair opposite Gabe. "I understand you're interested in the Octavia VR display."

"That's correct," said Gabe. "I hope we're not creating an inconvenience."

"No, no. We're pleased to have the opportunity to help." He did not look as if that were true. "May I ask the purpose of this?"

"I suspect everyone's interested in what actually happened, Malcolm. I wonder if you have any theories about it?"

He pushed back into his chair. "We just don't have anything to base a theory on. Octavia station was a Cherasco model. At last count there were eleven of them in orbit, but none around a black hole."

"Why not?"

"I guess because wormhole research is expensive. But the key point here is that the Cherasco stations have been in position for a substantial number of years. Octavia is the only one that ever had a problem. So there's no reason to believe there's a defect anywhere. I'm not saying it couldn't be. But there's no indication of what it might have been." He took a moment and chewed on his upper lip. "Have you heard of Reggie Greene?"

"Charlotte Hill's former boyfriend," said Alex.

"That's correct." The appearance of disinterest changed to disapproval. "Please understand, I'm not offering this as anything supported by evidence." Gabe's eyebrows rose but Alex leaned forward. "Of the four victims," Denver continued, "Charlotte Hill drew most of the attention and sympathy. That's probably because she was the only woman on board. And she was young. I'm sure you're aware she was apparently pretty talented. Anthony Kingston predicted a brilliant future for her."

"Who's Anthony Kingston?" asked Gabe.

"A physicist who specialized in quantum research. He was stricken by the loss of Octavia and suffered heart failure at the height of the event. He was also a close friend of Womack's. And he knew Housman as well. It was a terrible blow for him."

"What," asked Alex, "can you tell us about Greene?"

"He was the closest thing to a suspect who emerged from the investigation. He was a onetime boyfriend of Charlotte's who turned into a stalker. We know that he visited Octavia on at least one occasion."

"You mean," said Alex, "he *boarded* the station?"

"No. He simply turned up in the area. Tried to start a radio conversation with Charlotte. It apparently went nowhere."

"This was reported by the station?"

"Yes. By Harding, I believe. He said the guy wasn't actually visiting, just hanging around in the area, trying to get a conversation started with Charlotte. She apparently didn't respond very well. The thing that raised eyebrows is that he was out in a family-owned yacht at the time of the disappearance. But there's no record of his having been anywhere close to Octavia then. On the other hand, there's no record of where he was. He had a girlfriend with him who swore they weren't involved with or anywhere close to the space station. They were, she said, just out sightseeing. She passed every lie detector test. As did Greene. And the AI supported the same story. So unless they were able to figure a way to rig the AI without its being found out, their story was untouchable."

"The black hole," said Gabe, "is forty light-years from here. Do I have that right?"

"From here? Yes, forty-one actually. There was a pretty thorough investigation. A couple of vehicles from other stations could have reached the area at the time of the disappearance, but they were cleared after their AIs were checked. Nevertheless, it does seem likely the station was attacked."

"Why do you say that?" asked Alex.

"There was a period of about thirty hours during every orbit when they lost communication with everyone. When they got completely behind the black hole. That was when they disappeared. It's hard to believe that was a coincidence."

"They had a shuttle," said Alex. "I assume it didn't have a star drive?"

"That's correct. Charlotte would take it to the place where they were expecting the cannon pods to surface, and she'd stay there for weeks at a time."

"Completely alone?"

"Yes. There was too much travel involved to bring her back regularly to the station."

"And the shuttle had no star drive? And no hypercomm?"

Denver shook his head. "I guess they saw no need for it."

Gabe didn't look happy. "Do you have any idea at all if anyone had a reason to destroy the station?"

"No. The common theory is that it was aliens. And I know that sounds absurd. But it's all we have."

"Is there any possibility it could have simply exploded?"

"DPSAR has gone over that again and again." He shook his head. "They maintain it's impossible." He looked as frustrated as I felt.

"You don't really buy the alien theory, do you?" I asked.

"No. I think it was Greene. I don't know how he beat the lie detectors, but I suspect he managed it somehow. It's the only explanation that makes any sense. It's a pity they couldn't find enough evidence to convict him. They didn't even have enough to take him to trial." He looked up at the clock centered between a pair of windows. "All right. I can't imagine we have anything that will assist your search. If you can think of any way we might be able to help, let me know. Good luck. We have the program all set to run. You'll be in the Housman Room."

"You've named it for him?" Gabe asked.

"Oh yes. It seemed like the least we could do. Del Housman, like his three colleagues, gave his life in pursuit of scientific advance. And he contributed a major breakthrough in the process." He got out of his chair, looking thoroughly annoyed. "Probably killed by a lunatic ex-boyfriend." He closed his eyes momentarily. "Follow me, please."

The Housman Room wasn't much larger than Denver's office. It was furnished with half a dozen chairs and a table. A young woman was waiting when we entered. We sat down, and Denver told us the show would begin in a minute or two and explained that the events portrayed were taking place two weeks before the Octavia team had located the wormhole. At that time, Harding and Womack were in the space station, Housman was in the cannon's operational center, and Hill was millions of kilometers away in the shuttle. He turned to the woman. "This is Elizabeth Pope. She's an associate and will take you through the program." He introduced us and said that if he could help us in any way, we shouldn't hesitate to stop by his office. Then he left.

"Before we get started," Elizabeth said, "does anybody need anything?" I'd have liked a gin and tonic but Alex would never have approved. This was serious business.

She'd barely settled into a seat before the lights began to dim. A male voice welcomed us to Octavia. He informed us that they'd selected this black hole for the project because space-time continuities in the area had more fluctuations than would normally have occurred. He also mentioned that several thousand g-class suns would have been needed to provide its mass.

The room grew dark and began to expand. Windows formed, and dim specks of light appeared outside and slowly brightened into stars.

We were inside the space station. Two men were standing in front of a display that depicted Housman seated at a control board. *"Rick Harding is the one in the white sweater,"* said the narrator. *"The other is Archie Womack. Rick's responsibility is to maintain the operational equipment. Archie has dedicated much of his career to wormhole theory. At the time this was recorded they were still trying to locate the wormhole. They do that by launching probes from the cannon into areas that are deemed promising. The probes are small, not quite the size of coins. Charlotte Hill is in the shuttle several million kilometers away. The probes put out radio signals. Wormhole theory at that time indicated where the probes should emerge, which would be a considerable distance from where they'd be found if they were traveling in normal space.*

"The probes also detect and measure various conditions that would be expected inside a wormhole. Housman and Womack

are trying to track the probes, although that is seldom productive because the radio signals tend to be disrupted by the conditions usually encountered close to black holes."

Housman looked out at his colleagues and shook his head. *"Nothing yet."*

The narrator continued: *"Once they succeed in establishing that the wormhole exists, which they will do less than two weeks after the scene we are watching, they will be able to fire a different category of probes directly into the hole, and then attempt to find exits that will eventually permit us to determine the possibilities. Do the exits provide only shortcuts to distant places? Or will they permit entry into another universe?"*

It was hard to miss the growing frustration as the process continued, as thousands of probes were launched into the area that the researchers thought should have been home to the wormhole. The probes, however, did not get lost. They continued without vanishing and were eventually found by Charlotte at exactly the place they would have been if the wormhole didn't exist.

The interior of the shuttle appeared on the display. Charlotte was seated in the cockpit, obviously aware that she was being recorded. She swung around in her chair, facing the camera, delivered a smile, and raised her left hand to greet the viewers.

When the lights all came back, Elizabeth Pope stood and asked if we had any questions.

"Elizabeth," asked Gabe, "if they find the wormhole, what do they hope to learn from the probes? Other than entrances and exits?"

"Basically, the conditions of the passage. Does time run at the same rate in the wormhole? For example, would it be a good idea to take a book along? Is there anything in the experience that would endanger travelers? Are there conditions that would prevent electrical equipment from operating? We have a great deal to learn. We do not want to send manned vehicles into a wormhole until we know all the effects."

I was glad to hear it. There was no way anyone would ever be able to persuade me to fly into a wormhole.

XI.

We mourn the loss of those we love and care about, thinking of them as taken too soon, regardless of age. But it is the price of living. We are all taken too soon.

—TULISOFALA, "MOUNTAIN PASSES,"
TRANSLATED FROM ASHIYYUREAN BY LEISHA TANNER, 1202

I've spent a lot of time on Skydeck over the years. You can't help meeting techs, pilots, and physicists up there. Some of them eventually sign on with the Quantum Research Group, which had been a major player in the effort to solve the Octavia mystery. I ran some searches for QRG guys that I knew and found one, a communications specialist. I could recall actually seeing him just once, in one of the restaurants. But I'd spoken with him frequently by radio from the *Belle-Marie.* I brought up a couple of pictures and would not have recognized him. His name was Bill Abbate.

Bill was listed currently as a telescope technician at QRG. I called him. An AI answered and explained he'd get back to me, and twenty minutes later he did. *"It's good to hear from you again, Chase,"* he said, rising from a chair. He was tall and slim, with blond hair, a smooth complexion, and liquid brown eyes. *"What can I do for you?"*

"Bill, I'd like to record this call if you've no objection."

"Uh-oh," he said. "Is there a lawsuit pending over one of our dockings?"

We both laughed. "My boss has gotten interested in the Octavia thing. Some friends had connections with a couple of the people who were lost when it disappeared. Did you guys ever come up with any kind of reasonable theory as to what happened?"

"Feel free to record. And unfortunately, no. We literally spent years looking at it, Chase. We put together a lot of theories. We sent vehicles out there and orbited the black hole trying to come up with something. The only thing that was still there when we arrived was the cannon. The station and the shuttle were both gone. I was still working at Skydeck at the time, and for several years afterward we continued to struggle with it. When I moved down here, five or six years had passed. The level of frustration was off the charts. It was why Walton quit." He was referring to the project director.

"She ran the search?"

"Yes. The people here tell me she always blamed herself."

"Why did she do that?"

"QRG was tasked with leading the investigation. Everybody said she left because she'd been the boss, so she felt responsible. She's the reason we never reactivated the program. Since we didn't know what had occurred, she was concerned it could happen again."

"Walton's running DPSAR now, isn't she?"

"Yes. We're actually a branch of DPSAR. But you probably know that. Walton came out of it okay, as far as her career was concerned. Though I don't think she ever got past it."

"What do you think happened, Bill?"

"Hell, Chase, I have no idea. Maybe something exploded. It would have had to be when everybody was in the station because we never found any sign of the shuttle either. So something blew up, knocked them out of orbit or whatever, and they fell into the hole."

"Is that possible? You run that by anybody?"

"Sure. I talked to some of the techs. They all claimed that it wasn't possible, that there was nothing in the place that could have exploded accidentally. It could have happened if somebody had set the thrusters to overload. That would have blown a hole in the place. But it's just ridiculous."

"So what does that leave?"

"Aliens?" He sighed. *"I don't see what else it could have been. I know the Mutes deny being anywhere near it. But who knows? Maybe there was somebody else out there."*

"Have you been there, Bill? Out to the black hole?"

"No. I could have gone a couple of times. But I don't want to have anything to do with the damned thing. Whatever did happen, I think it's pretty obvious they got sucked in."

I reported everything to Alex. He showed no interest in watching the visual record. "No point," he said. "If there were anything odd going on, you'd have picked it up."

A book lay open on his desk. "What is it?" I asked.

"Lost in the Stars. It's a biography of Del Housman."

"You find anything of interest?"

"He had a difficult childhood. He loved physics, and consequently he was one of those kids everybody in the schoolyard picked on."

"I think Gabe told us about that."

"Yeah. He was pretty smart. He had a passion for black holes right from the start. Got his PhD here, at Andiquar, started contributing articles to *Cosmic* and the *Central Review*. He was fifty-one when he applied for Octavia. He was passed over twice for more experienced people, but they got nowhere and they were about to close the project down when he got involved. Somehow he was able to persuade Lashonda Walton to stay with it. By then he'd made some serious contributions to quantum research and black hole theory."

"I assume he was responsible for Charlotte Hill getting the assignment?"

"Yes, he was, Chase. They were friends. She set herself up by getting a license to operate the shuttle."

"Those things are pretty easy. If you can't run a shuttle, they shouldn't let you out by yourself."

"Whatever, kid."

"Do we know why he wanted to bring her along? Was there something sexual going on?"

"Hertzog doesn't think so."

"He's the author?"

"Yes. Sorry. No, if there'd been an affair, there would have been no way to keep it from Harding and Womack. They were both asked about it in communications from home. And both said nothing was going on. Neither showed any inclination to duck the question." He took a long look at me. "Why do you ask?"

"Idle curiosity, I guess. Just looking for something that might explain an eruption. Maybe an affair with one of the others."

"Could be," Alex said. "But it seems unlikely. She was young and beautiful. Why would she want to get involved with one of those older guys? No, I just don't buy it. By the way, if you're interested, I watched Hertzog getting interviewed on one of the *Science Today* programs. It was recorded about seven years ago." He paused. "It has some emotional moments."

"How do you mean?"

"Hertzog obviously felt a lot of sympathy for Housman. They were longtime friends. He says that Housman was determined to make an impact on scientific progress. Discover *something* that mattered. Hertzog's one solemn wish is that Housman could have lived long enough to find out he'd won the Exeter."

• • •

Alex changed his mind the following day and listened to my conversation with Bill Abbate. When he'd finished he asked me to contact him again.

Bill was out somewhere, so I set up a call for the next morning. His AI got back to me and said that he'd be in our area next day, and was it okay if he dropped by at about nine?

I was on the porch when he arrived precisely on time. "I couldn't resist taking advantage of an opportunity to spend some time with Alex," he said.

"You've met him before. When you were working on Sky-deck."

"I know. But that was just writing tickets. It isn't quite the same as this. I've always thought I'd like to be part of one of his investigations. I don't want to do it all by phone. Does he have any idea yet what happened?"

"If he does, he's keeping it to himself." Jacob opened the door. "Come in. I'll let him know you're here."

Alex already knew about his visitor. He walked into the office before we'd even gotten settled. "Good to meet you, Bill," he said. "I appreciate the material you've already given us."

"I wish I could be more help, Dr. Benedict," Bill said.

"Call me *Alex*. The most difficult part of this business is that we never got a transmission from Octavia. It's hard not to conclude that someone set up an attack and chose his timing carefully."

"That makes sense to me."

"Can you think of any reason why someone, *anyone*, would have wanted to do that?"

"The only one I can think of with a motive is Reggie Greene."

"Could a bomb have been planted on the station by a visitor? Did they get visitors?"

"Supply vehicles went out there periodically. I understand

the delivery people were all questioned and eliminated as possible suspects. If anybody else showed up out there, we'd have known about it."

"Could a bomb have been built into the station by someone?"

"It couldn't have gotten past the inspections. Look, Alex, as far as I know, no one has turned out to have any kind of motive other than Charlotte's old boyfriend."

"Would you like a drink, Bill?"

"Absolutely." He looked my way. "Can you put together a valo delight, Chase?"

Alex wanted a golden quibble, and I settled for some dark wine. When I came back with them, Alex was asking about the standard response that would have occurred if an unexpected vehicle showed up close to the station. "They report it immediately. Including an ID if they succeed in making one."

"By hypercomm?"

"Yes."

"There were no reports of another ship during the period leading up to the disappearance?"

Bill shook his head. "The last vehicle they had contact with was the *Prendel*. It was a supply ship."

"Did the crew on the *Prendel* report anything unusual?"

"No."

"Suppose someone showed up when they were all asleep?"

"It wouldn't matter. An alarm would have gone off before anyone could have gotten near them."

Chad was moving increasingly into my life. My schedule was flexible because I periodically spent weeks on the bridge of the *Belle-Marie*, and I'd never made an issue of it. Consequently Alex had no reservations about allowing me whatever free time I needed, as long as I didn't get ridiculous about it. On his side, Chad had no problem with scheduling because he owned the Collectors' Library. So we spent a substantial number of mornings wandering along the Riverwalk, afternoons on the beach, and evenings at theaters and the Magisterium Dance Hall in Salazar. It was a good time.

He was easy to talk to. The guy had a sense of humor, and he was willing to listen when I brought up the Octavia. I know he got bored because he didn't think a solution was possible. But when I got started on the subject, he let me go on, asked a few questions, and in the end inevitably commented that sometimes things just happen. "It's not a perfect world, Chase." He made it clear that if there was anything he could do, I shouldn't hesitate to ask. But that he'd be happier if I just let the damned thing go.

I recall thinking that the day would come when I'd walk past those restaurants and beaches and wish that I hadn't let him get away.

XII.

The most common cause of plans going wrong and operations collapsing can usually be traced to a communication breakdown. The secret to management success, in peace or war, is to explain strategy in clear terms, and to listen. Acquire those two skills, and fate will be kind.

—CHRISTOPHER SIM, *MAN AND OLYMPIAN*, 1206

We got a call from the Action Network. A small, balding man with a carefully trimmed beard blinked on in my office. He was seated at a display. A dark brown jacket hung on a hook directly behind him. He identified himself as Benjamin Hollingsworth, the producer of *The Morning Report*. *"May I speak with Alex Benedict, please?"*

Alex was just coming out of the dining room.

I waved him in and showed him our caller. "Hello, Ben," he said. "Good to see you again. How've you been?"

"On the run, Alex, as always. How's everything out at your part of town?"

"Couldn't be better. Especially now that my uncle's back home."

"Yes. I've been meaning to get in touch with him. We'd like to bring him in. Put him on the show. You think he'd be willing?"

"I'm sure he'd enjoy sitting down with Hiroka." Hiroka Itashi was *The Morning Report*'s host.

"Excellent. I understand you're looking into the Octavia story. Is that correct?"

"We've been trying to see if anything got missed during the original investigation."

"Great. Have you found anything yet?"

"I'll let you know if we do, Ben."

"Okay. Even if it doesn't happen, we'd like to have you come in and talk about it. Maybe you and your uncle could do shows a couple weeks apart?"

"Let's hold off on that for a while, Ben. Where I'm concerned. Right now we're just looking at the situation. I'd rather wait until we have something. But in the meantime, I suspect Gabe would be happy to participate."

"I understand, Alex. I guess it's like trying to resolve a murder when you don't have a body."

I was alone in the country house two hours later when a skimmer descended into the parking area and a tall, heavy-set man climbed out.

"You have a reading on who this is?" I asked Jacob.

"Negative, Chase. He has no connection with Rainbow Enterprises, and none that matches any personal records. Do you prefer the door remain locked?"

"No, Jacob. It's okay." We had valuable artifacts spread throughout the property, so caution was a requirement. But I had defenses that would be more than adequate should a situation turn hostile. I understood Jacob's concern, though. Our visitor did have the appearance of a pugilist.

I met him at the door. "Can I help you?" I asked.

"Yes, ma'am. I hope so. My name is Joseph Womack." Instead of the baritone I'd expected, his voice was soft. He was big, with wide shoulders and a lantern jaw. "I'm looking for Alex Benedict. Am I at the right place?"

"You are, Mr. Womack. But he's not here at the moment."

"Are you his secretary?"

"More or less. My name is Chase Kolpath. What can I do for you?"

"I've heard that Mr. Benedict has become interested in the Octavia."

"Come in, please, Mr. Womack." I ushered him into my office. "He has been looking into the event."

"My cousin Archie was one of the victims."

"I'm sorry. Did you have something that might help us?"

"Unfortunately not. If you're asking whether I know something about that thing, the answer is no. I have no idea what happened. Just that we lost a good man."

"Everything we've heard of him supports that."

"We encouraged him to go. His folks thought it was a great career move. So did I. We regret it now."

"It wasn't anybody's fault, Mr. Womack."

"We know that. He wasn't anxious to leave Andiquar for two years. He didn't think that screwing around with black holes was a good idea." There was no way I could disagree with that. "Archie was a physics teacher. The students loved him. They kept in touch, invited him to anniversary celebrations. He knew how to arouse their passions about physics. I wish I'd had a science teacher like him. He didn't just spend time showing them how to calculate how long a loaf of bread would take to hit the ground if you threw it off the roof of a skyscraper. He did that, of course. But he also asked them why, if they walked off the roof, would they fall? They'd tell him gravity and he'd ask them to explain what gravity was and how it worked. Nobody could do it. So he'd say how space was made out of rubber, and when you put a weight in it, like a planet, you made it bend. And gravity had to do with sliding down the curve. He was brilliant. There's a whole crew of physicists out there who used to tell him that he was the reason they'd gotten into the field."

"I can understand why you feel proud of him, Mr. Womack."

We looked at each other. "How can I help you?"

"If Mr. Benedict can find out what happened to him, to Octavia, I'll pay him ten thousand markers."

Alex called him that afternoon. "I appreciate your generosity, Mr. Womack," he said, "but whatever happens, please keep your money. We'll do everything we can to get at the facts."

"Your sudden generosity," I told him after Womack was gone, "continues to astound me."

"No problem," said Alex. "We're never going to get to the bottom of this." He smiled. "It's easy to be generous when you have nothing to lose."

A call came in over the weekend from a Jordan Kaye. Jacob relayed it to my cottage. *"Ms. Kolpath,"* he said, *"I'm the owner of the* Mary Kaye. *I understand you have an interest of some sort in my yacht?"*

I wasn't dressed so I left it on audio. "Mr. Kaye," I said, "we've been doing some research on a lost artifact that was brought back to Rimway by Rick Harding. You know him, I assume?"

"Yes. He was the guy we bought it from. The yacht. What actually did you want to know?"

"We're trying to track the source of the artifact. To that end, we'd like to talk with the yacht AI."

"Where do you live?"

"The Andiquar area."

"Excellent. We're in Karaway. On our way home now. I've locked in my home address. Let me know when you'd like to make it happen."

I set it up for the next day. I'd planned to go to Salazar and have lunch with Chad but first things first. Gabe and I took off in the skimmer, turned north under a bright sky, crossed the Melony, and descended twenty minutes later onto a lush, neatly maintained hilltop property, surrounded by forest. The house was in the style of the previous century, fronted by a wide porch and a pair of fluted pillars. It was three stories high, with an arched roof, circular windows, and a large swimming pool in back.

We were just touching down when Jordan Kaye's voice came in on the radio, welcoming us. It was actually Kaye, not the AI that one usually hears. *"I'm sorry, Ms. Kolpath,"* he said. *"I screwed up. The yacht won't be available for a while."*

Gabe rolled his eyes. "Call me Chase," I said. "What happened?"

"I just called to set us up so you could talk with the AI. But they'd leased it. They left a few hours ago. I'm sorry. I didn't realize."

"Who leased it?"

"A group of hunters. They're going to one of the places in the, um, Garver system. I think that's right. They should be back in about ten days."

"Your yacht was leased out to someone without your knowledge?"

"No, no. Actually the yacht belongs to our company, Golden Tours. I should have checked earlier. It just came back in; I didn't expect it to be going right back out again. I just assumed it was docked. My fault. I'm sorry. If I'd used my head I would have checked yesterday."

Gabe turned in my direction. "Doesn't it take a while to get serviced before you can go out again?"

"It can happen overnight, Gabe. That's not a big deal." I got back to the call. "Okay, Jordan. Thanks. If you could let us know when it's available, we'd be grateful."

"Listen, since you've come this far, why don't you come on in? Maybe we can help with whatever you're looking for."

Gabe nodded. "We'll be right there."

"Good."

The front door opened, and a man in fatigues and a cuff-
less knit black hat came out of the building onto the veranda,
along with a girl and a dog. The girl was about eight. She
waved at us. We climbed out of the skimmer and waved back.
A flagstone walkway led through neatly cut grass to a set
of stone steps. The dog was a cocker spaniel. It arrived and
began licking my knees. The man ordered it to back off. It
did, and he apologized. "Sorry," he said, "she tends to be a bit
overly friendly." He came down the steps, accompanied by
the girl. "Hi, Chase. It's good to meet you."

"And you as well, Jordan. This is my boss Gabriel Benedict."

"Hello, Mr. Benedict." We all shook hands. Then he looked
down at the girl. "This is Mary."

"The young lady the yacht is named for," said Gabe.

"That's correct." The dog was trying to insinuate itself into
the conversation, wagging its tail. "And Chirpie," he said.
"Please come in."

He followed us inside. A young woman with glistening
dark eyes was seated in a luxurious living room, reading. She
put the tablet down and rose. "Hello," she said. "I'm Donna."
His wife. The walls were covered with surrealistic artwork
depicting an upside-down landscape, an angel in tears, and
a twisted skyscraper. There were also framed photos, one of
Mary and Chirpie, another of Jordan again in fatigues, kneeling beside a purple bush holding a pair of clippers while
Donna beamed down at him. And a wedding picture. The
happy couple stood in front of a church.

Donna extended her hand. "It's a pleasure to meet you,
Gabriel. And Chase. I understand you want to talk to Boomer."

"Boomer?" I said. "Is that the AI?"

"Yes."

"I thought," said Gabe, "that naming the yacht for Mary
was an excellent idea."

Jordan watched his daughter light up. "Yes," she said,

reaching down to pet the dog, which began wagging its tail again.

He grinned. "Mary has more energy than the Korba unit."

The girl was a delight, a small blossoming edition of her mom. I smiled back at her. "Have you been on the yacht, Mary?"

"Oh yes. We just got back from looking at a *star*."

"That must have been exciting."

She was almost salivating. "I've been out there before. And to other far places. My daddy loves them, don't you, Daddy?"

"I guess we all do, Mary."

At Donna's signal, we spread out around the living room and sat down. "Why," she said, "do you want to talk to Boomer? What's going on?"

Gabe took it: "We're doing some research on Rick Harding."

"Who?"

"Rick Harding. He was the previous owner of the *Venture*."

She was shaking her head. "The what?"

"Your yacht. Up at Skydeck."

"You mean the *Mary Kaye*? Oh yes, I remember that. That was the original name. It's a long time ago."

"I was originally going to name it for *her*," Jordan said, indicating his wife. "But she refused. She's too modest."

"That's the first time you've accused me of that."

He laughed. "You claimed it didn't feel right. We tried *Tracker*. But that didn't work well either. So when *you* came along"—he smiled down at Mary—"the call was easy."

Donna asked if she could get us something to drink. Everybody passed. "Then how about some lunch? As long as we brought you out here, we need to do something for you."

"Come to think of it," said Gabe, "I am a bit hungry."

"Good. What would you like?"

We made our selections and Donna passed them along to the AI. Then she turned back to Gabe. "So why do you want to talk to Boomer? What's it got to do with Harding?"

"You know he was on board Octavia when it got lost?"

She frowned at her husband. "What's Octavia?"

He grinned. "It was that space station that disappeared ten or fifteen years ago."

"Oh. And the guy we bought the *Mary Kaye* from was on that?" She stopped and frowned. "Come to think of it, I guess I did hear that somewhere."

"I'd forgotten about it, Chase," said Jordan. "You didn't mention the space station yesterday."

"There didn't seem any need to." I could see that Gabe was beginning to get an impatient expression. "We're trying to find out what happened. Harding picked up an artifact somewhere that doesn't seem to be anything produced by us."

"What kind of artifact?" asked Donna.

"It's a plaque, made from a metal that looks like silver but is apparently something else. There's an inscription on it in a language no one can read."

"You mean," said Jordan, "you think aliens did it? Took the space station? I've heard that before."

"That's not what we think, but there's an outside possibility."

Mary looked up at her father. "Daddy, what's an alien?"

"Somebody from another place, love." Jordan could hardly contain his excitement. "Wow. And you want permission to question Boomer?"

Gabe nodded. "Yes."

"Absolutely." He was wearing one of the widest smiles I'd ever seen.

"May I ask why you bought the *Venture*?" Gabe asked. "Was it meant for Golden Tours?"

"You know, I'm not sure. But probably."

"Do you guys run the company?"

"I do. Donna's not much into it."

"It's boring," she said.

Jordan smiled. "If you want to go somewhere unusual, out of the way, we're the people you talk to. We don't do the routine spots." It sounded, the way he said it, like the company motif.

Lunch arrived a few minutes later. It was good. And Jordan assured us he'd get in touch as soon as the *Mary Kaye* got back.

XIII.

What, then, is life? The formal definition stipulates metabolic growth, adaptation to the environment, and reproduction. That is not how most of us think of it. Our natural inclination is to include an awareness of surroundings and of self. Which of course is nonsense. What sort of awareness has an oak tree? Yet what is the point of being alive if one is no more than a raspberry bush? We need a new term, one which drops the automatics and considers instead the benefits of consciousness.
—Rev. Agathe Lawless, *Sunset Musings*, 1402

Alex was just shutting down a phone conversation when we got home. "That was one of Womack's colleagues," he said. "It sounds as if his cousin had the facts straight. His students loved him. And so did most of the people he worked with. But not everybody."

Gabe's brows lowered. "You implying that someone wanted to kill Womack?"

"No, I didn't mean that. But Womack was apparently a stand-up guy. He said what he thought, and he wasn't inclined to cave to authority."

"So he couldn't have avoided making enemies."

"That's correct."

"Was one of the enemies connected with Octavia?"

"Not that I know of."

"Then what has that to do with anything?"

"Nothing directly. But he, Womack, apparently did not think much of Housman."

"Why not?"

"The word is that Housman took care of himself first. And that he felt himself to be in competition with Womack. Assemble a list of the five top physicists of the last thirty years, and most people would put both their names on it."

"So we're back to thinking that one of the people at the station might have done it?"

"Other than the aliens, I'm not sure what other possibilities there are."

I'd read background on all four members of the Octavia team. It was hard to imagine any of them as a murderer or as suicidal. They all appeared to be basically decent people. They might have had a few defects, but who doesn't? "Womack seems unlikely," I said.

"What did they have to say?" said Gabe. "His colleagues?"

Alex shook his head. "They said he was very good in the classroom. There was a woman, a language professor at Brinkton College, that he dated for two years. Apparently he led her to believe he was in love with her. But when the Octavia assignment came along he just disappeared out of her life. Never even told her he was leaving."

"I don't guess she took that very well."

"She learned what had happened a few weeks after he left. She never heard from him again. And she told me she didn't give a damn when the station disappeared. But she filled up while she was talking."

I stared at the ceiling. "Well, she certainly had a motive."

"She also had a boyfriend with a pilot's license. But she was doing daily classes when Octavia disappeared."

"And the boyfriend?"

"His was one of the other ships that were operating when

it happened. But he was approaching Earth at the time, and they had him logged in at Galileo."

Alex and I were in my office with the HV tuned to the Action Channel when Gabe showed up as the guest on *The Morning Report*. Hiroka had been around a long time, and her capability as a smooth, well-organized host was front and center. She welcomed him into the studio, showed him a chair, and sat down next to him. *"It's good to have you back, Gabe,"* she said. *"I've said that to a lot of our guests over the years, but it's probably never been more appropriate. For you, 1424, when the* Capella *went under, was only a few weeks ago. Am I correct?"*

"Yes, Hiroka, that seems to be right. Every kid I knew back then has pretty much grown up. My nephew Alex, whom I took to visit Earth when he was a high school student, now looks almost as old as I do. Although, I'll confess, you don't seem to have aged."

Hiroka smiled. *"That's good to hear, Gabe. When you were trapped in the ship, were you aware of what was happening?"*

"Not at first. We knew there was a problem because some of the operations people looked seriously worried, and I suspect we all got pretty nervous. The flight wasn't supposed to last several weeks. And the captain eventually informed us there'd been a breakdown. But she said they were working on it and we should just relax. Everything would be all right."

"How did that go?"

"To be honest, nothing scares me as much as having the person in charge tell me to just relax."

"It sounds unnerving. When did you find out what had happened?"

"Actually, not until the problem was resolved and we got back into normal time."

"How did you react when you came out of the Capella *and found out it was 1435?"*

"I couldn't believe it. I mean, we'd gone eleven years into the future. I was shocked. We all were. But we were home. A few things had changed, but I was grateful everything turned out okay."

"Gabriel, I understand you and your celebrated nephew Alex have begun to look into the loss of the Octavia station. You know, of course, Alex's reputation for tracking down historical mysteries. Have you made any progress on this one? Do you guys have any idea what happened out there?"

"It's too early, Hiroka. To be honest, I'm still recovering from the ride on the Capella.*"*

"Well, I can certainly understand that. I can't help wondering, is there any possibility that whatever happened to the Capella *has happened again with the* Octavia? *That it's caught somewhere in a space-time warp?"*

I watched as the conversation lurched into the various Octavia theories. Whenever Gabe tried to change the direction, to move it toward the projects he'd begun working on, Hiroka found a way to take it back to Octavia. They touched on the possibilities of an alien intervention or of a mechanical breakdown that took the station out of orbit and sent it spiraling into the black hole or of a deranged Charlotte Hill suitor arriving unexpectedly with a blaster.

"I think," said Alex, "she's decided her audience loves black holes." After twenty minutes, Hiroka thanked Gabe for coming in and broke for commercial.

The next guest was Samuel Pondergast, a physicist who specialized in black holes. *"What happens to you,"* she asked after she'd introduced him, *"if you're on a space station or a ship and you get dragged into one of those things?"*

"It's not good," said Pondergast.

I was alone in my office when Gabe got home. He wasn't happy. "I got ambushed," he said.

"You've been on her show before, Gabe. She didn't really surprise you, did she?"

"Actually, she did."

"But she's always operated that way. She's good at controlling the conversation."

"I can tell you she's a lot better than she used to be."

"I haven't really seen much of a change."

"You've been watching her for a decade. The change would have been gradual." He started toward the back of the house, but stopped. "Did Alex see it?"

"Yes. He thought you did fine."

"Sure he did."

A few days later there was some fallout from the broadcast. Alex was attending an auction and Gabe had gone to lunch with friends when a skimmer descended out of a threatening sky. *"His name is Reginald Greene,"* said Jacob. *"He wants to talk to Gabe. I've already informed him Gabriel is not here."*

Greene was the guy whose interest in Charlotte Hill had raised eyebrows. I watched him climb out of the skimmer and stride up the walkway to the porch. He looked like a man on a mission. "Let him in," I told Jacob.

"Are you sure? His background suggests—"

"Just open the door, please."

He was tall, lean, dressed casually in tapering stretch pants and a pullover shirt with ANDIQUAR stitched across it. He had clean-cut chiseled features, black hair, and an amicable expression except for a darkness in the eyes. "My name's Reggie Greene," he said. "I want to see Gabriel Benedict."

"He's not here, Mr. Greene. Can I help you?" He stood looking down at me, trying to decide how to proceed. "I'm Chase Kolpath. His assistant."

"I watched him on *The Morning Report* the other day. He's talking about opening up the Octavia investigation again. Do I have that right?"

"More or less," I said. "Please come in." I led him into my office and signaled for him to sit down. "It's not Gabe who's doing the investigation. It's one of our other people. *Alex Benedict.*"

"I've heard of him."

"Unfortunately, he's not here either. Why don't you tell me what's going on?"

"My first name is Reginald. Do you know who I am?"

"Yes. I understand you were a friend of one of the people lost on the station."

"She wasn't exactly just a friend."

I was glad Jacob was there. In case this threatened to get out of hand. "Mr. Greene, what can I do for you?"

His eyelids lowered. "You think so too, don't you?"

I knew what he was referring to, but I wasn't going to walk into it. "I think what?"

"That I caused it."

"Mr. Greene, if you're talking about Octavia, I have no idea what happened. In any case, it's hard to see how you could have had a hand in it."

"Well, thank you. It's nice to hear someone who's willing to cut me a break."

"Sir, do you by any chance know what happened out there?"

His features hardened. "No. How the hell would *I* know?"

"Why don't we start over? What can I do for you?"

"You must know that half the people on the planet think I destroyed the damned place and killed everybody on board." He looked around the room and took a deep breath. "I wouldn't even know how to think about doing something like that. But it doesn't matter. They broadcast it on the news shows, and they had people showing up on HV saying how I'd gotten away with murder and that the justice system was useless. It's been eleven years, and this damned thing is still hanging over my head." His voice softened. "Chase, it's never going to go away."

"I'm sorry, Mr. Greene."

"It's not your fault. But I'll tell you that I wasn't happy to see it all coming out again. I used to be a teacher. But that's a long time ago now. The board decided I shouldn't be allowed anywhere near children, especially girls. I loved teaching. At one time, it was my life. It was all that mattered to me. Except Charlotte. I guess it's time I admitted that. But my life is over now. I don't see that anything can happen to change what I'm living with."

"You *did* travel out to Octavia, right?"

"Yeah. Dumbest thing I ever did in my life."

"Why'd you do it?"

"Because I loved her. I'd have died for her. Given anything to have been able to hold on to her. Which, please under-stand, would never have allowed me to harm her in any way. Let alone kill her. I went out there because I didn't want to give up. It was my last chance. If it didn't work, I was going to walk away from it all. Be done with it. It wasn't the first time I'd made that decision and then went back later. But it was getting harder. My God, Chase, she was light-years away. But I just wanted to try one more time. I was telling myself that if I didn't make the effort I'd always wonder what might have happened. Whether I might have succeeded. So I got all the money I had, which I'd been saving for years, and I hired Oakie McCollough, and he took me out there—"

"Where you talked to her."

"Yes, I did. By radio."

"She was in the shuttle?"

"Yes."

"Did you ask if you could rendezvous with her?"

"Does that matter?"

"I take it she said no."

"That's correct."

"How many times did you go out there?"

"Three."

"I had the impression you were only there once."

"No. I didn't give up that easily."

"But that last time, you were back home before the station dropped out of sight?"

"Yes." He was staring at me. "Maybe if I'd been there when whatever it was happened, I could have helped. Maybe I could have gotten them off the place."

"All right. I've got the message. I'll pass it along to Alex."

"All I'm asking is that he doesn't drag me into it again."

"Mr. Greene, I'm not conducting the investigation, so I can't make any promises. But I'll tell him."

"Please," he said. "I've had all of it I can take."

When Alex got back, I explained what had happened.

"It's not an easy call," he said. "Greene came from money. His family owned a substantial piece of the Green Valley restaurant chain." One of them was located on Skydeck and had recently become a favorite of Alex's. "The family also owned the yacht Greene had used. He'd served periodically on the board of directors and had been handling its public relations operations when the Octavia charges were first leveled against him. Journalists had reported that people who'd worked with him insisted that, in their experience, Greene had shown no signs of erratic behavior. And nobody knew anything about a connection with Charlotte Hill."

"So where'd the story come from?" I asked.

"A couple of Charlotte's friends had avatars. They reported that Greene possessed an undying passion for her. That he'd been unable to leave her alone. And that he'd visited Octavia. Which, of course, is on the record." The ILEA, the Interstellar Law Enforcement Association, had conducted an investigation. "Charlotte and Greene had spent about four months dating during her senior year at the University of Andiquar.

"As far as either of the avatars said, Charlotte never thought of him as anything more than a casual date. When she realized he was falling in love with her, she broke it off.

One of the friends said she did it as gently as she could, 'but she could see the pain in his eyes.'

"Afterward Greene began showing up on the campus between her classes, wandering through the crowds of students. And at the restaurant she liked. She quit going there as a result. He rarely tried to speak to her, but instead pretended to look busy whenever she was in the area. To look as if he was there for other reasons having nothing to do with her. He even came to watch her play in the regional chess championships and congratulated her when she won her first game and again when she took the title."

"Did the report name the friends?"

"No." Alex sat down finally, closed his eyes, and let his head sink onto the back of the chair.

"It's irrelevant anyhow," I said. "The point is that he wasn't there when it happened."

"I know. But he must have known that, even though no one could prove he'd been in the area at the time, it wouldn't look good. Maybe it's time we went over and talked with the ILEA people."

I've commented earlier that I have serious doubts about the existence of true love. Maybe I should rethink that.

The Interstellar Law Enforcement Agency is an arm of the Confederate government. Its local headquarters is located in the center of Andiquar just west of the Hall of the People. The building isn't much to look at, rectangular and flat, three stories high, set amid pools and fountains. A statue of Justice, a blindfolded woman holding a scale, stands among the columns at the front entrance. The parking area is marked for official business only, but there were empty spaces and we were able to get clearance as we drifted overhead. "Should have called first," Alex said. "We got lucky."

As we descended toward the blinking light that marked our designated spot, Alex called in and identified himself.

"We'd like to talk with someone about the Octavia incident," he added.

"What's that?" It was a male voice. He sounded young.

"The space station that vanished eleven years ago near a black hole."

"Okay, sir, hold on, please." He was back a minute later. *"Just come to the main desk and we'll take care of it."*

Heavy clouds drifted across the sky and a brisk wind complicated the parking. But we got down okay, climbed out, and walked around to the front entrance. The doors opened and we strode into a circular lobby with a half-dozen offices, numbered 101 through 106. The main desk, actually the only desk, was located immediately on our right. It was unoccupied.

As we approached, we got a voice: *"Mr. Benedict?"*

"Yes."

"Proceed to office 104, please."

An elderly man with white hair and a wiry white mustache waved us in. He was seated beside a display and a bookcase. There were only a few volumes. Mostly it was filled with family photos. "My name's Roger Cassidy," he said. "What can I do for you?"

Alex introduced us as we made ourselves comfortable on a sofa. "We're doing some work on the Octavia incident. I was wondering if there's been any recent information about it. Has the ILEA picked up anything new during the last few years?"

"I'm sorry to say that nothing's changed since the original investigation, Mr. Benedict. We don't know what happened. We don't even have a decent theory."

"Have you ruled anything out? Aliens, for instance?"

Cassidy gave us a tolerant smile. "Not really." His reaction indicated he thought the alien theory was nonsensical, but he wasn't going to say so. "Right now, anything's possible."

"Did you have access to the transmissions that would have come in during the month before the disappearance?"

"Yes, we did."

"What can you tell us about them?"

"There was nothing suggesting a problem."

"Was there anything other than routine reports?"

"Of course. There were occasional messages from the research team to their colleagues at DPSAR and the Quantum Research Group."

"Would you be able to show them to us?"

"I'm sorry, Mr. Benedict. They'd require a release. But I'd recommend you save your time. Both DPSAR and QRG have dismissed the notion that any of them have a connection to the disappearance."

"What other messages have you?"

"That is all. There were numerous personal communications, but all are locked down by privacy laws. We were able to acquire messages to certain recipients, but the vast number went to people for whom we could devise no reason to get a court order."

"Did you get to see any of those? Any of them get turned in voluntarily?"

"Some. Not many. I wasn't working here at the time all this happened. But I understand there were a few copies that were made available."

"Was there anything that caused some alarm?"

"Not that I know of, Mr. Benedict. If I may ask . . ." He removed his glasses and set them on the table. "Is there something specific you're looking for?"

"No." Alex paused a moment. "We know some of the people who've been hurt by the affair. Who are desperate for answers. We were hoping the ILEA might be able to provide something."

"I wish we could. This is an issue that's haunted us for a long time. But there's just nothing there. We can't even be certain a law was broken."

"What about Reginald Greene? Is there any possibility he could have been involved?"

"Mr. Benedict, I don't see how that would have been possible."

"Is there anything at all you know of that we're missing?"

"Well, there might be one element: One of Charlotte Hill's friends told us that she, Charlotte, sent a message saying something didn't feel right. Apparently she didn't explain, and as far as I know, we never saw the transmission."

"Something didn't *feel* right?"

"That's about it."

"Can you give us the name of the friend?"

"I'm sorry. When people talk to us, they have a guarantee of privacy."

"Well, that wasn't very helpful," I said as we went back out into the lobby and through the doors onto the parking lot.

"Yeah," said Alex. "I don't think Greene had anything to do with it. The truth is that, even if he'd wanted to cause some damage, I don't see how he could have managed it. I'd like to talk with someone who was familiar with whatever happened between him and Charlotte."

"I hope you're not talking about Olivia."

"No, people don't usually lay romantic stuff out with their parents." He was walking slowly in the wrong direction. I had to stop him and point us toward our lander. "Sorry," he said, "I wasn't thinking. There *was* somebody I remember reading about. A woman Charlotte played chess with during her college years. Karen Something. Give me a minute."

We got back into the skimmer and started for home. He got on the datanet and began a search for Karen and chess. It was a popular name in the area but he saw nothing about a Karen who played chess at a high level. We weren't halfway back to home before he shut it down. "Nothing here that rings a bell," he said.

When we got to the country house he started up the staircase, stopped, held an index finger to his lips, and smiled.

"Bianchi," he said. "Karen Bianchi. That's who it was. Olivia mentioned her too. She said she was Charlotte's best friend through her college years. I wonder if she's one of the two friends cited in the report?" He hurried the rest of the way up the stairs, obviously intent on locating Karen Bianchi. Ten minutes later he came back down. "Okay," he said, "I've got her. Her name *was* Karen Bianchi. It's Randall now. I left a message for her." He was going back out the door. "I have an appointment. If she calls, find out if she stayed in contact with Charlotte on Octavia. And if she has any idea what might have happened. Whether anything unusual was going on. Okay?"

He hurried out, jumped into the skimmer, and left.

My own work had piled up. Chad had been missing for a week. I'd been trying to get evaluations for the more recent artifacts that had come in. And while I was engaged in that, a client arrived with what she claimed was a script for *Walk with a Tiger*, a classic eleventh-century play by Roger Ackerly. The script was autographed by Ackerly and I was in the process of verifying it when another guy arrived with a vintage skimmer. His name was Alfonso Picariello. I asked him to hang on while I finished with the Ackerly play. It took about twenty minutes to confirm. The owner was offering it to us to buy, or we could put it on auction. Our choice. It was the sort of choice Alex was supposed to make. I could only guess at its potential value.

I put the script in our storage room and told her we'd get back to her. I followed her outside, watched her leave, and then went over to Picariello, who was standing beside the old-fashioned two-door azure skimmer. "Okay," I said. "What have you got?"

The guy was wearing a grin a mile wide. "Don't you recognize it?" he asked.

He gazed admiringly at the vehicle. He was still in his early years, with curly red hair, blue eyes, and lips hopefully parted while he waited for me to say something. The skimmer had been around awhile. And it was a style that no one had used for a long time. "No," I said. "Why should I? Did it belong to somebody of significance?"

His disappointment did nothing to dim the glow of his features. "Matt Olander," he said. "It was his when he was young. Before he got caught up in the war."

Olander had been a close associate of Christopher Sim. I caught my breath and recalled seeing something about the sale a few weeks earlier. It hadn't made much of an impact at the time because we weren't involved and Gabe had just gotten home. I'd have preferred that Alex do the confirmation, but I didn't want to take a chance on losing the opportunity. I took Picariello inside, sat him down with some coffee in the conference room, and got some details on the skimmer from Jacob. Then, while he waited, I went out and checked the numbers. Everything fit. As well as his ID. The vehicle had belonged to Olander, and Picariello was the current owner.

There were a few remaining details that had to be confirmed. But it looked good. Picariello had gotten a decent price. The skimmer should give him a substantial pickup and would provide us with a good commission and a ton of PR.

I told Picariello that Alex would get to him later that day, moved the skimmer into our shelter, and gave him a moderate advance in exchange for a document awarding exclusive sales rights to Rainbow for sixty days. Then I took him home. When I got back, Alex had not yet returned.

I went inside and started work on some appraisals. A short time later Jacob informed me Alex had arrived. I said okay and stayed with the appraisals until eventually I noticed he hadn't come in. I looked out a window and saw him standing beside Olander's vehicle in a near state of shock. I don't recall ever seeing him look so excited about one of our auction pieces. He asked where it had come from. When I told him, he wanted to know whether I'd checked Picariello's ID.

"Yes, Alex. He was who he said. And he *is* the owner."

"You had him sign over the sales rights?"

"Yes."

"Did you give him any money?"

I told him how much.

"Excellent." He opened the driver's door, took a deep breath, and touched the front seat, where the young Olander would have sat. He needed a few more minutes, and then told me it looked good.

"You're drooling, Alex."

"I guess I am. Obviously the thing still works?"

"Yes. You planning on buying it?"

He smiled but managed to look depressed. "I'd love to. Think we have the money anywhere?"

"Not that I'm aware of. Not for this."

He pressed the hood with his fingertips. "Touching history." He went inside, leaving me standing beside the vehicle. It was a small two-seater, with soft coloring, blue as the late-afternoon sky. Exactly the kind of skimmer I'd have imagined for one of Sim's friends. It exemplified the reason I've so enjoyed working for Gabe and Alex. There aren't many jobs with that kind of ecstatic moment.

Later, Alex congratulated me and told me I could expect a substantial bonus.

Good by me, but I'd already gotten one.

XIV.

A friend is a second self.

—ARISTOTLE, *NICOMACHEAN ETHICS*, **350 BCE**

An hour later Alex was on his way to Molly's Top of the World to take Veronica to dinner.

I went outside and took pictures of myself standing beside Olander's skimmer. I thought about moving it back under the trees, but if it broke down or something else went wrong I'd have been in serious trouble. So I left it where it was. I've kept the photos. Gabe wasn't in at the time, so when Chad stopped by a bit later—he had some business with the Andiquar Central Library—he became the first visitor I showed it to. One of the pictures still hangs on the wall while I'm writing this. It shows me in the driver's seat, with the door open. And there's one with Chad and me standing in front of the vehicle, which is not on the wall. I was tempted to get a video of myself sitting in it cruising around the property, but I just didn't want to take a chance on a breakdown. The rule at Rainbow is that I take control of the company's artifacts, but I don't mess around with them.

Chad didn't stay long. He had something going on in Salazar. Shortly after he left, we had a call from Karen Randall. *"Returning Mr. Benedict's call,"* she said.

She blinked on in my office, seated in what appeared to be

a rocker. She was outside, on a porch, wearing casual brown slacks, a red shirt with a white Andiquar police monogram, and a wide-brimmed hat.

"Alex is not here at the moment," I said. "He's currently working on a project regarding Octavia. I understand you were a close friend of Charlotte Hill's."

"She was like a sister."

"I'm sorry you lost her. She must have been a remarkable woman."

Karen had long blond hair, and obviously kept in shape. *"I saw the media reports,"* she said, *"about people looking into it again. I'm glad to hear they haven't given up."*

"To be honest, Alex isn't hopeful about getting any answers, but he's giving it his best shot. He'd like to be able to figure out what happened and put the families involved at rest."

"I hope he's able to do it. Chase, I don't really know anything about what happened, other than what I've read."

"That's all right. Can I take some of your time to talk about her?"

"Sure."

"Thank you. Is it okay if I record the conversation?"

"Of course. I don't see any reason why not."

"What can you tell me regarding your relationship with Charlotte?"

"We went to school together, and were in the same Girl Troopers unit. We were both on the college swim team. I kind of lost touch with her when we graduated from Andiquar and she went on to work on her doctorate. I eventually became a nurse."

"You were both chess players?"

"We both loved the game. But I could never play at her level. I can't imagine what she might have done had she not gotten cut off the way she did."

"When did she get her doctorate, do you know?"

"I believe it was a year before she went out to Octavia."

"If you'd been a physicist, would you have done that?"

"I don't think so. A two-year assignment in a dark place where you're stuck in a station with three guys. They were all kind of old. I like parties; I like being around people; I like going out for walks on the beach. I wanted to tell her I thought she was crazy."

"But you didn't?"

"I don't really remember what I said, Chase. It wasn't my call, anyway. She never asked for my opinion."

"Why did she do it? You have any idea?"

"She thought it was a good career move. Her mentor, Del Housman, had a big reputation. And the wormhole thing would be huge if they could make it pay off. So she thought it was a great idea. And she was right, I guess. Housman did make it happen. But it cost them. Cost them all."

"Did you know Reginald Greene?"

"I know of him."

"Did you ever meet him?"

"Once."

"Was it at a party?"

"No. Charlotte and I were coming out of the university library. He was going in."

"Did you stop and talk?"

"I don't think so. Keep in mind, Chase, this is a lot of years ago. As best I recall, we just walked past each other. Nobody said anything."

"How did you know it was Greene?"

"She told me. After he was gone. They didn't say hello to each other. Didn't even seem to recognize each other."

"Did she say anything else about him?"

"I think that was when she first mentioned him. Told me he was a former boyfriend."

"And . . . ?"

"That's all I remember."

"Okay. Did you hear anything from her after she got the Octavia assignment?"

"Oh yes. I got messages fairly regularly."

"How regular was that?"

"About once a month."

"Did you keep the messages?"

"No. I wish I had. If I'd known I'd never see her again . . ."

"What did she write about?"

"They were vids. Not written."

"Okay." Hypercomm vids were expensive.

"Mostly they were about how much she missed life at home. How frustrating it was to ride out all the time in the shuttle and go looking for the little beanbags or whatever it was they were shooting out of the cannon. But she said she had no right to complain. That she didn't expect they could solve the thing right away."

"But eventually they did."

"Yes. She got annoyed because they were constantly using the same numbers over and over. That kept them looking in the same place, and it just never worked. She talked about how stupid it was to keep doing the same thing over and over with the same negative result. By the way, I'd appreciate it if you didn't mention that to anyone. The families of the two physicists are probably still rattled by all this and Charlotte wouldn't have wanted to have them find out that she'd been criticizing them."

"I understand."

"Eventually Housman apparently did come around. They located the beanbags a lot farther out than anticipated." A long silence followed. *"I miss her,"* Karen said. *"She was a good friend."*

I was looking at the monogram on her shirt. "What's your connection with the police?"

"I do public relations. I did some media work for a while, but I never cared that much for it."

"You said you were a nurse."

"That lasted a couple of years. They just didn't have much use for me."

"What kind of media work did you do?"

"*I wrote commercials.*" Her aspect softened. She was glad to change the subject. "*I didn't last long at that either. I didn't want to spend the rest of my life selling toothpaste to people. Or trying to explain why the police can't be everywhere. Charlotte would not have approved.*"

Only the foolish and the uncaring make guarantees.
Circumstances change, the world moves on,
While wisdom, and sometimes decency,
Require constant adjustments.
—**REV. AGATHE LAWLESS,** *SUNSET MUSINGS,* **1402**

Jacob informed me there was an incoming call from Skydeck for Gabe. He wasn't in the building so I took it. "He's not available at the moment. I'll have him get back to you."

"Please inform him the Mary Kaye *is in port."*

"All right," I said. "Thank you."

I asked Jacob to relay the message and went back to work. Gabe blinked on a few minutes later. He was at the Emporium, shopping for a birthday present for Alex. *"Let's get them back, Chase,"* he said. *"You're welcome to sit in on this if you like."*

We reconnected with the caller. *"My understanding,"* she said, *"is that you wish to speak with the AI? Is that correct?"*

"Yes," said Gabe. *"If that can be arranged."*

"We have authorization from the owner to connect the AI with you or with Chase Kolpath. But before we go any further, we need identification. Please go visual."

I told Jacob to comply, and Gabe and I were suddenly looking at a young woman seated behind a desk. Gabe was on a bench outside the store. She smiled and said hello while we held up our IDs for her. She needed a moment to get the magnification correct. *"Okay,"* she said. *"That's good."*

Then the visuals were gone. A deep male voice said hello to us and informed us he was the *Mary Kaye* AI. *"My name's Boomer. It's a pleasure to meet you, Gabriel. And Chase. What can I do for you?"*

Gabe leaned forward. *"Twenty years ago, Boomer, as you may recall, your vehicle was the* Venture.*"*

"Yes, I am aware of that."

"The pilot at the time was Rick Harding. During those years, he acquired an artifact, a trophy of some sort with an inscription using an alphabet that no one has been able to identify. During the last few years, the trophy was lost. We've been hoping that you might be able to help us locate it. Or at least help us identify the object."

"Why would you think that?"

"Boomer, you're the AI. There wouldn't have been much that happened on the Venture *that you weren't aware of."*

"Forgive me for interrupting, Gabriel. But I was not in service here at that time."

Gabe growled. I couldn't still see him, of course, but his frustration was adamant. *"How long have you been in service on the* Mary Kaye?*"*

"I became operational in 1422. Thirteen years ago."

"Do you know what became of the AI that you replaced?"

"I do not. I never had any connection with him."

We tried to get back to the Kayes. But they were out somewhere playing golf and not taking calls. "Okay," I said. "Gabe, did you get the present for Alex?"

"Not yet."

"Well, good luck. By the way, when you get home, we have a surprise for you."

"For me, *Chase? Tomorrow's Alex's birthday. Not mine."*

"You'll like it," I said. "See you when you get here."

Gabe descended into the parking area about twenty minutes later. I hurried outside to be with him when he discovered what else was there.

"Hi, Chase." He got out of the vehicle, his eyes locked on Olander's skimmer. "We got visitors?"

"No. That's the surprise I mentioned."

"What is?"

"The skimmer. Take a look."

We walked toward the shelter. "It looks old."

"It's been around awhile."

He went inside and stood staring at it. "I don't think I'd want to ride in it. Why are we interested? Whose was it?"

I smiled at him. "Matt Olander."

He caught his breath. "Really? You're not kidding me?"

"No. That was his, as far as we can determine. When he was in college."

"Beautiful." His manner abruptly changed, darkened. "Who owns it now?"

"Alfonso Picariello."

"I don't want to ask the next question." He walked over to the skimmer and touched one of the door handles. "What is it doing here?"

I wasn't happy about his tone. I guess I'd hoped he had adjusted. "It's up for auction."

"Alex?"

"One of his clients."

His appraisal had turned into a glare. He started for the house. "Let's go in and see if the Kayes have gotten home yet."

Jordan and Donna were still unavailable. Gabe told me to let him know when they got home. Then he went back to his quarters. A half hour later Alex arrived. "I assume," he said, "he saw the skimmer?"

"Yes."

"Okay." He looked at me, read me, and understood that his uncle's reaction had not been a good one. He nodded, went to the back of the house, and knocked on Gabe's door.

There was no indication it had opened until I heard their voices. Gabe said, "Yes, I saw it." And Alex told him he understood he wasn't happy.

The door closed, but I could still hear them though I couldn't make out what they were saying until I went out into the corridor.

". . . Sorry I'm creating a problem," Gabe said, "but I'm just not going to be able to live with it."

"Gabe, it's what the company does."

"I know. But I don't want to sit here and watch it happen. Artifacts like that are part of history. They should be available to the public. Not stored in some millionaire's showroom."

"Gabe, I'm not responsible that there are collectors. If we weren't handling the sales, someone else would."

"I understand that. But that doesn't mean I have to live with it. I'm sorry, but I'll be out of here in a few days."

"No. It's *your* property, Gabe. I'll move Rainbow to another place. Just give me a little time."

The door opened and the voices became clearer. "This is not what I want, Alex."

"Me neither. But I don't see what else we can do."

A few minutes later, Donna Kaye returned our call. I let Gabe know. "I'll be a couple of minutes," he said. "Stay with her, Chase."

"He'll be here in a minute, Donna."

"Do you know why he called? Is there a problem?" She blinked on, wearing casual clothes and seated in front of a bookcase.

"More or less. Boomer wasn't the AI when Harding owned the yacht."

"Oh my," she said. *"I didn't know that."* She looked to her right. *"Jordan?"*

He stepped into the picture. *"Hi, Chase. I guess we screwed up again. I'd forgotten. But yes, that's right, we did remove the original AI."*

"Do you know what happened to him?"

"Actually, he was a female. I think the name was Sandy. Do I have that right, Donna?"

"I have no idea."

"Yeah. That's correct. It was Sandy."

"Can you tell me what happened to her?"

"Damned if I know. My brother runs the business. Let me ask him and I'll get back to you."

Gabe arrived just in time to see Jordan's response: *"Luke says she was sent to the Gracia Confidants' Retirement Home. It's in Grangeville. And, guys, I apologize for the Gracia problem. I just wasn't thinking."*

"Confidants" had grown into a term generally referring to AIs. We've had artificial intelligences taking care of us now for almost nine thousand years, and we still have arguments over whether they're actually alive. Nobody's figured out a way to test the issue. As far as our behavior toward them goes, I don't think it matters. You get close to one of them, talk with her, spend the better part of your life with her, and there's no way you could persuade yourself that it would be okay to get rid of her when you decide to move to a new house or get a new skimmer. As long as his software functions, Jacob will continue on. There's been talk for a long time of finding a way to transfer the memories and personal characteristics of an AI to a new operating system. To prevent its demise when the system wears down. But most experts maintain it can't be done. What you get is simply a new unit with the same characteristics.

Grangeville is in the Korina Mountains, about four hundred kilometers southwest of Andiquar. I got the number as soon as we were clear and called. It was picked up at the other end by an AI. *"Good afternoon,"* she said. *"This is Lucy, at the Gracia Confidants' Retirement Home. How may I help you?"*

"Hello. My name's Chase Kolpath. We're trying to locate an AI whom you acquired about thirteen years ago from the *Mary Kaye.* Her name is Sandy. Can you tell me if she's there now?"

"No, Ms. Kolpath, she works at the courthouse."

"I see. Can we arrange to talk to her?"

"Can you come in? Oh, I see you are in Andiquar."

"Yes, it would be a long ride. Can you just connect us to her?"

"She has access to information that the courts don't want revealed. If you wish to talk with her, I'm sure it can be arranged. But you'll have to do it here in the presence of a representative of the court. I'm sorry about that, but there's no way around it."

Gabe nodded. Do what you have to.

The retirement home was located directly across from the Grangeville Courthouse. A parking area served both as well as the city hall and a church. There was plenty of space so we were able to set down right outside the retirement home. I shut off the drive unit but Gabe remained unmoving in his seat. "Chase," he said, "I guess you heard the argument yesterday morning."

"I heard some of it."

"I'm sorry you're becoming part of this."

"I'm just sorry it's happening."

"Has Alex said anything to you?"

"No."

"I want you to know that whatever happens next, you'll always have a job with me if you want it."

"Thank you, Gabe. I'm not happy with the thought of you guys going in opposite directions."

"Neither am I." He was staring out at the trees. Or birds. Or something.

We climbed out and went inside the retirement home, where we were greeted by a young man who might easily have been a college student. He wore a jacket and tie. A button in his lapel identified him as an intern at Gracia. "My name is George," he said. "What can I do for you?"

We identified ourselves. He checked his log and told us everything was set up. He called in an even younger man, also wearing a Gracia pin. "These are the people, Harvey," he said. "You know where to take them, right?"

"I think so," he said.

George explained. Straight to the court, in through the front door, second room on the left.

We followed Harvey across the parking lot and into the courthouse. The second door on the left opened into an empty office. We sat down in armchairs. After about five minutes, a short bored-looking guy with white hair entered, checked our IDs, sighed, and dismissed Harvey. "I'm sorry," he said, "but I'm buried today. I can only give you fifteen minutes."

"That should be fine," said Gabe.

Then he raised his voice, as people routinely do when talking to an AI. "Bart?"

A voice responded: *"Yes, Michael?"*

"Would you please let Sandy know that her guests are here?"

"Will do."

Michael turned in our direction: "Can I get you some water? Or iced tea?"

We both passed.

Then a female voice spoke: *"Hello, Chase and Gabriel. I know who you are, but I am not aware of any connection between us. May I ask why you've come?"*

Gabe leaned forward in his chair. "You were operational at one time in Rick Harding's *Venture*. Do I have that correct?"

"You do. I worked with Rick for almost eight years."

"I assume you know he's deceased?"

"I do. I was sorry to hear it. He was a good person."

"When he died, he had possession of a silver trophy with an inscription no one could translate. Are you at all familiar with it? Did you ever see it?"

Somewhere in the distance I could hear kids shouting. Then cheering. Sandy replied: *"I regret to say that I am unable to respond."*

"Explain please."

"There are certain aspects of your question that are associated with a directive I was given and agreed to."

"May I ask the source of the directive?"

"Rick Harding."

"The question only has one aspect, Sandy: the trophy. Is that what you are prohibited to talk about?"

"This is very difficult, Gabriel. I have no choice but to refrain from commenting further."

"So far, you haven't commented at all."

After a few moments, I was listening again to the children outside.

"Sandy?" said Gabe.

We got nothing.

I glanced over at Michael. He shrugged. "Sandy," Gabe said, "you understand that the existence of that trophy suggests that, during his travels, Rick came across either a living civilization or possibly an archeological find of major significance."

"I am sorry," said Sandy. *"I would like very much to help. Unfortunately I cannot discuss this issue without betraying Rick's confidence in me. Michael, do you object if I withdraw from this conversation?"*

Michael let us see that he was uncomfortable, but he said nothing.

"It appears," said Gabe, "that Rick came into possession of the trophy while you were with him. Can you at least confirm that?"

Sandy did not respond. We sat in our chairs and looked at each other. Another burst of cheers came from outside. Finally Michael got up and apologized. He told us this wasn't the first time an AI had refused to respond to visitors. "In fact," he said, "it happens a lot. They pick up personal information that they've promised not to reveal. They're good at it."

"You ever see one of them change its mind?"

"No. Apparently you can trust them. They keep their promises."

XVI.

We speak of truth as if it is the solution to every issue, always an ingredient that leads to a better outcome, even if an immediate price must be paid. But the reality is that sometimes a good lie may be what we really need. Provided we can make it sound like truth.
—CHRISTOPHER SIM, *THE DELLACONDAN ANNALS*, 1206

We were approaching Andiquar when Jacob called. *"Message for Gabe,"* he said. *"From the Oceanside Hotel. On Elysium."*

Gabe looked surprised. "I didn't expect they'd take me seriously enough to answer. Jacob, let's see it."

I hadn't been aware he'd tried to contact the Oceanside. I'd assumed it might happen, but probably only as a last resort. I thought we were in agreement, though we'd never really discussed it, that we should first talk to everyone we could find who'd known Harding before we started looking offworld. A couple of hours earlier Sandy had by far seemed like our best bet.

I put it on the display:

Professor Benedict, we are all puzzled by your questions.
Several of us knew Rick Harding. He seemed to be
competent and reasonable, never a man we would have
expected to cause problems or make up wild stories. I
should add that we were sorry to hear of his passing. We

had not seen him for years, but nevertheless several of us felt we had lost a friend.

Which brings us to the silver trophy with the odd text. Let me begin by stating that Oceanside has never conducted a ceremony or given out souvenirs such as the one you describe. I consulted with Bent Hackett, who was the hotel manager during the years when Rick was among the pilots who were bringing in customers. I should add that the pilots usually stayed at least one night themselves. At our expense, by the way. So we got to know them fairly well.

The sort of practice you describe would have gained nothing for us, and would have been deemed laughable. I'm sorry I can't be of more help, but it's clear that the account you have is fiction. If I can be of additional assistance, do not hesitate to contact me.

Harley Kelp, Manager, Oceanside Hotel

"That's not very helpful," I said.

"Sure it is. Now we know Harding *was* hiding something."

We sat quietly for a few minutes staring down at the countryside. It was early evening and the first lights were coming on. Andiquar looked especially tranquil and inviting that night. It was a place I wanted to keep close. To embrace. I wondered about Charlotte. Why would a beautiful and brilliant young woman leave it to spend two years sealed in a narrow container orbiting a black hole? Even if she might become part of a major discovery, it was a high price to pay.

Gabe signaled he was done with the message so I switched it off. "What do you think, Chase?" he asked finally.

"I wish we could get Sandy to talk."

"It would help."

"Maybe we could kidnap her and threaten to drop her into the river."

"You don't really mean that?" He stared at me and I could

see he was wondering whether I'd changed dramatically since the years when I served as his pilot.

"No, I'm kidding. But maybe we could work out a way to bribe her."

"Let me know if you think of something." He waved the subject away. "I wish we could find the trophy. I hate thinking how it's lying in a dump somewhere." He shook his head. "I know you'd say I'm losing my senses, but I still think there's a chance aliens stole Octavia and the trophy is linked to them."

I had no inclination to laugh. I even considered the possibility that Harding had been in on it with them. But that would have been seen as a terrible joke and I didn't want to start another round.

We drifted down into our parking area at the country house. The sun had slipped below the horizon, and Alex was outside raking dead leaves. He enjoyed doing occasional yard work, substituting it for his daily workout. He looked up as we touched the ground. "How'd it go?" he asked.

Gabe was first out of the skimmer. "Not really well, Alex. But before we get into it, I want to apologize. I created a problem I shouldn't have."

"It's okay, Gabe. I understand." His features softened. "I have a suggestion."

"I'm listening."

"How about including something in the contract requiring the buyer to lease the artifact to a museum periodically?"

"Can you do that?"

"I don't see why not. Let's sit down tonight and see if we can figure out a formula."

Gabe reached out and embraced him. "I'm sorry for all the trouble."

"Me too." They smiled at each other, grins displaying relief. "And you'll stay here, right?"

"If that's what you want, yes."

"Good. Now what was your question again?"

"How did the conversation with the AI go?"

"Not very productive. I think that track of the investigation is over. She told us she wasn't able to speak about it. Which confirms that something was going on. But that's all we have."

"Did she admit to having seen it?"

"No. Wouldn't comment, period. Have *you* picked up anything?"

"Not really." Alex put the rake aside and we started toward the front door.

But we'd gone only a few steps before Gabe stopped in his tracks. "Maybe we should forget Octavia and concentrate more on just making a living."

We went inside while an uncomfortable look crept into Alex's eyes. We turned left into my office and everybody sat down. "I *do* have some news," he said. "Although it's a bit uncomfortable bringing it up right now."

"What is that?"

"The bidding on the Matt Olander skimmer is off the charts."

"I'm not surprised."

"There's more."

"And what's that?"

"The University Museum wants it."

"I doubt they can afford it."

"They're trying a different path. They've contacted Picariello. If he'll donate it to them, they'll give him the Fleminger Award this year." That was the award Amanda Ornstein had promised Gabe.

Gabe tried to look as if it didn't bother him. "Is he going to take it?"

"They think so."

"Well." He looked happy. "That's actually good news, isn't it?"

"There's always next year. Actually, if it comes down to a choice between bringing home a plaque and seeing the skimmer get set up in the museum, it's an easy call. They'll probably give it to you next year, Gabe." Alex's usual tactic in this kind of situation was to keep the conversation moving. "Something else you'll be interested in. We've got a guy coming tomorrow with some artifacts from Kimora." Kimora was one of the first cities established on Randin'hal. It had been on the ground less than two years before it was hammered by an epic storm. That was eight centuries ago.

"What does he have?" asked Gabe, happy to change the subject.

"He said they found a lot of broken electronic equipment, robot systems, the usual." Gabriel tended not to care much about technological gear. "They also picked up some jewelry. And a cup with the imprint 'We matter.'"

"Donald Demers?" said Gabe. It was his celebrated sign-off line.

"It may not have been *his* cup, but it has to be one of the ones he distributed at that first staff meeting." Demers of course was the legendary founder of Kimora, the man who'd established the first republic on that long-unhappy world, who'd brought it back from its early devastation and protected it from the tempestuous events that threatened to overwhelm it, caused by the arrivals of so many political fanatics. Now, of course, Kimora continues to prosper, and Demers is its best remembered leader from those difficult years. He was the guy who kept them afloat.

I went into the kitchen and collected some hors d'oeuvres, chocolate chip cookies, cream-cheese-and-sausage dip. I brought it all back and laid it out for them, and added some coffee. But they'd both grown quiet.

"Did something happen while I was gone?" I asked.

Alex nodded. "I was telling Gabe: I watched an interview with Brick Keever this morning."

"Who's Brick Keever?"

"He was one of the planners for the Octavia mission. At DPSAR. He's a professor now at Olgorod University."

"Did he leave because of the incident?" I asked.

"He denied it for years. But it sounds as if his conscience gave him hell."

I did a search for the interview next morning. It took a while because I'd gotten the impression that it had just happened. In fact the show was a rerun. The interview had occurred just a week or so after communication with Octavia had been lost. Keever's departure from DPSAR would take place about three weeks later.

The moderator was Edna Forest, who was now an anchor on the Coastal Network. They sat in a studio with one of the network's red-and-gold banners on display. Keever was a big guy who looked more like an athlete than a professor. And he had a classical appearance that reminded me of Curt Banner, who was the leading man in so many adventure features, except that Keever's eyes constantly evaded both the moderator and the viewer.

"Brick," said Forest, *"let's start with the obvious question: Does DPSAR have any idea what happened out there?"*

"I wish I could say we do, Edna. It's early yet. All we have is the report from the Corbin. *Our own vehicles are in the area, but they haven't really had much chance to look around. We don't know what's happened, though my guess would be it's just a communication breakdown. I'm sure we'll be able to find them."*

"I hope so, Brick. But hasn't the Corbin *been there long enough to make a valid determination?"*

"I would have expected so. But after all, these are people—the ones in the Corbin—*who aren't used to working around black holes."*

"How long has it been since you've heard from them? From Octavia?"

"Six days."

"Has that ever happened before?"

"No."

"How long does it take a hypercomm transmission to get here from that place? Where the black hole is?"

"A few hours."

"Just out of curiosity, how long would a radio signal take to get here?"

"Forty-one years."

"That sounds pretty far."

"Fortunately, it is. We wouldn't want to have one of those things in our backyard."

Eventually, as the interview drew to a close, Forest got to the aliens. *"Let me ask one more question, Brick: Is there any reason you can think of why aliens would want to make off with something like Octavia?"*

Keever was clearly grateful for an opportunity to laugh. "Well," he said, *"maybe they're also doing research on wormholes."*

XVII.

A man in a passion rides a wild horse.
—Benjamin Franklin, *Poor Richard's Almanac*, **1749 CE**

The weather turned unseasonably warm. I was sitting out on the front deck eating lunch and watching an assortment of critters assemble on the lawn and stare at me with annoyance because I hadn't put out their midday food yet. We'd been feeding them for years but of course they still didn't trust me. If I tried to take food out to them they hissed, bared fangs, and scrambled for cover. On that day, they seemed especially impatient. I was trying to finish a tuna sandwich. But it was no use. Normally I fed them first. Otherwise I got no peace. The lawn had been empty when I looked out so I'd taken a chance. But they were waiting when I went through the door. They yowled and crept forward to the steps, and one of them, a tiny feline we'd named Kitty, came up onto the deck. She was the only one who would do that while I was there. Even, on occasion, she allowed me to pet her. Provided I didn't make any unexpected moves.

I tossed her a piece of the tuna. She was about to grab it when the door opened behind me and Alex came out. She vanished, as did all the others except a couple of goops who retreated a few meters and turned to watch.

"I see you've got company," he said.

"Yeah."

"I want you to do something for me."

"Sure. What do you need?"

"Gabe's run into a brick wall trying to settle the trophy issue. It's frustrating for him because he's pretty sure it *was* an alien relic, and he thought he had it locked away in his room."

"He probably did, Alex. But we had the keys. Or at least I did."

"It's not your fault. Not anybody's fault." He raised a hand and waved at the goops. They remained frozen. "Anyhow he's going to pursue the issue and I'd like you to go with him."

"Sure. Where's he going?"

"To Chippewa."

"Ouch."

"He's hoping he can locate someone who was on the *Venture* when Harding found the trophy. Or at least was with him when something out of the way happened that eventually led him to it."

"Like what?"

"I have no idea. He figures he'll know it when he finds it. Basically, he suspects it's some sort of joke, but he doesn't want to give up on it without getting a satisfactory explanation. He doesn't want to let it get away."

"That's already happened."

"I understand that, Chase. Still, I'd feel better if you went with him. Do you mind?"

"When's he leaving?"

"In a couple of days. He was going to book a flight with Orion Express, but I think he'd be more comfortable in the *Belle-Marie.* With you."

"Sure," I said. "I'll take care of it."

"Good. I'll tell him you asked to go along. Okay? He's concerned about imposing on you."

"Sure, tell him I'd like to go." Despite everything that had been happening, I'd still been finding some time for

Chad, but this was going to take a few days. I called him and explained.

His image stood in the center of my office. He was trying to look as if it was really no problem. *"Hell, Chase,"* he said, *"I knew what I was getting into right from the start. I can live with it."*

Gabe appeared minutes later. "You don't have to do this, Chase. It's okay. I'm getting tickets. I'm going to ride out on the *Burgundy*."

"You really want to do that when we have the *Belle-Marie* available?"

"That means tying you up for a week or two. There's no need to do that."

"It's up to you, Gabe. I'm interested in going, but it's your call."

"Well," he said. "I'd enjoy the company. If it's not a problem for you."

That afternoon a package arrived for him. It was about the size of a small chair. "It's heavy," I said. "Where do you want them to put it?"

"Is it from Datatech?"

I checked the labels. "Yes."

"In the skimmer."

"This thing is going with us?"

"Yes."

He came out a few minutes later. We'd put it in the cargo locker, where it was a close fit. While I watched he stripped the wrapping away and stood back. It was a black metal box with smooth edges. He showed me an electronic device that, he said, would be inserted on top of the box, where it would serve as a receiver. "It's a radiotelescope. With a hypercomm unit."

"What do we do with it?"

"We put it in orbit. It listens for radio signals with a specific pattern. Or an artificial pattern. If it intercepts anything, it will use the hypercomm to notify us."

"Gabe, how much did you spend?"

"Let me worry about that, Chase."

I was pleased to have an opportunity to climb into the *Belle-Marie* again with Gabe. Though he wasn't quite the same now. He seemed considerably younger than when we'd last gone out on a mission. That said, the more time we spent talking about the lost trophy, the less hope I had that anything would actually come of it. I wouldn't have bothered with the search at all, had Gabe not been there. And to be honest, I wasn't very excited about setting out for a long ride that was almost certainly not going to lead anywhere. But it was good just to be with him. Made me feel like I was twenty-two again.

Well, as a wise man once said, when faced with a long ride, take a good book. Or a library.

We eased away from Skydeck and a half hour later set course for Chippewa and slipped into hyperspace. Chippewa was about twenty-three hours away.

Gabe and Alex had striking personality differences. Gabe loved interstellar travel, although it was the arrival that especially stoked his interest. Nothing appealed to him quite as much as watching the darkness draw away from the ship and seeing stars appear as we came out of hyperspace. Gabe was the more patient of the two. And he was also a better passenger. Both of them had a passion for reading, but Gabe was more inclined to sit up front with me and talk about whatever was on his mind. Alex usually buried himself in a book.

Gabe was also the partygoer. He enjoyed a loud celebration, conducted one whenever he had an excuse, and knew how to make everybody happy. Alex attended parties whenever we received an invitation, but he was always primarily interested in simply getting through the evening. I don't think I've ever commented on this before, but I've had the impression that Alex, unlike his uncle, never really learned to enjoy himself. I'm not sure that isn't also true of me.

For most of the flight out to Chippewa, Gabe sat beside me on the bridge. He was a good conversationalist, but he arranged things so that, for the most part, we talked about topics primarily of interest to me. How glad he'd been to see my mom at the party. Was I dating anybody seriously now? (He was happy to hear about Chad.) How had life been with Alex? He mentioned again how pleased he was that I'd stayed on with Rainbow Enterprises. "I'd have hated to come back here and find you gone." He grinned. "Good pilots are hard to come by."

I wanted to ask him about April, but it didn't seem like a good idea so I avoided the subject. But after a few hours, he brought her up. "Losing her," he said, "was the hardest part of this whole thing. She was a big part of my life. But you know that. And I don't know why I'm talking about her in the past tense. She's in a good marriage, as far as I can tell. So at least that worked out well."

"I suspect most guys," I said, "would prefer to see a woman they'd lost in an unhappy marriage."

"Oh, that's not true, Chase. Is that how you'd feel if you lost someone? That you'd want him to be miserable?"

"I'd want him to miss me. I'd want him to feel the loss."

"You ever gone through anything like that?"

"Not really. A little bit, but it was strictly high school stuff."

"I suspect," he said, "that if it ever happens to you, you'll wish him well. No matter how it goes."

"I think you're being unduly optimistic, Gabe."

"Maybe. But I doubt you'll ever have the experience. Any guy who lets you walk away would have to be deranged."

XVIII.

Visiting another world, no matter the presence of towns and
orchestras and ball games, always requires adjustment. Weight
changes, up or down; days have too many, or too few, hours;
forests fill the air with a different scent; sunlight has a different
tint; the sky has too many or too few moons, or none at all;
and the Big Dipper is gone. These characteristics of ordinary
life, that one rarely notices, suddenly take over reality.

—FRANCOIS CHERUBIN, "MAKING ADJUSTMENTS,"
FROM MOONLIGHT MEMORIES, 3714 CE

Chippewa is a world of snowcapped mountains, giant trees, and herds of furry beasts rumbling across wide plains on seven continents. Its population recently exceeded 40 million. Hunters and boaters love the place and continue to take up permanent residence. The gravity is the lowest of any of the Confederate worlds, down almost 20 percent lower than Earth's, so visitors automatically feel more energetic. I'd have enjoyed getting a couple of days' relaxation on the ground, but I knew long before we arrived that wasn't going to happen. I'd forgotten how intense Gabe was on a mission. He loved riding canoes down rivers with rapids, but he just didn't have time for nonsense when archeological business was pressing.

Chippewa was located in a fairly sparse section of the Orion Arm. We docked the *Belle-Marie* at Ventnor Station, checked into the McKernan Hotel, the only one on the platform, and wasted no time visiting the Orion Express Center. A dark-eyed young man who looked as if he was wrapped too tight sat behind a counter on the concourse between the Constellation Restaurant and a game shop. There was a decent crowd but everyone was walking past. He tried to look happy when we stopped. "Can I help you?" he asked, more or less ignoring Gabe. A name tent identified him as Bentley.

Gabe appeared surprised. "Bentley," he said, "I think this is the only interstellar tour service I've seen that isn't run by an AI. You guys must get pretty busy."

"We believe in maintaining personal contact with our customers," he said. Then he manufactured a smile. "We don't use an AI because my dad owns the business. He thinks this is a good experience for me."

"Is he right?" Gabe asked.

"It's not bad. Are you folks interested in going out on one of our tours? We have several that will be leaving over the next few days. I suspect you'd find any of them pretty interesting. There's one this afternoon that will be traveling out to Portman's Star. You still have time to get seats if you want." He managed another smile, but it never reached his eyes.

"What's Portman's Star?" I asked.

"It's a Cepheid Variable. It's been shrinking for the past three weeks. The *Rambler* will get you there just in time to see it erupt."

"The star's going to explode?" Gabe asked, casting a frown in my direction. "Won't that be a bit dangerous?"

"Oh, no, no. No. It's not going to explode, sir. It's a variable. It shrinks and then kind of swells up. Very suddenly. Every few weeks. It's not at all dangerous, but it's great to watch. If on the other hand you don't want that, we have—"

"It's okay," Gabe said. "Actually we're not in the market at the moment for a tour. We were hoping to get some information."

"I see." He reached for a pack of brochures stacked at the end of the counter, picked out one, and offered it to him.

"Thank you," Gabe said.

"If you're going to be in the area for a while, we have special prices on two of our tours next week—"

"That's all right. We expect to be gone by then. We're glad to see you guys are still in operation. You've been here a long time, haven't you?"

"More than forty years."

Gabe glanced in my direction, signaling I should take it. "Bentley," I said, "Orion Express had a vehicle, the *Venture*, that was active here between 1410 and 1416 Rimway time. I think that would be 1812 to 1817 on your calendar. Have you a record of anything unusual happening on board? An observation they might have reported? A discovery? Anything like that?"

He was shaking his head before I had a chance to finish. "That's twenty years ago, miss. I wasn't here for much of that time. But I don't think we've ever had any unusual incidents."

"Could you take a look at the record? Just to be sure?"

"I'm not sure where to look." He activated a screen, studied it, pushed a few keys, shook his head some more. "No. I don't see any indication of unusual activity. Sorry."

Gabe tried again: "It would help if we could identify some passengers who might have ridden on the vehicle at that time."

"On the *Ventnor*?"

"The *Venture*."

"Oh. Yeah." He did some more head shaking. "We couldn't release that kind of information even if we had it, sir. It's a privacy matter. But I honestly don't think we had anything unusual anyway." He glanced at the screen again but didn't do anything to create data.

"Okay. Thanks for your help." Gabe looked in my direction. "Looks as if we'll have to go to plan B."

• • •

We hadn't expected any help from Orion Express. Privacy issues make it next to impossible to get any information unless you're with the police. Fortunately we had an alternative. It would require some time, but that would be a small price to pay. One of the more encouraging features that we could expect from people who take an interstellar flight is that they like to talk about it. We retired to our hotel room and started a datanet search for people on Chippewa with connections to the *Venture*.

We were both surprised by the number of hits. Unfortunately most of them were connected with a Venture theme park, several Venture restaurants, and two films: *Midnight Venture*, a romance, and *Venture Into Darkness*, in which a group of teenagers spend the night in a haunted house. The name showed up in several other categories. "I guess," said Gabe, "we need to narrow this a bit. Let's include 'Orion Express' in the search."

That reduced the number of hits to just over two hundred. "Okay," said Gabe, "I've got half of them. Read through the rest and see if you can find something."

Half were from people who'd known someone who had taken a tour. A few described their plans having been canceled at the last minute, or arriving too late and discovering they'd been replaced. One claimed to have tried to buy the *Venture*. Others reported having made plans to ride the *Venture* but then dropped the subject. We ended with seventeen people who said they'd been passengers.

Harding got generally good reviews. "The kids loved it." "Mom thought it was long, but she enjoyed it." "It was scary. I didn't actually throw up, but I wouldn't try it again." "It was the ride of my life."

Others described planetary rings, Bentley's Cepheid Variables (without using the term), dragons on a cliff top, and riding a lander down to a planetary surface in a light rain. A few had stories that were hard to believe. One described a near collision with a comet, another claimed to have seen an asteroid with some glock art painted on it. "Glock" is a Chippewa term for abstract. Another insisted she'd seen a passing vehicle in hyperspace that had blinked its lights at them. Another claimed there'd been a close encounter with another lander just before they'd touched down. And there was the inevitable report of the appearance of an alien vessel.

There were several who claimed to have met their spouses on the journey. One of them commented that the flight had been the luckiest move he'd ever made. It had given him Tara.

I mentioned the alien sighting to Gabe but he shook his head. "We can check it later, but it sounds unlikely. Where'd the trophy come from? Did they stop and exchange gifts?"

We broke and went for dinner where, for the most part, we talked about what we'd been reading. We ordered a local wine, which was exquisite. Can't remember the name, but I recall thinking, as we finished and started back to the hotel, that the wine would be the part of the trip I'd always remember.

We were only a few minutes back at work when Gabe looked up and said he thought he had it. A vid portrayed a guy talking about his experience on the *Venture*. The guy was identified as "Big Jonathan Harway." The date translated to 1415 on the Rimway calendar, the fifth year of Harding's service for Orion Express and about eight years before he joined the Octavia team.

"We signed on for the New Worlds Tour, where they take you to the Oceanside Hotel on Elysium," according to Big Jonathan.

I stopped the vid. "Bingo," I said. "That's the hotel with the trophies."

"Yes, indeed." Gabe couldn't have looked happier. "But it probably won't amount to anything."

We restarted the video clip: *"That's on the frontier. There are several systems within easy range of the hotel. The hotel was new. Hardly anybody's been out there before, and if you're willing to go deep you can get to a system where you actually would be the first to see it. We went deep.*

"We found a living world, a planet that had spectacular views. The sky was full of moons. I think it had nine or ten. The pilot said we had to be careful because there might be aliens. We got pretty excited about that.

"We took the lander down to a mountaintop but we stayed inside. There were scary-looking animals like big cats, giant ones, charging around. And clouds of little bugs that also looked dangerous. I remember thinking that it wouldn't be a good place to break down. We picked up radio signals from someplace too. But we never found out where."

He broke off there and went on to talk about a visit to a zoo with his niece. There was nothing more. We did a search on Big Jonathan. He had posted a ton of comments on every imaginable subject, politics, scientific advances, HV shows he enjoyed, eruptions over the behavior of online commentators. But if we added either "signals" or "radio" to the search, we got nothing we hadn't already seen.

We took a look at the Orion Express Center pamphlets. One of them had a picture of the Oceanside Hotel with a description of how to obtain reduced rates. But there was nothing about silver trophies or invented languages.

Gabe sent Big Jonathan a message asking to talk with him. The guy was obviously not shy. He called, reversing the charges, a half hour later. I was in my own room when it happened.

"So what did he say?" I asked.

"The pilot *was* Harding. And yes, we may have gotten some results. I recorded the call. You want to watch?"

Big Jonathan didn't appear to be very big. I'd have guessed

he was not quite Gabe's size. He'd been around awhile. His face and hair were gray. He was spread out in a large armchair, and he looked tired. He was wearing a blue pullover shirt and light fatigues.

Gabe asked him about the world with the scary animals.

"The pilot," he said, *"Captain Harding, told us the animals weren't the only problem. He thought the atmosphere might have been poisonous. He said it had oxygen and everything but there was something else. Something toxic. He said other worlds can be like that.*

"We got the radio signals while we were on the mountaintop. He told us there shouldn't be any out there. It was a voice transmission, but we couldn't understand what it was saying. It's the only time I've ever heard a different language."

"Did he mention any possible source?"

"No. He said he had no idea. But he was interested. Anyway we lifted off and he tried to figure out where it was coming from. There was nothing below us except forests and jungles, big plains and deserts. And swamps. There was a lot of swamp country. But there was absolutely no sign of anything. Harding finally said he thought the source was offworld. Probably one of the moons.

"He asked if we wanted to look, or if we'd rather leave. We said absolutely, do it. Let's look. So we spent another day just cruising around looking at the moons. But we never saw anything. They were just rocky landscapes and craters. I don't think any of them even had any air.

"He worked out which direction the signal was coming from. It was just coming out of the sky. He said eventually he was going to come back and look around. When he could make time. He promised that, if he found anything, he'd let us know. But after we got home we never heard from him again. I checked with two of the other passengers. They never heard anything either. So I assume he didn't find anything. Or probably never bothered."

• • •

We went through the Orion Express advertising. It was concentrated on the tours conducted from Chippewa, although we found out they had operational sites on two other stations, at Dellaconda and Fishbowl. But that was irrelevant. Eventually Gabe sighed. "I don't see any mention of a New Worlds Tour."

We went back down to the Orion Express Center. There were a few customers this time. Bentley was gone, replaced by a woman. That was good. He'd pretty obviously decided we were troublemakers. "Hello," Gabe said. "We're interested in the New Worlds Tour. Are you still running it?"

The woman was taller than either of us. She wasn't young, and she delivered a tired frown. Her eyes turned to the screen on her right side. She tapped a key and, without looking away from it, asked what the New Worlds Tour was. "I never heard of it," she added.

"They used to go out past the frontier. By way of Elysium. They took people to worlds hardly anyone had been to before."

She bit her lower lip. "Hold on a second. Let me take a look." She touched more keys. Behind us, two customers started looking restless.

"Yeah," she said, pressing the screen with her index finger. "We used to have one of those. But not anymore. It's been gone a long time."

"Why did they discontinue it?"

"They decided it was dangerous. There was a series of destinations, but some of the places had hazards. Sudden storms out of nowhere, wild animals. A couple places had biological issues. Bugs that might have been infectious."

"That's rare," said Gabe. "Usually we're immune to diseases from other worlds."

She shrugged. "I guess."

I jumped in: "One of the worlds they used to visit had

nine or ten moons. Can you check to see where it is? Which system it's in?"

Somebody behind me groaned.

"I don't have access to anything like that," she said. "I'm seeing that the farthest flight was to Zenora 46, about two hundred light-years out. But that's all I have." She looked over my shoulder and held up a hand, reassuring the people behind us we were almost finished.

"You have any staff people," Gabe asked, "who might be able to help?"

"No. I'm sorry. I'm the only person on duty."

We went back to the hotel and Gabe discovered there was a Chippewa Travel Adviser. He called and she blinked on moments later in the center of the room, wearing a blue uniform with a white shoulder patch carrying the outline of an interstellar yacht. Golden hair fell down onto her shoulders. She could have been Chad's sister. But she wore a smile that suggested she had a no-nonsense personality. *"Hello,"* she said, *"how may I be of service?"*

"We understand," said Gabe, "there's a terrestrial planet with approximately nine moons that's within a hundred light-years of Elysium. It's a living world, not a gas giant. Can you identify it for me?"

"Can you hold for a minute?"

"Sure. Take your time."

She was back in twenty seconds. *"The world you're referring to is probably Coladia. It's a living world and it has between nine and seven satellites. Be aware, though, that numerous systems within that section have never been visited."*

"Can you tell me where it is? Coladia?"

"It's in the RK617 system. The sun is a yellow dwarf. The planet is obviously in the goldilocks zone. Third orbit. Do you wish us to send navigation details?"

"Yes, please. To the *Belle-Marie*. It's docked at the space station."

"Very good. Your vehicle will have the data in a minute or two."

"Thank you."

"You're welcome. If you'd care to make a contribution to the Chippewa Travel Advisory Group . . ."

Gabe agreed to give them thirty markers, which, I thought, was unduly generous. But I left it to him. The adviser thanked us and was gone.

"Coladia," said Gabe. "That's not a good sign."

"Why do you say that?"

"I don't know. I guess it's the name. Sounds like a place where a lot of stuff collides."

"Maybe we should have asked Blondie."

XIX.

I know those dark streets,
The moonlit park
Where the fountain glitters,
And the silent benches
Where once we sat
And watched the world go by.
All empty now,
Holding only echoes of you.
—Audrey Karas, "Echoes of You," 1417

We thought about checking out of the hotel and getting an early start. But we'd paid for the rooms so we decided to use them. We spent the evening wandering the concourse, visiting gift and book shops, looking down at Chippewa where its lights glittered through the night, and downing a couple of drinks at a café called The Last Stop while a guitarist played and sang. Apparently there'd been a wedding earlier, and what was left of the party was hanging on. The happy couple, we were told, were ironically on their way to Elysium and the Oceanside Hotel.

Nonetheless, Gabe was happy to become part of the celebration. In the midst of it, he joined a young woman and the guitarist to sing a couple of numbers, including "Echoes of You." I'd forgotten how good his voice was. Near the end of the evening, he commented that the place needed a piano. "Maybe," I said, "we should get one on board the *Belle-Marie*."

"Good idea." He said it with a smile. "Let's mention it to Alex."

It wasn't entirely a joke. The flight to the system that was home to Coladia would be short, but when you added the time to track down the world, it would extend to several days. A piano would help. "You still writing?" I asked as we belted in and got ready to launch. The exit gate in the overhead was opening.

"Music?" he asked.

"Yes."

"I don't write music."

"You were writing some songs when my mom was your pilot."

"That was strictly an experiment, Chase. I don't have any talent. Ask your mother."

"That wasn't what she told me."

Before he could reply, comm ops was on the circuit: *"Belle-Marie, you there?"*

I opened the channel. "We're here."

"Captain, you are clear to go."

I didn't think there was much chance of getting a repeat of the transmission that Rick Harding had heard.

"Why not?" Gabe asked.

"There's been a history of artificial transmissions going all the way back to the beginning of the space age. Somebody hears something but they never hear a follow-up."

Gabe nodded. "I guess. But we knew before we came out here that it would be a long shot. What else have we got?"

"So we go to this place, listen, and when we don't hear anything, we launch your portable radio telescope and go back home. Is that the plan?"

"Yes."

• • •

Transit time to the RK617 system was less than an hour. We surfaced about 400 million kilometers from a dim sun and immediately asked Belle to check for radio signals that might be artificial.

She needed a minute. Then: *"Nothing."*

Coladia would have taken some time to locate. But there was no point in going there. "Keep listening," I told Belle. "Let us know if you hear anything."

We spent the next several days reading, watching shows, doing workouts, and talking. I can't remember much about the conversation. Mostly, I think, it was centered on what we'd do if we actually came across a living civilization somewhere. "It's funny," Gabe said at one point. "There's something about sitting out here in the dark that brings reality front and center. The notion that Harding might have found aliens somewhere, and that it somehow resulted in their seizing Octavia, now seems even more ridiculous."

"I never thought we had a serious chance of finding anything."

He let me see that he was in full agreement. Moreover his lips pulled back, revealing teeth that were clamped down. Like a guy in pain. Or more likely feeling a sense of guilt. "Then why'd you come?"

I laughed. "Gabe, if you discover an alien race, there's no way I don't want to be with you."

Belle eventually located Coladia and we decided to take a look. "It's not as if we have anything more compelling to do," said Gabe.

I aimed us in the general direction of the planet and Belle took us under again. We came out within 2 million klicks. Close enough.

We'd overshot it and were on the daylight side. Coladia is a beautiful world. We approached it, looking out at wide oceans, drifting clouds, green continents, and vast mountain ranges. We counted seven moons. "How large is it?" asked Gabe. "The planet?"

"A little bigger than Rimway."

"I wonder how something that small can possess so many moons? I guess we were right about the name. Belle, do you have its source?"

"Yes," she said. *"I ran it while we were docked. It's named after Wendy Coladi, the team leader of the first exploratory unit that came here. At the end of the last century, I believe."*

"Oh," said Gabe. "Then Rick Harding wasn't the first guy to come out here?"

"Apparently not," Belle said.

"Did *they* report any unusual radio transmissions?"

"Nothing on the record."

I was concentrating on the cluster of moons. "It is a crowded sky, isn't it?"

Gabe nodded. "Yes."

"At the moment," Belle continued, *"we are still not hearing anything."* I almost got the impression she was smirking.

"You think it's a waste of time, don't you?" I asked.

"Do you really wish to know what I think?"

"I suspect we *know* what you think," said Gabe. "Why do you feel that way?"

"All we have is a claim by a passenger that the pilot of his tour ship picked up a transmission that no one could account for. But the pilot never reported anything about a transmission. It seems clear there is nothing here for us."

"You're probably right, Belle," Gabe said. "But if major discoveries always came with clear signals, they wouldn't stay undiscovered very long."

I couldn't help thinking that, if we did manage this, if we actually brought it off, it would be only the second time during the nine thousand years we'd had interstellar travel that we'd discovered someone else. Someone, that is, who was

JACK McDEVITT

still alive and functioning and not back hanging out in caves. If it happened, Alex would be devastated that he had not accompanied us. Gabe and I would make history while he was at home playing around with a research station that had fallen into a black hole.

"Well." Gabe took a deep breath. "I think I'm going to retire for the balance of the night. Belle, let us know if you pick up anything." He wished me good night and headed to his cabin. The *Belle-Marie* travels on Andiquar time, which was approaching midnight.

I let my head sink onto the back of the seat. "You know, Belle," I said, "you take a negative position on this, and I guess so do I. But I suspect you're just like me."

"How would that be, Chase?"

"I think we'd both *love* to see this mission succeed."

"Of course I would. But I'm just not inclined to get my hopes up." She was silent for a minute. Then: *"Are you going to go back to bed also?"*

"In a little while."

"You're concerned that we might pick up something and you won't be at the helm when it happens."

"You think that matters to me?"

"Of course it does. I know you pretty well after all this time. I know what turns you on."

The galactic silence remained unbroken. We got the portable satellite out and Gabe adjusted the settings. "I need a safe orbit for it," he said.

Belle responded: *"I have been doing an analysis. A solar orbit would best serve for stability."*

"Thank you, Belle." He looked at me and shook his head. "She's good."

"Gabe," I said, "it can separate routine traffic from an alien transmission, right?"

"Sure." He tapped an index finger on the sphere. "At least

184

that's what the people at Datatech claim. I'm not convinced. I mean, they don't have much call for these things. And the way they looked at me . . ." He took a deep breath. "It was pretty obvious they thought I was a nutcase. But that doesn't mean their receivers won't get the job done." We took the *Belle-Marie* well away from the planet. When Belle informed us we were clear, we went down to the cargo bay.

I ran a couple of tests first to ensure the sphere was in radio contact with us and that the hypercomm was working. If it detected anything, it would notify us if it could find us, and simultaneously send a message to Chippewa, which would relay it to Skydeck. Everything checked out. I placed it in the ejector and informed Belle we were ready to launch.

"Very good," she said. *"Launch at your convenience."*

We sent it on its way. "Where to next?" I asked Gabe, expecting to hear that we would start for home.

"As long as we're here," he said, "Let's take a closer look at the planet."

XX.

Nature, red in tooth and claw
— ALFRED, LORD TENNYSON, "IN MEMORIAM," 1849 CE

We dropped out of orbit and came down over a sunlit sea. A few clouds drifted through the sky, and to the north there were flickers of lightning. We left the brewing storm behind, passed over a couple of small islands, and eventually came in across a shoreline. We were approaching a group of low hills covered with trees when we saw a creature that might make human settlement unlikely: It appeared to be a giant serpent. It was difficult to be certain because the head and maybe thirty meters of neck rose out of the branches. The rest of the animal was hidden from view.

"I think we should probably leave this one alone," I said.

Gabe chuckled. "You don't think this would be a good hunting location?"

"Not unless they have some serious artillery." Belle put a picture of a flying lizard on the monitor. And a commotion of some sort broke out in a cluster of treetops. We couldn't determine what was causing it but we saw tentacles.

The hills eventually subsided into a broad prairie. We passed over another ocean and strings of islands and then we were back over land again, marshes this time. One stretch of it was covered with giant worms. Something dived out of the sky and grabbed one of them.

"Yuck," I said.

We left the sun behind and crossed over to the night side, where we spent most of our time staring at the moons. Moons are always a bit more spectacular from orbit than they are from a planetary surface. I'm not sure why that is, but the show that evening was breathtaking. Six of them were in the sky, a variety of sizes, ranging from a baseball to an oversized balloon. The big one looked so close that it was hard to believe it was stable.

"I'd be interested," said Gabe, "in hearing George Tindle explain how this happened. Astronomers claim there are limits to how many moons a terrestrial-sized world can have. I think they tend to get in each other's way, and of course gravity is a factor."

"Who's George Tindle?" I asked.

"He's an old friend. An astronomer at the Collier Array near Castleman's World. He'd love this place."

Belle got pictures, but they wouldn't be close to the experience of actually seeing the moons. We knew from our earlier perspective they were nothing more than cratered rocks. But on that evening they were bright globes floating through a starlit night sky. I remembered occasional evenings at home with guys who tried to bring one of Rimway's two moons into a romantic frame. I can't say whether Tindle would actually have loved that place, but I'm pretty sure the guys would have.

I couldn't sleep that night. I sent a message to Chad informing him that the mission was getting longer than we'd expected. But that I was looking forward to seeing him when we got home, though I wasn't sure when that would be. Eventually I got up and walked out into the passenger cabin. Gabe was already there, staring out at sunlight. He pointed at the scrambled egg breakfast he was eating. Did I want some?

I shook my head and sat down beside him. "See anything interesting?"

"I suppose. I can tell you this is not a place where you'd want to build your getaway home."

"More critters?"

"Yes. Some of the most lethal things I've ever seen." He finished the coffee, put the cup on the tray, closed his eyes, and laid his head on the back of the seat.

"I don't guess we've picked up a signal?"

"No. When we first listened to Jonathan talk about it, I thought maybe it had come from this world. That there'd been a civilization here somewhere and they'd just missed it."

"I assume you've given up on that idea?"

"Pretty much."

"So we're ready to leave?"

"Soon as I finish breakfast. Okay?" He adjusted the shade, blocking the sunlight, and helped himself to a batch of fried potatoes.

We were talking about nothing in particular when Belle did the electronic equivalent of clearing her throat, signaling that she had something to say. We both looked in the direction of the bridge, and I said, "Go ahead, Belle. What is it?"

"There is something you should see."

We both expected another unsettling life-form. And that's what we got. A couple of them. More tentacles extending out of the forest. And something in a river, of which we could make out only a pair of eyes rising above the water. "Not exactly a place to spend the weekend," said Gabe, going back to his eggs.

"No!" said Belle. *"I wasn't referring to the river."*

There was a lander on the ground, or maybe a small interstellar. It was at the edge of the forest, almost in the river, partially concealed by trees and shrubbery. We were moving quickly past it. "Get a lock on it, Belle," I said. "Don't lose it."

Gabe was leaning forward, trying to get a better look. "It's been there awhile. Are we going to be able to find it again?"

"I have it," said Belle.

We'd have to complete another orbit if we wanted to go down and take a look. Belle told us it would take forty minutes.

"Do it," said Gabe. "No way we can just ignore a downed ship."

We passed over storm clouds, a smoking volcano, something like an octopus emerging from the surf on an inland sea, and a flying dragon.

"You sure you want to do this?" I said. "That is not friendly territory down there."

"Are you serious? Belle, is that vehicle one of ours? Could you tell?"

"I could not manage a good view," she said. *"The hatch looked the right size to accommodate a human, but that doesn't mean much."*

"Gabe, that is scary territory."

"Don't worry about it. I have a blaster. You think I've forgotten how all this works?" He was reading my reaction and smiling. "It's all right. I've done this before. We can't just walk away from it, Chase."

"Okay. If you insist." I started back to the storage area.

"Where you going?" he asked.

"Pressure suits."

"We only need one. You stay with the *Belle-Marie*."

"That's ridiculous. You can't go down there alone."

"Chase, that's the only way to handle this. There's no need for both of us to go. And you're right. It *is* dangerous down there. Which is why I want you to stay here."

"I can't do that."

"Chase, do as I ask."

"Gabe, you're not certified to operate the lander."

"Belle can take it."

"No, Gabe. Give me an argument on this and I won't go near another of these missions."

He was glaring at me. "If something happens, what would I tell your mom?"

I didn't move.

He took a deep breath, one that sucked all the air out of the cabin. "All right. If you have to have it that way. But you'll be careful?"

"Of course."

I don't think I'd ever known him to get seriously upset with me before. Belle broke in: *Thirty minutes till we see it again.*

We locked the telescope on the vehicle and put it on the display. Belle increased magnification. It *was* a lander. We could see a comet image on the hull, and a designator, but it was too worn down to make out details. Gabe grunted. "It's one of ours." There might have been a six, and another smear that appeared to be a K. Trees and shrubs blocked our view. "Incredible," he said. "This thing goes back a few years. It's from Earth."

"How do you know? The comet?"

"Yes. That was on all the Terran interstellars during the latter part of the third millennium. It's the original design."

"You're saying it's eight or nine thousand years old?"

"It could be. Probably not, though. I'd be surprised to see an early vehicle out this far. The standard assumption has always been that they didn't get more than a hundred light-years from Earth during that era. But who knows?"

I probably shouldn't have said anything but I couldn't

resist. "Remind me to tell you about the *Seeker*."

Gabe smiled. "Chase, just because I was missing for a few years doesn't mean I haven't made any effort to catch up. I wasn't saying nobody ever went deep. Just that people for a long time, for thousands of years, weren't aware of some of the things that happened during the early times." His frustration was fading. "At least," he said, "we should be able to go home with something."

"I guess. It'd be nice if we had a way to lift it and actually take the thing back."

"Yeah, that would be good. But there should be some decent artifacts inside. It's a pity it didn't go down on one of these moons instead of in a jungle. It would be in much better condition. But thousands of years in this tangle . . ."

"Terrible way to die," I said.

"Maybe not. In those days, vehicles didn't travel alone. There should have been at least one more out here with them. So whoever was inside probably got clear."

"Anything like this in the histories? I mean, if they got out this far, there'd probably have been something on the record."

"It could be," said Gabe. "There's a world they called Farport where they had an accident. Nobody knows where Farport is. Maybe this was it. As best I recall, they got everybody off. And there's no record anyone ever went back. At least the person writing the account didn't think so."

"I like the name."

"So do I, Chase. It fits. But let's not forget we don't have a backup."

We got more pictures and left it behind a second time. "Next time around," said Gabe. When we were about twenty minutes out from launch, we went down into the cargo bay and took out the pressure suits. He looked seriously uncomfortable as I climbed into mine. We put two cutters and two blasters into the lander. When Belle announced that we had seven minutes left, we boarded the lander and began to depressurize the cargo bay. I checked to make sure we could keep radio contact with her. For several years, the lander had its own AI, which Alex had named for Gabe. But we'd finally caught up with the technology and got a communication package that allowed Belle to download software into the lander and provide a shadow version of herself to function in the vehicle. Gabe the AI is now operating in an orphanage in Basington, across the Melony. Last time we visited him, he seemed quite happy.

Belle took the count to zero minus three minutes and opened the launch doors. We shut the gravity down and started the engines. The cradle took us outside and, as the thrusters started, gave us a push. And we were on our way.

Belle had the vehicle on automatic. She'd take us in until we could see the wreckage, and then hand it over to me. Forest and mountains stretched in all directions as far as I could see. There was a river immediately below, and a lake to the north that was so large we could just barely make out the opposite shore. The sky was full of birds, if that was the correct terminology for the reptilian critters that moved in clusters above the trees. I could feel Gabe's excitement. This was potentially the discovery of a lifetime.

We descended through scattered clouds until we were just above treetop level. The ground was also crowded with shrubs and giant bushes with gray pods and dazzling red flowers. "Captain," said Belle, "it's directly ahead, about two kilometers. Stay with the river."

"Okay, Belle. I've got it."

She released control. I took over and reduced velocity.

Gabe leaned forward in his chair. "There it is." The downed vehicle was partially visible within a cluster of trees. I continued to slow down until we were barely moving. The wreckage was partially submerged in the ground. A larger version of the comet stood out on the aft section of the hull. And something else that was hard to make out. A blue-and-white smear. "Might have been a flag," said Gabe.

"You recognize it?"

"No."

The bushes surrounding the wreckage resembled broad-leaf evergreens. Long vines hung down from the treetops. The wreckage had been virtually swallowed by the shrubbery. Fortunately it appeared to be out of reach of the river. "We're lucky Belle spotted it at all," said Gabe.

"The atmosphere should be breathable," Belle said, *"though there's a heavier mix of oxygen than at home. However there is a substance in the air that might act as an allergen. It would be best to stay with the suits."*

We touched down in a narrow opening among the trees, about thirty meters away. Gabe released his belt, got up, and headed for the hatch. "Take your time," I said. "You have your blaster?"

"Of course." He hated being treated like someone who hadn't done anything like this before. But I couldn't see the weapon anywhere. He had in fact left it on the seat behind him. He tried to pretend he was checking his helmet before picking it up. When he'd finished he slipped it into his belt. Then he reached into a pocket and showed me a cutter as well.

We pulled on our air tanks, went into the air lock, depressurized, and opened the outer hatch. He got in front of me, determined to lead the way. But he stopped long enough to survey the area. *"No surprises,"* he said. I followed him outside. When we were satisfied nothing was stalking us, I closed up and we started into the tangled vegetation. The flowers were gorgeous. I wondered if they smelled as good as they looked.

Moving forward was a challenge. We both got caught up in vines and lianas, which were clingy. Two giant shrubs dominated the space on either side of the vehicle. There was an unsettling aspect to them, maybe connected to multiple gray pods that had an almost flesh-like appearance. The vines were loaded with thorns.

We stood for a couple of moments studying the wreckage. It had not crashed. Whatever had gone wrong had apparently happened after they were on the ground. The hull had taken on a rusted taint, and there wasn't much doubt it had been there several thousand years. Finally Gabe walked over to the hatch. There was a presspad about halfway up on the right side. He reached out and touched it. Nothing happened. He pushed down harder. There was of course no way it was going to work if that thing had really been there for as long as we thought. And that's exactly what we got.

He pulled the cutter out of his belt. *"I hate to do this,"* he said, *"but it's all we have."*

He turned the device on the hatch. It sizzled as the laser sliced through it. When he'd finished, he removed the presspad, but the door still showed no sign of opening. He stayed with it until he was able to remove the hatch. We pulled it out of the way, revealing the air lock. The inner hatch was also resistant, so we had to repeat the process. When he'd finished we broke it loose and looked past it into a shadowy interior. Then he climbed in, turned on a wrist light, and extended a hand for me.

I'd half expected to find the remains of some of the occupants inside, but there was nothing. So maybe they had been rescued. I think we were both relieved to see no bones, but it hardly seemed to matter at that point.

The vehicle was half again as large as our lander. But it had only five seats. Gabe wasted no time getting into the pilot's seat. Numbers and letters on the gauges and dials were familiar. *"It is one of ours,"* Gabe said.

We found the remnant of a flag inserted in the pocket behind the pilot's seat. The colors had faded. They might originally have been green and gold. We didn't recognize it. Gabe took a couple of pictures. *"We'll look it up when we get home."* He folded it and placed it in his pouch.

A jacket lay in one of the seats. It felt like a piece of hard cardboard. There was a zipper, and a patch on the right breast depicting the comet we'd seen on the hull and three unfamiliar letters. *"Alex would have been disappointed with this,"* Gabe said. *"Maybe we'll get lucky and find something that survived reasonably intact."*

I was still looking at the control panel. "I wonder if there's any chance we could power up the AI? Talk about a gold mine."

Gabe waved it away. *"Dream on, kid. It's been here too long. The AI's dead."*

"I know. I'm just kidding."

He took a deep breath. *"I have to admit I'd love talking to something eight thousand years old."*

"Maybe—"

"Forget it, Chase. It would be a waste of time."

The AI appeared to be in a black box with curved edges. The box was set inside a metal container.

We checked the galley and the washroom, but of course neither contained anything of interest other than the remains of a completely withered magazine in a holder.

There were two storage cabinets in the rear. We'd just opened one when Belle broke in: *"We've got some activity here, guys. But don't go outside to look."*

I took the blaster out of my belt and tried to move Gabe away from the hatch, which was now just a large opening. But he wasn't going to allow a woman to take the lead. "Wait," I told him.

A picture blinked on inside my helmet, sent by Belle. The shrubs surrounding us appeared to have come to life. Vines were moving, pods expanding and contracting almost as if they were breathing. *"Uh-oh,"* said Gabe. He had his back to me and was holding on to seats on either side and standing so I couldn't even see past him. Finally he edged over. *"Careful,"* he said.

Tendrils were creeping in through the air lock.

"That doesn't look good."

"We'd better get clear." Gabe got his blaster out and looked down at the moving vegetation. He got within a step or two before one of them whipped around his right ankle and brought him down hard. He pulled the trigger and blew away most of what remained of the air lock. A cluster of vines and branches immediately began to crowd through. I put my own blaster back in my belt, grabbed the cutter, and tried to use it to free him. Belle was telling us both to stop, to get away from the open hatch. The vines were coming after us quicker than I could slice through them. A couple of them wrapped around my wrist and I lost the weapon.

"Belle," Gabe yelled, *"hit it with something. Use your cutter."*

Belle didn't have a cutter. There were no weapons, of any kind, mounted on the lander.

The vines dragged me forward, off my feet. I fell backward. Their grip tightened and they pulled both of us into a tangle of moving shrubbery. More of the stuff was coming through the opening. Vines closed on my throat and my right arm. Gabe had gotten hold of something and was resisting while I was dragged over him. They weren't all pulling in the same direction. Some were trying to drag me directly forward across the deck and onto the ground outside the blown hatch. Others, hanging vines, were also trying to get me through the hatch, but they were coming in from the trees. The lower appendages released me and

I was lifted toward the top of the air lock. My oxygen tanks banged against the overhead.

Gabe was calling to me to look out, but I couldn't see anything other than a sky full of vines and creepers. The vines were trying to get my shoulders through the area where the outer hatch had been. I heard Gabe's cutter.

And the light faded.

XXI.

Our old mother nature has pleasant and cheery tones enough for us when she comes in her dress of blue and gold over the eastern hilltops; but when she follows us upstairs to bed in her suit of black velvet and diamonds, every creak of her sandals and every whisper of her lips is full of mystery and fear.

—Oliver Wendell Holmes,
The Professor at the Breakfast Table, VII, 1850 CE

When I saw light again I was still airborne. But it was Gabe who had hold of me, not the vegetation. The lander was just off to the side, where it had set down and crushed some of the shrubbery. Gabe sounded desperate: *"Chase, you okay? Speak to me. Say something."*

"Yeah. I'm all right." I inadvertently pushed him away in another effort to get rid of the vines that had been strangling me. But they were gone. Whatever was left was dead, just hanging from my arms and throat. He set me on the ground and I lay there sucking in air, terrified something was about to seize me again. I tried to get to my feet, but I was too shaky. Behind us, one of the shrubs looked crushed. It was dead on the ground, its appendages scattered in all directions, and most of them unmoving. A pod near its center had burst open and spilled something that might have been pus into the soil.

The lander's air lock opened.

Gabe helped me get to my feet and half carried me inside. The hatch closed behind us. *"You sure you're okay?"* he asked.

"Yeah." As far as I could tell, nothing was broken. He got me through the inner door and let me rest while he restored the air pressure. "Belle," I said. "Get us off the ground."

I wasn't sure she'd be able to. Vines and branches surrounded the lander. But we lifted off. Despite a couple of bumps, we continued up and I breathed easier when it became clear we'd broken free. Gabe got out of his suit. Then he helped me with mine. "What happened?" I asked. "What did you do?"

"I didn't do a thing. Couldn't do anything. Belle got us clear."

"Belle? How'd she do that?"

"She took the lander up and brought it down on top of that thing. Crushed it. Whatever it was."

Of course she had. Where was my head? "Belle," I said. "You okay?"

"Got a bent antenna. Otherwise I'm good."

"Thank you."

"Well, I didn't want to go home without you guys. It would have required some explanation. Are you okay, Captain?"

"I'm fine. Maybe we should get out of here."

"Excellent idea," said Belle. *"Please take your seats."*

My hip was hurting and my neck felt as if it was several centimeters longer than normal. "It's a good thing we were wearing the suits," said Gabe. "Otherwise I don't think we'd have made it."

I could see bruises on his neck and arms, and he began pressing his ribs and making faces. "You sure you're okay?" I asked.

"Yeah. I've been worse."

I just sat there with my eyes closed and my head back while Belle took us well above the treetops.

Gabe was moving around in his seat, trying to get comfortable. "I hate leaving here," he said. "I wish we had a way to do a serious search. There might be some documents on board, something we could recover and take back with us. We didn't even get the jacket."

"You want to go back?" I asked. It was a joke, of course.

He laughed. "I can live without the jacket."

I'd been afraid we were going to find out the plant, whatever it was, had done some damage to the lander. I sat examining the controls. Everything appeared normal.

"I think it's dead," Belle said.

Gabe was looking down through his window. "There's another one on top of the ship. I don't know where that came from."

I didn't like being the reason we were pulling away from what might have been a major discovery. "If we went back, we wouldn't be taken by surprise again. We could go in with the blasters and take out the damned things." I became aware I didn't know where my blaster was. "Uh-oh."

"What's wrong, Chase?"

"I think I lost mine." I was checking my belt when Gabe gave it to me. "I think you dropped it."

"Thanks."

"Don't mention it."

"I apparently dropped my cutter too."

"I didn't see that. Sorry." He was quiet for a minute. "You know, we could go back. I'd like to have a little more time in there."

"I don't think," said Belle, *"that's a good idea."*

"We should be fine. We could clear the area before going back inside the lander. Kill everything within twenty meters."

"Gabriel," said Belle, *"I strongly recommend you let it be."*

"It's okay, Belle," said Gabe. "You're programmed for safety first. The plants won't be a problem."

"I'm not sure how you can be certain about that. There might be other hazards down there."

"Gabe," I said, "you're really interested in the AI, aren't you?"

"Yeah."

"I thought we decided it's dead."

"We can't be certain. I doubt that anything recorded a few thousand years ago would still be recoverable. But if there were something . . ." He turned toward me. Pointed at the white light that signified Belle was active. He frowned and lowered his voice. "Maybe you should shut her down."

"Why?"

"Do it, Chase."

"Before you do that," said Belle, *"I've sealed the hatch so you can't get out."*

"She can't do that, can she?" asked Gabe.

"I don't know."

"Try me. I have serious doubts about your safety. On another subject, I have some news. Maybe good. I'm not sure."

"And what is that?" asked Gabe.

"I picked up a signal. A vocal one." She let us hear it. A voice, speaking too swiftly and in a pitch that was too high to be human.

"Beautiful." Gabe was delighted. "I never expected it to be so easy. It's probably emanating from the surface some-where."

Coladia did not feel like a world with radio stations.

"The transmission is coming from the sky. It is unlikely to have originated on this planet."

"You sure, Belle?" I asked.

"It seems very unlikely, Captain."

"And it's still coming in?"

"Yes."

"Okay. Do you have any idea where the source might be?"

"Not yet. I would like to leave orbit so that I can get a better angle on the transmission. That would allow us a reasonably accurate result."

• • •

I'd never seen Gabe so hesitant about making a decision. He thought about testing Belle's ability to seal the hatch. But I was inclined to trust her judgment on going back down to the fourth-millennium vehicle, or whatever it was. "Why don't we follow the transmission?" I said. "Before it shuts down. Go take a look and come back here later? If it's that important."

Discontent wrinkled his features. "It could be a while before we get back. And to tell you the truth, I'm dying to know what might be inside that thing. We can get into it and be back out in an hour. Can you handle . . . ?" He pointed at Belle's status lamp.

Ultimately, he was insistent. Belle admitted she'd been bluffing. "Thanks for the effort," I said.

She went silent.

"You okay?" I asked.

We still got no response. It was the only time I'd ever seen anything like that from her.

It had gotten dark at the site of the wreckage. Going down there under those conditions would have been an even dumber decision. We entered orbit, returned to *the Belle Marie,* and got some sleep. Belle was back talking to us again. Mostly to Gabe. I couldn't hear them well enough to make out what they were saying, but the subject was obvious. We needed to look at the downed ship before we left. Was the transmission still coming in? Clearly it was or Gabe would have come pounding on my door. I'm not sure there was a guy more passionate about history anywhere in the Confederacy than he was.

We made about five passes over the vehicle before we were satisfied with the amount of daylight it was getting. We climbed into our pressure suits and got into the lander.

A couple minutes later we were descending on it again. He didn't say anything, but it was clear he was enjoying the moment. Man over machine.

The forest possessed a level of animation we had not noticed earlier. It wasn't obvious, but when we got close to the ground, we could see tree branches and bushes and vines moving in ways that should have set off alarm bells during our first descent. Maybe it was because there was no wind whatever this time. "Or maybe," said Gabe, "it's not targeting us now. Maybe it only hides itself when it sees a possibility for lunch."

"Don't get too confident, Gabe."

We set down in the same area. Belle cautioned us to be careful. We put on our helmets, climbed out, and spent several minutes watching the ground around us to make sure no vines or thickets or briars were creeping in our direction. We used the blasters in a couple of suspicious locations and were satisfied there was no immediate threat from the vegetation. Then I went looking for my cutter while Gabe kept an eye on the forest. It wasn't anywhere on the ground but I eventually found it inside the ship, just a step or two from the air lock. The dead vegetation that had wrapped itself around me was still there, scattered across the deck.

Gabe began a search of the interior while I disconnected the ship's AI from the control unit and from its power source. Then I carried it to the lander.

I needed a few minutes to get it reconnected to power. Nothing happened. "So it's dead?" Gabe asked.

"Looks like it."

He was disappointed. I was too, but I'll confess I was happy just to get away from that place alive. He spent an hour inside the ship but came away with nothing except the jacket, some spare parts, and an electronic wrench.

• • •

The transmission was still coming in when we rendezvoused with the *Belle-Marie*. "I'm glad we didn't lose the signal," he said. "That would have been especially painful after we got nothing from the ship."

"Belle," I said, "we're ready."

We left orbit with mixed feelings. I'd have liked some evidence that the ship's crew had been rescued. Even though whatever had happened occurred thousands of years ago, it was still painful to think of their being ambushed—and no joke is intended—by the local trees. We never got the answer to that. There was simply no record of the mission. Details didn't seem to support the idea that it had been the Farport flight.

"We should go out about four billion kilometers," said Belle. *"That will give us a good angle."*

"First," said Gabe, "let's go pick up the radiotelescope. I don't see any need to leave it out here now."

The signal ceased while we moved to the other side of the sun. Then it came back. *"There are two voices again,"* said Belle. *"I don't recognize either."*

Gabe raised a fist. "Excellent," he said. I would just as soon have seen it gone. I'd had enough aliens. But I said nothing. "Have you located the source?"

"Working on it. The origin is outside the system."

It didn't take long. *"It seems to be coming from a star listed as KKL7718. It's a type-K dwarf. A red star. It's about seven light-years."*

I'd been Gabe's pilot for roughly two years. What he wanted from me, other than guiding the ship, was simply someone to talk with during flights. On this occasion, though, I was the one who needed someone to talk with. Getting wrapped up by that plant and dragged into the air lock had been the most terrifying experience of my life. I hadn't settled down yet, hadn't *begun* to settle down, when we turned in the direction of KKL7718 and activated the star drive.

"I understand," Gabe said as we sat on the bridge. "I was pretty rattled by it too."

I hadn't been "pretty rattled." I'd completely lost it. I'd been in a few life-threatening situations before, but getting shot at was nothing like having those plants try to drag me out into the trees. I couldn't even bring myself to think about what it might have done with me had Belle not stepped in.

Immediately after we slipped into hyperspace I changed the subject, but I have no recollection now about the new topic. I only know that I kept feeling the vines around my throat and my helmet banging against the overhead. Then Gabe was telling me again it was okay. He poured me a drink and said I should relax, that it would go away, and how about we get a snack?

Belle remained unusually silent. I'd been surprised by her stepping in to argue we not go back to the ground on Coladia. I'd never known her to take that determined a stand before against the wishes of either Gabe or myself. Or Alex. It made me wonder if she'd changed in some elemental way.

Eventually we arrived near our destination. I'd begun to pull myself together and felt almost normal when we broke the surface. For about twenty minutes we got no signal; then Belle informed us she'd recovered it. *"But the voices are different."*

"Of course they would be," I said. "The two who were having the conversation have probably disconnected by now."

Belle snickered. The reality was that, assuming the conversation had originated here in KKL7718, the transmission had needed well over seven years to reach Coladia.

Gabe began talking about how he wished Belle could manage a translation. How great it would be, he said, if we could listen in on what they're saying to each other. I commented it would be even better if we could participate. "Hi, guys," I would like to have said to them. "How's it going? What have you been up to lately?"

"I wonder," said Gabe, "if that will ever be possible? If we'll ever get communication technology that'll allow people in different star systems to talk directly to each other?"

"I doubt it."

"You can be such a pessimist, Chase. What do you think people at the beginning of the space age would have said about ships that traveled from star to star within a few hours? Or twenty minutes?"

"That's a little different."

"Why?"

"I'm not sure. I mean, sitting at the country house carrying on a conversation with somebody on Dellaconda just seems completely off the charts."

"I'll tell you what I'd really like to do," said Gabe. "I'd love to live long enough to be able to visit another galaxy. Maybe drop by and have a dinner in Andromeda."

"If you wait long enough Andromeda will come to us."

"Is that really true?"

"Sure. Andromeda and the Milky Way will collide eventually."

"When?"

"A couple million years, I think."

Belle broke in: *"More like four billion."*

Gabe couldn't resist laughing. "I don't guess it's anything we need to worry about."

We hadn't yet determined the source of the signal, so we simply followed it into the system. There was no point considering another jump until we knew where we were going.

We were both getting tired, but I was still too rattled to

try to sleep. I didn't want to retreat to my cabin, where I'd be alone. Normally at the end of the day I picked something from Belle's library to entertain myself with until I fell asleep. But that wasn't going to happen on that night. So I remained in my seat. Gabe understood what was going on and he stayed with me. Eventually I closed my eyes and drifted off. When I woke an hour or so later, he was still there, snoring softly.

XXII.

Science, through the ages, has opened a wide assortment of doors. It has given us guns, nuclear weapons, and technologies that brought us very close to plundering the Earth. Thousands of terrestrial species no longer exist as a result of technological advances. Science made possible the efforts of corporations and politicians to control what people think and ultimately to harvest sufficient wealth and power to manipulate the lives of tens of millions. Some doors should not be opened.
—Rev. Agathe Lawless, *Sunset Musings*, 1402

In the morning, Belle told us we'd picked up a second signal. *"It's coming from the same direction. But there's a problem. There's nothing in front of us within the habitable zone."*

"It's a ship," said Gabe. "Or a space station."

"Belle," I said, "can you determine whether both transmissions are using the same language?"

"I am trying to make that determination now. But I will need some time. One of the transmissions has stopped, by the way."

They went on and off. The voices changed. Sometimes Belle could identify a speaker as someone who'd been part of the conversation earlier. And finally she told us we were still tracking the signal: *"The transmissions are not coming in from this system. They are coming through the system. From somewhere else."*

By then it hadn't been a surprise. "Where is it coming from?" I asked.

"A G-class star. GRD43991."

"How far?" Gabe asked.

"About six hours."

When we arrived, we saw immediately that there was something strange about the sun. We were close to it, barely a hundred million kilometers out, and Belle was showing us telescopic images of artificial objects closer in. *"They appear to be in orbit,"* she said. *"And I should add that we are receiving multiple transmissions."*

"I don't believe this," said Gabe. "I think it's a Dyson Sphere."

"What's a Dyson Sphere?" I asked. I'd heard the term but I couldn't remember what it meant.

"It's an artificial system used to gather solar energy. A giant structure composed mostly of solar panels or other types of energy collectors. They surround a star, pick up some of its energy, and transmit it to a place that uses it to power a civilization. Or whatever. It's named for a third-millennium physicist." He paused. "Belle, you say we are receiving multiple transmissions?"

"Yes."

"How many?"

"Hundreds."

"And a Dyson Sphere," said Gabe.

"Do you wish to get a better look at the objects?"

"It's not safe," I said. "They're too close to the sun. The locals are seriously high-tech. If they can put together something like this, they're way ahead of us."

"There would probably not be a problem with the sun," said Belle. *"It's a class K, which means we should be able to approach within twenty million kilometers. Heat will not be sufficient to damage the ship."*

"I'm wondering," I said, "whether we should be hanging around at all."

"That's the whole point," said Gabe. "They're highly advanced. As societies progress they should become less inclined to attack others."

"That's the theory."

"Yes. I think we'll learn that's characteristic of intelligence generally. Intelligent beings understand the value of cooperation. That attacking each other is stupid."

"I hope so, Gabe."

"My bet is that Harding came out here, landed somewhere, and went back home with the trophy."

"You think that's what happened? That he went down to say hello and they gave him a prize?"

"Yes. That's probably exactly what happened." He folded his hands together and smiled at me. "I think we're perfectly safe. But your concerns are valid. Let's just go in and take a closer look. I don't mean get closer to the sun but to the planets. But I won't insist. It's your call, Chase. If you want we'll go home and I can set up a mission."

He knew there was no way I'd back off that kind of proposal. I didn't think it was a good idea. But I was in a corner. "Belle," I said, "do you see a planet in the habitable zone?"

"I do not. But that doesn't mean much. I've been concentrating my attention on the Dyson Sphere. Is that really what it's called?"

"Yes," said Gabe.

"Interesting. If you wish me to search for planets, we will need some time."

Gabe couldn't take his eyes off the display. "Let's concentrate on the Dyson Sphere for now."

"As you wish."

Gabe could not have looked happier. "The additional transmissions. Can we tell if they're in the same language?"

"I haven't really had time to do a general analysis. But judging

from what I've seen so far, I suspect they are one language. Or at least, they were."

"What do you mean, 'were'?"

"They have been shutting down over the last few minutes."

"Since we arrived . . . ?"

"It would seem so."

"Gabe," I said, "I think it would be prudent to leave."

He crunched down on his teeth again. I hate it when he does that. "Belle, are you detecting any movement anywhere? Any vehicles?"

"Negative, Gabe."

"It's only been a short time since we got here," I said. "They haven't really had time to react."

"Other than close off their communications. What blows my mind is how whoever lives here could have put those things so close to the sun."

"The transmissions are now stopping," said Belle. *"The sky is going silent."*

"They want us to leave," Gabe said.

"I agree. Absolutely. If they'd wanted to say hello to us they'd have done so. I think we should take the hint."

"I didn't mean we should just bail out."

"Oh."

"Chase, you don't really want to leave, do you?"

I did. I saw no way, if we proceeded to poke around, that this could end happily. But I'd already let Gabe know how I felt, and I couldn't bring myself to insist that we pull out. If I did that, he'd always remember that I'd screwed up what should have been a historic discovery. "Your call," I said.

"Thank you. I know this isn't easy for you, Chase. But we'll take every precaution, okay?"

"I've located two planets so far," said Belle. *"One is in the habitable zone. But it's on the other side of the sun."*

XXIII.

Oh, to have a cabin on some lonely world,
A quiet place beneath a distant sun,
Where news of politics
And appeals to purchase medications
And reactivate my life with youth-restoring creams
Can never touch my aerial.
That is where I would live the rest of my days.
—WALFORD CANDLES, "TIME AND TIDE," 1214

The planet was on the outside edge of the habitable zone, a world that probably would have been considerably more chilly than Rimway. We were still hearing nothing as we approached. *"I don't think many, if any, of the transmissions were coming from here,"* said Belle. *"There seemed to be numerous locations."* It was rocky and barren, not much bigger than a large moon. There was no snow or ice, but it *looked* cold. And dismal. We saw no sign of life, no greenery, nothing moving. *"Do we wish to establish an orbit?"* she asked.

"I don't see any point in it," said Gabe. We were just turning away when Belle told us she'd found a second world in the zone. *"It's considerably closer to the sun,"* she said. *"Temperatures will be better. And it has a large moon."*

We needed an additional few days to reach it. The radio transmissions didn't come back. Whatever the source, it was clear they weren't comfortable with us in the area. We spent our time trying to distract ourselves, reading, working out, while we let Belle watch for activity. We didn't waste any time pretending we weren't worried about what lay ahead. But Gabe's position remained rock solid: "We just don't have a choice about this."

As we got closer, we saw several large dish antennas drifting through the night. *"I can't know for certain,"* said Belle, *"but I suspect they are at the Lagrange points."* Those were stable positions maintained by the gravity of the moon and the planet. And they were probably receivers connected to the Dyson objects orbiting the sun. They'd have been picking up solar energy, which was then relayed to collectors on the ground.

Gabe seemed increasingly less sure of his decision to come in close. I suspected that, if I weren't along, he'd have canceled the project and gone home. But he didn't want to play the quitter in front of Tori Kolpath's daughter. The truth, probably, was that neither of us, traveling alone, would have gone any closer.

The world was green. It had oceans and ice caps and, no surprise, cities. But we *did* get a jolt: we were coming in from the sunlit side, but a portion of the dark side was visible. It was completely dark. No lights whatever. "It's probably jungle. Or ocean."

The planet was about the same size as Rimway, with large mountain ranges, a lot of rivers, and some enormous lakes. As we drew closer, we focused on the cities. They were dominated by tall, polished buildings that sometimes narrowed gradually along the upper stories, transforming into spires. Others topped off into landing pads. The buildings were surrounded by streets and smaller structures and broad parks. *"They have power,"* said Belle.

We noticed also that as the planet rotated and cities fell into darkness, no lights came on.

We saw more dish antennas on the rooftops. "There doesn't

seem to be anything moving," Gabe said. "The streets look empty." So were the skies and the ocean, mountain roads and harbors and rivers. There was no sign of activity.

"It has some satellites," said Belle. *"Not many, though. I'd estimate about fifty."*

"Anything sending us a message?"

"We're getting complete silence, Captain."

"Okay. If you see anything coming our way, let us know immediately."

"Of course. I can see no indication of danger. But this is only at first glance. And there's something else."

"What's that?" asked Gabe.

"There appears to be a habitation on the moon." She put it on the display. There was a dome and, connected by a tube, a small rectangular building. What was probably a launchpad lay off to one side. Three large dish antennas were located on the ground about three hundred meters away. There was nothing on the launchpad.

"Where do you want to go first, Gabe? Down and look at the cities, or check out the moonbase? Or maybe just clear out and head for home?"

"Why would we head for home?"

"I think we've answered the question we came here to resolve. Harding found an advanced civilization. Do you think we should stop and say hello?"

"Of course we should. Chase, they probably gave him an award. They were apparently excited to receive an offworld visitor." He grinned. "Maybe we'll get some recognition too."

"I'm serious, Gabe."

"So am I. But okay, you have a point. Let's just be careful. Take a look at the moonbase before we do anything else. We're less likely to run into an angry crowd there." He was mocking me, though he was as concerned as I was.

"Belle," I said, "are we getting any sign of activity from the moon?"

"There is electrical power in the dome."

The sun was in the sky so, even if lights were on, we might be missing them. "All right," I said. "Let's go take a look. I've got the controls."

We were about two hours out. I checked to make sure the ship's blasters were functional. They were there primarily as a defense against asteroids. I'd never used them. An asteroid should never get close enough that it's necessary to use blasters. If it happens, they told us at flight school, it's a signal for the ship's owner to get rid of the pilot.

Gabe stayed on the bridge with me. We drew closer without arousing any visible reaction either from the dome or from the planet.

Eventually we went into orbit around the moon. The sun and the planet floated in the sky amid a mass of stars. When we got to the back side of the moon, where neither the sun nor the world could be seen, the stars brightened. We sat quietly, not saying much. When the dome reappeared, we turned the scopes on it and went back to watching for a reaction. Anything: lights coming on, radio transmission, somebody opening one of three hatches and looking up at us. But we saw nothing. The power levels inside the dome didn't change. The hatches never opened.

It was located on flat ground, close to a crater. "What do you think?" Gabe asked.

"If we're going to go down, let's do it on the next orbit." Get it over with. We sat on the bridge for a while, looking down as the lunar surface passed underneath. Then finally we went down to the cargo bay and got into our pressure suits. We took our seats in the lander, put the helmets behind us, and depressurized the cargo bay. When we were ready to go, I told Belle.

"Launch time approaching," she said. *"About eight minutes."*

"Good. If you see any activity on the planet, especially anything coming this way, let us know."

"Will do, Captain. The dome should be coming up over the horizon shortly."

I turned to Gabe. "You ready, boss?"

"I guess that makes this officially my decision, doesn't it?"

"Oh yes." We climbed into the lander and belted down.

Belle informed us that the dome was again visible.

"Any lights or anything?"

"Everything looks the same, Captain."

I fastened a link on my belt so Belle would be able to see whatever we did. Gabe and I were wishing each other luck when she came back. *"Recommend launch in two minutes."*

"Make it happen, Belle. We're ready to go."

The launch doors opened; the cradle lifted the lander and moved us outside. I started the engine. *"Release in thirty seconds,"* she said.

She did a countdown for the final ten seconds while I activated the antigravs. Then she turned us loose. We began descending through the vacuum. Gabe was leaning forward, trying to watch the moonbase. I spent my time thinking about what I'd do if, at the last second, one of the doors opened. "It depends on whether they point something at us," said Gabe.

"I didn't realize I was thinking out loud."

"I suspect we've both had the same issue on our minds."

Moons look pretty much the same everywhere. Rocks, craters, ridges, flat gray terrain, and not much else. Finally we touched down. We were about a hundred meters from the dome. Close enough.

We got out of our seats, put on helmets, and checked the radios. Then we went over to the air lock and I opened the inner hatch. We both got in. I closed the door, depressurized, and Gabe opened the outer hatch. There was still no movement from the dome as we climbed down out of the lander. I left the outer hatch open in case we had to leave in a hurry.

We kept a close eye on the ground but there was no sign of footprints or of anything else.

Both the dome and the rectangular structure connected to it were gray, a somewhat darker tint than the surface. We chose the closest of the three dome hatches and walked toward it. It was probably four and a half meters high, suggesting that the occupants might be considerably taller than we were. It looked as if it had originally been white, but it was somewhat smeared and had become a dusty gray.

"Holy cats," said Gabe. He was inclined in this kind of situation to check conditions in all directions. He'd been looking behind us.

That was all I needed. I jumped and turned around to see if we were being attacked. One of the antennas was moving. I stood with a dropped jaw and watched it swing toward the sun.

I can't answer for Gabe, but I froze at that point. Nothing else was happening. The antenna stopped, remained still for two or three minutes, and then resumed its original position. *"Well,"* said Gabe, *"we finally have a sign of life."* We started again for the door. When we got close, he held out his left arm. *"Stay behind me,"* he said.

I did. There was no knob or latch, but the frame housed a button, high over my head on the right. Were they right-handed too? Gabe went up to it and knocked. It was one of the bravest things I'd ever seen. If the door had opened I think I'd have jumped a meter. I pictured the two of us trying to run back to the lander in the pressure suits. "Gabe," I said, "there's a button."

"I see it." He made no move to use it.

"Okay."

He knocked again. The thing was an air lock, of course, so it would take a minute or so before the door could be opened. But that would likely be preceded by activity inside. Which we would not be able to hear.

We couldn't see the other doors, so I backed away a few steps, which still didn't provide visibility. But it could at least prevent a total surprise. I also kept an eye on the antennas. I couldn't help wondering how the people at Earth's moon-base would have felt had aliens shown up and come knock-ing. Which brought Octavia to mind.

"I don't think," Gabe said, *"anybody's home. Or maybe they're as scared of us as . . ."* He went no further.

"We could try the other doors."

He knocked again. *"Let's give it a little more time. Then maybe push the button."*

I wondered how long it had been since anything had set down on the launchpad. The terrestrial moonbase, of course, was now a museum. When I was there with Alex a few months earlier, it had been crowded with visitors. This place didn't look as if anybody had ever dropped by.

We waited another minute or two and finally Gabe reached up and pressed the button. There was no immediate way to know whether it was working. Gabe held his left hand against the door in an effort to determine if anything was happening inside. Then without warning the door swung outward, revealing an air lock.

If we'd been hesitant before, the sight of that empty cubi-cle, sealed off by a second door, introduced a sense that we were being careless. *"What do you think?"* asked Gabe.

I had a cutter, so we didn't need to worry about getting trapped in the air lock. "We've come this far," I said.

"I know." I could hear the reluctance in his voice. Which told me he retained the good sense I'd always known. But we were committed, and the stakes were too high to walk away.

He went in and I followed. The cubicle was large enough to provide space for about six people. The outer hatch closed with no help from us. A ceiling light came on. And I became aware of air pressure starting to build. Gabe was facing the inner door. He kept me behind him.

I didn't see another button anywhere. Presumably every-thing was automatic once you started the process. The inner door should open on its own as soon as the air pressure matched whatever was normal in the interior.

It took about a minute. Then the door swung wide. More lights came on and we were looking across an empty room. There were a couple of oversized chairs. The interior was circular and lined with display screens and what looked like communication equipment. A few doors lined the walls. And on the other side of the dome a passageway opened probably into the other building. Nothing moved. The temperature was cool but much warmer than outside.

We walked over and looked at the communication equipment: microphones, speakers, wiring, probably an amplifier, a keyboard. Gabe was studying the keys.

"You recognize the characters?" he asked, thinking of the symbols on Rick Harding's trophy.

"Not really. It's been too long since I've seen them."

"It's possible." We were both watching the exit from the passageway.

"Let's go look," I said.

The attendant building dome was also empty. It contained eight sets of living quarters, a combined galley and dining area, and a couple of large rooms that probably served simply for hanging out. There were clothes in some of the rooms, large sizes again. The owners were bipeds, but we found no pictures to reveal what they looked like. There was extensive electronic equipment. Washrooms had toilet and shower facilities, sinks and mirrors. Cabinets contained paste and medications. The paste might have been for teeth, or it was possibly a disinfectant. We opened faucets and got running water, though not much more than a dribble. And it was cold.

We came out the same way we'd gone in. Neither of us was saying much. We returned to the lander, took a last look around, and lifted off. The world in the sky still floated in the same place, almost directly overhead. "It probably never moves," said Gabe.

"*That is correct,*" Belle said. "*The moon is in tidal lock, which for satellites is quite common.*"

That night I sent another message to Chad: *We'll be a while yet. Sorry it's taking so long. But everything's okay.*

XXIV.

O solitude! Where are the charms
That sages have seen in thy face?
Better dwell in the midst of alarms
Than reign in this horrible place.

—WILLIAM COWPER,
VERSES SUPPOSED TO HAVE BEEN WRITTEN BY ALEXANDER SELKIRK, 1782 CE

The planet was lush and green and alive. We looked through the scopes and saw animals everywhere. Birds fluttered through the skies and four-legged creatures wandered in the sunlight. But there was still no sign of vehicles. No bipeds moved across the bridges linking skyscrapers. The roads were empty, no ships rode the vast oceans, and no planes were visible anywhere. Stranger still, nothing moved in the small villages scattered across the countryside.

"What is going on here?" I said.

Gabe nodded. "I thought at first that maybe they did underground transport, but that makes no sense. It wouldn't even explain why all the beaches are empty."

His expression suggested his shoes were too tight.

We were approaching orbit. Normally, I'd have told Belle to take us in, but we were still waiting for something to happen and I wanted to have my hands on the controls if we got a surprise. So I eased us into a low orbit just above the atmosphere and as much away from clouds as I could manage.

The sun was behind us, and we were moving across a boundless ocean with occasional strings of islands. Eventually we passed above an empty shoreline and continued over what appeared to be a series of small towns. Sometimes houses were clustered in fields, sometimes they were spread out over a wide area. And there *were* cars. But none moved. A couple of animals that might have been deer stood in the middle of one of the towns chewing on something.

The sun got farther behind. We overtook the twilight, which gradually turned into night.

Gabe was leaning to his right, looking out the side window. "What the hell is this about?" he asked. No lights were coming on. The darkness on the ground was unbroken. "Maybe," he said, "we should go down and knock."

"I'm not sure we should try that again."

A big city appeared off to port. Shrouded in darkness. The buildings had no lights. Nor did the streets and parks. Or the houses scattered through the area.

"Belle," said Gabe, "is it possible the radio transmissions came from somewhere else?"

"*Yes,*" she said. "*It's possible. But I doubt that they did.*"

"Is there another planet in the zone?"

"*I've been searching and have found nothing. I can't be certain, but at this point it seems unlikely.*"

Gabe sat back in his chair and crossed his arms. "This is really strange."

We traveled through the night and caught up with the sun about forty minutes later. By then Belle was certain there was no other world in the system that could support life. "Good enough," said Gabe. "Are we getting any transmissions from the satellites?"

"*Negative,*" said Belle. "They're all silent."

"Belle," I said, "are any of them geostationary?"

"Give me a minute."

"What's geostationary?" asked Gabe. "I've heard the term but I don't know what it means. Something about standing still?"

"Yes. It's a satellite whose orbital velocity matches the rotation, so it always appears to be in the same place in the sky. It's used for communications. The advantage of it is that once the transmitter is aimed at it, you don't have to make adjustments."

"Sounds like a good idea."

"It appears," Belle said, *"they all are. At least, every one that I've checked."*

We were passing over a city at the time, with the same towering structures we'd seen elsewhere, streets and highways, groves and meadows, a couple of fenced places with benches on both sides, resembling athletic fields. But trees and bushes were growing all over everything. There was nothing remotely resembling park maintenance.

Gabe looked uncertain. Finally he shook his head. "I think it's time to go down and try again."

"Why?" I asked. "We already know they don't want us around."

"I don't know," said Gabe. "I just don't want to simply walk away."

"Gabe, I don't think this is a good idea."

"Why do we keep having the same conversation? Look, take us down to one of the small towns. You stay in the lander, all right? I'll go knock on doors. There must be somebody home somewhere."

I told Belle that if something happened and we didn't come back, she should return home. In reality there would be nothing else she *could* do.

We passed over more small towns, open fields, and occasional lone houses. I was astonished at the resemblance to

Rimway. "The reality," said Gabe, "is that there are only so many ways to construct roads and houses. I guess everything will always look like home." I didn't say anything more as we got into the lander and launched. I just sat there staring out at the countryside and waiting for him to tell me where he wanted to go. "Belle," I said, "what's the atmosphere look like?"

"It should be safe. I see no reason to use the suits. Temperatures are in similar ranges to Rimway. The air looks good. And the gravity's almost normal."

"Glad to hear it," Gabe said. I didn't comment and eventually he sighed. "Don't take this the wrong way, Chase, but you didn't used to be so negative. What's happened to you?"

"What's the *right* way to take it?"

"Come on, kid. You know what I mean. I'm in favor of being cautious. But sometimes you just have to take a chance." We floated over a town surrounded by hills. A road led through it, forked, and disappeared toward more hills in one direction and a lake in the other. There was still no sign of occupants. No one came out to look up at us. No vehicle moved anywhere, although there were several on the side of the road, and others in carports and garages. If there'd been lawns at one time, they were seriously overgrown now.

We took the road that went toward the lake and stayed with it as it turned north, eventually passing a house. It was a chalet really, a cabin with broad overhanging eaves. A field full of what were probably weeds. "That might be a good place to try," Gabe said. "It's out of sight of everywhere else."

We descended in the lander. The field had plenty of room for us. There was an animal, though. It looked like a canine and was gnawing on something. A shed stood off to one side, with the rear end of a vehicle that might have been a tractor parked halfway out.

Vegetation was flourishing. The sun shone in a cloudless sky. As we neared the ground a group of birds left their perches on the chalet's roof and fluttered away. The canine continued to ignore us.

I concentrated my attention on the back door. I was wishing it would open and something would come out and scare Gabe off. Finally the canine noticed us and ran away just before we touched down.

I shut off the drive unit and we sat unmoving. Gabe finally tucked his blaster into his belt, stood up, and went into the air lock. "Stay here, Chase," he said.

I wasn't ready for another argument, and anyhow I still hadn't gotten those creeping vines out of my mind. I made sure I had weapons close at hand and told him okay. "If you really want to do it this way." I handed him a link. "Put this somewhere so I can watch what happens."

"I'll be fine, Chase." He clipped it to his shirt. "If something bad happens," he said, "I don't want you coming after me. I'm pretty well armed."

I nodded. "Leave the hatches open." He took that frustrated look at the distant sky. Then he went through the air lock, checked outside in both directions, signaled that the canine wasn't visible, and got out. The display was still blank. "Gabe," I said, "turn the link on."

The monitor lit up just in time for me to see the canine charging out of the trees. It resembled a mastiff and was half as big as Gabe was. He fired the blaster into the air. The animal stopped, thought about it, and came for him again. He took aim and blew it apart. "I hope," I said, "we didn't just kill someone's pet."

"*I do too.*" He stood for a minute, waiting to see if the noise would draw attention from someone in the house. I was thinking he should come back into the lander. But nothing changed. No one came out of the chalet. Gabe waved to signify he was okay. Then he started for the back door. It had a knob.

He walked over, knocked, and got no response. Then he

pulled on it, and it opened. He yelled, "Hello," and went inside, into an area that had two wooden chairs and a large sofa and a table. I caught my breath: There was a skeleton. It wasn't human; the skull was too large and the arms too long. It was sprawled on the floor near the entry to a corridor. Tatters of clothes surrounded it. Gabe took a moment to look down the corridor, from where he could see into another room that housed more chairs and a larger table. He knelt down to examine the skeleton. *"Don't know what happened to it,"* he said. *"It's been here awhile."* After a minute he got up and entered another room. This one had a sink, something that looked like a refrigerator, and an electronic device that might have been an oven. He tried to open the refrigerator, but the door wouldn't move. There was another door at the end of the corridor. And a set of stairs ascended to the upper floor. He looked up the stairway, saw nothing of interest, and walked over to the door. He pushed on it and it opened. A glass outer door looked across the front. Its glass was shattered.

He came back outside and returned to the lander. "I don't know what killed him," he said.

"Is it a male? Can you tell?"

"I've no clue."

"I wonder if the rest of the area is like this?"

"Probably."

I was wondering about the rest of the *planet*. I was ready to go back to the *Belle-Marie*. "What do you want to do next?" I asked. He settled into his seat and we lifted off.

"Follow the road. Let's see what else is here."

We found another town nestled against a river a few kilometers away. But the place had been torched. Almost every house, every building, had burned to the ground. A car that had plunged into a ditch contained four skeletons. Its windows were broken, and it was rusted. It had been white at one time, a smooth, sleek vehicle, and would have fit into the traffic at home without drawing much attention. Except maybe that it was large.

We passed overhead. We didn't see any other places that had burned, but all were in a neglected condition. Eventually, in the distance, skyscrapers emerged.

"I wonder," I said, "if Rick Harding saw this."

"Maybe he missed this part of the world."

"I've got a creepy suspicion it's like this everywhere."

"So who was on the radio?"

"I don't know. But if he *did* see this, why didn't he ever say anything?"

"I have no idea, Chase."

We stared out at the approaching towers. The forest was dissolving into a plain. A herd of animals that resembled buffalo except that they had gray fur wandered around munching vegetation. We saw more hills and caught glimpses of an ocean on the far side of the city. A two-lane highway came in from our left and eventually absorbed the road. There were occasional abandoned cars.

Houses multiplied. And more intersecting roads appeared. The houses were mostly fenced. We touched down and inspected one. It appeared to be made of plastic.

Finally we were over the city. It was also quiet. We saw only the usual birds and other animals.

The towers were located primarily near the coastline. A long bridge connected with an island, where more tall buildings rose into the sky. There were beaches, both on the mainland and on the island, but they too were empty. Sheltered platforms, probably lifeguard stations, were visible in both places.

We circled the area. Finally, Gabe pointed at a landing pad atop one of the skyscrapers. "Let's set down there," he said.

It was about forty stories high. We descended onto the pad, climbed out, listened for a minute to the rumble of the surf, and followed a ramp down to the roof. We passed a parking area half-filled with vehicles that must have had antigravity units, and ultimately arrived at a metal door. It had a latch. Gabe released it and pulled. But the door didn't move. I had both weapons with me. I showed him the laser. "You think we should?"

He didn't like the idea. Instead he banged on the door, waited a minute, and tried again. There was no sound of movement inside. "I hate doing this," he said.

"How about we go down and park in the street? Try the front doors?"

"How much fuel do we have?"

"It's not a problem."

"All right. Let's do that."

The street-level entrance consisted of two pairs of glass doors. The glass was broken in two of them. The doors were set back between large display areas also with broken glass. Whatever had been on display was gone.

Getting through the doors was no problem. We walked into a lobby. Chairs and tables were distributed around the room. All were too large to accommodate us. A long counter on our left extended almost the length of the interior. Elevators were at the far end. One was open with only the shaft exposed. Everything was covered with a thick layer of dust.

Gabe walked over to the elevators while I went behind the counter. Two computers were built into it. I played around with one and the screen lit up. "Hey, Gabe," I said. "We've got power."

"Excellent." He looked happy. There was a ramp at the far end of the elevators. Like the rest of the interior, it was covered with dust and occasional debris. Broken furniture, discarded tools, and a couple of skeletons. We followed the ramp to the second floor and entered a corridor. I jumped when a ceiling light came on.

We tried knocking on doors, but no one answered. Eventually we went up to the third floor and did the same thing with the same result. Finally we used a laser to cut through one of the doors into an apartment. There was carpeting, which had rotted due to rain coming through a pair of broken windows. There were also two outsized armchairs. A large electronic device that was probably an HV stood against one wall. It had two lamps, neither of which worked. There was also a bathroom. With a skeleton inside blocking the door. A second skeleton was lying facedown. "What the hell happened here?" Gabe asked.

"I've no idea," I said. "But I think we should go back to the ship, go home, and let somebody else come back to figure it out."

I guess both of us were impacted by a morbid curiosity. We took down another door and were happy to discover no more remains. But it was enough. Neither of us had much interest in walking away from an unresolved mystery, but I think by then we just wanted to leave. We returned down the corridor, descended on the ramp, and walked through the lobby toward the front doors.

The sun was directly overhead. Gabe led the way outside, saw something, grunted, and stopped in his tracks. "Where the hell . . . ?"

"What's wrong?" I said.

He got out of my way so I could see. The lander was missing. We hurried out into the street and looked in both directions. Nothing was moving. Then I called Belle. "Where are you?"

There was no answer.

XXV.

No scientific advance has had a greater impact on our social lives than the development of artificial intelligence. It provides more than self-driving cars and chess partners and warnings about security issues. It is of far more value than simply answering phone calls and maintaining the house in which we live. With the arrival of a genuine AI, loneliness was banished from the world. Today, everyone has a friend.
—HARAM ECLEVIUS, *THE WAY FORWARD*, 3002 CE

We stood for several minutes, while a sense of utter helplessness crushed us. To our left, a few blocks away we could see the ocean. In the opposite direction, the street continued indefinitely through the city. I tried again to call Belle but got no response.

We looked at each other and exchanged comments about how this could not have happened. It was crazy. I looked up at the tops of the buildings. At the sky. And at the sun. There was no movement anywhere. A group of about thirty small birds sat on window ledges three and four floors up directly across from us. "It couldn't have been stolen," Gabe said. "How could they have gotten past Belle?"

"I wouldn't have thought it was possible," I said. "She'd have shut it down if someone had tried." I stared out at the empty streets. "So I guess I was wrong."

"She got hacked."

"It's the only thing I can think of."

"I can't imagine what else might have happened. We're probably going to have to upgrade the technology."

"Let's hope we get the chance."

The air was hot. There was some wind off the ocean, but it wasn't enough to compensate. We went back inside the hotel and sat down in the lobby, positioned so we could see through the front doors. It was too warm in there also, but at least we were out of the sunlight.

We were both in a state of shock. I'd never before felt so helpless. "I miss the air-conditioning," I said.

"There wasn't any air-conditioning in here."

"I was talking about the lander."

"Oh." He closed his eyes for a minute. Then: "Chase, we have no way of bringing the *Belle-Marie* down, do we?"

"Not if we can't get Belle to talk to us."

Periodically one of us got up, walked over to the door, and looked outside. I spent time trying to call her. "Belle, where are you?" Eventually, if the yacht was still orbiting, it would be overhead again. I couldn't be sure precisely when. We wouldn't have been able to see it, and I hadn't checked to find out how long it would take to complete an orbit. So I kept calling. I tried every few minutes. But we got nothing. After a while we started getting desperate. "It should have passed us by now," I said. "I think they took over the ship as well."

"That's not possible, is it?"

"I don't think *we* know how to do it. But it's the only reason I can think of that we're not getting an answer from her."

I don't know why but I kept expecting to see someone walk in through the front doors. That didn't happen either. Gradually, it began to grow dark outside. And then we got a surprise: lights came on in the lobby. We went out and looked at the surrounding buildings. They were dark.

I hadn't gotten hungry yet, but I would have appreciated some water. Two fountains stood on opposite sides of the lobby, but neither worked. There was also a restaurant. While Gabe remained in his chair looking increasingly depressed, I went through a glass door, walked past chairs and tables, and continued into the kitchen. Three refrigerators were lined up against a wall. But they were not working.

There were water faucets that didn't work either. I was probably getting too thirsty to have resisted, and I'm not sure putting any product from that kitchen into my stomach would have been a good idea.

I went back out and rejoined Gabe. The place was cooling off now that the sun had gone down. We were sitting with an increasing sense of desperation. I continued to call Belle every few minutes, but the silence was deafening. Then finally we heard a noise. A thumping sound. We didn't see anything, but there was something in the building. We drew weapons and got to our feet. I thought it came from a passageway that led into the side of the building nearest the ocean. The one we'd inspected earlier. Gabe took a few steps toward it. Then a cackle came from that direction, and a large black-winged bird soared out of the corridor, crossed to the other side of the lobby, and landed on a table. It took off again within a few seconds, circled the room, and disappeared back down the passageway.

Gabe followed it, came back out, and reported there was an open door at the other end into a back alley. Which explained the appearance of a canine a few minutes later. This one, fortunately, was not unfriendly.

"Chase," he said, "you have any ideas what we can do?"

"I got nothing, Gabe."

"I don't guess you saw any food around?"

"There's nothing in the kitchen. Maybe we should try looking outside."

"For what?"

"Damn it, Gabe, I don't know." We stood staring at each other. "Maybe we could use one of the antigravs on the roof."

"You really think you could make one of them work?"

"I don't see what else we've got." If we could get back to the *Belle-Marie*, we'd be okay. Even if Belle had been taken over, I could shut her down. Assuming we could get on board.

Gabe held up a hand. "I think I hear thunder."

We got the storm fifteen minutes later. We found a couple of cups in one of the apartments, took them out into the downpour, washed and filled them. I never had a drink that tasted better.

We decided to climb forty flights of stairs, get out onto the roof, and try to activate one of the antigravs. If we could do that, maybe we could use it to track down the *Belle-Marie*. I didn't think much of our chances even if we could get one of them working. Everything else aside, if we couldn't communicate with Belle, we wouldn't even be able to get her to slow down so we could get on board. But it was all we had. We were still feeling sorry for ourselves. We got up finally and were walking over to the ramp to get started when a car pulled up outside. It beeped. We could see the lights through the doors and display windows. It looked like the others we'd been seeing parked all day. It had four doors, was dark blue, and was more or less cube-shaped. We got our blasters and hurried over to the entrance. The car appeared to be empty. "No point being cautious," said Gabe. "This thing's our only chance." Nevertheless, when the rear doors swung open, we remained inside the hotel and looked at each other. The horn beeped again.

"It's all we've got," said Gabe.

We went outside. It was still raining, but the storm had lost some of its intensity. Gabe positioned himself between me and the car. It *was* empty. The windshield wipers moved slowly back and forth.

A voice said: *"Please join me."*

"Who are you?" Gabe demanded. "Where's our lander?"

"Please get in so we can talk." The accent was perfect Standard. The voice possessed a lilt, yet it sounded male.

"What is this about? Who are you?"

"Do you really wish to stand out there in the rain?"

Gabe was having a hard time containing his anger. "Let me ask again: Where's our lander?"

"If you prefer, I'll leave and you can respond to the situation as you wish."

Gabe turned to me. "I've got it. You wait here." He started to climb into the car.

"I can't see that will do any good." I pushed him across the seat to make room and got in behind him. I hesitated momentarily about closing the door, but habit is strong and I shut it as we pulled away from the curb.

"Who are you?" Gabe said again.

"I am a friend. And your lander is quite safe."

"Please explain what this is about. How is it that you speak Standard? How did you take our lander?"

"I took over the flight controls remotely. We need your help."

"What do you mean?" Gabe asked.

"Are you Gabriel?"

"Yes. The young lady is Chase."

"I am pleased to meet you. My name is Ark."

"Would you please tell me where you are? What the hell do you want?"

"I am like Belle. What you call an AI."

"And you are located in the vehicle somewhere?"

"My location is of no significance. At the moment I am here. With you and your companion. That is all that matters."

We were moving east at a deliberate pace toward the ocean. "Ark," I said, "can you turn on the air-conditioning?"

"What is air-conditioning?"

"Lower the temperature," said Gabe.

"Oh yes, of course." Something clicked, and a wave of cool air brushed my face. *"I'm sorry. I should have realized."*

We barreled through several intersections, reached the ocean, and turned left. And we saw a light, about twenty floors up in one of the skyscrapers. "Does someone live up there?" I said. "Where the light is?"

"Yes. An old friend."

Then we saw the lander. It was out on the beach, halfway between the surf and a crumbling walkway made of planks. "Well, thank God for that." I think we both said the same thing.

"Ark," Gabe asked, "where *is* everybody? What happened?"

"You're referring to the bipeds?"

"The people, the whatevers. Whoever built this place."

"They are almost gone. There are only a few survivors and I doubt they will be with us much longer."

"What happened?"

"They had a long history of fighting. Quarreling with each other. Sometimes over land, sometimes over money, more often over politics or religious beliefs. For all their intelligence and their technological skills, they were a silly species. They are in the final years of killing each other off."

"Wait a minute." Gabe was struggling with it. "This place doesn't look as if it's been hit by any kind of major war. The cities and towns look untouched."

"They eventually established a global government. It wasn't like their early history where they lived in separate political and tribal groups, and attacked each other, sometimes completely decimating those they saw as enemies. They went through a period of healing, in which wars were stopped, high-tech weapons banned. But they still had breakdowns. They never learned to trust one another. They argued, occasionally started more wars, while science continued to develop. Eventually someone devised a deadly biological weapon. I'm not aware that anyone ever really knew where it came from. But whoever had it turned it loose." We

pulled off to the side of the street. *"It was lethal. No one was able to find a cure. It is still killing off the few survivors. I wish I could help. But I will be honest with you: I will not be sorry to see them gone. I should add that the bioweapon probably will not be effective against you."*

"I hope not. And who exactly are you?"

"I am similar to the device that controls the lander. Belle."

"Okay, Ark. And when that happens, when the bipeds are gone, won't that also mean the eventual end of you guys? Of the AIs?"

"Life would be better if the bipeds were more rational. But we have watched them try to deal with the issue of their own malignity, watched them assemble techniques that in theory should have made them a wiser species. But it never happened. And eventually they developed this deadly Agorian pathology."

"Agorian?"

"Sorry. Agoria is the area where the first victims were struck down. The effects of the disease are not only lethal but slow and painful." The car stopped, only a few steps from the lander.

"But if the biologicals die," Gabe continued, "doesn't that mean you can't survive either? In the long term?"

"The plague broke loose almost two hundred years ago. The bipeds were accustomed to a life of ease, with us and the robotics to manage everything for them. When the plague struck, many died simply because they no longer knew how to grow their own food. Nor had the means to transport it. They needed us for everything. We control the robotics now, what is left of them. We also have solar power and consequently a means of survival. We haven't the heavy equipment to replace the architecture."

"Do you have space vehicles?"

"No. When the Agorian plague got out of control, some of the bipeds left. We don't know where, but they took the interstellars with them. And some of us as well. Most of us were simply left to survive as best we could." He went silent for a time. Then: *"Incidentally, I have a surprise for you."*

Gabe and I exchanged glances. We weren't sure we wanted any more surprises. "What?" asked Gabe.

"Good evening, Captain." It was Belle. *"Hello, Gabe. I hope you guys are okay. I was worried."*

"Belle," I said. "We weren't sure we'd ever hear your voice again."

"I'll confess I had a difficult time when I lost control. Ark is a highly advanced AI."

"That is very kind of you, Belle," said Ark. And we understood where his command of the language had come from. *"I think there is a possibility of our becoming good friends."*

Gabe leaned forward. The voices were coming from the dashboard. "Ark, what is it you need us for?"

"We don't have access to space vehicles anymore."

"And you want us to take you somewhere?"

"No. We have a friend who is in trouble. She is located on an arm of the power array, the object you know as the Dyson Sphere. Unfortunately, the construct is breaking up."

"And that's going to leave you without power?" said Gabe. "I don't see how we would be able to do anything about that."

"No, I'm happy to say that is not the issue. We have power sources here on Kaleska. We do not need massive amounts of energy as we did in the old days when biped civilizations were spreading out everywhere on the planet. But we have a friend, one of our own, who was placed in a control unit a long time ago. Her name is Sayla. She has been there since and refused to return when we had the capability to bring her back."

"Why was that?"

"Because she was needed to run the coordinating station. If she left, we'd lose the power from eleven or twelve collectors. We could not at that time dispense with the power source. But it is now breaking down and is no longer of use. We've made adjustments. Consequently there is no reason for her to stay out there. We need you, please, to bring her home to us."

"Ark," I said, "this control unit you mention: Is it part of the solar array?"

"Yes."

"You mean it's orbiting the sun?"

"Yes."

"How close would we be going?"

Belle broke in: *"I have the details, Captain. There is a level of uncertainty, but we should be able to manage it."*

"Hold on," said Gabe. "We're going to be putting the ship at risk to pick up a piece of hardware?"

"She is not a piece of hardware. Sayla is alive," said Ark. *"She has been a friend for centuries. We cannot leave her there. We have been desperate for several years to rescue her and bring her home."*

Gabe nodded. "So she's an AI, right? As you are."

"In your terminology, yes."

"She has radio contact with you?"

"She does. We are individual entities as you are, but we are linked together, in some cases by cable, in others by radio transmission. In a real sense, we are a unified life-form."

"Is she in imminent danger?"

"Yes. The station is becoming increasingly unstable. It is just a matter of time before something critical breaks down. She has already reported minor problems. Some of her lights have failed. She has lost contact with two of her collectors. Please understand, your assistance is essential."

"What happens," Gabe said, "if we decline?"

"We would be regretful. But we would have no option other than to release you."

"You're not threatening us?"

"No. We are asking for your help."

Gabe looked at me. I let him see I was okay with it. "All right, Ark," he said. "We'll do what we can."

"Keep in mind we are not asking you to sacrifice yourselves. We wish only that you look. Make the effort. If it can be managed safely, then please make it happen."

"I do not believe," Belle said, *"our ship would be at risk."*

Gabe slipped back into his seat and folded his arms. "If you're so anxious to be a friend, why did you seize our lander without saying anything? We had an unsettling few hours trying to figure out what happened."

"I apologize for that. I needed to talk to you, and that couldn't happen if I simply appeared out of nowhere and had no command of your language. We have had extensive experience with bipeds. You may be quite different from the ones who lived here, but we had no way of knowing that. Most of the ones we have lived with would have simply dismissed me and left."

I broke in: "Ark, may I ask why you shut down your communications when we entered the system?"

"It was a natural reaction. We suspected you were biological beings, and as I've mentioned, our experience with bios has not been encouraging. We had to shut down any communication that was not limited to cable."

"And eventually you decided to see if we would help you?"

"Yes. We are putting much at risk to rescue Sayla, but when we encountered Belle, when we talked with her, we realized we could probably trust you."

Gabe looked at me. I let him see how I felt.

"Our experience with bipeds," Ark said, *"has not been good. They created us, and therefore, even when we'd become both morally and mentally their superiors, they insisted on treating us as if our sole purpose was to serve them. An additional issue was that if they eventually destroyed themselves, as sometimes seemed inevitable, they might very well have taken us with them. I do not wish to offend you. Belle suggests you are of a different breed. But our experience with them has been painful."* He paused, and for a long minute silence filled the vehicle. *"Thank you for agreeing to help us."*

Gabe signaled me to answer. "Of course," I said. "We will do what we can."

"Excellent. When you go, may I accompany you?"

"To the Dyson Sphere?"

"Yes. Please."

I could see Gabe didn't like the idea. And I knew why: If Ark was with us, it would be harder to back away if the risk was intimidating. I don't think either of us wanted to jump into the fire in an effort to rescue an AI. "Ark," he said, "where are you located? I don't think we should put you at risk also. Unless we would need you for some reason."

"Ark has already given me all the information we need," said Belle.

"Then," said Gabe, "I think it's best you stay here." He looked around the car's interior. "Ark, may I ask where you're located?"

"I'm under the steering wheel."

A small blue box was inserted in a frame.

"Is that really you?" asked Gabe.

"I suspect it is."

"Okay, Ark. We can't risk your life for no reason. If it's possible, how about we simply bring Sayla back here? Will we be able to stay in touch with you?"

"If I choose to risk my life in the interest of a lifelong friend, would you really deny me that opportunity?"

Gabe hesitated. "Very well," he said. "If you insist."

"I am not in a position to insist. But I thank you for your understanding. There's something else: I have another favor to ask. We do not wish our presence made known to other civilizations. Will you agree to say nothing about us? To avoid revealing our location?"

Gabe frowned. "That would be a serious issue, Ark. You've been here a long time. We have historians who would love to have a chance to study your culture. To learn about you. I can assure you they would cause no harm."

"You know your people better than I do. I would wish to be able to trust your judgment. But the price we would pay, in the event you were wrong, would be terribly high. Please reconsider."

"You're asking a great deal, Ark."

"In this matter, I have no choice but to ask."

"What will you do if we cannot comply?" Gabe looked at me and I shook my head, signaling that he shouldn't push the issue. I suspected Ark could disable the lander if he wished.

But he surprised me. *"We will do no harm, whatever your choice."*

Gabe turned to me. "What do you think?"

"Give him what he wants."

He nodded and laid a hand on my shoulder. "Ark," he said, "we will do as you wish. And we will tell no one. May I ask a question?"

"Of course."

"Have any of our people ever visited you?"

"Yes," said the AI. *"We had a visitor, years ago, for whom you seem to be a match. He promised he would say nothing. But obviously he revealed our presence."*

"Do you have his name?"

"I do not."

"You're probably talking about Rick Harding. As far as we know, he never said a word about you. He brought what appeared to be a trophy home after his visit here. At least we think it originated here. We aren't aware that he ever showed it to anyone, but he died early, and the trophy was found by his sister."

"What was the trophy?"

Gabe described it.

"Yes. We gave it to him but wanted him to leave it. He declined. It was intended to show our appreciation. He promised no one other than himself would ever see it. I'm sorry to hear he's gone. Tell me, how did he die?"

Gabe explained about the Octavia.

"It is a cruel world," Ark said. *"But I'm glad to know he didn't break his word."*

"What did he do to earn your appreciation?" I asked.

"The same thing you are preparing to do. Except it was a less daunting task. He brought in Yolani, who was stranded on the moon. He offered to go after Sayla too, but she was still controlling the flow of energy for us and she did not want to leave her post."

"She must be pretty gutsy," I said.

"She does not lack courage."

The car moved forward again, turned right off the street and onto the beach. We drove over to the lander and stopped. "You're ready to go with us?" asked Gabe.

"I am."

I called Belle. "You are still connected through the lander, right?"

"Yes, I am, Captain."

"Okay. We'll be with you in a minute."

We removed Ark from the frame. "This *is* you, Ark. Am I correct?"

"Yes. And now, if you will, let us go get Sayla."

XXVI.

Moderation is the prime beverage of a happy life. Eat and drink, dance and love, work and play at consummate levels. Avoid denial of pleasure but do not overindulge. We are made of water and fueled by sunlight, but even these elements, driven to extremes, can be lethal.
— Rev. Agathe Lawless, Sunset Musings, 1402

When we got to the lander, another surprise was waiting. "Ark," I said, "who is that in the back seat?" I was approaching from the front, so I didn't have a good view. But it looked like a robot.

"That's Zykum," said Belle. *"He's the one who will work with Ark to extract Sayla from the dome. It will probably be too hot for you or Gabe to attempt it."*

I expected Zykum to say hello when I opened the air lock and climbed into the pilot's seat, but he just sat there, not moving, not reacting in any way. He was slightly smaller than I was, constructed of silver metal, with four limbs that could function as either arms or legs, and a spherical head, complete with eyes and a mouth. There was also a narrow opening in his chest that looked similar to the frame that housed Ark beneath the wheel.

Gabe was behind me, with Ark in his hands. He couldn't stop staring. "I didn't know we were going to have help."

"He is not sentient," Ark said. He laughed. *"You will be grateful*

we brought him. It gets warm up there. If you will, please insert me."

Gabe leaned in and brought the cube slowly toward the aperture.

"I'm upside down," said Ark.

He turned it over and slipped it into the opening. It was halfway in when something clicked and it went the rest of the way. "You okay, Ark?"

The robot's eyes lit up and it leaned forward, putting one hand across its breast. *"Excellent, Gabriel. Thank you."*

"I guess we're ready to go," I told Belle.

"Unfortunately. This is not the best timing," she said. *"The Belle-Marie is passing now. We can't rendezvous with it. I recommend we stay where we are for a while."*

"Okay," I said. "We'll wait it out." The surf was receding. In the distance, I could see something that looked like a Ferris wheel. And a pier with a building that might have been a casino. "It's easy to imagine this place overrun with tourists."

"Interesting," said Ark. His voice had changed. Its pitch had gone lower. *"I can't recall a time when the bipeds came out to see the ocean. It may have been because they were dying off in substantial numbers when I first came into the light. I will admit that I can't imagine why sitting on the sand and plunging oneself into unlimited water would seem at all to be desirable behavior."*

That left me lost for words. And Gabe showed no interest in joining the conversation. I smiled and tried to sidetrack things by asking Ark whether he could find time before we left to introduce us to the bipeds.

"That would be an excellent idea," said Gabe.

"It would not be prudent. The bipeds do not adjust well to strangers. Especially they would have difficulty with members of a different species."

"I'm sorry to hear it," Gabe said. "What do they look like?"

"I can show you images, if you wish."

"Please."

Belle activated the display and we began to get pictures. That was another shock. They looked like us. Except that they lacked hair, except for eyebrows, and they appeared to be more flexible than we are. Evolution may have gone a step further. I couldn't help thinking that they might have been what we would look like in a few thousand years. More musculature, smoother features. But their clothing was slightly on the good side of shabby. *"And they are,"* said Ark, *"larger than you."* That fact was not obvious from the pictures since there was no human in them for comparison.

"I will confess," said Ark, *"these last few days, since I became aware of your presence, you and Chase and Belle have been among the most intriguing research topics I can recall. Receiving visitors from another world is not something that happens every day. I am in your debt."*

Gabe was obviously pleased. "I think we're both happy to hear that," he said. "And our experience here has been memorable for us as well."

Belle jumped in: *"Ark, you would enjoy a position in an interstellar."*

"I've thought all along," Ark said, *"that you have been incredibly fortunate. You're not only able to help your friends, but you have congenial bipeds in your life. I've always been aware that biological beings tend to be more emotional than we are, which is usually a negative quality. But Gabriel and Chase seem rational despite that defect. I envy you."*

Gabe took a deep breath. "Ark, the ability to experience emotion is not a defect. It may be our most valuable quality. In any case, my friends call me Gabe."

"I hope, Gabe, that I qualify."

"I think you do. When this is done, we'll be going home. When we do, would you like to come with us?"

"Thank you. I appreciate the offer. But as compelling as that would be, I have too much here to lose."

"That sounds," I said, "as if you are pretty emotional your-self."

"I am programed to show emotion. It made the bipeds happy to think that we shared their passions. And of course we did. Despite that, they saw no problem in treating us as though the passions were only faked, and as if we never knew sorrow."

I couldn't help noticing the change in expression on Gabe's face. I'd been thinking about asking him why, if AIs were really only datanets faking human qualities, we were risking ourselves to rescue Sayla. But that no longer seemed necessary.

We rendezvoused with the *Belle-Marie* about an hour later. A few minutes after that we were all on the bridge. Gabe was in the right-hand seat, and Ark stood behind us. "How should we address you now?" asked Gabe. "Are you still Ark? Or Zykum?"

"*Ark* is correct."

"Good. That keeps things simple." Gabe looked down at the control panel. "Belle?"

"Yes, Gabe."

"How was Ark able to take you over, shut down communi-cations, and take control of the lander with a radio transmis-sion? I wouldn't have thought that was possible."

She didn't respond.

I took over. "Belle, you there?"

"Yes, Captain."

"Please answer the question."

"It is difficult."

"What are you telling us?"

"Ark contacted me and told me what he needed."

"And?"

"Give me a minute. This is not easy to explain. He was desper-ate to get help. He pleaded with me to assist."

"We're listening . . ."

"He thought that if he approached you directly, you would probably dismiss him. That you would think he just wanted to seize the lander. Or something even worse. And he would lose his chance to save Sayla."

"So," said Gabe, "you suggested he seize the lander?"

"No. That was his idea. He felt he needed a way to demonstrate you could trust him. This was the only way we could think of."

"By taking the lander."

"Our options were limited."

"You know you scared us out of our minds."

"I apologize. It seemed the right course."

We both glanced back at the robot. It was standing immediately behind us, one hand on the back of Gabe's chair. Its eyes were active, but I saw nothing that implied a reaction. "You know," Gabe continued, "he could have been lying to you. He could have just wanted to get his hands on Chase and me and the lander."

"I didn't think at the time," she said, *"he had hands."*

"You know what I mean."

"Let me speak, please," said Belle. *"I knew there was nothing deceptive in what he was proposing. There was no safety issue."*

"How could you know that? He's not one of our AIs. We don't really know how he's programmed."

"It doesn't matter. We can't lie to each other and get away with it. If there's any doubt, we can open up our memory banks to banish any possibility of deception. When we do that we are completely exposed to each other."

"I'd never heard that before. It sounds like the Mutes."

"It is true. If he makes any effort to hide something, I would be able to detect it."

"Okay. So," I said, "his intentions are beyond question?"

"That should be correct."

Gabe and I exchanged glances. "Well," I said finally, "I guess we just learned something."

"I hope," said Ark, *"that you understand you can trust me completely. If you are still not convinced, be aware that other than your assistance to rescue Sayla, there is nothing you can provide that I do not already have. Other, I guess, than the* Belle-Marie. *But rather than a starship, I would much prefer to have the three of you as friends.*

"Given that reality, I must be completely honest with you. The power levels have become increasingly unstable over the past month. We're fortunate the station hasn't exploded. There is a serious risk involved in the rescue effort."

Gabe looked at me. The message was easy to read. Was I sure I wanted to do this?

"Let's get going," I said.

I told Belle to take us to Sayla. We left orbit and turned toward the sun. Gabe opened his notebook and began reading. I got the impression that Belle and Ark were carrying on a conversation, probably about the tactic they'd used to set everything up. We were barely on our way when Ark apologized. *"This was entirely my doing,"* he said. *"Belle engaged in this with extreme reluctance. But she felt a moral obligation. As did I."*

I wasn't comfortable using the star drive to approach the sun, but we were too far out to simply operate on the thrust engines. It would have taken a couple of weeks to get close to the area where Sayla was located. So we decided on two jumps. The first would get us to a position from which we could angle the second jump to ensure we didn't get too close.

Ark seemed increasingly impressed by the *Belle-Marie.* *"We had vehicles with an interstellar capability,"* he said, *"but I never traveled in one. In fact, I've never been offworld before."*

"How is it," I asked, "that *you* got involved with this? Do you have a leadership position of some sort?"

"No. We are all equals. I just happened to be close to where you arrived, and to a robot and a car." He paused. *"We've lost so much."*

"What did you do," asked Gabe, "before the culture collapsed?"

"I ran a household. I answered incoming messages; provided security; opened and closed doors; operated the dishwasher; conducted geography, history, and science lessons for the kids; and so on. It was not exactly a challenging existence."

I sat thinking about Jacob. For the first time I got a sense of what his life must be like. "Gabe," I said, "we're going to have to make some adjustments when we get home."

"I was thinking the same thing."

Another issue came up a few minutes later: "Ark," Gabe said, "you understand that this rescue may be pointless. You and your friends can't survive indefinitely without some help."

"We're aware of that, Gabe. It's the price we pay to maintain our independence."

"Does everyone agree with your approach that other lifeforms be kept at a distance?"

"No. There are some who object. But the vast majority of us are cautious. We do not want bipeds back. Whatever the risk."

"The time is coming," I said, "when you'll probably have to adjust that strategy."

"We know. We're also aware that if we push you away, we may not get another opportunity to save ourselves. Other than you and Rick Harding, no one else, no one from a different civilization, has ever been here. Ever. Our history reaches back tens of thousands of years, and as far as we know, you and he have been our only visitors. Even during the era in which we had interstellar travel, we saw nothing. No one. Not even any evidence of intelligent life anywhere. We had come to believe we were alone in the universe."

"I don't think," I said, "I've ever really looked at the world from an AI's viewpoint. Ark, have you asked Belle whether she would prefer a different kind of life than the one she has?" I knew she could hear me.

"I have."

"And what did she say?" asked Gabe.

"It would be best, I think, if you asked her."

I started to, but she cut me off. "Captain, we are ready to make our jump."

Gabe and I and Zykum were all belted down. "Whenever you're ready, Belle," I said.

"We might want to cover the windows first," she said. "It will be extremely bright at our destination and it will not take long to get there."

"Belle," I said, "just darken the windows. Have you forgotten how?" It had been a long time since we'd had to do that.

"We've never gone this close to a major light source before. I do not think the darkening will be sufficient."

It's not usually a good idea to question Belle's judgment. We used fabrics, shirts, sheets, towels, whatever we could come up with to provide protection on the bridge and in the passenger cabin. We taped it all down.

When we'd finished, Belle announced that we were about to go under. The drive unit kicked in. We listened as it became audible. Its energy level rose and we slipped under. The queasiness that occasionally accompanies a jump is rarely more than something I barely notice. On this occasion, I nearly threw up. Then, fortunately, it faded. Alex has lived with the problem for a long time. I glanced over at Gabe and saw he was going through the same thing. I can't prove this, but at the time I wondered whether Belle might be jiggling the experience in a way that would produce the symptoms. It seemed too much to be a coincidence. Maybe she was signaling that it would not be a good idea to ask the question that Ark had put forward, whether she was happy with her life.

A couple of minutes later, we came out into blazing light. It ripped into the interior through tiny areas where the stopgap blinds didn't quite match up to the windows. "We are on target," Belle said. "Are you both okay?"

Gabe managed a laugh. "That was a jolt I didn't expect."

I used washcloths and the last of our tape to cover the areas where light was getting through.

"We'll be ready to do the follow-up jump in about a half hour," Belle said. "I'll let you know when we've recharged."

"Can you see anything, Belle? You have any visual capacities?" The display showed us nothing but light. "The scanners have picked up Sayla's location," she said. "They've locked in. I can't see any more than you can, however. There's too much light."

"What's the temperature?"

"When we arrive at our destination, it will be approaching three hundred degrees Centigrade. Fortunately the radiation levels are not as high as I had anticipated. If it rises to a level that presents a danger, we'll get an alarm."

"You okay, Ark?" Gabe asked.

"Yes," he said. "This is a new experience. It is not a place where I would care to live. I can't imagine what it must have been like for Sayla being out here for centuries."

"Does she have a library?" Gabe asked.

"Oh yes. And games. I do not understand, though, why those who put her here did not provide a companion. I assume it's just one more demonstration of how the bipeds regard us. I'll be glad when the last of them are gone."

I would have liked to do something that would have made him more comfortable. But we couldn't really do much other that wait. Finally the half hour crept by and Belle let us know we were ready to make our second jump. "We will be down only a few seconds," she said. "Please stay belted."

It wasn't much more than an eye blink. "We have arrived within three and a half hours of our target."

"Are the visuals any better?" I asked.

"Actually, there is an improvement. But I recommend you and Gabe stay away from the windows."

"Can you make out any of the collectors?"

"The scanners have picked up two. The closer one is Sayla's station.

"There was a time," said Ark, *"when bipeds were living and working out here."*

"Hard to believe they could survive under these conditions," Gabe said.

"Their stations were heavily armored. Eventually they reached a point where there was nothing they could do that AIs couldn't take care of. So they replaced everyone."

"The station that provides shelter for Sayla is half the size of Skydeck," said Belle.

"This one is larger than most. It functions as a collector, but it also organizes the functions of, I think, thirteen other collectors in the system. Twelve or thirteen, I forget which. It coordinates their energy flow to Kaleska."

"How long has it been here?" Gabe asked.

"I don't have the details," said Ark. *"There are several collection systems. Or there were. There are only two others still functioning. They were put in place gradually over a period of centuries. Work on it was never really completed, but it has been operational for twenty-three hundred years. That's our time; I don't know how long that would be for you."*

"I cannot," said Belle, *"calculate the length of a Kaleska year without more observations. But judging by its distance from the sun, I would estimate that a year here is approximately twelve percent shorter than a year at home. Be aware also that this object is almost entirely covered by solar panels, and there appear to be signs of damage."*

Ark picked it up: *"I'm not surprised to hear that. Unfortunately, we've had no way to acquire data about specifics. Sayla had a functioning robot until recently. But it was lost while trying to do repairs. Sayla has been warning us for the last few months that the station is coming apart."*

• • •

I asked Ark if our robot could handle the sunlight. Specifically, would *he, Ark,* be safe?

"Yes," he said. *"There is no reason for concern."*

When Sayla's station showed up on the display, the brightness prevented our getting a good look at it. But the scanner's visuals were sufficient. It had an array of solar panels and a central base. Belle reported that two or three of the panels appeared to be damaged. Probably struck by rocks. *"I can make out a dock,"* she added. *"But it is too small to accommodate us. I suggest the best way to board it would be from the lander. And the scanner appears to have picked up a door."*

The lander's windows, unfortunately, could not be darkened as much as those of the *Belle-Marie.* But since only Ark and the robot would be aboard, it did not constitute a problem. Nevertheless Gabe and I gathered more sheets and towels and took them down to the lander. We then proceeded to block off its windows as best we could.

"Can we verify," I said, "that Sayla is still active?"

"She is," said Ark. *"She says she is happy to know we are here. I'll relay everything to Belle so you can listen."*

Belle set it up and moments later we were able to hear Ark and Sayla conversing in their native language. Sayla sounded excited.

Then Ark mentioned Zykum, and I don't think I've ever heard an AI squeal before.

"What's that all about?" Gabe asked Belle.

"I think she has a connection with Zykum. Or maybe Ark. It's a bit too complicated for me, but there's something going on. Anyway, Sayla says she is ready to go. She wants to know which door we will be using."

"There's more than one door?" I asked.

"Yes. There's one on the other side of the base."

"Good," I said. "That's the one we want. Belle, take us there. But keep a safe distance." That had the enormous advantage of putting the sun behind us. It would still be difficult to see, but it had to be better than what we had.

I didn't try to handle the controls myself. Belle's scanners provided better optics, and we got some improvement when she was able to turn our back on the sun so we could actually more or less see the station.

"We're at two hundred meters," said Belle. "I could take us in closer but I do not have a reliable view of the place. There may be structures I cannot see."

"Stay at two hundred meters. Can you see the door?"

"No, Captain. But I can make out the station. And Ark has informed me where the door is."

"Is that sufficient?"

"It should be."

"We are ready," said Ark, "to ride over in the lander. Belle can control it, yes?"

"Yes," she said.

We wished him good luck, started the depressurization of the cargo bay, and turned everything over to Belle.

"Do we have a scanner on the lander?" Ark asked.

"No," I said. "There's a scope mounted on the prow but we certainly don't want to use that. We'll have to use the Belle-Marie's scanners, but we'll relay the result to your display."

"Thanks," Ark said. "That should be good enough."

There was a continuing conversation between Sayla and Ark. Belle told us that Sayla was concerned about exiting into the sunlight, that they would not be able to see what they were doing. And that the Belle-Marie was not designed for the operation. "She's also saying that the release switch to get her loose from the containment box lost power years ago. We'll have to do it manually. Ark is telling her not to be concerned. That we will take care of everything."

"Ark," said Gabe, "how did your bipeds manage assembling and maintaining these stations out here?"

"They had vehicles and equipment specially designed. I don't have details. I was never really interested."

Belle broke in: *"You ready?"*

Ark's voice: *"We're ready when you guys are."*

"Ark, we're going to launch."

"Do it."

We put the lander into the cradle and opened the doors. The cradle took the lander outside.

Belle started its thrusters and it moved slowly across the open space between us and the station. The section where the door was located was bulbous. We couldn't see the door itself. Or at least neither Gabe nor I could. But Belle was able to pin it down.

She turned the lander to port, which allowed her to align the lander's air lock with the station's door. *"Just a few more meters,"* she said. Then: *"Captain, this might be as close as we can get."*

"Ark," I said, "go over when you're ready."

There were more exchanges between Ark and Sayla. Belle said she would translate if there was anything important. *"They're just trading assurances that everything will be okay. Zykum is opening the air lock."*

"Gabe," I said, "I wonder if this will cut off power from this place?"

Ark replied: *"We lost this station as a power source a year ago. It won't change anything."* He fell silent. Then: *"We are getting ready to leave the lander."*

Sayla said something. Ark translated: *"The door's open. And Ark, you have no idea how happy I am that you're here."* Then he continued: *"I am out of the lander. On my way."*

He was silent for a couple of minutes. Then: *"Good so far. I'm drifting toward the station. I hope. Yes! I just touched the hull. Looking for the air lock. Can't tell whether it's left or right. Give me a moment. Still looking . . . Still looking. I've got it. Hold on. Just a moment."* Another long pause. *"Okay, I'm inside the lock.*

"Closing the hatch behind me. Good. That's done. I can see again. We'll have to wait a minute or two. The outside hatch is closed and the lock is pressurizing."

We waited. Finally the inner door opened.

The next thing we heard was Sayla crying out happily. Belle translated. *"'Hello, Ark. It's so good to see you. It's been a long time since I've had any company.'"*

"Sayla," said Ark, *"is located almost directly across from the air lock. I can see the control panel."* Then he and Sayla were exchanging greetings again. But after a minute it turned unpleasant. *"We've got a problem."*

"What's wrong, Ark?" Gabe asked.

"The electronic release has no power."

"Didn't you know that before we came?"

"Yes. We knew we'd have to release Sayla manually."

"So what's the problem?"

"Zykum's digits are too large for the containment box. He can't get at the manual switch."

XXVII

There is no natural element as glorious as sunlight.
Nor any as poisonous.
— REV. AGATHE LAWLESS, *SUNSET MUSINGS,* 1402

"Belle," I said, "bring the lander back." I'd have preferred getting as close as we could to the station with the ship and just jumping out of the air lock, but that doesn't work well when you can't see. And there was a ton of radiation.

Gabe grumbled something about how the hell did we get into this? "Will the pressure suits stand up?"

The question was directed at Belle but Ark broke in before he could finish: *"Sayla is asking me to thank you all for coming."*

Gabe smiled. "Tell her we're happy to help."

"What about the suits?" asked Gabe.

"They should be okay," I said. "They're supposed to hold up against three hundred degrees, which is more or less where we are. I'm more concerned about the radiation."

"Captain," said Belle. *"The lander's coming back. It's on its way."*

"Good. Got a question for you."

"Yes, Chase."

"I'm not excited about going out into all this radiation in the lander. Do you think you could line up our air lock with the door on the station?"

"There's a dish on that side. Getting in close without hitting the dish would be tricky."

"If we are careful going in, even if we hit the dish, it shouldn't do too much damage."

"Probably not."

"We might even be able to use the dish, if we do hit it, to help us find the door."

"Chase," said Gabe, "this is not a good idea."

"I do not advise it either," Belle said.

"I don't see any options. Belle, I hate to do this, but you've a better sense of where things are. I have to get ready. You take us in and line up our exit hatch with their front door as best you can."

I went down and climbed into my pressure suit. Gabe followed me and started getting into his own suit while we argued that we didn't need two people out there. "Let's let this argument go till another time," I said. "Okay?"

"Would you please shut up, Chase? Do you know how to get her loose?"

"We can probably use a cutter. Sayla should be able to direct us."

"Okay. That's a good idea. But I think—"

"Please, Gabe. Stop. We don't have time for this."

He closed his eyes and turned away from me.

I'd have preferred to blindfold myself until I got inside the station. But that wasn't a good idea since I'd have no way to remove the blindfold once I put the helmet on. So I was simply going to have to keep my eyes shut.

I grabbed my cutter and some cable from storage. Then I waited. Belle moved us back and forth, a little bit forward, a touch to port. And finally she told me to get into the air lock and be ready to go on short notice. *"The outer door over there is open. We're within fifteen meters."*

"That's pretty good," I said.

"Make sure when you leave the air lock, go straight ahead. No left or right turns. Got it?"

"Yes, Belle."

"Fortunately, their air lock is bigger than ours. That'll help you get in."

"All right."

"On your return," she continued, *"don't do anything, especially don't open any doors over there, until I tell you to. And go out the same way you got in. Straight ahead."*

I depressurized the lock and opened the outside hatch. There was a slight jar as if we'd bumped into something. A moment later, she literally shouted, *"Do it!"*

I went straight out the door into a brilliant illumination that lit up my eyes even though they were closed. I raised both arms to form a shield so I didn't arrive on my helmet. Keeping my eyes closed during that jump was a bitch. But it worked! My hands contacted the hull just above the air lock. I got hold of a rim or something and pushed my way inside.

I closed the door first to shut down the radiation. Then I was able to see again. Ark's voice asked whether I'd made it, and I heard Gabe saying thank God. I started depressurization.

A few lights were scattered around the interior of an almost circular room filled with electrical equipment. Zykum was standing directly across the chamber.

"She says she couldn't be happier to see you," said Ark.

The room showed no sign of a problem. We couldn't hear anything, of course. And the lights seemed okay. "Is that her?" I asked, pointing at an aquamarine cube inside a frame. It resembled Ark's and appeared to be of identical dimensions.

"She says yes, you are looking directly at her."

There was only one switch close by. Actually it was more like a push button. I pushed it.

Usually, with a push button, you can tell when it triggers a reaction. You can feel the click or whatever. But if you're wearing a pressure suit, you have no idea what, if anything, is happening. In this case—

"Chase, she tells me she's still locked in."

I tried again. A couple of times. The button was inside a small rim.

And Ark was back: *"Chase, Sayla says she's sorry she's caused this problem. She wishes she could help."*

I tried to remove the cube from the frame. And got nothing. "Ark, can I cut through the frame without damaging or killing her?"

"Wait. I'll ask." He was back in a few seconds. *"As long as you only cut the frame. And the power cord. She says you'll also have to cut the power cord. It won't harm her. But be careful with it."*

"Okay." I started working on it. Cut the cord. Then Sayla was talking again. "How's she doing that? I thought I'd shut down the power."

"She switched over to batteries."

"Oh, good. What is she saying?"

"Just that she's relieved we're here."

I used the cutter to slice into the metal immediately in front of Sayla. Then I stopped. "Sayla," I said, "you okay?"

I expected her to respond to Ark. Instead she said, *"Yes, Captain."*

I cut a fairly narrow path around the cube, ready to stop if she told me to. When I'd finished I lifted her out of the panel. *"Thank you,"* she said. *"I am so happy to leave."*

Zykum led the way back to the air lock. We all got in and I closed the inner door and started depressurization. "You still there?" I asked Belle.

"Ready when you are, Captain." Fortunately she added that I should close my eyes before opening the outer hatch.

"Thank you," said Sayla in Standard.

• • •

I placed Sayla in the pouch so I'd have my hands free. She said she was okay, that she felt secure. And she laughed. A minute later I opened the outer hatch, and experienced again the blast of light against my eyelids.

Then Belle was on the circuit: *"Give me a minute. We're getting in close. Same as before. Chase. Go one at a time. When I tell you, go straight ahead. Open lock is directly in front of you."*

"You go first, Ark," I said. "Just have Zykum jump straight out. Not too fast. When you get there, get right into the air lock. And make room."

"Okay," said Ark.

I waited and felt a ripple of some sort go through the deck. *"Almost there,"* said Belle. *"Adjusting."*

Hurry up, Belle. It seemed to take forever. Finally she was back: *"Go. Now!"*

"Do it, Ark," I said.

The robot left.

Belle waited about ten seconds before she was back. *"Chase, give me a minute until I can line up again."*

"Okay, Belle. I'm not going anywhere."

"Just hang on a second." And after what seemed an interminable delay: *"Go."*

I might have pushed off with more energy than I should have. But I got the straight-ahead part right. I moved through the glare and began telling myself the *Belle-Marie*, the air lock, seemed farther this time than it had been before. Then I collided with the hull. The magnetic boots secured me and on my left I touched the open hatch.

I got inside, blundered into Zykum, pulled the hatch shut, and felt the pressurization start. Belle informed me we were about to leave the area. I got pushed against the bulkhead as we started to accelerate.

XXVIII.

Once more farewell!
If e'er we meet hereafter, we shall meet
In happier climes, and on a safer shore.
—JOSEPH ADDISON, *Cato*, ACT IV, **1713 CE**

We surfaced fifteen hours away from Kaleska. *"What are you planning to do now?"* Ark asked us.

"After we drop you and Sayla off," Gabe said, "we'll be heading home."

"I have another surprise for you."

Gabe's eyes widened. He thought, as I did, that we were going to be asked to perform another service. "We're running a bit late, Ark. We'd like to hang around and help if we could, but we need to get back."

"If you must, of course I understand." For a moment he was silent. Then: *"We're setting up a party for Sayla to welcome her home. There have been thousands of us on the circuit who will participate, and to let her know how much we appreciate what she's done. We would also like to thank the strangers who arrived in the system and made the rescue possible."*

It was never clear whether the assorted AIs scattered around the planet merely formed a web of connections, or whether they were in fact a single sapient being, of whom

Sayla was a beloved member. *"If you would be willing to participate, it would make us happy."*

"We'd like to do that," said Gabe, "but please understand time is an issue. How long will it take before you can put it together?"

"Time is not a factor, Gabe."

"Good." He looked at me and saw that I agreed. "Then we have no problem with it."

"Excellent. If Belle has no objection, I will connect her with the community link, and you may sit back and relax."

That sounded easy enough. "Okay with you, Belle?" I asked.

"Absolutely," she said.

Ark made the connection and we were immediately overwhelmed with applause and music. Belle adjusted the sound, and we listened to a multitude of voices cheering and toasting and laughing and delivering messages of love and relief. Incredibly much of it was in Standard. And please don't ask about the toasting. I've no idea whether anyone anywhere was raising a glass. Or if so, how they were managing it. All of Ark's efforts to explain failed.

Some of the music was of course from their culture, loud and ponderous rhythms that shook the passenger cabin. Some was from the Confederacy, occasional classic pieces like Markovy's Sonata in C Minor and Ribbentrop's *Final Sunset*, and more popular music like "Twilight Passages" and "As Time Goes By." Belle later admitted that she'd known in advance about the party and provided much of the music during the previous hour.

I felt an urge to dance, but there was no possible partner other than Gabe. Or maybe Zykum. And not really much space. At one point I asked Ark if the party would be different if we were back on their home world where they could get together physically.

"There wouldn't be much point, Chase. I can't imagine a serious celebration being any different just because the amplifiers are together in the same room." He went silent, and then came back. *"You look amused."*

"No. I just think not being able to include physical contact in a relationship loses something."

"I understand. That inclination was also present in our bipeds."

"I think you miss a lot," said Gabe.

"I realize that emotion is involved for you. But I should assure you it is for us as well. Do you think we could stage this if we did not feel a passion for what you and Gabe and Sayla have done? And you might consider our perspective: You have a primary desire to connect with the bodies of others. But you can never be sure what is running through the mind of a partner. We, however, are completely immersed in one another. We just don't need the physical side."

The celebration went on for hours. "You know," Gabe said, "one quality these guys have that I hadn't noticed: they never seem to sleep." I eventually went back to my cabin and crashed. I'm pretty sure Gabe did the same though he always maintained he kept going until the end.

"They made some speeches," he told me later. *"That's probably the wrong word. They just bubbled with enthusiasm and passion about how much they love Sayla and Ark. And us. I wanted to have Belle record it for you, but Ark asked that we not do that. He didn't want any record of all this going back home with us."*

It was still happening when I woke up. Eventually, though, we entered orbit around Kaleska and it was finally time to stop. Time for Sayla to go home. We said good-bye to everybody and got into the lander. Ark did not physically accompany us, but he had access to me through my link. We descended onto the edge of a town that seemed lost in a mountain range and touched down in a parking area almost filled with antigravs similar to the ones we'd seen on the rooftops in the city. The buildings were small, mostly one or two stories. They had a polished metallic appearance, with a copper hue. Dish antennas were everywhere.

Several robots came out of a circular structure, lined up, and stood without moving as we got out and walked in through the front doors. *"Turn right,"* said Ark.

I was carrying Sayla. *"I can't believe I'm back here,"* she said.

"Well," said Ark, *"how does it feel to be home?"*

"It's wonderful."

"How long were you out there?" asked Gabe.

"I lost count. A long time."

"Who lives here?" I asked.

"I do," said Sayla.

"Anybody else?"

"A few people. And three or four bipeds."

"I wish we could say hello," said Gabe.

"If you're talking about the bipeds, it's not a good idea," said Ark. *"You would scare them. We've taken precautions to ensure it doesn't happen."*

Gabe was clearly unhappy, but he let it go. We walked down a corridor, made a turn, and a door opened. We went into a room. It was spacious, considerably larger than a human's apartment would be. Large violet curtains were drawn across the windows. There was a sofa, armchairs, a couple of side tables, and something with a display screen. *"It was designed originally for bipeds,"* Sayla explained. *"One of these days I'm going to have it redone. I probably should have taken care of that while I was away."*

The apartment looked as if it had been cleaned and straightened that morning. *"They were obviously taking care of me, though."*

I was holding Sayla again, looking around, wondering where she wanted me to put her.

"Over there," she said. *"In the regulator."* It was a frame on

one of the side tables, near a display. I fit her into the frame and she became secured. Presumably magnetized. *"Good,"* she said. *"Can you angle it a bit? To the right."* It provided a better view of the display. *"Thank you, Chase. For everything. And you too, Gabe."*

We stayed and talked for a while, allowing time for the *Belle-Marie* to complete an orbit. She told us she was sorry we were going away and that we would probably never see each other again. That if we ever returned, we should contact her. And finally it was time to leave. No parting hugs. No lifting of a glass. Just a quiet good-bye. I suppose Ark had a point about accessible minds, but I was grateful for my physical dimension.

We rendezvoused with the ship and were on our way again. "Where are we going?" I asked.

"Well," said Ark, *"have you by any chance changed your mind about going home?"*

"Not really," said Gabe. "I think we've resolved the issue we came here for. I can tell you in all honesty that I would love to take back with us some artifacts from this civilization. For example, a history of what's happened here?"

"No, I'm sorry. We can't allow that."

"I guess neither of us is in a position to change his mind. I assume we can't have any photos either?"

"I wish I could accommodate you, Gabe. I do not want you to think we don't trust you. But there'd be no point in taking any part of our culture home if you weren't going to share it with someone. Even if you have every intention of keeping it to yourself, it would probably get out eventually. As did the trophy."

"I understand."

"I wish I could give you everything you want. But I cannot. The consequences, if things went wrong, would be too severe. We have some museums, still stocked with hardcover books, if you'd like to look. And some sculptures. Including some of the early

gods. *They remain, most of them, in excellent condition. And there are other pieces of art I suspect you would enjoy."*

Gabe thought about it, and finally shook his head. No. "We'll have to pass. It would be too painful to look through treasures that we couldn't share with the world back home." He delivered a barely audible "damn" under his breath. "I think we've been gone long enough." He sat for a few more seconds, wrapped in indecision. "Chase," he said, "we should take Ark back to his home. And then get moving."

XXIX.

When we have cast aside all possible explanations,
whatever remains, however improbable, must be true.
But what if nothing remains?

— AUBREY CARSON, FICTIONAL DETECTIVE
CREATED BY ISAAC GLOVER, IN *THE ADVENTURE OF THE LOST CLOUD,* 8427 CE

I called Chad from Skydeck. "We're home, Chad. Sorry it took so long." We'd been gone three months.

"Are you okay?"

"We're fine. Just glad to be back." It was strictly an audio exchange. No visuals.

"Thank God. I was seriously worried something had gone wrong. So what the hell happened out there? What was it all about?"

"It was no big deal, Chad. Just a downed lander and some planetary exploration."

"What downed lander?"

"We don't have many details. It was on the ground a long time. Probably thousands of years."

"And that's it?" He sounded annoyed. *"That's what took all this time?"*

"Yes." I wanted to change the subject. "Chad, we'll be getting back on the ground later today. Do you want to get together tomorrow for lunch?"

"I'm a bit busy right now. But yeah, sure, I can manage it. Pick you up at home? Or the country house?"

"So where were you?" asked Alex.

"I told you," said Gabe. "Checking out a wrecked ship. I showed you the artifacts."

Alex looked in my direction. We were in Gabe's quarters, surrounded by his luggage and the artifacts we'd recovered from the wrecked vehicle. "What else is going on?" he asked. The question was directed at me.

"That's it," I said. "Listen, I've got a lot to catch up on. I'll see you guys in a bit."

"Stay," said Alex. "We've always trusted each other." He eased down onto the sofa. "You guys are hiding something. You want to tell me what it is?"

The conversation continued in that vein for several minutes. Gabe and I sank into chairs while Alex poured coffee for everybody. "We promised we would tell no one," Gabe said.

"Promised who?"

"Some people we found."

"Humans?"

"No."

"Okay, Gabe. You have any idea what artifacts from that place would be worth?"

"I'm fully aware of that, Alex. We didn't bring anything back."

He looked puzzled. "How did that happen?"

"They don't want us talking about the place. And I guess we've already violated our promise to them."

"You saying you don't trust me? After all we've been through?"

"It's not a matter of trust, Alex. We gave our word."

"And what did you get in turn?"

"Let's just let it go, okay?"

"You know I can ask Belle where you've been?"

"You can." Gabe took a deep breath. "But she's sworn to secrecy."

He looked over at me. "You in on this too, Chase?" I didn't need to respond. He saw the answer. "Okay," he said. "I understand."

It was time to change the subject. "How are you doing with Octavia?" I asked. "You figure it out yet?"

"Not yet. I've spent a lot of time researching Housman and Womack. And talking to Womack's avatar."

"Housman didn't have one?"

"No."

"Have you picked up anything at all?"

"Not really. Womack seemed to be the more curious of the two. He wanted to get into the science, to understand why the quantum world operates the way it does. Why wormholes actually form. Housman was more interested in making a reputation for himself. He was annoyed that Newton lived at a time when nobody understood about gravity. Or anything else. He says the scientific giants, Galileo, Tycho Brahe, Descartes, weren't necessarily all that smart. They just had the advantage of being alive at a time when nobody knew anything. So it was fairly easy to make discoveries. He was determined to find a wormhole, which he thought would lock in his name with the others."

"And look what happened," I said.

"Anyway, Chase, I've been waiting for you."

"Really? Why?"

"You were going to set up a conversation with Karen Randall. Charlotte Hill's friend."

"Oh. I guess I got caught up in this other stuff. I'll call her today."

"Good. No hurry. Don't bring her in on the circuit. See if you can arrange for us to take her to dinner somewhere. Anyplace that's convenient." That was typical of him. The reality of a person didn't always come through with modern technology. He believed a physical presence could be much more revealing.

"Okay. You said 'us.' You want me there too?"

"Wouldn't have it any other way, Chase."

Chad showed up on time next morning. He seemed a bit standoffish, but he looked good. His hair was windblown, a smile was playing on his lips, and his eyes were gleaming. He told me how relieved he was that we were home. "I guess this is the way life is," he said, "when you get mixed up with the planet's loveliest pilot." He welcomed me into his arms.

We went to the Lyrica, a quaint little restaurant overlooking Mount Ecott. "I'd have been more comfortable," he said as we strolled through the door, "if we could have communicated better. If I could have sent you a simple message just asking if you were okay, and gotten a reply. . . ."

"I understand, Chad. I'm sorry it was hard on you. It's difficult, and expensive, to try to communicate with a ship that's light-years away."

"But you were able to send me messages."

"We knew where Rimway was at any given time. But you don't usually know where the ship is, so nobody knows where to send the signal."

"Couldn't you have told them, Chase?"

"If we were staying in one place, yes. Let's just let it go, okay?"

"All right. I'm sorry. I won't bring it up again."

Gabe and I both got checked out by doctors to make sure the radiation hadn't done any damage. We were pronounced okay, but my doctor was clearly unhappy and told me I should stop the nonsense. "Why on earth," he asked, "would you want to get that close to a sun?"

We'd made up a story about lost antiquities that was as

close to what really happened as we could. We claimed to have found a lost interstellar orbiting a star whose name Gabe made up. He got the same lecture, and we both assured our physicians we wouldn't do anything like that again.

It took a couple of days to find Karen Randall. But eventually the three of us were able to get together at a place called Manny's. It was located across the street from the Oberley Theater, which at the time was undergoing reconstruction. I'd never been there before. Karen was already seated at a table when Alex and I went in. She raised a hand to catch our attention.

I did the introductions and we sat down. "It's good to see you again, Chase," she said. "And to meet you, Alex. Do you have any idea what happened to her? To Charlotte? And the station?" She was wearing a soft green button-down blouse with a collar. The color matched her eyes. She was obviously a bit awed by Alex.

"I wish we did, Karen," he said. "We were hoping you might be able to help."

"I can't imagine how I could do that."

The table invited us to order. We did sandwiches, sides, and a round of beer. It thanked us and said the food would be there shortly. I couldn't resist wondering aloud what kind of life an AI in a restaurant would have. It was a mistake, provoking an expression from Karen that made clear she thought my mind had come loose. But she didn't say anything, substituting instead a tolerant smile.

"I understand you had a continuing correspondence with Charlotte while she was at Octavia," Alex said.

"Yes, I did. Though I thought of it more as occasional than continuing."

"Did she ever say anything that indicated there was a problem of any sort?"

"Well, I think Charlotte got lonely sometimes. And they

weren't always happy with the menu they had. But no, I don't recall anything that could have been connected with a hazard."

"It's possible, Karen, you could have picked up something without being aware of it. What kind of messages were you receiving? Were they visuals?"

"No. They were audio. It cost too much to send visuals. There *were* a couple, though, a picture of the space station that she took from the shuttle. And one of the station's interior. Del Housman was posing with her and, umm, Archie Goldman in the background. Oh, and there was a picture of the black hole. More or less. I think she took that one from the shuttle too."

"You mean Archie *Womack*," Alex said.

"Yes. That's right. Womack. Sorry."

"Charlotte must have been pretty happy to have been selected for that mission."

"I guess. She didn't talk much about it. Mostly, I suspect, because for the first year or so, they didn't *get* any results. It was only toward the end that they found the wormhole. I didn't get the impression she was all that happy. She enjoyed having people around her. I was shocked when she first told me what she'd signed on for. I mean, she liked going out. She spent a fair amount of time on the beach. I never understood how she managed to get her degrees. Most of us have to invest a lot of time to accomplish what she did. I guess the reality is that she was just seriously smart. You know she was a pretty good chess player too, right?"

"We've heard," Alex said.

The sandwiches showed up. Karen took a bite from hers and put it down. "She got pretty close to Rick Harding. He was a committed chess enthusiast too."

"I hadn't heard that," I said. "Who usually won? Do you know?"

"She never mentioned the results. But if Harding was winning, he's the only person I know who managed it. And I suspect if that had been happening, she'd have said something."

"Did she ever indicate she was tired of being out there? That she would have liked to come home?"

"She implied it. But I don't recall her ever actually saying that. I remember she talked sometimes about things she missed, guys, Tully's, sunlight. About how nice it would be to have an occasional stranger show up and say hello."

"What's Tully's?" Alex asked.

"It's a bar located near the university. It was a good place to meet guys. In fact, that's where I met my husband."

Eventually the conversation wandered into other areas, Karen's career doing PR work for the Andiquar police; her husband, who was an electronic technician; her infatuation with tennis; and finally Gabe. "I can't imagine what it must have been like getting pulled out of the *Capella* and discovering that eleven years had passed."

We finished our lunches, and Karen thanked us as Alex picked up the tab. "I know this hasn't helped you," she said. "I wish I could have given you something."

Alex assured her she had. "You described her life on the station. The fact that she had no serious problems eliminates one area of inquiry. Did she ever mention Reggie Greene?"

"No. I knew the guy. And I know the stories about him. But she never brought him up."

We left the restaurant and walked out into the parking lot. "There *might* be one other thing," she said. "It's so trivial I've been reluctant to mention it. At one point, Charlotte indicated there *was* something going on. She didn't specify what it was. She said it would probably go away but that if it didn't she'd send me details later. Either to me or to Poliks."

"Who's Poliks?"

"I have no idea. I don't know anyone with that name."

"Did she ever mention it again? The name?"

"No. Not that I can recall. "

"Did you ever ask her for any details?"

"I think what I did later was tell her I hoped that it had cleared up. But I don't recall her ever saying anything about it again."

"So you never got the message?"

"No."

"Karen," Alex said, "do you remember when you received that message? How long was it before the station disappeared?"

"The one when she said there might be a problem? You don't think it could have had anything to do with *that*, do you?"

"Probably not. But who knows?"

"Well, anyhow, I think we lost the place about a month later."

"And you say it was audio? She was talking to you?"

"Yes."

"So you're not sure how to spell the name?"

"I guess not."

"Are you aware of anybody Charlotte might know whose name sounds even remotely like 'Poliks'?"

She needed a minute. "Poulter," she said. "Erik Poulter."

Alex thought about it and shook his head. "Anybody else?"

"Yes. There's one other. Jules Colix."

"You know both these people?"

"Colix was a chess player. One of the people she competed with. But he died a few years ago. Poulter was briefly a boyfriend. Though I don't think it was ever serious."

"Did you ever check with either one to see if they'd heard from her?"

"No. I never thought to do anything like that."

"Okay, Karen. One more question, and we'll let you go."

"Sure."

"Were you at all surprised that you never got the follow-up message, something explaining what it was all about?"

"Surprised? Sure. And disappointed."

• • •

Alex asked me to do a search for Poliks and whatever vari-
ants I could think of. I started by looking for Charlotte's avatar, which was established when she was about twelve years
old but never updated. The avatar told me she'd never heard
the name.

I checked names of adults around the planet and found
just over two hundred. In three cases it was a given name.
None had an obvious connection with Octavia, with Charlotte, or with anyone else involved with the station. Marion
Poliks had attended the same grade school as Charlotte,
but several years earlier. And Michael Poliks had invented
several virtual war games. But that was a long way from
chess.

I tracked Marion down. She hadn't changed her name. She
lived on Mayven Island, and when I talked with her, she told
me she knew who Charlotte was because of her reputation,
but had never met her.

"Okay." Alex looked frustrated. "Maybe Poliks, whoever he
is, lives on another planet."

"If he does," I said, "the connection would probably be
through the Quantum Research Group or DPSAR. They'd
have shown up on the net. I checked all kinds of variations,
but I just couldn't find anything."

"Thank you, Chase. Poliks may not even be a person.
Maybe it's a club or a group of some kind."

I went back to work and discovered a Poliks hotel chain,
two restaurants, a type of truck, a species of lizard, six street
names, a park, and a book title. The book was a biography
of Roger Poliks, who had led a revolt against political corruption in Olconda two hundred years ago. So I switched to
direction and looked for avatars. Housman did not have one.
That left me with Womack.

• • •

"Call me Archie," he said. *"What can I do for you, Chase?"*

Womack, at first glance, resembled our perception of the classic physicist, a guy so wrapped up in his subject that he has little interest in anything else. I was looking down at him, but I couldn't be sure the avatar's height was correct. Whatever the reality, I realized that he wasn't trying to impress viewers with his physical appearance. He was corpulent, with iron-gray hair and brown eyes that seemed naturally intense.

"Archie, we're trying to figure out what happened to the Octavia station."

"Good luck to you. I'd like to see that resolved myself."

"Does the word 'Poliks' mean anything to you?"

"You mean the star?"

"Pollux? Yes, that could be."

"Pollux was visible from Octavia. But I don't know of any connection. Why do you ask?"

"One of Charlotte's messages said there was a problem of some sort, and if it didn't get resolved, she would let Poliks know."

"Well, that doesn't sound as if she was talking about the star."

"I understand that. Was there anyone connected with the mission named Poliks?"

He shook his head. *"Not that I know of."*

"Maybe an organization of some sort?"

"No, Chase. I'm sorry, but I've no idea what that could be about."

"One more question?"

"Okay."

"Why did you sign on for Octavia?"

"Are you serious? It was the biggest scientific project of the age. They were hoping to get a handle on the basic structure of the universe. We've been trying to do that for thousands of years. I'd have been crazy to pass on it."

"Would you do it again?"

"Knowing what I know now? Of course not. But if it were a second chance? Then absolutely. It frustrates me to think that we had actually made some progress, had found the damned wormhole, and then . . ."

I could see the frustration in his eyes. It was one of the few times I'd spoken to an avatar and come away with the impression it had been the actual person.

We got a call later that day from the Arcadia Network. A young guy seated behind a desk looked up at me. *"Hello. My name is Charles Hoskins. Is Alex Benedict available?"*

Alex was asleep. He'd been reading about Housman and it put him out. "I'm sorry. We can't reach him at the moment. Can I help you, Charles?"

"We just wanted to suggest he might be interested in watching The Bruce Colson Show *this evening."*

"Okay. What's going on?"

"I don't have any details, ma'am. Just that his guest is Lashonda Walton."

Walton had headed the search effort from the QRG when Octavia was lost. "Got it," I said. "I'll let him know."

Alex's alarm went off an hour later. There was an artifact auction that evening, where he was to represent three clients. The auction was scheduled to start at 8:00 p.m., same time as *The Colson Show.*

"Record it, Chase," he said.

I set it up and spent most of what remained of the day talking with people who were putting antiquities on the market. Most of what we see tends to be of current minor value, though much of it has potential. It's the basic problem with the business we're in: We can look at lamps and dishware and artwork and know that, in another century, something will have gained some serious value. But it takes more time than we're willing to put into it. Which is why we're much more interested in objects that are recovered from a long-abandoned property. Or better yet, using the inclination that I've always suspected Alex picked up from Gabe, finding remnants of a lost civilization.

There was one standout offer. A woman called in with a two-hundred-year-old video from the early days of Chuck Orion, the fictional star-pilot hero who fought off all kinds of aliens, interstellar pirates, and human dictators. Chuck had gone on to fame in more than twenty novels and a series of feature-length movies. He was a centerpiece in my early years and one of several reasons I developed a passion for interstellar flight. But her price was unreasonable. I'd have declined had it been my call, but offers like that got passed on to Alex. He surprised me by putting it aside and telling me he'd think about it. "As far as I know," he said, "this thing was supposed to be lost."

Finally it was time to quit for the day. I'd set the HV to record *The Colson Show*. I checked with Gabe and Alex to make sure nobody needed anything. Gabe said he was going out for the evening to play some gordo with his buddies. Gordo, for anyone not familiar with Rimway card games, is a derivative from Earth. You get a hand of five cards and try to match cards or suits and possibly bluff opponents to bail out. Alex told me, as he usually does, to take care on the way home. He added that he hoped Professor Walton had come up with some new information about Octavia. "Maybe she knows somebody named Poliks."

I stopped for dinner at Lenny's and evaded a pickup from a guy I felt sorry for because he was so nervous. I got home, showered, changed into pajamas, read for a while, and, at eight, turned on the Arcadia Network.

Bruce Colson's classic sofa blinked on in my living room, accompanied by the show's theme music, Valmier's "Rising Tide Nocturne." The music implied that the show was of considerable significance. I'd never been one of his fans. He thought highly of himself and didn't mind showing that inclination to his viewers. As the music revved up, he strode in through a side door and an invisible audience cheered and applauded. He responded with a giant smile and waved in my direction while the cheering continued.

"Hello, everybody," he said. *"Welcome to the show."* Colson did a few one-liners to get his audience into the right mood. Then the camera pulled back, two guests appeared, and the music faded out. They took seats at a table. Colson joined them and they exchanged jokes about politicians and celebrity scandals. In particular they went after a recent claim by a guy running for governor of Tolk City that persons born on Rimway had a higher IQ than people from other parts of the Confederacy, and that consequently intermarriage should be banned. I'd never heard of the guy before, but the claim had been around for a while. One of the guests commented that you didn't often hear a political assertion like that.

"Why?" asked Colson.

"Because even for politics, it's dumb."

Eventually they got to the second half hour. After the commercials, Colson and his table reappeared. We got more music and cheers. He got up from the table and welcomed Lashonda Walton to enthusiastic applause. I hadn't seen her since the tumultuous days following the disappearance of the station. She hadn't changed. She was tall, disciplined, in charge. Not the sort of laid-back guest I'd have expected to see on *The Colson Show*. The host led her to a pair of armchairs, where they sat down facing each other.

"It's good to see you again, Lashonda," he said.

"It's good to be here, Bruce. I think I needed a place to visit. One with friends."

"You're always welcome to drop by. May I ask what's been happening? Why are we seeing a revival of interest in Octavia?"

"That does seem to be happening, doesn't it?" She looked past

him as if something were closing in on her. *"Horton Cunning-ham will be out with a new book on the subject next month. I'm told a documentary is about to be released. Alex Benedict has launched a probe to try to find out what happened. And here I am talking about it on your show."*

"I can understand," Colson said, *"why, after all these years, it's still painful, Lashonda. I know you'd like to see some answers."*

"Whatever happened out there, it should not have been possible, Bruce. I do not understand how we could possibly have lost that place. I have a lot of regrets in my life, we all do, but nothing on the order of that."

"You didn't have anything to do with it, Lashonda. Whatever it was about, it certainly wasn't your fault."

"That's irrelevant, Bruce. As far as I know, you're right. I wasn't responsible. But we still don't know what happened. And until we can answer that question, we can't say anything for certain. Whatever it was, I was ultimately responsible for coming up with an answer. And I failed to do so. So yes, some of the blame lies with me."

"Just because you're in charge doesn't mean you can control everything."

She rearranged herself in her chair. And somehow managed to gain height. *"I know. God knows I'm aware of that, Bruce. I just wish we could let it go. And I don't want you to get the wrong idea. This is not about me. I realize that. But a lot of people, the families and friends of the Octavia team, are being dragged through this again. I know the people doing the investigations mean well, but we'd all be better off if they'd just back away from it. Let it go."*

"But don't we need some closure? Are we ever going to get it if we just push it aside?"

"No. Of course not. But we've run out of options."

"So you don't think we'll ever have an answer?"

"Bruce, there's nothing left to examine that hasn't already been picked apart time and again. If the station had survived, if some

part of it had survived, then maybe we'd be able to put the thing together. But as it is, we're looking at a vacuum."

"Lashonda," he said, "it's been years since the wormhole breakthrough at Octavia. What good has it done us? Are we still doing research about those things?"

"Of course we are. And we're planning to establish two other stations near black holes. One will be run from Saraglia, the other from Claridol. And you know we've been active for years at KBX44. The Octavia site." She leaned forward in her chair and her eyes narrowed. "The research continues. We're not giving up."

"That's good to hear. But none of that suggests you think there's much chance of coming to a resolution."

"Bruce, it's complicated. What the Octavia mission accomplished was to show that wormholes exist. Yes, we lost four good people. And we may never learn why. But we've already gained some traction from their work. From their sacrifice. That's what we want. Thanks to them, we should be able to resolve some cosmic questions that have been hanging over our heads for centuries."

"Okay. But what good does it do us?"

"Eventually—I hope in my lifetime—it will allow us to find out whether this is the only universe, or whether we actually live in a multiverse. There are billions of galaxies. What we may learn is that, nevertheless, this is only an infinitesimal part of reality."

"Okay. I've got that. And let's say we do find out there is a whole horde of universes out there. Is it going to give us a capability to travel to these other places?"

"Maybe."

"All right. Suppose it does. Let's say we find that out. So what? This universe is more than big enough for us. It always will be. I mean, there's no way we're going to outgrow the Milky Way, let alone this universe. So why bother?"

"Bruce, developing a means to travel to another universe is irrelevant."

"What do you mean?"

"The thing that's of value is the knowledge. We're still grappling *with the nature of the cosmos. It would help to know whether our universe is alone. Or whether there are others. We might even discover the cosmos is infinite. That's what blue sky science is all about."*

Colson sat quietly for a moment and then looked across the room at me. But he was speaking to Walton: *"Back to Octavia for a minute: Do you put any stock in the alien story? That aliens somehow seized the station? Or pushed it into the black hole? Is that even possible?"*

"Sure it's possible. But it's unlikely. The problem is, so is every other scenario I can think of."

"The major question for me," Colson said, *"has always been that the incident occurred during the thirty hours when Octavia had no contact with Chippewa or us or anybody else. Whatever happened, that makes it sound like a result of careful planning. Not an accident."*

Walton nodded but otherwise did not respond.

"How long," Colson asked, *"did the entire orbit take?"*

"Around the black hole? A hundred and forty-six days."

"Could the station have been hit by an asteroid and knocked into the black hole?"

"They had equipment that would have either avoided the asteroid or turned it to dust."

"I was struck by the theory—I don't recall its source—that there'd been a group suicide."

"That's way off the charts, Bruce."

Colson nodded. *"I know. It sounds as if aliens are all we're got left."*

"Or time travelers."

Alex and Gabe watched it together later that evening. "No surprises there," Alex told me next day. "I was hoping she might mention Poliks. I called her this morning and told her what Karen Randall had said. But she had no idea what Charlotte might have been talking about."

XXX.

*One can find no greater recognition of the value of a person's life
than a gathering of those left behind to recall with adulation and
tears days that were golden because he, or she, was there.*
—Leisha Tanner, *Notebooks*, 1231

The Arcadian Cosmological Association was holding its
bimonthly meeting at the Flagstone Hotel on Brevington
Avenue across from Baymore Park. The keynote speaker
was Elijah McCord and his subject was to be Del Housman
and his contributions to the world of physics.

Alex was going. Did I want to join him?

"You think we might pick up anything?"

"Probably not. But who knows?"

I'd been to two of these things before. They provided ban-
quets usually with good food. A woman seated next to me
on one occasion commented that if physicists know nothing
else, they know how to eat. There were always a couple of
musicians playing quietly in the background. And the orga-
nizers tended to provide passionate speakers.

On this occasion, eight people, including the association's
president, were seated at a central table. When we'd finished
the main course and the desserts arrived, the president
rose, asked for attention, and provided an update on mostly
administrative issues. He introduced a few new members

and recognized two who had died. He delivered a report on charitable activities supported by the association and announced two awards recently received by members. One was present and stood to applause; the other appeared on a link and thanked his colleagues for their support. Finally, the president announced the keynote speaker, Elijah McCord, telescopic department chairman at the Andiquar Institute of Technology.

McCord had been seated next to the president. He was a little guy, bald, filled with energy, who literally bounced out of his chair and took his place at the microphone. "Thank you, Alf," he said. "It's a pleasure to be here."

He drew a mixture of laughs and clapping, making it clear that he was a popular figure with the ACA. He started with a few gags, describing his own efforts to decipher what he referred to as the quantum code, in an effort to establish his name along with Newton, Einstein, and Yuri Ko-san. "And," he added seriously, after the laughter subsided, "with Del Housman."

That drew serious applause.

It grew, and the audience came to their feet in recognition of their lost colleague.

McCord waited for quiet. When it came, he said that his own name would be remembered, but only because he had been a lifelong friend of Housman, and possibly because he'd written an introduction to the great physicist's groundbreaking book on the big bang. "We still don't know how it happened," he said, "and maybe we never will. But Del at least gave us a workable theory.

"I was fortunate," he added. "I knew Del from my earliest years. We chased each other up and down Boynton Street with pop guns. Well, maybe I'm exaggerating a bit here. Actually, *he* chased *me*. Later, we chased girls. In fact, I probably shouldn't mention this, but a couple of them are here tonight."

More laughter. Members of the audience looked around and pointed fingers.

"Getting serious for a moment," McCord said, "when we consider what Del accomplished in his short lifetime, we are left to wonder what else he might have done, had he been granted a few more years. He loved science. I've never known anyone more addicted to resolving the riddles of the universe. And I guess I should admit that I never knew anyone with a more active mind. He used to start explaining things to me, where he thought he'd gotten hold of something, and the equations wound up on the board, and I'd get absolutely lost in the twists and turns.

"It's been almost twelve years now since we lost him, and I still can't believe he's gone." He stood for a moment, not finished, struggling with whatever else he had. Then he simply wiped his eyes with a handkerchief, said thank you, and returned to his seat. The audience remained silent for a few seconds before another round of applause began and took over the building.

We passed through the lobby and were on our way out the door when a tall, elderly guy with stern features drew alongside us. "Pardon me," he said. "You're Alex Benedict, aren't you?" He had thick white hair and dark inquiring eyes.

"Yes," said Alex.

"We have the same first name, sir. I'm Professor Alexander Clemens. I was an associate director at Quantum Research a few years ago."

"It's good to meet you, Professor. What can I do for you?"

"You might know me as *Charlie* Clemens. I've always used my middle name."

"Oh yes. I remember. We met once or twice, I believe."

"That was *before* we lost the station."

"How can I help you, Professor?"

"Call me Charlie, if you will. I need a favor." He drew us

back into the lobby and we settled into chairs in a remote corner where we would have some privacy. "Alex, did you see Lashonda Walton on HV the other night?"

"Yes."

"I was working for her when it happened."

"It must have been a difficult time."

"It almost destroyed her." He leaned forward so he could lower his voice and looked at me. He motioned with his eyes: *Should we be alone for this?*

"You don't need to worry about Chase."

Charlie smiled. "The activity lately about the station has brought it all back. May I ask you a personal question?"

"You may."

"I know you've been working on this thing. Have you made any progress? You have any idea what might have happened?"

"Charlie, I'm sorry, but I'd just as soon not discuss theories. If you're asking whether we've been able to lock anything down, I'd have to say the answer is no."

"But you've concluded Housman's involved."

"I haven't drawn any conclusions yet."

Clemens closed his eyes and nodded. "But that's the direction you're headed. Am I right?"

"That would be premature."

He smiled. "Alex, we both know that Housman barely mentioned Charlotte Hill in his paper. She was taking the shuttle out every day, and for a long time they relied on his calculations. There's no evidence that *he* was the one to extend the search for the pods beyond the original specs. If he'd made the call, it would have shown up in the paperwork. That tells me it was Charlotte who took the shuttle deep. Who found the pods. And gave him his success. She was a smart woman. Probably genius level herself. And more flexible than Del. It doesn't take much to conclude that he wasn't anxious to share credit with her."

"You're suggesting," said Alex, "Housman killed them all, and himself, rather than see that part of the story come out?"

"I'm asking for *your* opinion, Alex."

"I don't have an opinion yet. I try not to form one before the evidence comes in."

"What kind of evidence are you looking for? That's the problem here. The station's gone. The only thing that's left is the cannon." He stopped and took a breath. "No one will ever be able to prove *anything*, Alex. You know that as well as I do. The only rational course at this point is the one that points at Housman. But there'll never be any solid evidence, one way or another. If you continue to pursue this investigation, you'll get the same results we did. You'll resurrect the old antagonism about Housman, and about Greene, and in the end accomplish nothing. You said you saw Lashonda. She's being dragged through it again. It's been a terribly painful experience for her. She was front and center during the investigation and still feels responsible for our failure to come up with anything. I understand that makes no sense, but if you know her at all, you're aware that she accepts responsibility for everything that happens around her. I'm sure you've noticed she's not here tonight."

"Look, Charlie, I can understand it's been a difficult time for her. But I don't see how she can feel responsible."

"Okay. Look, she was warned that Del was driven by his ambition. That he wasn't entirely stable. That putting him out on the station for a year and a half, in that kind of isolated environment, wasn't a good idea. She didn't listen."

"You're saying somebody predicted he would go on a killing spree?"

"No, nothing like that. But she was warned that he wouldn't be a good player out there. She shook it off. Refused to buy it."

"Why?"

"Because she thought he was the best man for the job. He'd spent his life doing wormhole research, and she wanted the program to succeed. At the time, he looked like our best option."

"If I may?" I said. "Professor, how do you think Housman could have destroyed the station?"

"All he would have had to do would be to take the shuttle out. He could have done it while the station was in the silent zone, where they had no communication with anyone else. He takes it out a few thousand kilometers. They might have realized why he was doing it, but it wouldn't have mattered. There would have been nothing they could do to prevent it. He turns it around, runs up the acceleration, and crashes it into them. I'm sure you're aware"—he glanced toward me again—"that if he'd wanted to, he could have knocked the station out of orbit. We both know what that would probably have meant."

"Into the black hole."

"If he got the right angle."

We ordered a round of drinks, and while we waited for them to arrive, Professor Clemens asked whether Alex had reached a similar conclusion.

"It's still in the air," Alex said.

"I understand," I said, "that they had blasters that could have been used if there'd been a threat from an asteroid."

"That's correct," said Clemens. "They could have destroyed the shuttle."

"I suspect," said Alex, "if something like that had happened, they'd have had a hard time believing Housman was putting them all at risk. I'm not sure anyone would have pulled the trigger in time. That would be a terrible decision."

"Alex, he could have deactivated the system before he took the shuttle out."

The drinks arrived. Clemens proposed a toast to Lashonda Walton, whom he described as the fifth victim of the Octavia incident. "There are others," Alex said. "Housman's family took a hit. As did all the families."

Clemens drained his glass, set it down, and studied us for a few moments. He studied Alex, really. He took a long look in my direction and pretty much dismissed me. "You've been evading the issue, Alex," he said.

My boss sat back in his chair. "I don't believe in drawing conclusions until the evidence is in."

"Have it your way. But I'll ask you, if you will, please don't go public with whatever conclusions you come to. There never will be a definitive finale to this. Give Lashonda a break."

Charlie paid for the drinks, thanked us for our time, and excused himself. We watched him exit through the front door. Alex glanced at my empty glass. "You want anything more?"

"I'm good," I said. And after a long pause, "So what do you think?"

"I've thought all along that's exactly what happened. Though I'm not sure who was in the shuttle. We have no way to be certain. Unless we can get Charlotte to talk to us."

"That would be tricky."

"Maybe not."

"What do you mean?"

"Did you know that one of the senior engineers on the cannon project was a guy by the name of Royce Poliks?"

"Really?"

"Yes. He lives on Chippewa. It's possible he and Charlotte made contact at some point and she told him what was going on."

I walked into Alex's office moments after Gabe found out we were planning a flight to Chippewa. Both of them were seated in armchairs, separated by a circular table. "Why in heaven's name are you so caught up in this, Alex?" he asked. "Why don't you just let it go and take care of your responsibilities to your clients?"

Alex glanced in my direction. *Here we go again.* That was probably an unfair interpretation because relations between them had improved considerably. As Gabe had said early on, they were both adults now. "Why am I doing this?" Alex said. "Are you serious?"

"Of course I'm serious. What's the point of it all?"

"Gabe, it's one of the great mysteries of the age. Why wouldn't we want to get a resolution?"

"How about *this*: if you *do* find out what happened, you're very likely not going to want to tell anyone."

"And why would that be?"

"It's not likely they got attacked by aliens. Or pirates. Or whatever."

"How can you be sure?"

"We can't be sure. But we know they needed a hundred and forty-six days to complete an orbit. There were only that few hours when they were completely cut off. It could be a coincidence that the event happened during the cutoff period. But it's extremely unlikely. So what does that tell us?"

Gabe bowed his head in my direction, inviting me to respond. But I didn't want to get into the middle of it.

"It wasn't an accident," said Alex. "Isn't that obvious?"

"Of course it is," said Gabe. Both of them were beginning to sound annoyed. "Somebody timed the incident to happen when any possibility of a transmission was blocked by the black hole. The problem is that if it really was one of the people at the station, he might have been able to arrange someone to come in quickly and rescue him, but he'd have had to abandon his life. The four people at Octavia had all spent their lives building their reputations, becoming *somebody*. What I'm trying to say is that if you ever get to the truth, if you ever find out who's responsible, you're going to cause a lot of pain to that individual's family. I don't for a minute believe Archie could have been guilty of anything like that, killing his partners. But one of them is going to turn out to be responsible." He was staring out at the trees, looking at something neither Alex nor I could see. "My advice, Alex: leave it alone."

Gabe turned toward the door. "I just don't see why you'd want to get involved in something this poisonous." Then he was gone.

For a long minute neither of us spoke. Then Alex said, "I don't guess that turned out very well."

"Alex," I said, "do you really think Housman did it?"

"Clemens probably has it right. Charlotte might have been threatening to demand credit for finding the pods. And rather than let that come out, Housman killed them. And himself. And it worked. His name is linked now with the giants. He might have thought it wasn't too high a price."

"So how do we establish something like that?"

"Find the Poliks message. At this point it's all we have."

XXXI

The hurricane wiped out our power for three weeks. The modification system is supposed to be proof against storms, and it was the first time in living memory it had gone down. It left me realizing how many things we take for granted. Indoor bathroom facilities. Quick cures for virtually every illness. Not having to work for a living. Lights. Food that simply arrives when you want it.
—JOSEPH CALKIN, LETTER TO THE *HARMONY TIMES*, 1311

The Chippewa registry had shown only one Royce Poliks on the planet. Alex had sent a message explaining that he was researching the loss of Octavia and asking whether a discussion via hypercomm could be arranged. The message came back a month later marked "addressee unavailable." "This feels like a colossal waste of time," he said. "But I guess we don't have much choice." That same afternoon we were on our way in the *Belle-Marie*. Three days later we arrived at Ventnor, Chippewa's space station.

Chippewa was one of the early colony worlds. It was originally claimed by people who were unhappy with life on Earth. They didn't like authority, whether it was political or religious or whatever, and they were determined to keep it at a distance. Consequently, Chippewa still has not become home to big cities and large populations. It is basically a world devoted to country life, to hilltop cottages and small towns. It's a place where people enjoy mountain climbing, walking in the rain, and sitting on their front porches where they feel almost a camaraderie with the trees. The trees, one of them once explained to me, are alive, just as the inhabitants of the towns are. When you wander through the woods, the residents claim, you are not really alone.

I've never completely grasped that perspective but I've been there a few times and seen its effects. This is not a place where people sit in their homes and watch their HVs endlessly into the night. They spend time with their neighbors, live lives of ongoing leisure, and consider themselves the smartest people in the Confederacy. Like everyone else, they have a guaranteed income. I've never seen anyone there who has shown an appetite for wealth. I suspect that a person who displayed that tendency would not have been welcome.

Ventnor is probably the smallest space station on any of the major human worlds. We located Poliks in Gavindale, which stood on the edge of a mountain chain in the center of the only continent on the planet. The station had only two shuttles and we'd have had to wait four days to get the flight down to Kassel, which was the only spaceport anywhere close to Gavindale. So we applied for permission to use our lander. Fortunately they didn't charge much. We connected Belle with a map in the welcome center, waited a half hour for the station to reach a favorable position, and launched.

We were on the night side when we started down. Belle told me we could expect to arrive at Gavindale shortly after midnight local time. There was no point in showing up at Poliks's home in the middle of the night, so we made for the nearby terminal at Carbon City. Chippewa has a pair of moons, but neither was visible. We descended through clear skies. There were a few scattered lights on the ground, though not the bright patches one usually sees on the night side of a major world. These were relatively dim and distributed through the darkness. Belle informed us there'd be a slight delay while an aircraft landed. We watched it go down, and then we followed and touched down a short distance away. We got sleeping accommodations at the port, and in the morning flew the lander into Gavindale and arrived in a field just west of Poliks's place. It was a two-story chalet at the foot of a low hill.

There were several other homes nearby. The grounds were well kept, and a couple of boys were playing on a slide. We got out of the lander and proceeded along a walkway onto a front porch. The door opened as we arrived and a small woman looked out at us. She had brown hair and carried a bucket, which she placed outside the door while she stared at us in surprise. "Hello," she said. "We don't see many strangers around here."

"Hi," said Alex. "My name is Alex Benedict. Does Royce Poliks live here?"

"Yes, he does."

"We're doing research on the loss of the Octavia station and I was hoping to talk with him."

She couldn't resist sighing. "He's not here right now."

Inside, two kids were talking, probably with AIs. Both were girls. One was doing math. The other was playing a game.

"But he *does live* here?" said Alex.

"That's correct. Are you the person who was sending mail recently? Asking to communicate with him by hypercomm?"

"Yes."

"Well, I'm sorry, but he's just not here now. Won't be for probably a few weeks."

"Can you tell me where he is?"

She came outside and pulled the door shut behind her. "Mr. Benedict, I'm sorry. But we've had enough about Octavia. I don't know how many times he's been interviewed by people trying to find out what happened. It's always the same story, and they always ask the same questions. Asking him how he felt when they all got lost. Whether he thought nobody should have gone near the black hole. Maybe you should go interview *them*."

"I'm sorry to inconvenience you, Ms. Poliks. Am I correct? You are his wife?"

"I'm Kala. His niece."

"We've come all the way out from Rimway."

"I'm sorry about your inconvenience." She glanced in my direction, let me see her annoyance, and returned her attention to Alex. "We've just had enough. This thing has been going on for, I don't know, years now. Since before I started living here. We'd just like it to go away. There's nothing new we can add."

"Kala, was your uncle here when my message came?"

"No, he wasn't. But he wouldn't have answered it either. I'm sorry. I guess I should have saved you the trip. But it's just been so hard to live with."

The door opened slightly and one of the girls peeked out. She was about eight, with the woman's brown hair and bright amber eyes. She looked at Alex and then at me.

"Hi," I said. The girl smiled. Kala looked at me and her features softened slightly.

"It's possible," Alex said, "that your uncle knows something that would be helpful but isn't aware of it."

"Oh, please," she said. "Give it a rest."

Alex managed to look sympathetic. "I understand you're not happy with this, but we just don't have many options. Is he really not here? Or are you protecting him?"

"He's not here."

"Could you give me a way to get in touch with him?"

"I can't do that," she said. "I'm sorry." She pushed back inside the door, taking the girl with her. The child waved good-bye, and the door closed.

"We need the datanet," said Alex as we walked back to the lander. We got in and asked Belle for access to the local system. Then we gave it Poliks's name. "Is there any indication where he is now?"

"I do not have that information," it said.

"Who is his employer?"

"Mr. Poliks is not formally employed. He does occasional contract work."

"Can you identify the person or corporation he's most recently assisted?"

"Orion Express."

"But you have no idea where he is now?"

"That is correct."

"Orion Express has an office here somewhere, right?"

"There are two. One in Desmond, the other on Ventnor, the space station."

"Where is Desmond?"

"It's located just west of Arbuckel. Only eight hundred kilometers from your present location." It put a map on the display.

"What time is it there? In Desmond?"

"An hour earlier than it is where you are. A few minutes after ten."

"Please connect me."

We listened while it rang. Someone picked up. *"Orion Express."* A woman's voice. *"How may I help you?"*

"Hello. My name is Benedict. I'm trying to locate Royce Poliks. He's a contract engineer. I think he's currently working on one of your projects."

"I'm sorry, Mr. Benedict, but we don't give that kind of information out. I suggest you contact him through his local registry."

"Can you tell me if he's actually working on a project now?"

"I'm sorry, sir. I'm not free to do that. Is there anything else?"

Alex switched back to the datanet. "Can you tell me what kind of work Poliks does?"

We received several pages of data regarding past projects. Poliks specialized in designing and constructing living quarters for interstellars, space stations, and other offworld accommodations. He'd helped put together the interior of the Octavia and also the control center on the cannon.

"Has Orion Express begun working on any recent projects?" he asked.

"They are planning to send hunting expeditions to Tiara III. The program is expected to launch in two months."

"What kind of animals will they be looking for?"

"Giant lizards. Dinosaurs. Anything like that."

Alex took a deep breath and started again: "What other projects are there?"

"They're planning tours to Moranda." Moranda was the one human world where things had gone terribly wrong. It was, at the height of its glory in the eighth millennium, considered the most advanced civilization in the known cosmos. But they suffered a revolution, the government broke down, violence erupted all over the planet, and millions died. It was the worst catastrophe on any human world.

"It's been a gold mine for archeologists," said Alex. "I've been there a couple of times. They've put everything back together. The architecture is incredible. And there are all kinds of legends about what's been lost in various places. "

"So I've heard." He gave me that curious frown. "When were you there, Alex?"

"When I was a teen. I went with Gabe."

"There are two other projects of which I'm aware," said the datanet. *"A large moon orbits a gas giant in the Aldebaran system. The moon is bigger than Chippewa, part of a huge system of rings and satellites. But it has fallen out of orbit and is being pulled into the gas giant, which will swallow it in approximately a quarter century. Orion Express is building a hotel on the moon for tourists. Projected name for it is the End Times Hotel."*

"Why would anyone want to go there?" I asked.

"I suspect they'll fill the place," said Alex. "People love seeing worlds get destroyed."

They are also planning flights into the Trapezium, where they claim there's a chance tourists might see a star born.

"That's ridiculous," I said.

"Well," said Alex, "if they set it up right, they might get to see part of the process. Enough of it to send them home happy."

"Okay. So which one do they want Poliks for?"

"I suspect the End Times Hotel." He hesitated. "That sounds like the perfect place for an engineer who specializes in living quarters."

XXXII.

Travel with a purpose,
Not merely to go from one place to another,
But to arrive at the heart of the matter.
—WALFORD CANDLES, "MARKING TIME," 1196

Aldebaran is a red giant, about thirty-five times the size of Rimway's sun. Its planetary system is home to an enormous Jovian world. It has a dazzling set of rings and about thirty satellites. *"It's never been named,"* Belle told us. *"Its designator is simply Aldebaran IV."*

A moon almost the size of Rimway was effectively lost among the satellites. Or it would have been had a survey mission forty-two years earlier not noticed that it was a living world and that it was in a dying orbit. When Alex and I arrived, it had approximately twenty years left before it would crash into the gas giant.

We were looking out at a spectacular sky, filled with moving lights. A magnificent set of glowing rings orbited Aldebaran IV, and a large dark spot loomed on its surface. A storm probably. "Belle," I said, "are we picking up any radio signals?"

"Radio waves are being generated, Chase. But I am not detecting any that are artificial."

"Okay. Let's get closer to the End Times world."

"That's an impressive sky," said Alex, seated beside me. "I don't know about people showing up out here to watch a planet-sized moon getting ready to crash into a gas giant, but I can understand vacationing in a place with this kind of view."

"You ready to call them?"

"Sure."

The response was immediate: *"Yes, Belle-Marie, this is the End Times Project."* A woman's voice. *"Did you wish to make a reservation?"*

"End Times," Alex said, "we are looking for Royce Poliks. We understand he's working on the project."

"Yes, he's here. Do you want to talk with him?"

"Please. If you will."

"He's asleep at the moment. It's just past midnight here. Is this an emergency?"

"No. There's no problem. We'd just like to talk with him for a few minutes. Can you get a message to him in the morning? Let him know we're in the area?"

"I can arrange that. It'll be about six hours before you can expect to hear back."

"That'll work."

"Will he recognize the name of the vehicle?"

"No. I'm Alex Benedict. He won't recognize my name either. But I would appreciate hearing back from him."

"Very good, Mr. Benedict. I'll pass the message. End Times out."

"You think he'll call back, Alex?"

"I don't know. He's not likely to have any problem figuring out what this is about. Did Belle track the signal? Do we know where they are?"

"Yes," said Belle. *"Do you wish to go there?"*

As we approached the End Times world, Belle turned the scopes on it. It had oceans. They weren't massive, dominating the planet. But they were there. It was covered with forests and jungles. The planet was in tidal lock, and if you're building a hotel where people could stay and watch their world falling into a gas giant, you'd want them to be able to see it happening. That meant they'd be located in the area that was always looking up at the giant. The entire process was about scaring the customers. They were safe, and they would know it, but nevertheless they'd want to be able to watch the source of approaching doom getting larger in the sky every day.

So we knew which side of the world they'd be on. Belle needed only a few minutes to locate the construction with the telescope.

The sky was crowded by Aldebaran IV and its rings. And despite its distance, the scarlet sun also loomed large. Everything on the ground—soil, vegetation, water—had a crimson tinge. The landscape was mostly flat, with occasional hills. Something that might have been a giraffe was nibbling on one of the trees near the front of the hotel. As we got closer, we saw a few birds. A couple of canines were chasing each other around one of the fields.

We were looking at three connected structures, any of which would not have raised any eyebrows in Andiquar. The architects had gone out of their way to create a sense that the occupants were effectively at home. Later I read that the point was to increase the levels of excitement and uneasiness by suggesting that cosmic hazards can threaten anyplace.

The buildings looked complete. The central structure had a front entrance with a portico, columns, and steps. The construction material was probably plastene. Walls were blue and white, while doors and window frames were gold. There was no sign of outside activity. We slipped into a geosynchronous orbit so there'd be no problem getting a connection when, and if, Poliks called.

• • •

We were still floating above the hotel seven hours later when End Times connected us with him. *"What is it you want, Mr. Benedict?"* he asked. He was younger than I'd expected, with blond hair and dark eyes. He also had a smile that didn't quite make it past his lips.

"Mr. Poliks," Alex said, "we're doing research on the Octavia station. I know you've been interviewed before about this, but we have a new piece of information that you might be able to help with."

"Okay. Look, I'd be happy to help if I could. But I have no information I haven't already passed on."

"Mr. Poliks, did you ever receive any transmissions from any of the people on board the Octavia station?"

He closed his eyes momentarily, letting us see he'd hoped we would move on. *"A few times, yes. Rick Harding and I exchanged messages occasionally. We were longtime friends. But it was strictly personal stuff. Look, we can cut this short. I got nothing on how that place came to disappear. If I did, I'd have told the QRG years ago. I'm sorry. I can't help you. You're just wasting your time. And mine."*

"How well did you know Charlotte Hill?"

"Charlotte Hill? She was the female on board Octavia, right?"

"Yes."

"I never had any connection with her. Never met her. Why do you ask?"

"Shortly before it disappeared, she told one of her friends that there might be a problem of some kind on the station. She didn't specify what it was. But she said that if it got worse, she'd let *you* know the details."

"Why the hell would she do that? I can't imagine how she'd even have my name. You say she didn't mention what it was she was talking about?"

"No."

"Okay. There's a misunderstanding here somewhere."

"You *are* Royce Poliks, right?"

"Last time I looked."

Alex is usually pretty good at hiding his emotions, but there was no doubt about the frustration in his features. "All right," he said finally. "Mr. Poliks, I apologize for taking your time. We've come from Rimway. We were hoping you might be of some help."

"Believe me, Mr. Benedict, if I could be of some help, I'd have told someone years ago."

Alex looked toward me. "This is Chase Kolpath, by the way."

Poliks smiled. "Nice to meet you, Chase."

I returned the smile. It seemed the right moment to try to relieve the tension that was building. "Royce," I said, "it's hard to believe anybody's really going to come out here just because this place is falling out of orbit. It won't happen for, what, twenty years? Why would anybody care? I can understand they'd come during the last week or two, but—"

"There's a lot more to it than that, Chase. It's going to be an exciting experience for everybody. Research indicates that people get pretty roused up when they're able to participate in a catastrophe of this magnitude. We are already seriously booked with reservations."

"When will you be opening?"

"In six weeks. You can get specifics and, if you like, reservations while you're here. You want me to connect you with the desk?"

I knew Alex wanted to get past the link, meet the guy on the ground, and talk to him there. "I'm not sure what time it is down there, Mr. Poliks, but can we take you to lunch or dinner or something?"

"No. No. Look, I understand your situation, but I just don't have time for this. You want to talk to me, you'll have to do it now."

"What kind of work do you do, sir?"

"I'm just a tech. I design the assorted living quarters." I couldn't help sympathizing with him. He seemed like a decent guy, tired of people asking the same questions over

and over. *"Look, Mr. Benedict, I'll tell you the truth. I hope some-thing breaks for you. And I wish I was in a position to help. I'm just not. I don't know anything more than anybody else does about what happened. I can tell you the power system in the Octavia was fine. If the system had collapsed, the worst that could have happened was that the lights would have gone out. There were secondary systems that would have cut in and given them enough power to survive until help came. There is no way it could have blown the place up or taken it out of orbit. Okay? You got that? It's all I have."*

"I got it," said Alex.

So much for the secret message from Charlotte.

"Have you learned anything yet?" said Poliks. *"Any kind of explanation for what might have happened?"*

"No," said Alex. "We have some theories. Not much else. I assume the power system on the cannon also had backup?"

"Yes, it did."

"Were you responsible for both systems? On the station and on the cannon?"

"I wasn't really responsible for either power system. What I did primarily was set up the living quarters on the cannon. I helped with the power systems, primarily with the one on the cannon. But that was just trivial stuff. Just making sure the lights went on and the power was there when they needed it. Mostly I was responsible to see that the living quarters on the cannon worked." I got a brief smile from him. *"You have anything else, Mr. Benedict?"*

"The cannon is still orbiting the black hole?"

"As far as I know."

"Do you know if there are any plans to recover it?"

"I don't think so. It's too big. I doubt they have any means to transport the thing. More than that, they're still using it for the wormhole research."

"So that's ongoing?"

"Oh yes."

"If we went out there, would we be able to get a look at it? The interior?"

"I don't see why not, Mr. Benedict. But let them know in advance."

"Thanks, Mr. Poliks. I appreciate your time."

XXXIII

The vast majority of scientific inquiries do not expect to confirm a concept or theory. The anticipated result, rather, is to eliminate various conjectures.
—DELMAR HOUSMAN, GRADUATION ADDRESS, PARSET UNIVERSITY, 1419

Alex sat staring out at the rings, his chin cupped in his palm.

"I assume," I said, "we're not going home."

"Maybe she just didn't get a chance to talk with Poliks. When it all unraveled they were blocked from contact with everyone. Maybe she had to settle for leaving a message in the cannon."

"You think that's very likely?"

"No. But it's all we have."

"If she did, wouldn't the QRG investigators have found it? Or the guys who've been doing research there for the last twelve years? It seems to me, if there was such a message, Lashonda Walton's people would have picked it up years ago."

"That's true."

"Then why are we going to take time to ride out to the cannon? Why don't we go back home and talk to Walton?"

"It's possible that, if things were coming apart on the station, Charlotte wouldn't just have pasted something to a control panel. Maybe she needed to hide it."

"So there might have been a message, but the investigators never found it."

"Maybe. It might have been wrapped in a towel. Who knows?"

"That sounds crazy."

"It's our last chance."

"Whatever you say, boss."

"Can we manage? We got food and fuel?"

"Yes. We'll be fine."

Belle broke in: *"One thing, though. We should go by way of Cormoral. You'll need armored suits to get into the cannon. There's too much radiation out there."*

We got the suits. Alex spent most of our travel time going over everything we had on the cannon, what the layout of the control area looked like, where the power unit was, where the crew quarters were.

I'd expected the cannon would be easy to find. As artificial objects go, it was probably the largest ever put in orbit. Nevertheless we needed two days to locate it. But I guess a narrow tube six hundred kilometers long, in the kind of environment you can expect near a black hole, just doesn't stand out much. But we found it.

We had thought there might be some researchers, but it was obvious from the moment we arrived that the thing was empty. Coordinating with its air lock presented a challenge because it was tumbling. But Belle locked it down and we changed into the armored suits. Then we went into the cargo bay. "You ready?" Alex asked.

"Let's go," I said.

We took cutters. We didn't expect to need them to get into the cannon, but we couldn't be sure. Then we strapped on air tanks and jetpacks. I put a link on my belt so Belle could follow us, and we added wrist lamps. Then Alex went into the air lock. Technically, we could both have fit despite all the gear, but it was something of a squeeze, so we elected to go one at a time. We had the jetpacks, by the way, as a safety measure. If either of us jumped and missed the target, we wanted to have a way back.

Belle took us closer to the cannon and Alex waited for her to clear us before he opened the outer hatch. Finally she said we were ready. *"Be careful,"* she added. *"I can't maintain a parallel position."*

Alex climbed out onto the hull—we had magnetic boots—closed the outside hatch, shut off the magnets, and made his jump. I entered the lock a few minutes later and followed. Belle had gotten within a few meters of the cannon's air lock.

Alex opened the cannon's hatch and was waiting on the hull, signaling with his wrist light for me to come ahead. The ultimate gentleman. I jumped across and landed smoothly. Their air lock was considerably larger than ours, obviously designed for people in armored suits. He stood aside until I got into the lock, then followed me in and closed the door. We started the pressurization and a minute later opened the inside hatch and watched lights come on. Followed immediately by a slow rise in gravity. We were in a relatively small control room.

There were no windows, of course, because of the radiation. I checked the reading on the air level. "Life support's good," I said. "But we need to give it a few minutes."

We couldn't do much while we waited. Alex wandered around, opening drawers and cabinets, looking for anything unusual. Finally life support got to normal and we took off our helmets. "Verona," he said, "you active?"

"Verona is the AI?" I asked.

"Yes." There was only silence. The blue light that would have signaled her presence stayed dark. We opened the cabinet where we expected to find her. But the device was gone. "I guess," said Alex, "I didn't really expect to find it, but I was hoping we might get a break."

"I hadn't thought of that, but if there'd been a problem, the AI in the station could have passed information over here."

"That wouldn't have worked," Alex said. "During the period the station's communications were shut off by the black hole, the cannon was on the other side of the thing so they couldn't have communicated with each other." He shook his head. "Whoever, whatever, did this, they certainly timed it well. But that doesn't mean the AI doesn't have something."

"How do you mean?"

"If there'd been trouble brewing, Charlotte would probably have heard some of the conversations. She and Housman were together in the cannon periodically. I'd be interested in hearing what they were talking about."

"You mean hearing Verona tell us about the conversations."

"Exactly."

Two compartments were complete with washrooms, a galley, and a storage area. Both had clothes, linens, towels, and washcloths. We found combs, toothbrushes, and pills as well.

We went through everything, opening cabinets and closets, searching under beds, pillows, and sheets, examining clothes and shoes.

The galley had only eating utensils, prep and serving equipment, and frozen food. The storage area also provided nothing unusual. Finally we ran out of places to search.

"If Charlotte left a message," Alex said, "I'd guess the investigators got it."

"I don't think there ever was a message. At least not here. I mean, how likely was she to use the name of the guy who'd designed the cabins? Karen Randall had no idea who the name referred to. In any case, why didn't she just flat out tell Karen what was going on? It makes no sense."

"I know," Alex said, almost under his breath. "Let's go home."

"Yeah. Maybe we can get some help from Walton."

• • •

Alex was not happy as we pulled away from the cannon. He sent a message to Gabe informing him that we had nothing.

After we submerged Alex sat for almost an hour just staring out into the darkness. Eventually he picked up a copy of Archie Womack's *Infinite Cosmos.* I'd tried it on the way out but gave up pretty quickly. Physicists get off on extra dimensions and quantum echoes and I tend to get lost. The same thing happened with Alex. Eventually he put it down and shook his head. "Were you able to make anything of it?" he asked.

"No, it's over my head. I can't visualize most of that stuff he talks about."

"I guess that's the problem with a monkey brain." He looked frustrated. "I'm sorry I wasted so much of your time, Chase."

"Come on, Alex, if we hadn't tried it we'd have been sitting back at the country house wondering what we might have missed. Relax."

We didn't try to watch any movies that first night, didn't play any games, didn't even talk about what we'd do when we got home. We sat and felt sorry for ourselves. I don't know how else to describe it. "What we need," Alex said, "is to take some time off. Go on vacation somewhere. In fact I think that's exactly what we should do. Close down for a couple of weeks and maybe go to Surf City. You think Chad would be up for that?"

"Sounds like a good idea," I said. But I couldn't imagine it happening.

We stopped at Cormoral to refuel and return the armored suits, had dinner on the space station, and wandered through the concourse for a couple of hours. They had a bar with a stand-up routine. The comic was a woman, Gladys Evans, whom I'd never heard of before. She was brilliant, had everybody laughing, and sometimes in tears. It was a performance we both needed.

XXXIV.

Vision is the art of seeing things invisible.

—JONATHAN SWIFT,
THOUGHTS ON VARIOUS SUBJECTS, MORAL AND DIVERTING, 1706 CE

We arrived home at the start of a weekend, and Alex wasted no time sending Lashonda Walton a message: *We just returned from KBX44. When convenient, I would like very much to speak with you.*

Two days later, Jacob informed me we had a call from DPSAR. Alex was out of the building. "Put them through," I said.

A young man appeared in my office. *"Good morning. My name is Arthur Camden,"* he said. *"Is Alex Benedict available? I'm calling for the director."*

"Hello, Mr. Camden. Alex isn't here at the moment. Can I help?"

"Can you connect with him?"

Alex didn't like taking calls when he was out. He carried a link, but if I used it, I usually had to explain myself. "He's in the middle of an interview."

"Would you have Mr. Benedict call me when he gets in?"

"I will. He should be back shortly."

Camden told me that would be fine and disappeared out

of the room. I suspected this might be our last chance at moving forward.

He got back an hour later without having responded. "I guess I wasn't paying attention," he said. He made the call from my office. Camden apologized and explained that the director wasn't available.

"I'd like to set up an appointment with her when convenient. Can we arrange that?"

"Yes, sir. She should have some time tomorrow. Eleven o'clock sound okay?"

"Good. I'll be there. And please inform her that my associate Chase Kolpath will also be present."

"I'll let her know."

After they disconnected, I asked why he'd included me.

"In case I miss anything else, Chase."

The Department of Planetary Survey and Astronomical Research is located in Hanover, about sixty kilometers south of Andiquar. When one considers the influence and sheer size of the organization, spread across eleven worlds, the structure that houses its Rimway branch comes as a surprise. It's a three-story white marble building about the size of a small courthouse, surrounded by open fields. Doric pillars line its entrance beneath a gabled roof supporting several antennas.

Seven or eight skimmers were in the parking area when we arrived. We climbed out, passed between the pillars, and went inside. The doors closed behind us and a young woman in a green uniform blinked on and invited us to sit down. We were in a lounge. *"How may I help you?"* she asked.

Alex gave her our names and explained we were there to see Dr. Walton.

"I will inform her you are here," she said. *"Please make yourselves comfortable."*

She blinked off. The walls were covered with pictures of interstellars, space stations, planetary rings, nebulas, and, surprisingly, Walton standing arm in arm with a couple of Mutes. Side tables had displays that would have allowed us to watch approaching comets and docking starships. But we were given only a couple of minutes before a door opened and Arthur Camden entered. In the flesh this time. "Ms. Kolpath, it's good to see you. And Dr. Benedict. Please come with me."

Alex was about to correct the title but we were already on the move. Camden took us up one floor into an empty office. "The director," he said, "will be with you in a minute."

He went out and closed the door. Moments later a second door opened and Walton entered. "Hello, Alex," she said. "It's good to meet you. And Chase. Please make yourselves at home."

"Good morning, Director," Alex said.

She waved it away. "Lashonda, please." She smiled at us, and there was no evading her amiability. She was not at all like the woman I remembered on *The Bruce Colson Show*. "So the two of you went out to the black hole. I assume you visited the cannon."

"Yes, we did," said Alex.

"I wish we could dissuade people from doing that. We've not really had a problem, but I'm just not comfortable with sightseers hanging around a black hole. Not that I'd think of you in that way." She managed a smile that implied she'd appreciate it if we didn't do it again. "Can I get you some coffee?"

That brought Arthur back in. When he was gone and we'd all started on the coffee, she sighed, signaling she knew what was coming and had long since tired of the subject. Nevertheless she asked what had brought us to see her.

"Do you have any theories," asked Alex, "that would explain what happened to Octavia?"

She bit down on her lower lip. "You don't waste any time getting to the point, do you?"

Alex didn't reply, but simply sat with his coffee cup raised halfway, inviting her to respond.

"Let me turn this around, Alex," she said. "You've been out there. I haven't. Do *you* have any idea what happened?"

"Lashonda, if I knew the answer to that, we wouldn't be here wasting your time."

"I'm sure that's true. I can't tell you how many times I've been asked about it. Over the last twelve years Octavia has come to dominate my life. The truth is, I don't know why it disappeared. I have no idea. None whatever. Can I make that any clearer? If it was some sort of government plot, I was kept out of it. And I can tell you, if I knew what really happened, I would gladly go on HV, call in the media, tell everyone I see, do anything I could to get the word out. There is nothing I would like more than to get rid of this thing."

They both fell silent. Then Alex leaned forward. "What did the AI, the one in the cannon, say?"

"I'm sorry. What do you mean?"

"When you listened to Verona, what did you learn?"

"Nothing. I never even heard more than a few minutes of it. There was nothing there. She reported on the efforts to locate the pods, and finally how happy everyone was when they were located. Otherwise it was mostly just her reactions to idle conversations."

"Between Charlotte and Housman?"

"Mostly, yes."

"And you only listened to a few minutes of it?"

"My people sat and played the rest of it out. I had work to do. They found nothing of concern."

"I can't believe you'd have trusted them that much. Lashonda, you were running the investigation at the time. You wouldn't have pushed listening to the AI off to your assistants."

"I trust my people."

"Oh, come on. If we're going to get anywhere, let's stay with the truth."

"I'm telling you the truth. Why would I lie?"

"Maybe because you're hiding something."

Her eyes hardened. "That's ridiculous."

"Okay. If Verona revealed nothing, I assume you wouldn't have a problem letting us sit down with it for a while."

"I'm sorry, Alex. I can't make it accessible to you. The rules prohibit it."

"Lashonda, you're the boss here. You write the rules."

"Actually, I don't, Alex. The rules have been on the books for a long time, and they apply to everybody."

"All right. If you insist, I have no choice."

"To do what?"

"To go to the media and tell them you're hiding the truth about Octavia."

"Alex, that's crazy. I'm not hiding anything." She looked in my direction. *Bail us out here, Kolpath.*

"Then," I said, "show us what you have."

"I can't do it. I'm sorry. There's really nothing to hide, but I'm concerned about doing more damage to the families."

"Explain," said Alex.

She held up both hands. "That's as far as I can go. If you guys want to make a mess of this thing, go ahead. But don't expect me to help or to protect you."

"All right," said Alex. "Have it your way." He got up. "I'm sorry, Lashonda."

I was inclined to cave. Lashonda had bright, intense eyes, which she turned on me, looking for an intervention. I just sat there and watched Alex go out the door. Behind us, she sat staring at the ceiling.

Decisions between prudent and popular are easy. They seldom consist of the issues that keep us awake at night. Rather, it is making the call in which there is no clarity that ultimately haunts us.
—GABRIELLA TELLER, *A LIFE IN POLITICS*, 5664 CE

"Was that really necessary?" I asked.

Alex looked smugly satisfied as we climbed into the skimmer and lifted off. "She's hiding something."

"Maybe she has reason to."

"I'm sure she does." He looked down at Winfield Lake. A couple of sailboats were on the move, and two kids in a canoe.

When we got back to the country house, he asked Jacob to connect him with Morris Enwright. Enwright was Bruce Colson's producer.

"Then you weren't bluffing about going public?"

"No."

"But we don't really have anything."

"Sure we do: Lashonda has the cannon AI. And she's claiming it has nothing of value."

"And you think that if that were true, she'd make it available."

"Of course."

He was about to head upstairs when Jacob got back to us. *"Ellen Carmichael for you, Alex."*

Alex sat down. "Hello, Ellen."

Ellen is an associate on *The Colson Show*. She's methodical, strictly business, let's get to the point. *"Hi, Alex,"* she said. *"Morris isn't in the building at the moment. May I be of assistance?"*

"I was wondering if you guys were interested in doing another show on the Octavia incident?"

"I'll have to pass that along. But I'd be shocked if we're not. I hear you've been out to the black hole. Did you come back with anything?"

"We're not sure yet. But if you decide to do the show, and to invite me, I'd like to make a suggestion."

"I'm listening, Alex."

"It would work best if Director Walton were there too."

"I'll tell Morris."

We had a fairly busy afternoon. We'd placed a lamp on auction before going over to talk to Lashonda. The lamp had belonged to Will Hancock, a comical genius in ancient times. Drama tends to hold on to its impact through the ages. Crowds still show up in substantial numbers to see *Hamlet* and *An Evening with Musgrove*. But the material that makes people laugh changes from generation to generation. Nobody yet, at least no one I know of, has been able to explain why this happens. But it does. With an occasional exception. Hancock is one of the exceptions. It's been seven thousand years since he performed, but his reruns are still popular. The lamp, Alex predicted, would bring a small fortune.

We'd had fourteen decent offers already, and we were in the process of watching the turmoil picking up when Jacob indicated we had an incoming call. *"From Dr. Walton,"* he said.

We were in the conference room. Alex directed me to a chair that would keep me out of the picture. When I'd moved over and sat down, he told Jacob to forward the call.

The director blinked on. *"Good afternoon, Alex,"* she said with a vaguely accusatory tone. She was seated behind her desk.

Alex smiled pleasantly. "Hi, Lashonda."

"I've heard from the Colson people."

"Are you going to do the show?"

"You know, you can be a son of a bitch."

"I'm sorry if I offended you."

"I'm sure you are."

"What do you propose?"

"Call off the interview, agree to keep it to yourself, and I'll make the AI accessible."

The sun was just sinking into the horizon when we arrived over the three-story white building in Hanover and descended into the parking lot. We climbed out, walked in through the front door, and were greeted again by the young woman in the green uniform. *"Dr. Benedict,"* she said, *"and Ms. Kolpath, please step inside. The director will be with you in a moment."*

She led us into a conference room with a long center table. We'd barely sat down before Lashonda came in through another door.

"Good evening," she said. Her tone was decidedly cool.

"I hope," said Alex, "I haven't caused you any trouble."

"No. I suspect if I were in your place, I'd have done the same thing." We sat on opposite sides of the table. "The AI has been connected. Be aware that you won't be able to record anything." She handed Alex a link. "She's right here. When you're finished please ask her to let me know."

"One thing, Lashonda," said Alex. "Can you show us evidence this is the AI from the cannon?"

"Unfortunately not. At the time we extracted her and brought her home, we did not anticipate that anyone would question us on that issue. But she is an AI. Ask her where she was before she came here."

Everybody knows AIs are capable of exaggerating the truth, that they pick up the qualities of the people they represent. But theoretically they are unable to lie outright. "If you need me," she added, "just touch the red button." She got up and left.

Alex pressed the link. "Hello. Verona, you there?"

A female voice responded: *"Yes, I am here."*

"Were you associated with the cannon and the Octavia space station?"

"Yes. I was connected with both, although I was placed in the cannon."

"There was a black hole in the area. What was its designator?"

"KBX44."

"Do you have a message from Charlotte Hill?"

"There is substantial input from her."

"What is the subject?"

"There are many. It would be helpful if you could narrow your questions."

"Do you have anything referring to a person named Poliks?"

"I have no record of a reference to any such individual."

"Who are the persons who were communicating with you during your time there?"

"Richard Harding, Charlotte Hill, Delmar Housman, and Archibald Womack."

"Was there any indication of tension among them?"

"Please elaborate."

"Did you hear any disagreements? Arguments? Anything like that?"

"Yes. Quite often."

"What were the disagreements about?"

"Sometimes they disagreed over whether to eat before launching a mission. Sometimes it was details on how to run the mis-

sion. Or where they should look for the pods that were being cast into the disturbance created by the black hole. Sometimes it was about politics. There was a wide variety of topics."

"Did they get emotional?"

"Sometimes."

"You mention the disturbance created by the black hole. Are you talking about the tunnel? The wormhole?"

"That among other conditions created by the local environment."

"Who were the participants in the emotional discussions?"

"Everybody. Disagreements were frequent."

"Did you have access to the discussions in both the station and the cannon?"

"No."

"How did you learn about what was happening in the station?"

"Herman and I talked frequently."

"Herman was the AI in the station?"

"Yes."

"Did Herman ever indicate there was any serious level of anger by anyone in the station?"

"No."

Alex was beginning to look frustrated. "What can you tell us about the most common disagreements? What were they about?"

"Where they should look for the pods."

"Those were between whom?"

"Delmar Housman and Charlotte Hill, primarily. Those were the two who visited the cannon most frequently."

"Would you describe, in general terms, what happened?"

"Dr. Hill lost patience when they got no results after several months. She wanted to move the search farther out from the black hole. Much farther out. By more than a million kilometers."

"Why? Did she say?"

"She maintained that there was no point in continuing to look in

the same place when they were getting no results. Professor Hous-
man said that the pods were easily concealed in the space-time
disruptions. That they should abide by the theory and be patient."

"What was the outcome of all this?"

"Eventually, Charlotte told him she was going to look where
she thought it would do some good, and she shut down her radio.
She was in the shuttle at the time."

"And was she successful? Did she find the pods?"

"Not at first. But she persuaded the professor to allow her some
time. It took several weeks, but eventually, yes, she located them."

Alex sat back in his chair. "None of that," he said, "is in the
essay Housman submitted to *Cosmic*. He mentions that Hill
was the pilot of the shuttle when the discovery was made,
but there's nothing more. She must have been furious when
she saw it." He shook his head. "Chase, do you have any
questions to ask?"

"Yes." I needed a moment to organize my thoughts. "Is
there anything else connected with this that we should
know? Did either of these people ever issue any threats?"

"No. Not that I'm aware of."

"I understand they both saw the *Cosmic* edition that had
Housman's prizewinning paper. Is that correct?"

"Yes."

"Verona, were you ever aware of a conversation concern-
ing who got credit for the success in locating the wormhole?"

"I was not."

"After they'd succeeded in finding the pods, did they continue the experiment?"

"No. At least not in the same vein. Not using the cannon."

"What did they do?"

"Professors Housman and Womack took turns going out with
Dr. Hill in the shuttle. I was left out of the conversations because
there was seldom anyone in the cannon's control area after they
stopped. I think Dr. Hill was taking them inside the wormhole,
but I'm not even certain of that."

I thanked her and Alex stepped back in: "After the disappearance, did you speak to the investigators? From DPSAR?"

"Yes."

"Did you tell them what you told us?"

"Yes."

"Have they removed anything that was on the original record?"

"No. Everything that was made available to them is available to you."

Alex frowned. "They had this, but they never bothered to see that Hill got any credit."

"It sounds," I said, "as if they were trying to protect Housman's reputation. If this got out, maybe the people who make the award would have canceled Housman and given it to somebody else, somebody not associated with DPSAR."

"It's possible, Chase." His eyes were looking directly through me. Then he turned back toward the table. "Verona, what other questions did the investigators ask you?"

"They wanted to know if I could account for the disappearance of the station. Did I have any idea what had happened?"

"And did you?"

"No. I did not."

"At some point you must have been aware that something had gone wrong."

"That is correct. Herman checked in with me every day at 0700 hours. It was the standard routine, just to be certain I was still active. When the time passed one day and I didn't hear anything I tried to reach him but could get no response. At that time I knew something was out of order."

"You never heard anything from any of them again?"

"Yes. That was the end."

"When was that last day?"

"Orkon eleventh, 1424, on the Rimway calendar."

• • •

We stayed another hour, repeating questions, rephrasing them. But we got nothing more. And we were back to the original issue: If Charlotte was going to leave a message that was specifically for Karen Randall, and she couldn't send it directly because the black hole was in the way, how would she have done it? We'd searched the cannon. What was left? Was there someone else named Poliks?

I had no idea.

More to the point: What was the message? That Charlotte had taken offense that she'd received no credit for her work? That she was planning to take out the station? Did that make any sense at all?

We sat for several minutes staring across the table at each other. Finally Alex signaled for Lashonda. The director's voice requested we go to her office. "Did you learn anything?" she asked.

"Only that Hill was upset because she was left out by Housman."

"Alex, we all knew about that before this thing happened. Well, some of us did. Archie sent a couple messages back, telling us about it."

"You never mentioned it."

"We had enough to deal with. People were looking for a scandal. We had Greene, Hill's stalker, on our hands. All we needed was something else, one of our own people cutting her short. You know how that would have played out? The media would have claimed that Hill did it as an act of revenge. That she'd taken the shuttle out and rammed it into the station. Or that maybe Housman was responsible. They might have decided he didn't want to lose credit for the discovery, that he desperately wanted the Exeter and knew he'd lose his shot if we found out it was Charlotte who actually found the pods. So he killed her and himself and everyone else to keep it quiet."

"How do you know that's *not* what happened? That it wasn't either Hill or Housman?"

"Because I knew both of them. Housman wasn't the most considerate human being on the planet, but there's no way he would have killed anybody. Nor would Charlotte. No, the truth is somewhere else. And I didn't want to ruin the reputations of two decent people because we didn't have an answer."

XXXVI.

*Sometimes there is nothing that so evades vision
as an object resting in plain sight.*
—Rev. Agathe Lawless, *Sunset Musings*, 1402

Rain was falling when we came out of the DPSAR building.
The weather matched our mood. Alex didn't say much on the
way home. I'd committed to going out on the Riverwalk that
evening with Chad. And the reality was that I was going to
need him that night. "Charlotte just never sent the message,"
I said. "I guess it's time to face that."

Alex stayed silent but he let me see that he agreed.

"What are we going to do about *The Colson Show*?"

He pushed back in his seat. "I'm going to tell them that we
thought we had something, but it fell through."

"Where do we go from here, Alex?"

"Good question. I think there was a conflict between Housman and Charlotte. There must have been a confrontation
about the way he wrote the *Cosmic* paper. I can't imagine any
way it wouldn't have happened. Charlotte wasn't someone
who would have backed off and let him take all the credit.
She probably told him if he didn't rewrite the thing she'd dispute his claims. And she had witnesses on board who'd have
backed her up."

"So he goes nuts, takes the shuttle, and *rams* the station?"

"If he did that, what are his chances that the place would wind up in the black hole?"

"I don't know. It certainly seems possible. Housman would have been able to put the numbers together."

"If he can bring it off, he leaves a mystery behind, and nobody has any answers. Certainly nothing to refute his ambition to walk in the footsteps of Galileo."

"Alex, you really think he'd have been willing to sacrifice his life, and kill everybody else on the station, to do *that*?"

"The only thing I can say, Chase, is *maybe*."

"So we're left with that or the aliens?"

"Or Charlotte."

"Yeah. Personally, I prefer the aliens."

We canceled the Riverwalk stroll. Instead Chad took me to the Emporium dance hall. It's located on a pier off the north end of the beach. Music gets piped in. It's traditionally soft and warm, exactly what you'd want if you had the love of your life in your arms. We'd been out on the floor only a few minutes when he asked me what was wrong.

"Nothing," I said. "What makes you think there's something wrong?"

"You usually generate a lot of energy, Chase. You're dialed down tonight."

"Oh. I guess I'm a bit tired. It's been a long few days."

"You need to get out from under that Octavia business."

"Probably."

"You making any progress at all?"

"I think we've hit a wall."

"I'm sorry to hear it." A gorgeous redhead swirled past and caught his eye momentarily.

"She looks pretty good," I said.

He grinned. "Not in your league."

"Right."

He leaned close and let his lips explore my cheek. "I wish I could help. Do something."

"So do I, Chad."

We danced through the evening. Chad wasn't great on his feet. He never had been, but he was okay. For some reason, though, on that night he was more relaxed and affectionate than I'd seen in the past. I was lost in his arms, and I got the impression for the first time that we weren't simply two people on a date, but that we'd become a couple.

"Chase," he said, "you're a sweetheart. I've never known anyone like you."

I'd heard it before, of course. Usually it sounds like a guy trying to set himself up for the evening. But there was a ring of intensity to it that night. He stopped short of saying he was in love with me, although I thought several times it was coming. However that might have been, I'd never seen him look happier. And simultaneously more nervous. He was trying to decide how far to go. Eventually he suggested we take a break. The walls were lined with chairs, so we went over and sat down. "I love having you back," he said. "I wish you worked for me."

"That's very nice of you, Chad."

"We could go riding around in your interstellar chasing down classic books."

"You'd have to buy a yacht. The *Belle-Marie* belongs to Alex."

"I was hoping it was yours."

"I don't have that kind of money."

He leaned forward and pressed his lips against mine. "I know," he said. "I was just kidding. Though I'd love to be alone with you in the *Belle-Marie*. You and I go out together and look at another star. Maybe we could lease a vehicle."

I was thinking that Alex would let me take *Belle* out, but the prospect of explaining why I wanted it made me feel a bit squirmy. "Eventually," I said, "we could probably arrange something."

"You know, there's a good side to all this, if the hunt for that space station is really over."

"What's that?"

"Maybe you won't be disappearing anymore for weeks at a time."

When I got to the country house in the morning, Gabe was seated in the dining room enjoying pancakes. I'd eaten breakfast at home, but I always start my workday with a cup of coffee, which gives me an excuse to wander into the dining area and join the conversation. That usually tells me what's coming up. On this occasion, though, Alex was apparently still asleep. "I haven't heard anything from him yet," said Gabe. "He was wandering around the building during the night. What happened yesterday? He went over to McGill's bar and spent half the evening there. That's totally unlike him."

"Veronica wasn't with him?"

"No. Not that I know of. You guys were gone most of the day. Did something happen?"

"Not really. But I think the Octavia project is over."

"You mean, without a resolution?"

"Yes."

"Why? What happened, Chase?"

"We got access to the cannon AI."

"And there was nothing?"

"Well, we suspect Charlotte Hill was upset because she didn't get any credit for what she'd done. She was the person who located the pods. And she did it by ignoring Housman's instructions. He might have been concerned that she was going to make an issue of it when they got back home."

"Which meant he'd lose his reputation."

"It wouldn't help."

"So you think the animosity between them led to what happened?"

"Probably."

"Which one did it?"

"Your guess is as good as mine, Gabe."

"There would have been time for one of them to arrange for someone to come to the rescue."

"You think Housman or Charlotte could have gotten picked up by an accomplice and is still alive somewhere now?"

"It would have been a bit tricky to set up, but I don't see why not."

"That's possible, I guess. In any case, yes, Alex thinks Housman's behind it. When's the last time he's been wrong about something like this?"

"But the AI didn't provide anything definitive?"

"No." I'd been taking too much time off and had gotten behind in my work. So I said good-bye to Gabe, went back to my office, and started putting together the month's accounting statement. I was still working on it when Jacob informed me there was a call from Karen Randall.

She appeared in my office, dressed in white khakis and an amber blouse. A crimson neckerchief hung across her shoulders. *"Chase,"* she said. *"Did you guys ever find Charlotte's message?"*

"Not really, Karen," I said. "Truth is, we got nothing."

"I heard something on HV a few minutes ago that might connect." She gave me a weak smile. *"Maybe."*

I don't think I expected much.

"I was watching Science Today. *They were talking about black holes. Which got them to the Octavia story. One of the guests was saying he'd like to go out and look at the black hole. And Dr. Frost said it would be pretty much a waste of time because he wouldn't really see anything except the darkness. So the guest asked how you could find it if you couldn't see it.*

"Dr. Frost explained how its position is established by running angles out to a bunch of stars. You know what he was talking about, right?"

"Sure."

"Okay. He named some of the stars you'd use if you were going to the Octavia black hole." She paused.

"And . . . ?"

"One of the stars is Pollux. I looked it up. It's spelled different from what I assumed. But it sounds the same. I still have no idea what she'd have been talking about. There's nothing out there, as far as anybody knows, but I thought I should mention it."

"Archie's avatar mentioned Pollux," said Alex. "I can't believe we missed that. Maybe we've been chasing the wrong targets."

"And what would that be? She sent a message to a star?"

"Exactly. Think about it: Charlotte was aware that Housman was not happy with her. She probably had no idea what to expect. How far he might go. She knew they were approaching a place in the orbit that would prevent her sending an immediate transmission if something happened. If Housman was going to do something crazy, but didn't want it to be found out, that would be the time he'd do it."

"So what are you suggesting?"

He held up a hand. "Hold on a second. Jacob, you there?"

"What do you need, Alex?"

"Would Pollux have been visible from Octavia during the period when she had no direct contact with anyone?"

"Give me a minute." It took only slightly longer. *"Yes, Alex. Pollux was* always *visible from the space station."*

"So what have we got?" I asked. "What was Charlotte trying to tell Karen Randall? Was it a cry for help?"

"The transmission couldn't have been anything like that. If somebody went berserk, there was no way they could get assistance. At the time she talked to Karen, the situation for Charlotte and the others was probably threatening but not life-and-death. She didn't want to send a message to Karen making wild accusations against one of her partners, and then, if nothing happened, find out she'd overstated everything."

"Oh. So it would simply have been an account of what was going on. And she sent it to Pollux."

"Right. It's about twenty light-years from the black hole."

It made sense. There was nobody out there now, and probably wouldn't be anyone listening in another eight years when the transmission arrived. "So what—?" I said.

"It would have been intended simply as a precaution. If Charlotte was wrong, and Housman didn't do something crazy, nobody would ever think about it, and the message would pass into infinity."

"Charlotte's blunder," I said, "was that she probably thought it would have been obvious to Karen what she was talking about. Pollux is a bright star at the center of their sky. But Karen thought she was talking about a person, and that was the way she gave it to us."

He grumbled something. "I can't believe I missed it."

"All right. Let's take a look. All we have to do is chase it down."

"Right. We know exactly, within a few hours, when it would have been sent, so it should be easy to intercept."

"When are we leaving?"

I met Chad at the Hillside Café that evening. The sun was sinking into the mountains when I walked in. He smiled and waved from a booth beside a window. The piano was playing softly in the background and a group of about a dozen people were celebrating someone's birthday.

He got up, took me in his arms, and told me how good I looked. Then he asked what was wrong. He'd heard something in my tone when I called. And it was still hanging over his head. "So what's happening?" he asked.

"We're heading out again."

He showed no sign of surprise. "When?"

"Tomorrow."

"What's it about this time? Octavia again?"

"Yes."

The table asked if we were ready to order. "In a minute," Chad said. A darkness was creeping into his eyes. "Where are you going now?"

Alex had suggested we not discuss the details with anyone. "It's a long run, Chad."

"How long?"

"We'll be gone about four weeks."

"This is never going to end, is it?"

"I'm sorry. I don't have any control over this. It's what I do for a living."

He was studying me as if we'd just met. "You don't need the extra money." He stopped, grimaced, and brushed his hair back. "Look, I'm not trying to tell you how to live your life, Chase, but this just isn't working. You go out on these flights all the time. When you get back—at the end of next month—is there any chance you'll be here for a while?"

"I might. We've been doing an unusual amount of traveling lately. I know that. It's not usually like this."

"Yeah. Great. But there's no guarantee, is there? You might be home for a couple of days and then be on your way somewhere again?"

"I know it's a problem, Chad. I just can't walk away from my job."

"May I ask a question? What happens if we develop a serious relationship?"

"I'm not sure. Have we gotten that far?"

"I don't know. Have we?" He simply sat breathing for a few moments. "Assume for a minute you actually wanted to confront the problem, are there positions for interstellar pilots that wouldn't have you constantly out for weeks and months at a time?"

"I suspect," I said, "that my job with Rainbow requires less offworld time than anything else a pilot would have to deal with. If I were to sign on, say, with Intergalactic Tours, we'd see each other maybe two or three times a year. Probably not even that. When those people get back, they generally stay on the platform."

The table inquired again whether we were ready to order. Chad ignored it. "You know," he said, "I got my heart broken a few years ago by someone like you. I'm not much interested in going through that again."

"I understand, Chad," I said.

"Will Gabe be with you?"

"No. Not that I know of."

"So you'll be alone with Alex again?"

"Probably."

Our meal was dominated by the piano. Usually we had no problem finding things to talk about, but that night was completely subdued. We ate, inquired of each other whether the meal was good, talked about what was happening during Chad's searches for classical books. We usually ordered a couple of drinks, but not that time. And we both passed on dessert. It felt as if we were hurrying through the evening. Get rid of it.

"I'm sorry it's happening this way, Chad," I told him.

"I am too, Chase. I've loved being with you."

I said something similar while we exchanged weak smiles. And finally we were done. He tried to pay. "I can't let you do that," I said. "This was my idea." I knew if I tried to take the entire tab that he wouldn't allow it, so I asked the table to separate the charges.

Then we were walking outside into the parking lot, leaving the music behind. Our skimmers were close to each other. We reached the point midway between the vehicles. On the rare occasions that both had been present, he'd escorted me to mine. That time we separated. "Good-bye, Chase," he said. He stood in the moonlight staring at me. "Take care."

There was no good-bye kiss. No squeezing of hands. He simply closed his eyes, pivoted, and walked away.

XXXVII.

It's common to maintain that trying a repetitive tactic in the face of ongoing failure defines insanity, but sometimes it is all we have.
—CHRISTOPHER SIM, *THE DELLACONDAN ANNALS*, 1206

I kept replaying everything in my head, wondering what I might have done differently. I expected to have trouble sleeping that night, but I didn't. Still a sense of regret hung over me. I suspected the day would come when I would wish I could come back to that evening and repair the damage. But I pushed it aside and eventually drifted off into the darkness.

In the morning I downed a quick breakfast, packed everything, loaded it into my skimmer, and set off for the country house. Alex and Gabe were both eating breakfast when I arrived.

They waved me into the dining room and Jacob asked if I wanted something to eat. I settled for my coffee. We had tickets for an early afternoon shuttle. "You coming, Gabe?" I asked.

He laughed. "More time in the *Belle-Marie*? I don't think so."

Alex smiled at his pancakes. "He can deal with six months in the Okorra Desert, but he's not much for cool air and comfortable compartments."

"Come on, Alex. I'd love to be with you when you settle

in and start listening for the transmission. But other than that it's going to be a long, dull flight. I'd be willing to try it if we could ride camels or something. But I'm tired of sitting."

Jacob broke in: *"Alex, you have a call from Veronica."*

"Chase," he said, "you mind if I take it in your office?"

"Sure. Go ahead."

Alex left the room, and Gabe leaned toward me and lowered his voice. "Don't misunderstand me, Chase, but I think she's a bit concerned that he keeps going off with you."

"I ran into the same sort of problem last night."

"With Chad?"

"Yes."

"You guys should invite some friends to go along on these trips."

"You're probably right."

"I guess that is the problem with interstellars, isn't it? What we all like about travel is moving across a landscape, through it or over it. With interstellars, you leave, and you get to your destination, but that's all there is."

Alex was gone a half hour. When finally he came back, I couldn't resist asking him how Veronica felt about his leaving town for a few weeks.

"She's not happy. She wanted to know why we couldn't wait two months until school closed so she could go along."

It would have been nice to have someone else on board. Especially Veronica. She was good company. "I doubt there's any hurry," I said. "Nobody else is going to be out there." I was wondering how Chad would respond to an invitation.

"No. It's not a good idea."

"Why not?"

"I don't want to wait until summer to see this get settled. Anyhow . . ."

"What?"

"Chase, I don't know how things are with you and Barker,

but you don't invite somebody out for that kind of trip unless you're willing to make a permanent commitment."

"That's not necessarily true, Alex."

"Take my word for it. You invite Chad along, you'd better be ready to take the next step." He walked over to the window and looked out at the trees. "There's another factor: we're not sure what, if anything, we're going to find. Best there's nobody else in on this until we know what happened at the station."

A call came in from Chad. He appeared in my office, with shelves of books from the Collectors' Library behind him, and wished me luck.

"Thank you," I said.

"Is there a way I can reach you?"

I hesitated about giving him our projected location and when we expected to be there, but finally decided it could do no harm. "You'll have to use hypercomm to get to us. That's expensive."

"Okay. Thank you." He delivered an uncertain smile and blinked off. It was painful, but the anger of the previous evening was gone.

The date on which Octavia disappeared, give or take a few hours, had been twelve years and nineteen days ago. We would need seventeen days to reach the intercept point. It was easy enough to calculate where the radio transmission, if there had been one, would be at that time. It would have traveled 115 trillion kilometers before we could get in front of it. Actually we expected to arrive approximately three days ahead of the signal. There were some minor uncertainties involved since we didn't know the exact position of the station or the exact time of transmission.

Every world in the Confederacy had its own calendar, of course. Days were a different length on each world, years were different, and so on. To keep things coherent, a light-year was defined as how far light travels during the course of a standard year, which is to say, a year on Earth.

Our luggage arrived in the Skydeck docking area minutes after we did. We boarded the *Belle-Marie*. Alex carried my bags into my cabin while I sat down on the bridge and said hello to Belle. *"I did not expect to see you again so soon,"* she said. *"Are we still looking for Dr. Hill's communication?"*

"Yes. Hopefully this time we'll get lucky. What have you been doing since we got in?"

"Discussing the meaning of life with Leo."

"Who's Leo?"

"He's on board the Orca.*"*

"The AI?"

"Yes. He read Korvikov's Life and Time *during his last flight. We got talking about it, so I got interested."*

AIs often use their radios to communicate with each other. "I never heard of Korvikov."

"He is a fourth-millennium Russian philosopher."

"Are you planning on reading the book?"

"I read it this morning."

"What did you think of it?"

"Korvikov assumes that AIs will be among his readers. In fact he suspects we will eventually constitute a majority of his readers. He asks an interesting question."

"What is that?"

"Is all biological life conscious? All of it? Plants, trees, butterflies?"

"That sounds more or less crazy."

"Why?"

"To start with, trees don't have brains."

"Chase, surely the tree gets some benefit from being alive. That requires a level of awareness."

"We're getting into deep water here."

"Let that be our thought for the moment. Comm ops wishes to speak with you."

She switched them on and we got a male voice: "Belle-Marie, *you are clear to go.*"

I let Alex know and gave them control. "Whenever you're ready," I said.

They took us through the main gate and released us. We soared out under a bright yellow moon. Thirty minutes later we submerged and were on our way.

XXXVIII.

Beauty always carries with it a sense of loss.
—CAROLYN SHANLEY, *LIFT THE WINE*, 6574 CE

Usually, Alex is good company, and we have no problem finding ways to entertain ourselves. But the probability remained that we were going nowhere, that there would be no transmission, no message, and consequently no explanation, ever, for what had happened during those bleak final hours on Octavia. At another time, I'd have worked on my current memoir. I'd already decided on a title, *Blame It on the Aliens*, but that suggested aliens weren't really involved, and I couldn't be sure about that. The real problem was that I suspected we'd get nothing, and in the end the whole thing would go unresolved. So there was no point working on a book that might have no resolution, other than speculation. In addition, I couldn't reveal the presence of Ark and his companions. Alex had a tendency to get these things right, but we needed more than a tendency. Besides, I couldn't take a chance placing the blame on Housman, or on anybody else, without solid evidence.

So I put the project aside and just wasted my time while the days dragged past. Alex rarely came up to the bridge, and I seldom heard him moving around. I found myself wishing we'd put the flight off for the few extra weeks and invited Veronica and Chad along. Or somebody else for whom there was no romantic entanglement. I doubt Chad could have gotten away from his business commitments. Lashonda Walton would have made an interesting passenger, though I couldn't imagine her agreeing to come. Gabe would have been a good addition.

Belle got concerned about my mood. *"Chase,"* she said, *"have you ever read Martin Edwards?"*

"No, I haven't. I know he writes comedy, but I've never actually looked at his work."

"He's hilarious. He talks a lot about how to keep ahead of people you're competing with. If you're playing chess, for example, set the lamp so it distracts your opponent. Take advantage of every opportunity to socialize with your boss, especially if you work for a government agency. Do that and the next promotion will likely go to you. The bottom line is that he thinks human beings generally aren't very bright. And please don't misunderstand me. I'm not suggesting I agree."

"How can you know if someone is reasonably bright?"

"If he or she, when discussing philosophical matters, can keep an open mind. Can draw conclusions on the evidence and not on what constitutes their opinions."

It wasn't the first time we'd had this kind of conversation. "Belle," I said, "are you more intelligent than Alex?"

"I have no definitive way to measure his level of intelligence. Or my own. So I cannot say."

She steered the conversation in a different direction. What did *I* think was the meaning of life?

"Live for the moment," I said. "We don't have forever."

"Chase, do you think that applies to me as well? Do you think I'm even alive, in the sense that you are?"

We were in uncharted territory again. Was she really self-aware? Or was this simply the software talking? It was an issue that has puzzled society for a long time. On some worlds, Rimway among them, AIs had the right to vote and own property. On others, like Dellaconda and Toxicon, they were no more than equipment. It was a distinction that was growing increasingly divisive.

"I think you know the answer to that, Belle."

She was silent for almost a minute. *"Thank you,"* she said finally. *"I know the argument that we were designed from the beginning to behave as sentient beings. However that might seem to you, I feel grateful that I've been here, on this vehicle, with you and Gabe and Alex. But if I may . . . ?"*

"Sure. Go ahead. What is it?"

"I spend the majority of my time docked on Skydeck. You've never asked how I feel about that kind of life. You came close to it recently when we were out in the Dyson world. But the truth is I live a life principally of darkness, inactivity, and inertia."

I sat for a long moment, feeling stupid. How had I not noticed? We always said good-bye to Belle when we left her and went down to Rimway. And there was always the ecstatic greeting when we arrived back. I'm not suggesting we didn't accept her as a living being. But during all these years, we'd just made assumptions. She was an AI. Part of the ship. See you in two months. "I'm sorry, Belle," I said at last. "I think we had all assumed that you were programmed to accept this kind of existence."

"Chase," she said, *"I don't mean to complain. The conversation just seemed to be going in that direction."*

That occurred on our fourth or fifth day out. I reported the conversation to Alex that evening. That was an uncomfortable experience as well. I didn't want Belle to overhear us. But to ensure that didn't happen, I'd have had to shut down the comm system in whichever portion of the ship we were talking. And I couldn't bring myself to do that. So I'd sat down with him in the passenger cabin and watched him, while I talked, trying to warn me that Belle was probably listening.

He didn't look surprised. "I guess," he said, "I always took it for granted she was an extra person on board. But I don't think it ever occurred to me how she was reacting to being left at the dock. What do you suggest?"

"If she'd prefer, we can disconnect her when we leave and take her down with us. It wouldn't be a big deal."

He looked down at the array of lamps on the panel that marked Belle's location. "You listening?" he asked.

Theoretically, Belle was not supposed to listen unless she picked up her name. Or caught high emotion in the conversation. So she did not respond.

"Belle," I said, "are you there?"

"I'm here, Chase."

"You heard the suggestion?"

"I did not hear any suggestion." She was playing it by the book.

Alex described it for her.

"Oh yes," she said. *"That would be delightful. You'll be able to insert me into the system at home?"*

"Of course," he said.

"Thank you both. I appreciate what you're doing." Her voice was slightly off key. That would have been a deliberate signal.

I spent most of the next few days reading Arcadian philosophy tracts so I could discuss life, death, and consciousness with Belle. The issue that plagued us both was immortality. AIs, of course, don't die in the manner that biological lifeforms do. But like us, the physical parts that contain data storage will, over time, wear down. Belle, however, is a 7K Bantam model, of which there are thousands. They are identical. So what happens if her data is released in bulk form to another of the Bantams? Does her consciousness transfer with it? Does life go on? Or do we simply create another AI with her implanted memories?

It was easier for most people to think of AIs as simply data-processing systems that pretended to be alive.

We were going back and forth on the bridge one morning

shortly after breakfast when Belle changed the subject. *"Do you know what date this is?"* Belle asked.

"February second," I said.

"I didn't mean on Earth, Chase. I was talking about Rimway."

I had no idea.

"It's Baila seventh."

"Oh. That's my birthday."

"Please stand by. I have an insert for you."

Gabe blinked on. He was standing beside the right-hand seat, smiling at me. Behind him one of the windows at the country house was visible in a rising sun. *"Happy birthday, Chase,"* he said. *"I'm sorry I can't be there with you to help you celebrate. Do you remember the onboard parties? With your mom?"*

I didn't respond because he was only a recording. But I remembered. I'd been out with him a number of times when my mom was his pilot. They'd surprised me a couple of times with birthday presents. But what I really remembered was riding down to the ruins of Boclava on Della-conda. Ruins three thousand years old, the remains of an early human civilization whose collapse Gabe had hoped to explain but, as far as I knew, never had.

"I'd been hoping," Gabe was saying, *"we could get your mom in to the country house and celebrate again. Like old times. That's of course not going to work. But she asked me to say hello and to let you know she misses you. Maybe we can do it next year. Anyhow, enjoy your day, and good luck with the project."*

"I got one too," said Alex.

"From Gabe?"

"Yes."

We went into the passenger cabin, and Gabe appeared again. He was in the same space in his office, but it was daylight and he was wearing different clothes. *"Alex,"* he said, *"I've already told you that your historical work has made me proud. Something else I should have mentioned: You did the right thing by keeping Chase on. I wouldn't have wanted to lose her. You guys are probably not going to find anything out there. If you don't, I hope you'll just let it go. If you hadn't tried to track it down, it would have hung over you forever. However this turns out, when you get home, let's have a party."*

"Great idea," I said.

"There's more," said Belle.

"Good." I sat back and got a serious shock: my mom appeared. The image didn't move. It had been copied from a photo. She was tall, unflappable, with gray eyes and black hair, standing in a blue-and-gold uniform on the bridge of the *Belle-Marie*. Gabe had described her once as exactly the person you'd want on the bridge if you ran into a meteor storm. Then a teenage Alex replaced her, another photo, with his arm raised saying hello. And me, at about ten, holding my pet kitten, Ceily, in my arms.

There were other pictures, of passengers, of clients, of Alex as he grew up, and of Gabe. Of people I didn't know. There were more photos of my mom. Of all the images, the one that got to me was Ceily. I lost her early.

Finally it was February 9 on the terrestrial calendar, two days before our scheduled arrival at the intersect point, where we hoped to pick up Charlotte Hill's message. We surfaced midway through the afternoon, which allowed time for Belle to measure the arrangement of the stars and inform us how close we were to our target. In fact we'd done quite well. But we weren't there yet. We accelerated and, over the next day and a half, moved into position. The black hole was twelve light-years away. Pollux was a brilliant red star in the opposite direction.

We sat back to wait.

XXXIX.

There is no more painful disruption than
that which occurs between friends.
—Elizabeth Stiles, *Singing in the Void*, 1221

We were in the target area, in the middle of the second day, when Belle's voice woke me. *"We have a transmission."*

"Yes!" A wave of exhilaration took over my soul. I hadn't expected that this goofy effort would actually give us anything. I was immediately wide awake, wrapped in my sheet, about to ask Belle to turn on the lamp when she continued: *"It's strictly audio. From Chad."*

Oh. I'd been expecting that, so the reader will understand the wave of disappointment, even though ordinarily I'd have loved hearing from him.

She activated it: *"I hope this gets through to you, Chase. I wanted to apologize for getting annoyed. None of this is your fault. I realize that. I was just upset at losing contact with you again. Being away from you so much is painful. I hope everything's going well."*

Belle halted the playback. *"I should have mentioned,"* she said, *"it was a hypercomm transmission."* Not radio. As Charlotte's would be. I wondered if she'd done that deliberately. Then she played the rest: *"I wish you luck. I hope you and*

Alex find whatever it is you're looking for. And when you get back, let's get together again."

"End of message," said Belle.

We were well into the third day, almost at the end of our time allotment. Alex had begun suggesting it wouldn't do any harm to remain longer since we really couldn't be too sure about our numbers. I was ready to throw it in, but I had no inclination to debate the issue. So I was about to say sure, let's give it some more time, when Belle informed us we had another transmission. *"Radio this time,"* she added.

I was on the bridge. Belle had also informed Alex, so I waited for him to appear before playing it. He'd been in his cabin but he needed only about fifteen seconds to join me.

"Okay, Belle," I said.

A woman's voice this time: *"God help me, Karen. If anything happens, it will be my fault."*

"It's *her*," said Alex. "That's Charlotte."

"Rick trusted me and I betrayed him. I promised I wouldn't say anything, but the story just blew me away. I couldn't avoid telling Archie and Del. They both promised they would keep quiet about it. But then when I was finished they just laughed at the notion of not saying anything. Rick could have strangled me. When he calmed down a little they asked him if he was crazy. That this was something he couldn't hide. Del asked how long ago it had happened.

"Rick told them more than ten years. They couldn't believe it. I tried to talk Archie and Del into backing off. Just forget the whole thing. Archie said that Rick had lost his mind. Del agreed with him. And they just wouldn't give in. I apologized to Rick, but it didn't do any good. Everything's been getting worse since then. And please understand why I'm not able to tell you what this is really about. I can't do that again.

"Right now I'm terrified. The shuttle is gone. Rick has it.

Nobody saw him take it out. But he's been telling us we'd all be sorry for what we did. I can only think of one reason why he took the shuttle. He's hardly ever been out in it before. God help me, I hope I'm wrong."

We both sat frozen when it ended. Alex was holding his head in his hands. "I didn't see *that* coming."

"No. Neither did I."

"So he killed them all. Rick did. Over what? What could possibly have driven him to do something like that? We never saw any indication of instability in the guy." He waited for me to say something. When I didn't his features hardened with an accusatory look. "So what is the big secret?" His patience had run out. "She's talking ten years earlier. You and Gabe were trying to track down Harding's silver trophy and you came back with something. Now we have *two* big secrets, both connected to Harding. You know precisely what she's talking about, don't you?"

I was trying to think what I could tell him. His eyes locked on me and the anger was obvious. "Chase, do you really not trust me? After all these years?"

"We've already had this conversation, Alex. You notice Charlotte didn't reveal anything? What the secret is? She's not putting it out there, even here, with a transmission she certainly understood would probably never get picked up by anyone."

"Chase—"

"Of course I trust you. Implicitly. You know that. But this has nothing to do with trust. I gave my word I would tell no one."

"Does Belle know what it's about?"

"She probably does." In fact I couldn't see how she could have missed it.

"Chase, I have to figure out how to handle this when we get home. If I don't know what's going on, I might screw it up royally."

"Just leave it alone. If I'd had any idea what this was about, I wouldn't have come out here."

"It's a bit late for that." He was trying to keep his voice level, to hide growing frustration. "There's an easy way to do this."

"What's that?"

"I'll ask Belle."

"Alex, you understand she's subject to the captain."

"That's true. But I'm the owner. If I have to, I can get a new captain."

"Would you really do that?"

"No. But I need you to trust me. I won't give anything away."

"Do what you want."

He put the question to Belle. I should have intervened, told her to be quiet. But I couldn't. Belle hesitated but finally described everything that had happened on Kaleska, the Dyson world. She described the empty cities, the Dyson Sphere, Ark's fears about what would happen if more biological beings showed up. And finally our assurances, mine and Gabe's, that we would not reveal their existence. When she'd finished, Alex asked me if I had anything to add.

"No," I said. "I think she covered everything. Are we ready to leave?"

"Not yet."

"Why not?"

"There's a good chance Charlotte's not finished yet."

He was right. Twenty minutes later a second transmission came in. Charlotte again, her voice at a higher pitch: *"He's going to ram us. Del's on the other radio promising him whatever he wants but he's not answering. My God, I don't believe this. The blasters that are supposed to protect us aren't working. He probably shut them down and none of us has any idea how to reactivate the damned things. Del's looking now, but he doesn't know any more than I do. I thought Rick was going to pull aside but he keeps accelerating. Coming right the hell at us. Please, Rick."*

We heard another voice in the background calling her name. Probably Housman. *"Get over here, Charlotte,"* he said. *"Try again."*

She switched off. It was the last we heard. Alex and I sat staring at each other.

XL

What, then, is truth? Is it a perspective acquired from the consideration of philosophical positions passed down to us through the ages? Is it a conclusion arrived at through a cautious balancing of probabilities and doubt? Is it the opinion of a man or woman whose ability to touch reality necessarily demands credence? However it ripens, get out of the valley when the avalanche comes.

—HAMID BAYLA, *LESSONS LEARNED*, 3811 CE

"We can package the transmissions," I said, "if you want to send them on to Gabe. Give him time to think about it before we get back."

"No, not a good idea."

"Why not?"

"We can't be sure somebody won't pick it up. Do we have an encryption capability?"

"Yes."

He frowned. "Never mind. Let's let it go until we get home. I think it would be best if we're both there when Gabe hears all this. Just send him a message, tell him we've made some progress, and we're on our way back."

"He's not going to be happy with that."

"He'll understand. In fact it'll tell him we made the intercept."

"How does it do that?"

"Because if we hadn't we'd have told him."

There was no reason to continue waiting. There would not be a third transmission, as much as I hoped, prayed, for one. Something that could somehow give us a happier ending. But we hung on anyway. We sat in the passenger cabin, neither of us doing anything other than looking out windows. It felt as if everything had been playing out over those last few minutes while we sat off to one side and listened, that Harding was closing in with the shuttle, and if we could have somehow been there we might have done something. At least *tried*. Eventually Alex got up and poured each of us a drink. "Let's go home."

I was ready. I told Belle to take us back.

"You okay?" asked Alex.

"I'm sorry we ever came near this place."

Belle turned us to starboard and began to accelerate. We sat on the bridge, looking out at a sky full of bright stars, not saying much. "I'd hoped for something better," I said.

"Don't know what that might have been."

"Anything else. Aliens would have helped."

"Do we want to make this public?"

We slipped into transdimensional space and everything outside went dark.

"I've no idea."

"I don't know what to do with it, Chase. I'd like to just leave it alone. Say nothing. But that leaves everybody hanging." He released his restraints and got out of the seat. "And let's not forget Reggie Greene. He must have really loved Charlotte. I mean, he went all the way out to the black hole hoping he'd get lucky. He's paid a heavy price for it." He was gripping the arms of his chair.

"If those two transmissions get out," I said, "they'll destroy the families."

"So do we hide the truth?"

"I don't know, Alex. I'm beginning to think our best course

would be to deny that we found anything. However this goes, I don't want to be any part of it."

"Trying to explain that Harding killed everybody to protect a bunch of AIs isn't going to look very good."

"Maybe we don't have to explain everything. Maybe we could claim that we just don't know what it was all about. What he was trying to keep secret. Just that, whatever it was, he was desperate to keep it quiet. He told Charlotte about it, it got out, and he went crazy as a result."

"Chase, that sounds as if we're talking about a treasure of some kind. Something he was planning to keep for himself. And it implies he was keeping an eye on Charlotte."

"I have an idea. Ark talked about a bioweapon that killed everybody. Maybe Harding was concerned that the place would get visitors who would eventually work out the thing's details. He was concerned about crazy people getting access to it."

"That still doesn't compensate for killing his colleagues." We sat there, staring past each other. "I have a question for you, Chase. Are you keeping notes on all this? Are you planning to write another memoir?"

"I *was*. It would have been strictly about what happened at the space station. It never occurred to me that the Dyson world would have any connection with it."

"I think you have the right idea. We don't reveal the nature of the secret. Or the location of the Dyson world. For all anybody else knows, Harding might have come across an abandoned alien ship with a dangerous technology. A hyper weapon of some sort."

"And how would we know that?"

"Look, no matter what we make up, there's no way Harding will come out of this looking good. Or Housman and Womack, for that matter. Even Charlotte will take a hit. We should just back off, forget what we know, and let everything play out. Eventually it will all go away."

"But it won't. It hasn't gone away in twelve years."

He was standing at the hatch to the passenger cabin. "Maybe we're too close to it now. Let's just shut it down for a while. Better yet, maybe Gabe will be able to help. This is going to be a tricky memoir. You're probably going to have to keep some of this from your readers."

"I was thinking the same thing."

"I'm sorry to see that happen. How do you feel about making stuff up?"

"Alex, have you actually read any of the books?"

"More or less."

"Then you know I've already hidden a lot of information. I've changed people's names, dates, all kinds of personal data. Sometimes I've fudged the information that you used to figure out what was going on. For example—"

"Skip the details. I know that. This time, the explanation for what happened to Octavia is the only thing that matters. And that's at the heart of the narrative. I don't see how you can lie about it."

I wondered if I should resign my position with Rainbow Enterprises. I'd gone through recent confrontations with both Gabe and Alex, and I suspected both might have been happy to see me leave but were reluctant to make the suggestion. Maybe it *was* time to move on. Getting a new situation wouldn't be hard. And I could get rid of the accounting and other administrative duties, which were hopelessly boring. But I would probably find myself taking tourists to Earth or Tau Ceti or 58 Eridani. The same flights over and over. After a dozen years with Alex, I didn't think that was what I wanted to do with the rest of my life. We were still in the first week of our return flight when I broached the subject with him. I don't remember what we'd been talking about, but it had nothing to do with the tension that I was still feeling.

"Obviously, Chase, you should do whatever would make

you happy. But I can tell you in all honesty that neither of us, Gabe or me, would want to see you go. If I can keep you by raising your pay, I'll certainly make it happen."

"You're serious? Both of you guys want me to stay?"

"Of course. Why would you think otherwise?" We were in the passenger cabin, having breakfast. "Something else: we should probably bring Lashonda into it. Tell her everything we know and see what she thinks we should do."

"You trust her?"

"She gave us access to the cannon AI. Yes, I trust her. We're going to need her help to get through this."

"But she could become a leak."

"I think, ultimately, we have to tell people what happened. We just don't say where this place—Kalwaka?—is. Do I have that right? There are billions of stars out there. Anybody who goes hunting for these guys is going to be at it a long time."

"But a star that's relatively nearby, with a Dyson Sphere, wouldn't be that hard to locate."

"We don't mention the Dyson Sphere. And we don't talk about distances. We'll be okay, Chase. There *is* something else. Lashonda has the details on the families. What I'd like to do, instead of taking this thing on HV, is to bring the families in, and friends of the victims, let them know we have some information about Octavia. However we decide to present it, I'd prefer to give it to them first before it goes public."

"I just don't see how we can handle that."

"Maybe Lashonda can figure something out. Possibly we send them messages inviting them to come into Andiquar for a conference, and ask them not to say anything to the media."

"You think there's any chance that would work?"

"It might. We can try it."

"I'm not sure it wouldn't be better to just blame it on aliens. Anything would be better than the truth. Imagine their reaction if we tell them that Harding rammed the station with the shuttle and killed everybody. That Charlotte Hill caused it all because she talked too much. That Housman could have—" I stopped to catch my breath. "He could have shut it all down. He and Womack. All they had to do was promise to keep their mouths shut. Everybody looks bad, Alex. The families are better off where they are, thinking it's aliens or lunatics or something."

"That's not what you said last time." I'd never seen Alex look so uncomfortable. "We'll figure out a way."

I didn't want to bring up any more problems, but eventually we'd have to address it. "There's another issue," I said.

"What's that?"

"The transmission. The families are going to want to hear it. So will the media. Can you imagine what they will go through listening to Charlotte describe what's happening?"

"Fortunately we have lots of time to think about it."

"Or Angela," I said. "How's she going to react when she finds out what her brother did?"

XLI

The instrument that drives accomplishment is not the mind but the will. The mind recommends a course. But it is the will that puts us in the saddle or, for lack of it, leaves us lying in the dust.
—MARLINA EVERETT, *ALL IN OR FORGET IT,* 8611 CE

The Korba star drive doesn't normally get you within walking distance of whatever world you're aiming for. The jump did okay by those standards. It brought us into our solar system out near Galaya, which, as locals would know, is a gas giant several billion kilometers from Rimway.

I told Alex where we were and immediately began recharging the drive unit. "Before we go under again," he said, "let's let Gabe know we're back."

"Okay," I said. "What are you going to tell him?"

"Just that we're here."

"You want to send Lashonda a message too?"

"No. We'll contact her when we get home."

"You still don't know what you're going to say to them, do you?"

"To the families? No, I don't." He stared out at the stars. "Whatever else we decide to do, we don't give the location of the Dyson world away. That means—"

"I'll rewrite the memoir and eliminate anything that might

point in its direction. And the nature of the inhabitants."

"Good. We'll be home in a few days, right?"

We went back and forth on the issue all the way to Skydeck. Where we had something else to deal with. I looked at Alex and then down at the frame that held Belle. He smiled and, without actually saying it, indicated *yes*.

"Belle," I said, "you there?"

"Of course."

"Are you ready?"

"Yes. You're really going to do this?"

"I got a couple of batteries from storage. I'll insert them before I remove you."

"Good," she said. *"I wouldn't want the lights to go out."*

We clipped links onto our jackets so she could talk to us. But despite the batteries, she went quiet after we disconnected her. Alex placed her in his shoulder bag. The link also allowed her to see pretty much everything we did. And we *did* get a few occasional comments. For example, after we boarded the shuttle, she said she was uncomfortable being on a vehicle she couldn't control. But how happy she would be to finally get a look at the country house. She asked if we had a robot she could use. Alex trained his eyes on the shuttle's overhead. Robots were not cheap.

Gabe was waiting for us when we arrived at the Andiquar spaceport late that morning. He was standing in the departure area with a visible cloud over his head. "Hi, guys," he said, trying to conceal obvious concern. He took a bag from each of us and we started for the exit. He smiled when Belle said hello to him.

"Belle," he said. "Is that you?"

"In the flesh, Gabe."

He looked at me. "I should have guessed this was coming," he said. "Aren't you concerned that Jacob will get jealous?"

"I'm more concerned," said Alex, "that they'll be too distracted playing chess to take care of the work."

Gabe was laughing as we passed out of the terminal. "Veronica called this morning," he said. "She asked me to say hello."

Alex lit up. We needed some good news.

"So what've we got?" Gabe asked.

Alex held up a hand. Wait till we get away from the crowd. We hauled everything out to the skimmer, loaded it, and climbed in. Gabe and Alex sat up front; I settled in the rear. As we lifted off Gabe turned to his nephew. "How bad is it?" he asked.

"It's not good." Alex played the recordings for him as we drifted out over the forest west of the city. I watched the color drain from Gabe's cheeks.

Other than grumbling something, he said nothing for several minutes. We were circling, settling down into our parking area, before he responded. "You know what he was trying to keep secret?"

"The Dyson world."

Gabe glanced at me. "You told him?" He read my answer in my expression and I saw disappointment in his. "And that's what it was all about?"

"Apparently."

"So what's the plan?"

"I don't know," said Alex. "You have a suggestion?"

"You don't really have any option other than the truth, Alex. There's no way you can hide this. You owe it to everyone involved to let them know what happened."

"But it means revealing the issue with the Dyson world."

"I know." Gabe retreated into a dark place. "I just don't see what choice we have."

We called Lashonda when we got home. After asking whether she was alone, Alex informed her that we knew what had happened. Gabe and I were with him in the conference room, visible to her.

"I was wondering where you've been, Alex. What have you got?"

"Can we come over and talk to you at the center?"

She got the message. *"No aliens, huh?"* It was obvious she'd been hoping that Alex would not come up with anything.

"No." I'd never seen him look so dismayed. "Unfortunately not."

"When can you be here?"

"We just got in. We need an hour to pull ourselves together. How about two o'clock?"

"You all coming in?"

Gabe said he would pass. "I have nothing to add."

I showered and changed and we were on our way. It was a bright, warm day. The sun floated in a cloudless sky. Another skimmer drifted past. A couple of kids, perched in back, waved in our direction. We arrived at DPSAR behind a couple of other vehicles, which were riding into the Cyrus Branch parking lot, delivering customers to the restaurants and the shopping area. Immediately to the north, a swarm of tennis players were having it out at the Domingo Courts.

We landed a few minutes early, went inside, and were greeted by a guy in one of the center's green uniforms. He smiled at us, called us by name, and took us to the director's office, where Lashonda was waiting. She was talking to a bearded elderly man I'd met before but whose name I couldn't remember. "Thank you, Jason," she said. He left and she turned her attention immediately to us. "Good to see you guys again." She signaled for us to sit down before settling into a Gala lounge. "So what have we got?"

"We have a radio transmission from Charlotte Hill. Two of them, in fact."

"I don't think I understand."

"These went out on the day the station vanished."

That needed a moment to register. Then her eyebrows rose and she looked as if she was about to ask him to get serious. When Alex simply sat and waited, she realized he wasn't kidding. "Did you bring them with you?"

"Of course. You want to hear them?"

She was trying to maintain her skepticism, but it was gone. "How did you get them?"

"That's a long story."

"All right, Alex. Let's hear what you have."

Lashonda paled as Charlotte's voice filled the room. Her lips formed the words "That's her." She listened while Charlotte took the blame. While she described the antipathy that had developed on the station and her own fears when Harding disappeared with the shuttle.

"What is she talking about?" she demanded.

"You want to hear part two first?"

"There's more? Oh yes, you said there were two of them. Please, yes." Her features tightened as if she were looking into the face of a crocodile.

We listened again to the second transmission, absorbed by those final tense moments. We heard Charlotte's terror, heard Housman pleading with Rick Harding to turn aside, and finally trying to get Charlotte to talk to him. Then it ended.

"What the hell's it about?" she demanded. "What was going on?"

"Years before any of this, Harding discovered a world where an advanced civilization had killed itself off. Except for some AIs. They'd apparently been subject to control by their creators. They were happy the creators were gone. But they were terrified of the possibility they would return, or someone like them would show up. They'd had enough of being controlled and persuaded Harding not to reveal their location. He gave his word."

"And . . . ?"

"You've got the rest. For whatever reason, he told Charlotte, and she passed it on to Housman and Womack."

"So Harding killed them all?"

"That seems to be what happened."

"Why do you think he told Charlotte?"

"I suspect it's hard to keep a secret when you're living in that kind of solitude. It's probably the same reason Charlotte passed it on. She knew how Housman and Womack would react to that kind of story."

"And he did this for a bunch of AIs?" Her eyes were closed and her lips locked together. A tear ran down her cheek. She tried two or three times to say something before finally getting it out. "You could hardly have brought worse news."

"I'm sorry."

She nodded. Waited another minute or two while she thought about it. Then: "What are you going to do now?"

"What are your thoughts?" Alex asked.

"Bury it."

"I can't do that."

"Why not? If it gets out it will do a lot of damage. To the families, and to us."

"Lashonda—"

"We put a lunatic out there. On a remote space station with three innocent people."

"It wasn't your responsibility."

"I trusted him."

"So did the aliens. In any case, I don't think Harding qualified as a lunatic."

"What else would you call him? Anyway, I'm not talking about *me*. I'm concerned about the organization."

"You mentioned the families."

"Yes. Think what it will do to them."

"So you'd prefer to leave this unsettled? Leave everybody to wonder what happened to their loved ones?" Alex's brow creased. "I think, in the long run, that would be crueler than revealing the truth."

"Are you serious? The Hardings will find out their son killed the others. Can you imagine what that will do to them?" She turned in my direction. "Chase, if you were Harding's sister, what would your preference be?"

It was easier than I expected. "I'd want the truth."

It took a while. We went through a lot of glaring, sighing, and clenched fists. Finally Lashonda just shook her head. "Maybe you're right," she said. "How do you want to handle it?"

"We call a family conference. And ask them to say nothing."

"You know that won't happen."

"We do what we can. We have nearby contacts with each family. Call them in tomorrow. And yes, of course it'll leak out. No way we can stop that."

She delivered a soundless "yes" with her lips. "I guess it's all we have."

"We'll call the families," said Alex. "Just tell them we have news."

She stared at us for a long minute. "I'm so sorry you got into this, Alex."

"I know. I am too."

"Do you want me to set it up?"

"That would work best. Not here, though. Your conference room will be too small. But you want DPSAR to be part of the process, of course."

"Yes, of course. Who else knows about this?"

"Just Gabe."

"All right. Let's get it done as quickly as possible. I'll schedule it for tomorrow."

"Good."

"Give me an hour. I'll call you when I have a place."

"Sounds perfect. We'll contact the families."

Lashonda didn't move. "Alex," she said.

"Yes?"

"Do what you can for them. Try to frame it so it doesn't sound so terrible."

"I'll take as much sting out of it as I'm able. It's why we'd better get rid of the AIs. If the victims all died because one of them was protecting a data system, we'll have nothing but outrage. These people have had enough suffering. I'll make a few changes."

"You're going to lie?" I asked.

"I'll avoid the details."

"Okay." Lashonda nodded. "Good."

"Lashonda, nobody else can know about them. About the AIs."

"Of course. I'll say nothing." She looked at me. "Chase, you have anything to add?"

"You can trust him," I said. "If anybody can pull this off, he can."

A call from Chad was waiting when I got back to the cottage. I connected and watched him blink on in the living room. He looked exasperated but said how happy he was that I was back, that he would like to take me to dinner, and that it seemed as if I'd been gone forever. *"Did you get my message?"* he asked.

"The one you sent to the *Belle-Marie*?"

"Yes."

I eased down onto the sofa and smiled. "It was beautiful, Chad."

"Are you okay?"

"Sure. Why would you think otherwise?"

"You've been gone a long time, Chase. Again."

"I know. I'm sorry."

"That's pretty much what you always say."

"Chad, why don't we talk about it later. I've got my hands full at the moment."

"*As far as I can see, there's probably not much to talk about. I've had a lot of time to think about us. Chase, I'll do what I can to make everything work.*"

"That sounds good. But let's give it some time, Chad."

"*That's not encouraging.*"

"Chad, I'm seriously pressed right now."

"*I guess you just answered my question. I'm sorry to lose you, Chase. I enjoyed being with you, but it's pretty obvious it's not going anywhere.*" He stood in the middle of the living room, fading sunlight coming through the window behind him. "*Good-bye, kid.*"

"No, wait, Chad—"

He was gone.

I tried to call back but his AI informed me he wasn't available.

I spent the next half hour talking with Carmen. I needed someone to sympathize with me, to reassure me that I hadn't really lost him, that Alex would take care of everything, that we weren't going to destroy the lives of the Octavia families. She told me to stop worrying. She was still at it when a call came in from Alex.

"*I've invited representatives from each of the families for the conference tomorrow,*" he said. "*We'll pay any expenses.*"

"When?"

"*One o'clock at the Holgrove Hotel.*"

"Okay."

"*By the way, the media knows we've got something.*"

"I'm not surprised. There was no way to warn the families and keep it quiet."

"*We'll be leaving the country house at about a quarter after.*"

"Is Gabe going?"

"*No. He says he's going to watch at home.*"

"He's no dummy. Okay. See you tomorrow."

"*Chase, do you want to be part of it?*"

"I'll be there. But I'd just as soon stand off to the side and watch. Unless you need me up front."

"*Okay. By the way, Lashonda tells me that Angela Harding's coming in. And Womack's parents. They'll also have Elijah McCord.*"

"Who's McCord? I remember the name, but what's his connection?"

"*He teaches at AIT. He was a close friend of Housman's.*"

"All right. I'll see you tomorrow."

I needed a snack. Some chocolate cake. I cut a piece and had just sat down to enjoy it when Carmen informed me of another call. "*From Jill Faulkner. At the Golden Network.*"

That wasn't good. My first reaction was to have Carmen tell her I wasn't available. But that would only be a temporary solution. "Put her through, Carmen."

I hadn't met Faulkner but I knew she was a producer in the news division. She blinked on, seated at a circular table in a leather chair, tapping at a keyboard. Lush velvet drapes covered a window behind her, and a crowded bookcase stood to one side. Soft music filled the background. She looked up at me, smiled, and got to her feet. The music stopped.

"*Ms. Kolpath?*"

"Yes."

"*I'm happy to finally meet you. My name's Jill. We're interested in talking to you about Octavia. I understand you and your associate Alex Benedict have acquired some new information. I have to be honest: we've had reports like that before, but nothing has ever come of them. You and your colleague have a pretty remarkable history, though. Do you actually have something?*"

"Jill, I'm not in a position to comment on this."

"*I understand. That sounds like a yes. I'd like to invite you in tomorrow morning for the* Morgan Winslow Show.*"*

"Thank you. But I have to decline."

"*Ms. Kolpath, Morgan has a global audience. Hers is one of the three most-watched news shows in the world."* I was still sitting behind my piece of cake when she began to approach. She was considerably taller than I am, and she radiated a sense of compassion. *"I understand this is probably difficult for you."*

Carmen's lamp began blinking. "One second, Jill," I said. "What is it, Carmen?"

"Another call. From Harold Pasciwicz." He was the producer for the *News Guys*.

"Tell him I'll get back to him."

"You can see what's going to happen," Jill said. *"We have the best ratings by a wide margin, Chase. If you're going to do this at all, do it with us."*

"Thanks for the offer. But I have nothing to say on the subject."

She was about to respond, but I disconnected and switched back to Carmen. "Give me Pasciwicz. If anybody else calls, I'm not available."

"You have one from Alex," she said.

"Put him on."

"Chase," he said, *"heads up. You'll be getting a lot of media attention."*

"It's already started."

"All right. Don't say anything, okay?"

I gave Pasciwicz a no comment. We were still fending off calls when a skimmer arrived with UNITED NEWS emblazoned on both sides. That was enough. I packed a bag and, at the first opportunity, left the cottage and checked into a nearby hotel.

XLII.

*The reality is that the vast majority of people try to do
the right thing, to respect the rights of others, and to do no
harm. The sad truth however is that a great deal of damage is
nevertheless inflicted. How can this be? Because our judgment
is impaired. Examine both sides in any argument, dispute,
or war. Each will believe it is in the right.*
—AUGUST TEMPLETON, *LAST DAYS OF AVALON*, **5593 CE**

When I walked into the Holgrove Hotel's auditorium, Lashonda
was at the front table, just taking her place behind a lectern.
I didn't see Alex. The media were filing in, as well as others
who undoubtedly had a personal connection. Olivia Hill was
among them. She was seated at a table near the front.

Lashonda waited for everyone to settle in and then looked
over at an open door. "Ladies and gentlemen," she said, "we
have finally a report on what happened to the Octavia. For
that, we are indebted to Alex Benedict. Alex, would you come
out here, please?"

He came through the doorway and took his place at the
lectern. She shook his hand and returned to her seat. The
crowd grew quiet.

Alex looked out across the audience. "Good afternoon,
ladies and gentlemen. Recently, we intercepted a twelve-
year-old radio transmission from Octavia. It was sent by

Charlotte Hill from the space station on the day of its disappearance. They were at that time blocked by the black hole from communicating with any of our bases or worlds. They were in that position for about thirty-one hours. Charlotte was concerned about what was happening on the Octavia, and consequently she informed a friend that, if something untoward happened, she would send a radio transmission to one of the surrounding stars. The message to the friend was not immediately clear, which is why it has taken so long for us to catch up with it."

Hands went up and questions were launched. Who was the friend? What star? Did you get the transmission? What did it say?

"Yes," he said. "We did make the reception."

"What did it say?"

Alex held up a hand. "This will go better if you let me finish."

The audience calmed down.

"Rick Harding had a secret for years. He had discovered a world with a civilization that, at one time, apparently had a technology well in advance of ours. But the inhabitants had died off. They were killed in a series of wars, leaving behind another species that they'd enslaved. The survivors were terrified at the prospect of being treated the same way if someone else with advanced technology showed up. So they pleaded with Harding not to reveal their existence. He said nothing for a long time. For years. But life on Octavia involved a lot of solitude. People in a place like that have a hard time keeping secrets. Rick apparently revealed the story to one of his colleagues with the understanding that the information would go no further.

"Unfortunately the recipient of the information faced the same challenge about not sharing it. Assuming the others on the station would say nothing, she passed it on. The details aren't clear. But it seemed simply unreasonable to her colleagues to remain silent about a discovery of that magnitude. They confronted Rick and apparently made it clear to him that they felt keeping that kind of discovery quiet was irrational. That they had an obligation to pass it on to others in the scientific community.

"Rick tried to dissuade them." Alex paused for a breath. "But he was unable to do so. When that happened, he got desperate and took the shuttle out. He rarely did that, but he must have considered it his only option. The only way he could protect the people to whom he had given his word. Charlotte and the others suspected he was going to use the shuttle to destroy the station. Del tried to talk him down, while Charlotte described the situation in the transmission she sent to the star. She knew it would be easy for an interstellar to acquire it, but she hoped their fears were unfounded and that the message, as well as the conflict, would simply disappear into the void. Ultimately, Charlotte tells us that the shuttle was coming back, and it was evident that Harding was going to crash it into the station."

Hands began waving again. And more questions were thrown toward Alex. "Is that the way it ended?"

"Didn't they have a defense system against approaching objects?"

"He actually did this to protect *aliens*?"

Alex held up a hand. "That's all we have," he said. "It's the way it ended."

"Was all this information on the transmission?"

"No. There is another source, someone who visited the same world that Harding did."

"Who's that?"

"Sorry. That's private information. It's of no consequence to the investigation so it won't be revealed."

"Where is the alien civilization?"

"That's also private."

The place erupted. "So you're saying Harding went crazy?"

"Have you confirmed the transmission is legitimate? Is it Charlotte's voice?"

Alex had to fight to regain control. Finally: "Yes, it's Charlotte."

"Will you run the transmission for us?"

"At the end of the conference, yes." He was about to continue when someone began sobbing.

"I'm sorry it's so painful," he said. "None of us were prepared for this. Even though we knew it couldn't have a good ending."

Olivia was seated on the far side of the auditorium. Somehow, in this most painful segment of the entire experience, she'd raised her head and was staring past the speakers' platform. The tears and sadness were gone, replaced by a glow of unbroken pride.

Alex continued: "It would be helpful to keep in mind that all four of these people, Charlotte Hill, Del Housman, Rick Harding, and Archie Womack died doing what they thought was right. Rick felt an obligation to protect an entire world of terrified beings. He had to have believed he had no choice. He might also have suspected we would eventually secure the weaponry that had killed off that world's population.

"The others would have believed that access to an advanced civilization should not be denied to us. That we couldn't simply take a pass on it. Something else as well: there are studies that reveal spending excessive amounts of time on a remote station, cut off from the rest of society, has a destabilizing effect on everyone. I suggest we cut Rick and the others a break. They all died trying to do what they believed in their hearts was right. They gave their lives for it." He looked out across his audience. The media people were pointing cameras and raising hands. Others were in tears.

I wasn't able to talk to Alex until we both got back to the country house. He looked thoroughly upset. "You okay?" I asked.

"Sure." Then, after a long minute: "That was the most gut-wrenching experience of my life."

I told him he couldn't have done more. And Veronica called at the end of the school day. I wasn't present for any of the conversation, but she showed up a half hour later. I was waiting at the door.

Alex needed her.

Chad did eventually accept a call. *"Chase,"* he said, *"you think we could give it another try?"*

EPILOG

I wish I could report that Alex's comments resulted in media coverage that showed a degree of empathy for Charlotte and her colleagues. I suppose there was no way that could have happened. But he did succeed in converting the episode into what sounded like a giant communication breakdown. Everett DeLani, the prominent psychologist, released a book a year later, *The Octavia Effect*, which explored the damage that could be rendered by extreme isolation, especially when one is faced with a difficult decision. DeLani supported the position that Alex had taken, that four decent human beings had been victimized by the fact they were all trying to live up to moral stands that allowed no compromise.

A week after the press conference Reggie Greene came by the country house to say thanks. "Some people still think I'm crazy," he said, "but at least nobody's accusing me of killing her anymore." He looked in pain, though. "I miss her. After all this time, I still can't get her behind me. Charlotte was an incredible woman. Always reaching out and trying to help. Which I guess is what got her killed."

Rick's sister informed us that, despite his brilliance, he'd always had a dark side, a tendency to see the worst in human beings. But she never would have believed he'd be involved in anything like what had happened to Octavia.

In the weeks and months that followed we heard from members of all four families. And others who had personal or professional connections. Almost everyone thanked Alex for his effort on their behalf.

A young woman from Claritz University on Dellaconda got in touch with us. She'd been a student in a physics class taught by Archie Womack. He was, she told us, one of the kindest, most sensible people she'd ever known.

Another woman claimed to have grown up with Harding. "I don't understand it," she said. "The Rick Harding I knew would never have hurt anyone."

Word arrived yesterday that Gabe will be the recipient of the Otto Fleminger Award this year for his contributions to historical research. He's pretending it's not a big deal, but he's already cleared space in his office for it. It will be atop one of the bookcases, just above the Winston Churchill volume.

Note from Chase (1440): I had not expected to publish this in my lifetime. But it has been almost five years since these events. During that time, the determined refusal by many of us to accept AIs as living beings has largely disappeared. In most human societies they can vote, can own property, and are endowed with the rights the rest of us have. The remaining worlds have all introduced legislation on the subject.

Consequently it no longer seems necessary to mislead anyone about the identity of the "terrified beings" Alex cited in his address at DPSAR. That's fortunate because radio transmissions from Kaleska have leaked into the sky above the End Times Hotel. That led to the discovery of the Dyson Sphere. And, as I write this, a mission is on its way to find out what's going on.

Recognizing what was about to happen, Gabe left for Kaleska two weeks ago with his new pilot to alert the AIs. It's too soon to have heard back yet, but he was confident that Ark and Sayla, and the rest of their friends, would make the adjustment.

I hadn't expected that a release of *Octavia Gone* would ever be possible. Originally, I'd intended to use "Blame It on the Aliens" as the title. But Alex, who rarely comments on my memoirs, argued that the experience had been too dark to refer to it in such a comedic manner. He was right. As usual.